Jackie Ashenden writes
alpha heroes who've just
only to have it blown wi
heroines. She lives in Au
husband, the inimitable I
When she's not torturing alpha males and their gutsy
heroines she can be found drinking chocolate martinis,
reading anything she can lay her hands on, wasting time
on social media or being forced to go mountain biking
with her husband. To keep up to date with Jackie's new
releases and other news sign up to her newsletter at
jackieashenden.com.

Formerly a video and radio producer, **Christy McKellen**
now spends her time writing provocative, passionate,
seductive romance. When she's not writing she can be
found enjoying life with her husband and three children,
walking for pleasure and researching other people's
deepest secrets and desires. Christy loves to hear from
readers. You can get hold of her at christymckellen.com.

KING'S RANSOM

JACKIE ASHENDEN

GOOD GIRL

CHRISTY McKELLEN

MILLS & BOON

First Published in Great Britain 2019
by Mills & Boon, an imprint of HarperCollins*Publishers*
1 London Bridge Street, London, SE1 9GF

King's Ransom © 2019 Jackie Ashenden

Good Girl © 2019 Christy McKellen

ISBN: 978-0-263-27377-9

MIX
Paper from
responsible sources
FSC® C007454
FSC
www.fsc.org

This book is produced from independently certified FSC™ paper
to ensure responsible forest management.
For more information visit www.harpercollins.co.uk/green.

Printed and bound in Spain
by CPI, Barcelona

KING'S RANSOM

JACKIE ASHENDEN

MILLS & BOON

To the cat.
For absolutely no reason at all.

CHAPTER ONE

Ajax

I WAS TEN years old the first time I suspected my father was a criminal.

At thirteen he showed me the truth.

That's when I decided I was going to take him down. But if you want to take down a man like Augustus King you have to do it right. You can't leave anything behind. A crime empire is like a Hydra—cut off the head and twenty more sprout.

It took me nearly two decades to cut off every single head. Yet I did. And I put that prick in jail once and for all.

But surviving decades of being the oldest son of the biggest crime lord in Sydney doesn't leave a man without scars, and mine ran deep.

That was okay, though. Scars were reminders of the big picture and my big picture involved keeping my brothers and my city safe. Staying vigilant for danger. Always on the lookout for threats.

Threats such as William goddamn White, my father's enemy and the last head of the Hydra.

Dad had been in jail five years and I'd been legit

ever since, running one of the fastest growing property development companies in Sydney, and, as much as I wanted to, I couldn't simply cut that head off the way I preferred. Not if I wanted to avoid jail myself.

No, I had to use other methods.

I leaned against the wall of the ballroom of one of Sydney's top hotels, studying the glittering, couture-wearing crowd all gathered to celebrate the formation of a new charity.

I hadn't been invited—no one would invite a King to a swanky charity ball like this one—but I'd shown up anyway and they'd been too afraid of me to turn me away.

The King past was something my two brothers and I were trying to overcome, but it came in handy at times. And I wasn't above using it, especially when it came to driving home to the cream of Sydney society that the King brothers were up-and-coming and they couldn't ignore us any more.

But that wasn't the only reason I was here.

That other reason was sitting across the ballroom from me, at a table surrounded by goons in suits trying hard not to look like goons in suits and failing.

Miss Imogen White, William White's daughter and the most guarded heiress in the entire city.

The chick was like Rapunzel in her tower—no one was getting inside. Both figuratively *and* literally. She was the apple of her father's eye and he made sure she stayed pure and pristine, his perfect Princess.

Sadly for White, I was about to storm his daughter's pretty little castle and sully the fuck out of it.

He'd managed somehow to stay out of the law's reach following the collapse of Dad's empire and he'd been waiting in the shadows ever since. Not drawing attention, quietly trying to resurrect Augustus King's filthy legacy.

A legacy I was going to destroy once and for all.

That motherfucker was going *down* and I was going to use his daughter to do it.

I tilted my head, studying her as she sat on her chair, all alone apart from her goons.

Five foot nothing, long blonde hair the colour of pale corn silk. Big green eyes that watched the rest of the room and the people in it like they were a cage full of tigers and she was a goat tethered to a stake.

Interesting that her father had managed to get her an invite and that she was attending without him. Almost made me think that she *was* playing the part of a goat tethered to a stake.

Bait. To lure someone out.

Me, perhaps? But then, probably not. As far as White was concerned, I was too busy running King Enterprises, my property empire, to worry about him—an illusion I'd worked hard to cultivate to hide my real motivations.

Whosever bait she was, Imogen was pretty in her plain white cocktail frock. A perfect little doll. Pale and virginal and pure. Except not totally pure, not with the kind of sulky pink mouth that would look great wrapped around a man's cock.

Yes, she was lovely, but she was also nothing but leverage.

Her father's weapon that I was going to turn back on him, using her to ensure that whatever he was doing in those shadows, whatever plans he was hatching, he needed to stop immediately and get the hell out of Sydney.

Only then would I release his daughter.

And if he didn't? I'd take that carefully guarded virginity of hers and make her mine. Because if there was one thing I knew about William White, it was that he'd rather slit his own throat than have a King touch his daughter.

Especially me. As far as he was concerned, I was still rough and brutal, still only a few steps away from the violence that had made me.

He wouldn't want his daughter anywhere near me.

As plans went it wasn't all that subtle, but I'd been searching for some legal way to take that bastard down and hadn't managed to find anything I could use against him.

No, his daughter was it. My plan to protect everything I'd built.

Ten years ago, I could have headed over to her and slung her over my shoulder and no one would have stopped me. Even the police would have given me a wide berth—they didn't want to mess with a King.

But it wasn't ten years ago. It was now, and even though I'd never have considered using Dad's kind of tactics—I was, after all, a different man—the stakes were too high to risk failure, which meant the end justified any means.

Such as kidnapping William White's daughter from a ballroom full of people.

Oh, yeah, and not get caught.

I glanced away from the scaredy-cat Princess and looked towards the bar area of the ballroom. Sure enough, there was my younger brother Leon, along with his wife, Vita. They were commanding a lot of attention, which was the reason I'd demanded the pair of them attend the ball with me.

They could take the heat while I did my thing unnoticed.

Leon would be pissed if he knew what I was planning, especially given his own past, but what he didn't know wouldn't hurt him. This was my idea and not telling him would allow all the responsibility to fall on me if it turned to shit.

The only person who'd get hurt here was William fucking White.

I shifted against the wall, checking on Imogen again.

She was sitting up so straight and still, her hands clasped in her lap, holding herself rigid, except for one little white-satin-covered foot that was tapping to the music that filtered through the ballroom. Then it stopped and she looked down at herself, colour staining her pale cheeks. As if she'd only just realised what she was doing and caught herself. As if tapping her foot to the music was a bad thing.

Another man might have felt sorry for her sitting there all by herself, not even able to enjoy the music. But I didn't. I couldn't afford to. She was a tool for me to use. That was all.

On the table near her was a glass of iced water that I'd paid one of the waiters to keep refilled. Eventually, given the amount of times she'd emptied the thing, she'd need to visit the bathroom and when she did...

Right on cue, she glanced at her bodyguards and slid off the chair, gesturing towards the exit to the bathrooms. One of them nodded and jerked his head at the man standing next to him, the two of them then falling into place behind her as she moved towards the exit.

Good.

Taking on five of them would be tricky, but two? Easy.

I stepped away from the wall and ducked out through a nearby doorway that led to the same corridor where the bathrooms were located, reaching the ladies' bathroom in time to see her vanish into it. The two guards stationed themselves outside.

Giving them a minute or two, I took out the cap I had in the back pocket of my suit pants and put it on, pulling it down to hide my face, then I moved in for the kill.

I took them down as quickly and as quietly as possible then shoved their unconscious bodies into the empty men's bathroom, pulling shut the door behind me and breaking the handle so they couldn't get out.

That done, I moved over to the ladies' and stepped inside.

Luckily it was empty, apart from White's little Princess, standing at the bank of sinks opposite the door. She was in the process of washing her hands, her head bent.

I closed the door silently behind me and locked it for good measure, then I leaned back against it, watching her, waiting to see how long it would take her to notice me.

A good minute as it turned out.

She was humming something under her breath, a cheerful-sounding pop song, completely distracted. And it wasn't until she'd dried her hands and had leaned forward to study her reflection that her gaze met mine in the mirror.

The humming stopped, her green eyes going big and filling with shock.

'Don't scream,' I said calmly. 'I'm not going to hurt you. However, I might change my mind if you try to call for help. Is that understood?'

Her eyes widened even further, her mouth in a soft pink O. But she gave a very slight nod to show me that she did, staring at me in the mirror all the while as if I was the devil himself.

I stared back.

Her skin was pale, like cream, and her eyelashes were tipped with gold. She had a conventional prettiness that was saved from being bland by that quite frankly carnal mouth and the delicate little mole sitting just above it.

There was an energy to her, an electricity that reminded me of a live wire about to spit sparks.

Somewhere deep inside me, interest tightened.

What would it feel like to put my hands on her and touch that electricity for myself? Would it shock the dead parts of me back to life?

Shit, touching her wasn't the point of the kidnapping, no matter the threat I was going to deliver to her father. Besides, pure princesses—live wires or not—had never been my type. I liked a woman who knew her way around a man's cock and who didn't mind getting rough with it, not a wide-eyed virgin like this one.

I dismissed the thoughts. Right now, getting her out of here with the minimum of fuss was my priority.

'W-where are my bodyguards?' Her voice was clear with an inexplicably sexy roughness to it.

'I dealt with them.' I stepped away from the door-frame and straightened to my full height, her gaze following every move I made.

The shock had begun to drain from her pale face, leaving behind it an expression I didn't recognise. '*Both* of them?' She sounded incredulous, as if I'd done something incredibly difficult.

'Yes. They're in the men's room with the door locked.' I took a step towards her. 'They're not coming to save you, little one.'

She didn't move. 'You're Ajax King.'

'You've heard of me.' I took another step.

'Of course. My dad hates you.'

'The feeling's mutual.' I was close now, standing right behind her, watching her face in the mirror.

Her lashes lowered. Then she turned around, her head tipping back, looking straight up at me.

She was very small, the top of her head barely reaching my shoulders, and the pale skin of her cheeks had gone pink, deepening the vivid green of her eyes. They were glowing. They were full-on fucking glowing.

Maybe that's when I recognised her expression, the one that wasn't fear or shock or anger, or any of the other emotions I'd expected when I'd first stepped inside.

No. What I saw in her face was unconcealed awe.

Not the reaction I normally got. People were either afraid of me or they loathed me. But not this green-eyed virginal Princess. She looked at me like I was the second coming of Christ.

For some reason, my cock liked that very much indeed.

Fuck. That was all I needed. Desire wasn't supposed to be part of this plan and I didn't want it to be. The goal was protecting my city and my brothers, not screwing a wide-eyed little ingénue.

Ignoring my disreputable dick, I gave her the stare I usually gave to those who thought they could argue with my decisions. 'Okay, here's the deal,' I began. 'You're going to need to—'

'Why are you here?'

I blinked at her interruption. Another thing that people knew better than to do. 'What?'

'I mean, why are you here? In the women's bathroom?'

'Well, I—'

'You *do* know it's the women's bathroom, don't you?'

'Yeah, I know it's the—'

'Are you here for me?'

I gritted my teeth. 'You're going to have to stop interrupting me.'

A line appeared between her pale silky brows, the electric energy of her intensifying somehow. 'Sorry, I didn't mean to. I just really need to know.'

Hell, what was I doing, standing here letting her pepper me with pointless questions? I was supposed to be kidnapping her, for fuck's sake.

'Yeah,' I growled, taking another step closer, looming over her, hoping she'd get the idea she was supposed to be scared and not keep looking at me like I was Captain fucking America. 'I'm here for you.'

Her eyes glowed even more and she'd gone even

pinker, as if I was the man of her dreams and I'd just asked her out.

'Don't look so fucking pleased,' I said harshly. 'I'm not asking you to dance. I'm here to kidnap you.'

That gorgeous mouth of hers dropped open. 'Kidnap me?' she echoed, looking astonished. Then, before I could speak, she grinned. 'Oh, my God, that's excellent!'

CHAPTER TWO

Imogen

'WHAT DO YOU MEAN, "excellent"?' Ajax King's mesmerising blue eyes had narrowed into shards of ice and there was offence in his deep, rough voice.

Weird. You'd have thought he'd be happy that I wanted to go with him without making a screaming fuss.

Obviously not.

Then again, I didn't have time to be thinking about whether he'd be offended or not. All I was conscious of was finally—freaking finally!—here was the opportunity I'd been searching more than two years for.

The opportunity to get away from my bloody father.

My shuddering heartbeat was going hell for leather, adrenaline pulsing through me.

'There's no time,' I said hurriedly, tilting my head to the side so I could see past his massive, broad figure to the door. 'Dad's other guys will notice I haven't come back and they'll come after me. So if we're going to leave, we have to leave now.'

'Now wait just a fucking minute—'

But I had no fucking minutes to waste.

I reached for his hand and pulled him over to the door. Or at least I tried to. Bit difficult when he wouldn't let himself be pulled.

Dammit.

I turned back, fear beginning to thread through my excitement. 'Please. If you're going to kidnap me then you have to do it now. Come on!' I tugged on his hand again.

He didn't move, only pinned me with those icy blue eyes. 'You actually *want* me to kidnap you?'

Seriously? He was asking me stupid questions now?

'Would I be asking you to do it if I didn't want you to?' I pulled on his hand yet again. 'Come *on*.'

But it was like trying to pull on a mountain. The damn man wouldn't budge.

Fear tightened inside me. If we didn't leave now the rest of my bodyguards were going to come looking and they'd find me. And then they'd try to stop me, and my chance of escape would be gone.

I'd be back to living in my gilded cage, where I couldn't move a muscle without five guards springing into action. Where I had to watch my behaviour so assiduously that it was easier to stay in than go out. It was a cage I hadn't noticed get smaller and smaller as the years progressed. Not until the day I'd realised exactly what kind of man my father was and that if I stayed in the cage any longer I was going to get crushed.

I'd go back to being powerless. Back to being used. Back to being so lonely it made my soul ache.

No, I couldn't do it. I wouldn't.

Right here was my opportunity to escape and I was taking it.

Ajax King was my father's greatest enemy so who

better to help me? He'd been watching me all evening—I'd noticed since I'd nothing else to do—and now I knew why.

It couldn't have been more perfect.

Right then, someone knocked on the door and I froze, fear an iceberg floating in the centre of my chest.

'Miss White?' a male voice asked. 'Are you in there?'

Shit. It was Colin, one of my guards.

I turned back to Ajax, standing near the vanity unit, so tall his head almost brushed the ceiling. He stared at me from underneath the cap he wore, his expression impassive. His rough features were intensely compelling. A sharp, hard jaw and strong blade of a nose. High cheekbones. Those deep set, amazing blue eyes. Not typically handsome. Very, *very* masculine, and the look he was giving me...

I felt an odd flash of something. A crackle over my skin, like electricity. It was unexpected and strange so I ignored it, too worried about what he was going to do to pay attention to it.

Would he change his mind? Give me back to them?

I swallowed, my mouth dry, and I gave him a pleading look. *Please help me. Please.*

'Miss White?' Colin asked again, sharper this time. 'Are you in there?'

Ajax shot a glance at the door then back at me.

Then suddenly he pulled me towards him so I was only inches away from his massive, muscular figure. He lowered his head, his mouth near my ear. 'Do as I say,' he murmured. 'And I'll get you out of here.'

I blinked at the wall of white cotton in front of me. I hadn't been this close to a man in years. Possibly I hadn't been this close to a man *ever*.

It was weird. He was very, *very* warm and he smelled good. A spicy, woody scent that for some reason made the iceberg in my chest start to melt and calmed my rising panic.

'Now, put your arms out. And don't say a word.'

His breath on my skin made goosebumps rise along my neck and shoulders, that crackling sensation getting more intense.

I didn't have time to think about it so I put my arms out obediently. Quickly, he shrugged out of his black suit jacket and, before I could figure out what he was going to do with it, he'd put it on me.

Nearly forgetting that I wasn't supposed to speak, I opened my mouth to ask him what he was doing. But he whipped the cap off his head and put it on mine, then, with surprising skill for a guy, he coiled my hair up underneath so it wasn't showing.

I blinked up at him. Way, *way* up at him.

His eyes were the most incredible blue. The pupils had a dark ring of midnight around them before lightening up towards the iris, a shade that was exactly the same as the sky on a perfect winter's day. They were made even more noticeable by the straight black brows and thick black lashes that framed them.

My heart gave a weird thump.

I didn't know much about him, only that my father hated his guts because Dad and Augustus King had been rivals until Augustus had finally gone to jail. Dad had been hoping that once Augustus had gone he'd be able to grab what was left of his empire and take it for himself—he was nothing if not opportunistic.

But apparently Ajax King kept getting in the way.

Maybe that was why I hadn't screamed when Ajax

had appeared in the bathroom. Why I'd believed him when he said he wouldn't hurt me.

He might have once been the heir to the biggest crime empire in Sydney, but he wasn't now and any enemy of my father was a friend of mine.

Of course, I hadn't been thinking straight when he'd appeared in the doorway and clearly I wasn't thinking straight now if all it took to make my heart thump was one look into his eyes.

Forgetting that I'd promised not to speak, I opened my mouth to ask him what was going on but, before I could, he bent and picked me up in his arms.

My stomach dropped away, the world lurching around me; every question I'd been going to ask vanished from my head.

I'd never been held by a man. Couldn't remember the last time I'd been held, full stop.

Had it been this hot? Because that's all I was conscious of. An intense, stunning heat surrounding me. From the hard torso I was lying against and the strong arms locked around me. It made something restless and antsy inside me go utterly still.

I caught my breath.

'Hide your face against my chest,' Ajax murmured before heading straight to the door.

My brain didn't seem able to process the instruction. Hide my face? Why? And what was he doing? Didn't he know that—

There was a sudden crash as he kicked the door open and I caught one glimpse of Colin and the other guy—a new guard whose name I could never remember—and instinctively I turned away, hiding my face against Ajax's broad chest, just like he'd told me to.

The cotton of his shirt had been warmed by the hot skin beneath it and his scent filled my senses. Sandalwood, maybe, and…cedar? I'd taught myself about perfumes once and remembered the scents. Anyway, it was amazing. I pressed my cheek against the fabric, feeling firm muscle beneath it, and inhaled, the smell of him going straight to my head.

'What?' Ajax demanded, his deep voice making his chest vibrate against my cheek. 'Get the fuck out of my way.'

Silence.

I should have been paying attention to what was happening, but being in his arms was way too distracting.

The warmth of his body was soaking through the stupid white cocktail frock Dad had insisted I wear tonight, and I was conscious of how hard he was. Like he'd been carved out of rock, not muscle and bone.

The restless thing inside me had curled up and gone to sleep, as if it felt safe. As if it knew that he would protect me if anything went wrong, which was strange since I knew that men in general weren't particularly safe to be around.

'We're looking for Miss Imogen White,' Colin was saying. 'She was in the—'

'Don't know, don't give a fuck,' Ajax said casually, continuing to walk with me in his arms down the corridor. 'Go check the damn bathroom yourself. There's no one in there now.'

'But you must have—'

'If you hadn't noticed, I'm busy.'

There was more silence after that and, given that Ajax hadn't stopped, it must have meant my guards hadn't realised it was me in his arms. The suit jacket and cap now made sense; he'd been trying to hide my identity.

I'd relaxed totally against him, but curiosity stole through me and I began to turn my head, only to have him say gruffly, 'Keep your head where it is. We're not out of the building yet.'

I nodded and closed my eyes, inhaling warmth and spice and the faint smell of laundry powder from his shirt. His heart was beating beneath my ear and I could hear the rhythm of it, steady and strong and sure.

Like him.

Odd thing to think about a man I'd only just met and didn't know. Maybe I was drunk. Maybe I was high. On him and his magical scent. Whatever, I accepted the thought without protest.

Not that it mattered. He could have been Jack the Ripper and I would have been okay with it if he could get me out of the building without being seen.

The thought of freedom being so close made excitement surge through me and if I hadn't been held so securely in his arms I would have wriggled.

Keeping still was something I found difficult at the best of times, but most especially when I was excited or angry or sad.

A fidgety chatterbox, all the nannies had said about me.

A mess, said my father, looking at me with the disapproval that used to cut me so badly when I was a kid and longing for his attention.

My mother had died when I was born and if she hadn't, things would have been different. Dad would have been different. But she had and he wasn't, and all I remember wanting was his love.

He didn't like my insatiable curiosity or the way I couldn't stop moving. I used to try to stay still, to not piss him off by jogging my leg or humming or asking questions, or any of the other things I did that irritated him, but it had always been a constant battle.

But it wasn't until I was eighteen that my inability to check myself had consequences. Terrible consequences.

Since then I'd tried to stay in the box Dad had put me in, but the fight against my restless nature was never-ending and quite frankly exhausting.

I didn't feel exhausted now, though. Now I could have lain quiet and still in Ajax's arms all day.

I rubbed my cheek absently against the cotton of his shirt, wanting to get closer to him, and he made a growling sound. 'Fuck's sake, don't move until I tell you. Your hair will come down and people will see it and they'll guess who you are.'

I stilled obediently. 'Who do they think I am now then?'

'Some girl I'm carrying back to my cave to screw.'

The words travelled down my spine like an electric shock. 'Really? Do you often carry girls out of balls to screw?'

'You can stop talking now.'

'But what about—'

'Quiet.'

There was a note of deep authority in his voice that calmed me, not that I needed extra calming right now. I was so calm I was nearly catatonic, lulled by his heat and the feeling of being held gently and carefully. As if I was something precious he didn't want to drop.

A large group of people passed by us, their conversation loud, and then cooler air brushed against my bare legs, the glare of neon and streetlights illuminating the white of Ajax's shirt.

We must be outside.

It felt like we were walking down some steps and I could hear cars.

Regret gripped me. Being outside meant he was going to put me down and I would lose his heat and that blissful sense of peace.

I didn't want to. I wanted to stay here, in his arms, against his hard chest, listening to the certainty of his heartbeat.

There was the sound of a car door opening and his arms were loosening, and sure enough I was being let go and bundled into the back of a featureless black van.

'Go,' Ajax ordered the driver as he climbed in behind me, slamming the door closed. Then he pushed me down onto one of the bench seats, grabbed a seat belt and buckled me in as the van took off in a screech of tyres.

I clutched the seat belt as the van lurched, while Ajax sat down himself and did his own belt up.

The warmth that had held me so safe and still was seeping away, making me feel cold, the restless part of me stirring to life again.

'Please tell me that's it.' I stared out the window as the building receded behind us, my heart racing, waiting for my guards to come spilling out. 'Please tell me they're not going to come after us.'

'Oh, they might come after us,' Ajax replied with

infuriating calm. 'But locating us is going to be a different matter.'

I turned to find his gaze on mine, satisfaction gleaming in his icy blue eyes.

My breath caught again.

He was sitting in a casual, arrogant sprawl, long legs outstretched, the material of his shirt pulled tight across his muscled shoulders and chest, as if he didn't care that he was taking up as much room as possible. As if he was expecting *me* to move if I didn't like it, but he certainly wasn't going to.

He was like a king on his throne, staring at me as if I was a new country he'd just conquered.

Through the remains of the warmth left over from his touch, a shiver shot through me.

And all of a sudden it crashed down on me what had just happened and what it meant.

I was free of my father, but I wasn't free. Not when I'd been kidnapped by Sydney's baddest billionaire.

And I had no idea what he was going to do with me.

CHAPTER THREE

Ajax

I SAW THE moment the realisation hit her. The realisation of exactly what she'd got herself into. And, for the first time, wariness crept into her gaze.

It wasn't fear, but I'd take wariness and about fucking time.

She'd been curled up in my arms, all warm and soft, relaxing as if I was her own personal hero all set to save her. And that shit wasn't happening. Not when I wasn't anyone's goddamn hero.

Especially not when all I could think about was that tempting mouth of hers with that fascinating little mole just above her top lip. I wanted to kiss it. I wanted to lick it. I wanted to bite her bottom lip then suck gently on it, watch it get even redder and fuller than it was already.

Not that I would. She might be proving to be unexpectedly tempting, but I had a plan and I wasn't going to deviate from it. Not when her continued virginity was such an important part.

She stared at me, that mesmerising energy she threw off still crackling all around her.

It was good that she was wary. Because I *was* dangerous.

Everyone treated me with caution, the more nervous giving me a wide berth. It was a reputation I cultivated because if there was one thing Dad had taught me, it was that fear kept people in line better than being nice ever did.

And people had to fear me. I didn't want another Augustus King rising in this city and fear of what I might do to any pretenders to Dad's empty throne kept the more ambitious at bay.

'So,' Imogen said, her long delicate fingers clutching at her seat belt. 'This is fun.' Then she had the gall to smile—a bit uncertain but a smile nonetheless. 'Do I get to know where you're taking me? And what you want with me? What about Dad? Won't he be—'

I put a finger across her velvety pink mouth, silencing her, purely because I could.

Her eyes widened.

She looked ridiculously cute swamped by my jacket, with the cap pulled down over her pale hair, staring at me with those big green eyes.

I could still feel the imprint of her in my arms, the warmth of her body nestled against my chest. She'd rested there so quietly, yet I'd felt that live wire quality to her, a subtle vibration that had somehow crawled under my skin and stayed there. It made me think that she wasn't the fragile little thing she'd first seemed. Certainly, when she'd pulled at my hand back up there in the bathroom, there had been a surprising strength to her grip. And even now, after I'd kidnapped her, I could see a glimmer of determination beneath the wariness in her gaze.

Curiosity flickered into life inside me, smouldering alongside the undeniable physical attraction. But I crushed both. Hard. She was a tool, a means to an end, and I couldn't afford any distractions, not now.

'We're going to my house.' I let my finger linger on her lips a fraction, to show her I meant business. Nothing to do with how soft they felt. 'And I'm going to keep you there a little while.'

Her mouth turned up, giving me a smile that had no hesitancy in it whatsoever, the wariness draining from her clear gaze.

And for a second I didn't quite know what to do with that. I was her father's mortal enemy. She had to know who I was—*what* I was. She should be cringing in fear, not giving me bright smiles like I was her best friend.

'Yay.' Her lips moved against my finger, brushing against my skin, the warmth of her breath making me catch mine. 'I was hoping you'd say that. Where do you live?'

Yay? What the fuck? And why the hell was I breathless? Luckily, physical attraction was the easiest appetite to control so I controlled it.

I dropped my finger. 'That doesn't concern you right—'

'What kind of house do you have? Does it have a pool? Is it by the sea?'

'It's not—'

'Can I go outside? Does it have a view?'

'You're not going to—'

'How long can I stay? Will you be there?' Her eyes were glittering with excitement and there was a flush in her pale cheeks, the live wire spitting sparks.

You'd think I'd just promised her the trip of a lifetime, not that I was going to hold her prisoner until her father did what I wanted.

Losing patience, I stared hard at her. 'Interrupt me again and there'll be hell to pay.'

Her lips pressed together obediently, but her eyes didn't lose that excited sparkle. She didn't even have the grace to look ashamed of herself. 'I'm sorry. I always talk when I'm nervous.' Then, clearly picking up on my irritation, she added, 'I didn't interrupt this time.'

'This is a kidnapping. You do understand that, don't you?'

She laughed. 'I know. And?'

Laughing. She'd been kidnapped and now she was *laughing*. And, even worse, the husky, joyful sound sent a hot pulse down my spine, jump-starting something inside me. Something that had been dead a long time.

Shit. Just what I *didn't* want.

I ignored the feeling and scowled. 'You should be frightened of me.'

An arrested expression crossed her face, as if the thought had never occurred to her. 'Should I? I mean, I was a bit unsure a moment ago. But…' Her forehead creased. 'Do you want me to be?'

The thing that had sprung to life inside me burned, her complete lack of fear for some reason more powerful than any aphrodisiac.

Dammit. I wasn't looking to be attracted to her, for fuck's sake. That kind of shit only got in the way and I was *not* looking for distractions right now. Not that I ever had. My own desires were irrelevant when I had a goal in mind and I let nothing distract me from that goal.

Including the bolt of electricity in human form sitting next to me.

I fixed her with a 'don't fuck with me' look. 'Anyone ever tell you that you ask too many questions?'

The colour in her cheeks deepened. 'Kind of.'

'Listen. You know who I am. You must have heard the rumours. They're all true, understand? And yes, you should be scared. Because you have no idea what I'm going to do with you when I get you home.'

'What are you going to do with me?' She didn't sound as if it worried her. At all.

Christ. If ever a woman needed a lesson in proper kidnapping etiquette, it was this one.

I leaned forward fractionally, letting my physical size intimidate her. 'I'm going to ruin you, little one. That's what I'm going to do.'

Or at least I would if her father didn't do what I wanted.

Far from being intimidated, though, Imogen only frowned. As if I'd handed her a fascinating puzzle to work out. 'Ruin me? Like…how?'

This was ridiculous. Did I really have to explain a sexual threat?

'Like this…' I reached out again and this time I brushed my thumb along her lower lip to illustrate my point, because the day I had to explain myself was the day I'd hand in my scary motherfucker badge.

Her mouth was just as soft and warm as it had been when I'd touched it not a minute or so earlier, and the burning thing in my gut flamed like a fucking firework.

Mistake. You shouldn't touch her.

Bullshit. I didn't make mistakes and I wasn't a damn

fifteen-year-old boy touching a woman for the first time. I could control myself. She had a pretty mouth but that was all. Pretty mouths were a dime a dozen and if I wanted one that badly, I'd find one. Later.

Her eyes went huge as I touched her. 'Oh…' The word was warm, exhaled against my skin. '*That* kind of ruin.'

So she understood. Good.

Yet she still didn't look scared. Wary, yes, but there was definitely no fear in her expression.

Hell. What did I have to do? Pull a gun? A knife? A fucking bomb?

'So how exactly do you ruin someone sexually these days?' she went on, her eyes alight with interest. 'It's a bit nineteenth century, if you know what I mean. Virginity isn't the big thing it used to be.'

'That's it?' I dropped my finger from her mouth, ignoring the warmth that lingered on my skin. 'That's your response?'

'Should it be different?' A crease appeared between her brows. 'If you're going to ruin me or whatever—' she waved her hand as if the 'whatever' was negligible and not the threat it very much was '—I'd like to know how you're going to do it. Seeing as how I have a vested interest and all.'

'Screwing you, that's how I'll do it,' I growled, my patience starting to run even thinner than it was already, hoping that would quell her.

'Oh, sure.' She shrugged, very much unquelled. 'Screwing goes without saying. But I'd still like to know how that ruins me.'

Shit, this woman was either simple or…she was playing me.

I was beginning to suspect it was the latter and if that was the case, she'd regret it. I could play that game better than she ever could.

'You're a virgin—'

'Hey, how do you know that?'

'Interrupt me one more time and I'll give you back to your father's men.'

Her mouth closed up tight. Interesting. She really didn't want to go back. I filed that fact away for future reference.

'As I was saying,' I went on. 'You're a virgin and your father has been guarding that very jealously for a long time. You may not think it's important, but it is for him because if he wants to make alliances with potential friends, he's going to use you and your pretty hymen to do it. But how will that work when his virginal daughter has been in the hands of his enemy? Make no mistake. The ruin I'm talking about will make you mine and mine completely, and once you're mine you'll be useless to anyone else, including him.'

Emotion shifted in her eyes, gone so fast I wasn't sure what it was. Not fear, something more complicated than that.

This girl seemed open and sincere, but maybe she wasn't. Maybe there was more to her than there appeared.

The curiosity I thought I'd crushed earlier smouldered back into life, making me want to know exactly *what* more there was.

I'd always enjoyed a complicated woman—I was a man who got bored easily—and I hadn't had complicated for longer than I cared to remember.

But no. This wasn't about what *I* wanted and never had been.

Imogen took a soft breath, the fabric of her strapless white dress pulling tight across a pair of quite frankly beautiful little tits. The dress moulded to her generous hips too, outlining her rounded thighs.

Nice. Very nice. Not usually my type—tall, athletic women handled me better than small kittens like this one. But she was soft and strokeable, and undeniably sexy. What would she be like in bed?

Fucking wildfire.

Another pulse of heat burned through me, making my cock twitch.

'So what does that mean exactly?' She frowned. 'Am I a threat or a tool for you?'

'Both.' I ignored the heat in my groin. 'I want your father to leave Sydney. Only when he's gone will I let you go.'

She glanced down at where her hands clutched at her seat belt, a lock of pale hair falling out from underneath the cap I'd put on her head and down over her shoulder. It gleamed like watered silk in the light coming through the windows. Pretty.

What would it feel like coiled around your finger?

Nothing. Because I wasn't going to touch it.

'That still doesn't really explain this ruin thing,' she said. 'And you haven't said what it involves exactly.'

'What do you want? A fucking diagram?'

A flash of green glinted from underneath her pale lashes. 'Actually, that would be super helpful. Especially since I don't know anything about fucking.'

The heat I was trying to ignore burned a little hotter. Was she…flirting with me? Toying with me? If so, she was playing a dangerous game.

This wasn't a date and I wasn't some harmless boy desperate to kiss her hand. I was the oldest and most feared son of one of Sydney's worst criminals, and I had things in my past that would wipe that expression off her face. That would make her look at me as if I was the devil himself.

Maybe it was time she learned that this wasn't a fun night out and that I wasn't some tame house cat she could stroke, who'd curl up in her lap. I was a wolf and I'd eat this Red Riding Hood alive.

'You really want to know?' I leaned right into her space, getting a kick out of the way she had to press herself against the window to keep the distance between us. 'Are you sure?'

Her eyes went wide, her sulky, pouty mouth opening. And for a second I thought I saw fear there, but then it was gone and something else glittered in the green depths of her gaze.

Yet more excitement.

Shit.

'Seriously, I am *so* sure.' Her voice was on the edge of husky. 'Tell me, Ajax. I'd really like to know how you're going to ruin me.'

CHAPTER FOUR

Imogen

HE WAS VERY CLOSE, inches away. His broad shoulders blocked out the streetlights coming through the opposite window of the van, his body in that pristine white shirt and black suit trousers, a hard wall of muscle in front of me.

And his eyes. Electric blue, so vivid against his olive skin. Fascinating in a way I couldn't describe.

He was so compelling. He made my heart shudder behind my ribs for reasons I didn't understand.

This talk of being ruined... It was all I could think about.

Since I'd been taught at home by tutors, I'd never gone to high school, never dated. I'd never had a teenage crush, except once, on a guy I'd seen through the window of the car while I was on my way somewhere. I'd constructed a whole set of dreamy fantasies around him for at least a week until I'd lost interest in the whole idea.

If I'd had any girlfriends I'd have discussed my lack of a sex life with them. But I didn't even have girlfriends.

What I did have, though, was an insatiable curiosity about pretty much everything, including all the things I wasn't allowed to have.

Such as sex.

I'd learned how to get around the blocks Dad had put on my Internet years ago and I'd looked stuff up. Sexy stuff. Enough to have an idea of what I might like when it came to men.

One thing I hadn't realised, though, was that looking at sex on a computer screen was *very* different to having an actual man right in front of you, looking at you so intently it made you want to burst into flames.

Like me, right now, with him.

'S-so,' I stuttered, unable to keep quiet, my heart racing. 'You know, how does it happen? Do I have to take my clothes off? Do you touch me or—'

'I don't have to touch you to ruin you, little one,' he said in that dark, deep voice I felt right down low inside me.

Okay, wow. That was…intense.

My heartbeat ratcheted up another notch. 'That's a bit patronising, you know. The whole *little one* thing.'

God knows why I was arguing with him. Probably stupid given my situation and the fact that me not being afraid of him clearly annoyed him.

But too bad. I wasn't afraid. He might think that all of this would frighten me, but what he didn't understand was that I didn't see this as a kidnapping. No, this was a rescue.

He'd bloody well *saved* me.

And, for all his talk of ruining me, I knew he wouldn't hurt me. Not a man who'd carried me so gently; close to his chest; holding me as if I were precious.

He was scowling now, not liking that I was arguing, and maybe I was completely crazy but I loved how growly and fierce he was, though I didn't really know why. Maybe it was simply the fact that I could get a reaction from him. Me. The sheltered virgin who could never sit still. Who was of no use to anyone except as a tool.

You're Ajax's tool now.

Yeah, but it felt different somehow. For a start, Ajax was a complete stranger. Unlike my dad, he wasn't supposed to love me and I wasn't supposed to love him. I could push back at him with impunity and it wouldn't matter.

'I don't give a shit whether it's patronising or not,' he said. 'You're my prisoner and I'll call you whatever the fuck I want.' He paused, his gaze like a searchlight finding all my secrets, all my hidden desires. 'Besides,' he added, 'I think you like it.'

I went red. Sadly, I *did* like it. I'd never had anyone refer to me as anything but Imogen and being called *little one* made me think of being curled up in his arms, safe.

Not knowing what to say, I frowned instead.

He smiled, all satisfied like he'd won a point off me. 'Of course you do. But that's not what you wanted to talk about, is it?'

'You were going to tell me how you can ruin me without touching me,' I reminded him. 'How does that work? Is it possible to screw someone without touching them? Do you just talk at me? I mean, maybe I don't know how these things go, but—'

He leaned forward even more, making the rest of what I'd been going to say catch in my throat.

The glass of the window was cold against the back of my head, the door handle jabbing my spine painfully. Yet those sensations seemed quite distant, even irrelevant.

There was only Ajax and his electrifying blue gaze. 'It's very simple.' His voice brushed over my skin like soft black fur. 'First I'd get you to lift up your dress. Then I'd tell you to spread your legs and pull your knickers to the side.' The words became even deeper, even rougher. 'Then I'd get you to slide your fingers over your pussy, rubbing that little clit in exactly the way I tell you to, and not stopping until you come. Hard. While I watch.'

All my breath had vanished, my heartbeat out of control. I couldn't tear my gaze away from his. My cheeks had to be scarlet and there was a definite pressure between my thighs. A pulse. An ache.

Those things he said were shocking and yet…they made me hot and restless and I…wanted to do them.

Except I had a suspicion that he hadn't said them to get me off. He'd said them to frighten me.

Unfortunately for him, fear was the last thing I felt right now.

And it hit me in that moment that Ajax King wasn't a choice my father would *ever* have made for me. It was why I'd been at that stupid ball in the first place, to meet a guy that Dad had decided might be a potential ally. To charm him, be the bait in the honey trap Dad had set up.

Ajax telling me that Dad was using me wasn't anything I didn't know. I'd figured out what my purpose was for Dad after what had happened with Cam, and it wasn't simply to be his treasured daughter.

I was the Princess, the prize he'd use to set various people off against each other, and whom he'd award to whoever was the strongest.

It was like a medieval marriage bargain, where I got no say and my feelings on the subject were irrelevant.

Dad didn't care whether I wanted to be used like that or not. The only aspect of me he cared about was the debt I owed him for being the cause of Mum's death.

A debt I had no choice but to try and repay, even though it wasn't my fault.

But I had a choice now.

I could try and escape, or I could choose to be ruined by Ajax King, Dad's most hated enemy.

Dad would be *so pissed*.

It was perfect.

'Okay,' I said thickly. 'Do you want me to do those things now? Or should I wait till we get to your place?'

He blinked. Rapidly. 'You did hear what I said, didn't you?'

'Uh, yeah. A bit difficult *not* to hear, to be honest.'

'And you understood what I wanted you to do?'

'Of course. I'm not stupid.' I swallowed, my throat dry. Oh, I wanted to touch him. Feel that hard chest I'd been held against, test all that delicious muscle with my hands.

I had a whole folder of hot guys on my computer at home, inspiration pics for when I got too lonely. But having the reality right in front me…

He was so intent, studying me as if he'd never seen anything like me in all his life. 'This doesn't frighten you at all, does it?'

'No,' I said honestly. 'I'm sorry, but it doesn't.'

His straight black brows drew down. 'Why not? It should.'

'Well, it might if I didn't want to do it. But…' I stopped, belatedly self-conscious about what I was admitting to. I was attracted to him, but he might not feel the same way about me. After all, he didn't know me from a bar of soap. 'It's okay, you know,' I went on in a rush. 'You don't have to ruin me if you don't want to. I mean, you might not actually want me and I don't have any experience and—'

'Quiet,' Ajax said for the second time that night, the note of authority in his voice making me fall silent. 'You really have no idea what the fuck you're talking about. If you think playing with a man like me is a good—'

'Playing with you?' I interrupted yet again, shocked. 'I'm not playing with you. I just don't know—'

Ajax took my chin in one hand, his thumb silencing me the way he had earlier. And, just like earlier, I swear I could feel every single whorl of his thumbprint on my lips. As if I were a lock and he the only key.

'Listen,' he said quietly. 'First, you need to shut up and do as you're told. Second, I'm not ruining anyone in the back of a bloody van. I'm not fifteen any more. And third, if you think I don't want you then you're very much mistaken.'

I ignored everything he said but the last part.

He *did* want me.

I shouldn't have done it but, next thing I knew, my hands had let go of their death grip on my seat belt and were reaching out for him, my lips parting so I could taste his thumb pressed against them, the flavour of his skin salty and sharp on my tongue.

My fingertips made contact, pressing against his chest. So warm, so hard…

Ajax made a sound and I felt the vibration of it in my fingertips. And I looked and saw flames. Blue flames.

'Little virgin.' His voice was very soft. 'What the fuck do you think you're doing?'

Oh…

I looked at my hands on his chest, the heat of him burning through my fingertips. Perhaps touching him had been a mistake.

Damn. I'd been trying so hard to modify my behaviour and *not* simply do the first thing that came into my head. I was supposed to think things through, restrain myself, because I knew what happened when I didn't. I'd seen the consequences. And they were terrible.

My cheeks were burning as I snatched my hands away, a combination of shame and embarrassment gripping me. 'I'm sorry,' I muttered against his thumb. 'I didn't mean to. I just…wanted to t-touch you.'

His grip on my chin tightened.

And, before I knew what was happening, his head bent, his mouth brushing lightly over mine.

I'd never been kissed on the lips before, and for a second my brain simply ceased to function. There was softness, a fleeting pressure and heat. Lots and lots of heat.

A current of electricity crackled over my skin, goosebumps following along in its wake, and my hands were lifting once again, reaching for him, but he was gone, my fingers closing on empty air.

Panting, I realised that the sudden darkness meant

my eyes were closed, so I opened them to find his wintry blue gaze staring into mine.

'You kissed me,' I said stupidly. 'Why?'

His beautiful mouth quirked. 'How else was I going to shut you up?'

'I wasn't—'

'And to get a taste of what we're working with here.'

I couldn't think. What was he talking about? 'I don't understand.'

'Of course you don't.' That quirk became a smile, satisfied and somehow very male. 'But you'll find out.'

'What do you mean?'

He didn't answer. He merely straightened up and sat back in his seat, getting out his phone and looking down at the screen.

Dismissing me.

A million questions swarmed but, perhaps for the first time in my life, it was easy to stay quiet. Because I could still feel that kiss, the imprint of his lips on mine, tingling, burning…

I'd only known him half an hour. God.

Turning away, I stared sightlessly out the window of the van at the neon of the city outside, not even thinking about how cool it was that I was out without an entourage, on my own for the first time in my life.

Out from under my father's thumb.

My own woman at last.

No, all I could think about was Ajax bloody King and that kiss.

And, for the second time that night, I wondered if maybe I was in way over my head.

CHAPTER FIVE

Ajax

I SAT BACK in my chair on the big stone terrace that looked out over the sea, nursing an espresso. The sun was warm on my face, the ocean busy throwing itself against the rocks below the house I'd claimed after Dad had gone to jail.

Last night I'd shown Imogen to the bedroom I'd set aside for her and she'd gone quietly, without peppering me with any more questions.

Satisfied she was secure for the night, I'd then sent texts to my two brothers, telling them that I wouldn't be around for a week or so and that they were to handle any emergencies that might crop up.

Luckily their personal lives had settled down recently with two lovely women keeping them on the straight and narrow. God knows it was about time someone other than me stayed on top of things, and I was appreciative.

It certainly helped me now when I had to concentrate all my attention on a lovely woman of my own.

A strangely fascinating young woman, who was not in any way what I'd anticipated.

The virgin part, yes. The questions and the excitement and the sheer vibrating energy of her, not so much.

I hoped that wouldn't become a problem.

But that was an issue for later. First I had to contact White, let him know I had Imogen, and deliver my ultimatum.

I picked up my phone and pressed a button, waiting until the contact I'd been given answered the call.

'Yeah, who is this?' It was one of White's thugs.

'Ajax King,' I said curtly. 'Tell your boss I have his daughter. If he wants to see her safe and sound, get him to call me at this number.'

I didn't wait for a response, cutting the call then putting the phone back down on the table and ignoring it as it began to ring almost immediately.

I wasn't going to answer him right away. He could stew for a couple of hours.

Glancing down at my watch, I checked the time.

Nine-thirty in the morning.

Jesus Christ, just how long was Imogen going to sleep?

Kidnapped women were not supposed to have long lie-ins when their captors were waiting to inform them of the rules of their captivity.

In spite of my satisfaction with how easily my plan had come together, a thread of annoyance wound through me.

I couldn't believe how unafraid of me she'd been in the van last night, even when I'd deliberately been explicit, thinking that would scare the shit out of her.

But the bloody woman only seemed to find that even more exciting. And then she'd touched me, laid those delicate little fingers on my chest, pressing lightly, *feeling* me.

As if she had no idea about the chemistry flaring between us.

As if I was no fucking threat to her at all.

That touch shouldn't have affected me in the slightest.

But it had.

Given that, I shouldn't have kissed her and Christ knew why I had. Perhaps it was simply the way she'd looked at me, as if she'd never seen anything so fascinating in all her life, and then the assumption that I didn't want her, like she'd be disappointed if I didn't…

Nice justifications. You just wanted her.

But since when had what I wanted ever mattered?

Except her lips had been as soft as I'd known they would be, and she'd smelled of something sweet, something that had made my heart twist inside my chest. Roses. My mother's favourite flower.

Ah, fuck, what was wrong with me? It was just a kiss from a wide-eyed virgin. Nothing to get wound up about.

Whatever my own feelings on the subject, though, one thing was clear: her virginity was the only leverage I had and so it had to remain intact.

I had to stay focused on my end game, because that was all that mattered.

Even if some other things get broken?

Yes, even then. Years ago, I'd had to stand by while my middle brother, Leon, had been kidnapped and tortured at the hands of my father's enemies, and let my youngest brother, Xander, be used as some kind of evil financial genius to grow Dad's empire.

That was my fault, my responsibility.

But my goal had always been to take Dad down, to save my city, and that outweighed everything. Even if it meant pretending I was on board with everything Dad did, no matter how it had sickened me.

The end justified any means.

And even now that end had been accomplished, the story wasn't done. We still had enemies. And I would keep protecting my brothers.

I'd do the hard things so that no one else had to.

I sipped my coffee, gazing out at the sea, white-capped and with a few boats sailing here and there. It was a peaceful view and one I'd always loved when I was a kid, imagining I could just get in one of those boats and sail the fuck away, escape my father and his legacy for good.

A dream.

Despite the small yacht I kept in the boathouse at the foot of the cliffs, I'd never escaped and I was never going to.

Dad might be in jail, but he wasn't the only one with a life sentence. That was fine, though. It was something I'd accepted long ago.

I glanced down to check the time again.

Quarter to ten.

Time for my prisoner to get the hell up.

I put my coffee down on the table and went back into the house, making my way into the wing that had once housed my stepsister and Dad's second wife, and which I'd had renovated as guest quarters.

There was room enough to house an entire football team, though right now there was only the one occupant.

The unexpected little virgin I'd kidnapped the night before.

I strode down the hall that ran the length of the wing, the polished floorboards shining in the sunlight coming through the windows.

Arriving at Imogen's door, I stopped outside it and knocked lightly.

There was no response.

Jesus, she'd better still be in there. Not that she'd be able to escape even if she wanted to, not given the security I'd surrounded the house with. The place was a fortress. Nothing got in or out. Including her.

Still, it was better to be safe than sorry so I didn't wait, pushing the door open and stepping inside.

The room faced the ocean, one wall just glass to enhance the view. A king-sized bed had been pushed up against the wall at right angles to the glass, and in the centre of the bed, all curled up like a sleepy cat, was Imogen.

Sunlight fell over the bed, her long, silky pale hair tangled across the white linen of the pillowcases, a sheet wrapping around her middle, leaving the rest of her uncovered. She hadn't even bothered to undress, and was still wearing her white dress.

Her hands were tucked under her chin, her pale lashes lying motionless on her cheeks, deeply asleep. A smile curved that pretty mouth I'd kissed the night before, as if she was tucked up in her own bed and having a lovely dream, not a prisoner of Sydney's most infamous King.

Lust flickered to life inside me, dark and dirty. I wanted to go over to the bed, pull away her dress, uncover her satiny, strokeable skin and ravage her carnal mouth. Find out whether she'd be as wild and electric with my dick inside her as I thought she'd be. Whether she'd shock those long dead parts of me back into life with a touch…

Ignoring the lust, I leaned against the doorframe instead, taking a moment to study her uninterrupted.

Last night she'd been happy that I'd kidnapped her and even though her lack of fear of me had been annoying, it did tell me one thing: being captured by me was preferable to being her father's prisoner.

I wondered why. Her father had his own fledgling crime syndicate going on, extortion and violence the means he used to keep his followers loyal, and being related to someone like that wasn't exactly going to be a picnic. Hell, I should know. I was related to a prick like that myself.

But why was being *my* prisoner preferable to being his? I didn't use violence, not these days, but I was going to use her the way he had—for my own ends. The only thing that distinguished me from him was that my goal was ultimately to protect people.

Pushing myself away from the doorframe, I moved over to the side of the bed. She slept on, completely unaware that her kidnapper was standing beside her, staring at her.

Hell. The woman had no sense of danger whatsoever.

You like that. You like that a lot.

Imogen shifted, making a sexy noise and snuggling into the pillow. The top of her strapless dress had pulled down, her rounded breasts pushing against it.

My cock, the predictable fuck, hardened at the view. I ignored it.

'Wake up, little one.' I couldn't keep the growl out of my voice. 'I'm getting tired of waiting for you.'

She made another of those noises, then her lashes fluttered and she sighed, a sliver of green appearing as she opened her eyes.

Automatically, I searched her face for any signs of fear but there were none. Apparently, waking up to find me standing beside her bed wasn't frightening or even all that surprising.

In fact, as her gaze found mine, that delicious velvety mouth turned up in a slow and sleepy smile.

She's delectable.

The heat I'd been fighting tightened its grip.

'Oh,' she said, the word exhaled on a long, relieved-sounding breath. 'Thank God. I was afraid you were a dream.'

'I'm not a dream,' I said flatly. 'I'm a nightmare.'

She grinned then threw her arms above her head, stretching unselfconsciously in the sunlight like a sleepy cat. 'No, you're not. And it was definitely *not* a nightmare.'

The top of her dress dipped even lower, revealing lots of pale silky skin, and, despite myself, I couldn't stop staring. My hands itched to tug that fabric down, to see what colour her nipples were and what they might taste like if I sucked on them.

'Are you sure?' I finally dragged my gaze from her chest, but looking into her eyes wasn't any better. They were wide, the colour of new grass, and I caught a hint of her scent—roses and heat…

Delicious.

'Oh, I'm sure.' She blinked at me, apparently unaware of how close to the knife-edge I was. 'I can even tell you about it if you want.'

'I do not want.' I kept my voice cold, trying to force away the ache in my groin. 'What I would like is for you to listen. I have some things I need to say to you.'

'Really?' Her tongue crept out, small and pink, touching her top lip. The move wasn't flirtatious but I was riveted anyway. 'What things?'

I knew I should turn away, look at something other than that small pink tongue and soft mouth; that tiny mole near her upper lip; the pulse at the base of her pale throat.

But that would be to admit I wasn't in control of this situation, that somehow she had the power here, and there was no way in hell I was doing that.

So I continued to stare at her. 'Your father. I've told him I have you.'

Her gold-tipped lashes swept down, veiling her gaze. 'Oh. I see.' Slowly she pushed herself up so she was sitting on the bed, tugging up the top of her dress as she did so, which was probably a good thing considering the state of my damn cock. 'And what did he say?'

'I didn't give him a chance to say anything. Once he's got the message he'll call me.'

She sat with her head bent, looking down at her hands twisted in her lap. Her pale hair lay over her shoulders and streamed down her back, gleaming in the sun like new minted gold.

There was a stillness to her now, that vibrating energy muted. 'So what's going to happen now then?'

'What do you mean, what's going to happen now?'

I frowned. 'Nothing's going to happen now. You're my prisoner and you stay here. End of story.'

'I don't care about that.' She lifted her head. 'What I want to know is when you're going to ruin me. I mean, that's what you said you were going to do.' Something that looked a lot like disappointment glittered in her eyes. 'Or did you not mean it?'

CHAPTER SIX

Imogen

YES, I WAS disappointed and, even though I tried, I couldn't hide it.

Last night when he'd shown me to my room and told me there was no point escaping because the whole house was surrounded by his men, I'd been expecting him to continue what he'd started with that kiss.

But he hadn't. He'd pointed out the en suite bathroom then left.

It was a bit of an unhappy surprise after I'd decided that he was the perfect way to get my revenge on Dad.

I'd decided not to argue about it, though. I was tired anyway and consoled myself with the thought that maybe I could ask him about it the next day.

So I'd lain down on the bed fully dressed, shut my eyes and had gone out like a light.

It had been the best sleep I'd had in years, and that dream I'd had about him had really helped.

My very *naughty* dream.

I'd had sex dreams in the past, usually involving faceless men who would touch me and then walk away, leaving me hot and aching and restless with feelings I didn't understand.

But not last night. Last night I'd dreamed I'd stayed in that van and this time the man wasn't faceless. He had rough, blunt, handsome features and eyes the colour of a winter sky. And he'd watched me as I pulled up my dress, telling me what to do in his deep, harsh voice…

God, so *hot*. And now there was an ache between my legs, a throbbing heat. I wanted him to touch me, to make good on all the threats he'd delivered the night before, but, given the way he was standing there, the expression on his face utterly impassive, it was obvious he had no intention of doing so.

Dammit.

Did that mean that my one and only chance for getting back at Dad, of having any kind of choice about being with a man *I* wanted, was gone?

To make matters worse, Ajax looked unbelievably good in the white T-shirt and jeans he had on, the short sleeves exposing heavily muscled arms and inked olive skin. I hadn't realised he was tattooed and I could barely drag my gaze from all those black lines snaking around his biceps and forearms. That and his beautiful mouth. And the way the cotton pulled over his broad chest…

I could barely drag my gaze from him, full stop.

He was just taunting me now, wasn't he?

'No.' He crossed his arms across that incredible chest. 'I didn't mean it.'

It was strange to feel the hurt so personally, but I did.

'So you lied,' I said, only just stopping myself from crossing my arms too.

Ajax frowned, the mesmerising blue of his eyes sharpening. 'I'm not sure I like your tone.'

I should have stopped arguing, but I wasn't good at hiding my feelings and the disappointment was biting unexpectedly deep. 'You told me you wanted me. Was that a lie?'

'You should be more worried about the fact that you're my prisoner, not whether or not I'm going to fuck you.'

I lifted my chin. 'You know, for an ex-criminal mastermind, or whatever you are, you're not very smart. I don't care about being kidnapped or about being your prisoner.'

'You should care.'

'Why? I just wanted to get away from Dad and you helped me do that.'

'I did *not* help you.'

I sniffed. 'Whatever, dude. As far as I'm concerned, you got me away from Dad and that's the only thing that matters to me.'

A muscle leapt in the side of his impressive jaw. 'You don't care that all you've done is swap cages?'

'No. Anyway, you told me last night you'd let me go when Dad leaves Sydney.' At least Ajax's cage wouldn't end up crushing me. Probably.

He stared at me for a minute, not saying anything. As if he couldn't quite figure me out. Which I liked. Especially considering I got nothing but dismissal from Dad.

'If he doesn't,' Ajax said, 'I'm going to take your virginity. You do understand that, don't you?'

Seriously? He thought I didn't understand? Maybe I should have told him what I'd decided, but if he was grumpy now, he'd definitely be grumpy about the fact that I wanted to use him purely as a way to get back at Dad.

I gave him an exasperated look. 'And do *you* understand that I'm okay with you taking my virginity? I mean, why do you think I didn't mind any of what you said to me last night in the van?'

'Little one, you barely know me. And you've certainly got no fucking idea what losing your virginity to me even means.'

'Okay, first, like I told you last night, I'm not stupid. I have some idea what losing my virginity means. Second, I've read about you. I know about your reputation.'

He remained motionless beside the bed, his eyes glittering strangely, his big body radiating tension. 'Whatever you heard about my reputation, just know that it's twice as bad and twice as fucked up as any of the rumours. I'm not a man you want anywhere near your bed, Imogen.'

That didn't sound like a 'no'. More like a…warning. Too bad I didn't care about warnings.

'Why not?' I asked. 'The rumours said you once took down a drug ring all by yourself and that you broke the kneecaps of—'

'Enough.' His voice was as hard and cold as the look in his eyes. 'You'll remain my prisoner until your father leaves Sydney. That's all.'

I bit my lip, trying to hold my tongue and hide my disappointment.

Except I could see my chance for revenge slipping further and further away and a question came out all the same. 'So all those threats last night were empty ones?'

His scowl became thunderous. 'Don't push me.'

Another warning. Which I also ignored.

If I couldn't change his mind now, then I'd be returned to Dad like an unwanted present, free to be handed to whomever pleased him the most.

And I would never, ever have this chance, this choice again.

'Why not?' I asked. 'What are you going to do to me? I know you won't hurt me—'

'You don't know that.'

'Yes, I do. You didn't last night when you kidnapped me, which means you're not going to now. I mean, you could have used my life to get Dad to do what you want, but you didn't. You used my virginity. Which is a whole lot friendlier than, say, actual murder.'

His expression shifted, the look in his eyes sharpening. 'Tell me why you were so pleased to be kidnapped by me.'

The change of subject caught me off guard. Should I tell him everything? Maybe I shouldn't.

It said something about me that I hadn't realised how prescribed my life had become until I was eighteen, and I was a bit of ashamed of that. And then there was the fact that it had almost taken a man's life to make me see it.

Yeah, I wasn't too keen to share that with him.

I'd had one attempt at a normal life, where I'd tried to have friends, a job, go to uni—all the things a girl my age should have. And it had been great—until I'd impulsively asked a guy I liked out for coffee, only to have poor Cameron beaten half to death in an alleyway.

Dad had called me into his office afterwards to inform me that it had been him who'd ordered it and that I needed to be more careful with whom I associated. That had been a wake-up call for me about how far he was prepared to go to keep me out of anyone's reach.

I'd wanted to leave ever since, but the opportunity had never presented itself until Ajax had showed up.

'I was tired of being a prisoner,' I said, deciding to keep some of the truth to myself. 'I'd been trying to figure out how to get away from him for ages and you came along at just the right time.'

His gaze roamed over me and I felt it like the sunlight falling on my skin. No, hotter than that. Way hotter. 'You don't act like a woman who's been a prisoner for years.'

'How is a woman who's been a prisoner for years supposed to act?' I shifted on the bed, restless all of a sudden.

I didn't want to sit here and talk about Dad and how he'd curtailed my life. Or about how I'd been so desperate for his approval that I'd let him. Or about Mum and the constant reminder of the debt I had to pay.

You can't pay it now.

And I never would. But surely that didn't mean I wasn't allowed to have a life? I wanted to have a taste of all the stuff I'd missed out on. Stuff like exploring having sex with Ajax King.

Surely that was allowed?

Except Ajax completely ignored my slightly pissy tone. 'Did he hurt you?'

'Who? Dad?' I moved to the side of the bed and slipped off it. Not physically.' Emotionally, yes. Another thing I didn't want to talk about.

I walked past Ajax and went over to the massive

windows that looked out over the sea. It was so beautiful. The only thing I'd seen from the windows of Dad's
isolated house in the Blue Mountains, where I mainly
lived, was trees and paddocks and yet more trees.

'Wow,' I breathed, staring at the ocean and white-
capped waves and the yachts sailing on it. 'What an
amazing view. Can I go outside and see it? Do you
have a boat?'

'No, you can't go outside, not yet. And yes, I have
a boat.'

I could feel the pressure of his stare against my back
but I didn't turn around, keeping my gaze on the sea,
enjoying the way he was looking at me. 'Oh, good.
Can I go out—?'

'What did he do?' Ajax's deep voice cut through
mine like a hot knife through cold butter.

The damn man had a one-track mind.

'Can we not talk about that?' Slowly I turned
around. 'Can't we talk about what you promised me
in the van last night?'

Ajax had remained by the bed, but was now facing
me, his arms folded across his chest. The expression
on his hard features was difficult to read, but something steely glinted in his eyes. 'I'm not sleeping with
you, Imogen. I've already made that clear.'

He said it so…flatly. As if that kiss he'd given me,
that small taste of pleasure, didn't mean a thing.

*Of course it didn't. He just told you he didn't mean
it. The real question is: why does it mean so much to
you?*

Wasn't that obvious? Dad had told me what to do my
entire life and now I had a chance to do what *I* wanted
for a change, I couldn't—wouldn't—give it up.

'You're not going to sleep with me *yet*,' I amended for him. 'But why can't we do it now? Dad will never know.'

'He will if he demands a doctor's examination.'

My face went hot because, knowing Dad, that's exactly what he would demand.

How humiliating.

'As it stands now,' Ajax went on ruthlessly, 'he's going to have to take my word that I haven't touched you.'

'You could…lie, maybe?' I tried not to sound too hopeful.

But that was clearly the wrong thing to say because the blue of his eyes became ice. 'My word as a King means something to men like him. And I won't put that at risk with a lie simply because you want to lose your virginity.'

I blinked, feeling like he'd thrown a bucket of cold water over me, with an extra helping of shame following along behind it. I'd gone full Imogen on him last night, not even bothering to try and contain myself. Asking questions and interrupting. Touching him without asking and then getting annoyed when he told me to stop.

I'd made it all about me. I hadn't even thought about him.

'I'm sorry.' I shoved away my disappointment, trying to regain my dignity. 'You don't want to sleep with me and that's fine. I respect that.'

But something in my tone must have given me away because the muscle in the side of his jaw leapt again. 'You're a sexy woman, Imogen. And it's not about your lack of attractiveness, understand? But nothing gets in the way of me achieving a goal, and that includes any personal distractions.'

I didn't take offence at being lumped under the heading of 'personal distractions'. I was too curious.

'The goal being to get Dad out of the city?' I asked. 'Why?'

'Why do you think? Your father is trying to set himself up as a pretender to Dad's empty throne and that's not happening. Not while I can still fucking breathe.'

A whisper of cold swept through me. I knew who my father was. I knew that the money we had didn't come from him working hard. I understood that my mother's death had left a hole inside him that he'd been struggling to fill. I'd once wanted to be the one who helped him fill that hole, but that had been before he'd made it clear that I could never be that for him.

He didn't want the child his wife had died giving birth to.

He preferred money. He preferred power.

Of course he'd want to be the new Augustus King.

At that moment, Ajax's phone started buzzing.

He pulled it from his pocket and checked the screen then he hit the answer button and raised it to his ear. 'King.'

Silence fell as whoever was on the other end of the call talked.

Ajax simply stared at me. 'Listen,' he said eventually, his voice ice-cold. 'Here's what's going to happen. The only way you'll get your daughter back is if you get the fuck out of Sydney and stay out. And if you don't? Then I'll take her precious virginity and make her mine.'

Another silence fell, Ajax's gaze burning.

Was it weird to find the way he'd said that hot? Not that I cared if it was weird or not. It *was* hot. Especially the way he'd said 'make her mine'.

Calm down. You've known him approximately twelve hours or less.

So? It wasn't like I was going to fall in love with him or anything. This was all about attraction.

'Yes,' Ajax went on. 'She's alive.' He held out his phone towards me. 'Say something to your father, Imogen.'

I looked at the phone and everything I'd been thinking vanished from my head as a wave of dread swept through me.

I didn't want to talk to Dad. He'd be disgusted with me for allowing myself to be taken. And it would be my fault. Everything was my fault.

Why do you still care what he thinks?

I didn't know. But that didn't change the fact that I cared.

Ajax's blue gaze narrowed then, as abruptly as he'd pointed the phone at me, he lifted it back to his ear. 'She'll speak to you later. Remember what I said.' Then he disconnected the call without another word.

I cleared my throat, feeling like an idiot, but Ajax spoke before I could say anything. 'Take a shower if you like—I've asked my housekeeper to leave you some clothes. There's breakfast on the terrace for you when you're done. You're allowed to go anywhere in the house including outside, but the top floor is off limits.' He paused, giving me a look that pinned me where I stood. 'I'm going to be out the rest of the day, but don't worry. You're safe here. Understand?'

'Yes,' I croaked. 'But where are you—?'

'Later,' he said. 'We'll talk more later.'

And, before I could ask him any more questions, he turned and walked out.

CHAPTER SEVEN

Ajax

I ABSENTED MYSELF from the house over the next couple of days, using the time to have meetings with people who should have known better than to fuck with me. Meetings that involved gentle reminders of who was boss…and that wasn't William White.

The reminders weren't of the violent kind—it wasn't necessary when threatening people's money worked just as well—but that didn't mean I was kind. I'd ruin every last son of a bitch in this town if they even so much as kept White's name in their contact list, and they knew it.

I also tried not to think about Imogen, an impossible task seemingly.

My brain kept returning to the look on her face when I'd handed her the phone that morning. She'd stared at it like I'd handed her a snake, making every one of my protective instincts sit up and take notice.

She'd told me her father hadn't hurt her physically, yet she *really* didn't want to talk to him. In fact, the only time I'd seen her scared was when I'd given her that phone.

Why? What had he done to her?

Knowing what the story was between her and White didn't affect my overall goal and technically it could be called a distraction. But I couldn't stop thinking about it.

I couldn't stop thinking about what a delicate thing she'd seemed that morning either, with the light falling on her hair, turning her from white and pale into sun-drenched gold. She was fragile and vulnerable, a woman in need of protection.

Yet that's not all she was. There had been a demanding element to her, flashes of a strong, stubborn will, plus an honesty I hadn't experienced in a long time. The world I moved in—even now it was totally legit— was full of bluffs and façades and gambles and trade-offs. Games. That's what doing business was all about.

But Imogen didn't appear to have a façade at all. She didn't strike me as a game-player either. There was no artifice to her, no guile. She wanted me and she'd been totally straight up about that.

Hot.

It was probably a good thing I'd stayed out of the house. God knew my dick could sure as hell use some time out.

Two days later I stepped out of the building where I'd had my last meeting, heading to the featureless black sedan where Andy, my assistant, was waiting for me.

Getting into the car, I settled myself then slammed the door shut behind me.

As Andy pulled into the traffic, my thoughts drifted back to my little captive. I hadn't seen her for the past couple of days, though my housekeeper had been giving me daily updates, which consisted of Imogen roaming around my house being bored, apparently.

Too bad. Then again, Imogen kept asking my housekeeper questions which annoyed Mrs Jacobs because I'd forbidden her to answer them.

I probably needed to give Imogen a few more things to do.

You could think of a couple of things.

I scowled at the traffic. Yeah, there were a lot of things I could think of for her to do. Particularly things involving a bed.

Sadly, that wasn't happening. I had to keep my eye on the big picture, that's what I'd always been about. I couldn't get obsessed with the details and, right now, Imogen White was merely a detail.

Like your brothers were details?

Shit, my brothers had never been details. No, I hadn't been able to stop what had happened to them, not when I'd had to keep up the façade of the loyal first son to Dad, but it had been vital that Dad thought I was on his side. That way he wouldn't see me working in the background to take him and his filthy empire down.

Yes, Leon and Xander had got caught in the crossfire, but they were better now. They had the lives they'd always wanted and all because Dad was no longer in the picture.

It had all been worth it in the end.

My phone buzzed in my pocket.

I hauled it out and looked down at the screen. Yet another call from White. Should I answer it this time or leave the prick to stew a little longer?

I hit the answer button but didn't say anything.

'King?' White's voice vibrated with fury. 'You'd better be answering this time, you piece of—'

'Are you ready to give me what I want?' I interrupted. 'Or am I going to have to disconnect yet again?'

There was a silence, White evidently trying to get himself under control. 'I'll call the police. Tell them you have my daughter.'

'No, you won't. You can't afford to have the police getting into your business and we both know it.'

He muttered a curse. 'I'm not leaving this city. It's impossible.'

'Then I'll make sure your pure Princess isn't so pure any more.'

'You can't. She won't let you touch her.'

I laughed. 'Oh, you'd be surprised. She seems to quite like the idea.'

'If you've even so much as—'

'Relax, I haven't done anything to her.' Apart from a kiss, but that didn't count. 'Her virginity is quite safe.'

'I've only got your word for that.'

I watched the city moving past my window. 'And my word is all you'll get.'

'The word of a King.' He spat the words down the phone, my name dripping with contempt.

'You respected my father's,' I said coldly. 'You'll respect mine.'

'What makes you think I care enough about her virginity to pack up my life and go somewhere else anyway?'

'Because you need it. Once she's mine, she'll be useless to you. And you don't have anything else of value to get people on your side, do you?'

'You have no idea—'

'I've done my research, White. Believe me. You don't have the finance, not these days. All you have is your daughter.' I leaned back against the seat. 'Except you don't even have her now, do you? I could make her mine, get a couple of kids on her. What do you say to having a couple of King grandchildren, hmm?'

'Fuck you.' His voice was bitter. 'I'll leave and when you free her I'll take her somewhere else. A new city. Melbourne, maybe.'

'Fine. I don't care where you go.' And I didn't. There was only one thing that mattered to me. 'Just stay the fuck away from what's mine.'

There was silence from the other end of the phone, though I could feel his fury.

'I want proof of life,' he said eventually. 'In person.'

Something inside me tightened. 'A meeting?'

'Yes. Alone.'

'No.' I didn't even need to think about it. 'There will be no meeting.'

'Listen. You let me talk to her for five minutes, just so I know she's okay and unhurt. And if she's fine I'll leave Sydney. I'll even take a few people with me so they're out of your hair.'

Interesting. He was clearly desperate to have her back if he was prepared to negotiate. And I'd certainly be happy with fewer troublemakers to worry about. 'That could work,' I allowed.

'Once I've gone, you can let her go and we'll go elsewhere. But only on condition that wherever it is I go, you stay out of it.'

My smile widened. 'Like you can tell me what to do. I dictate the terms here, White. Not you. But I'm feeling magnanimous. I'm sure a five-minute meeting with your daughter can be arranged.'

'Good. Tonight. Bring her to—'

'As I was saying. *I* dictate the terms. Which means I'll be in touch.' I didn't wait for him to launch into yet another round of protests, I simply disconnected the call then put my phone back in my pocket.

Good. This was proceeding much more smoothly than I'd planned. If all he wanted was a meeting with his daughter, then that was easy enough to arrange. Of course, he might want to meet with Imogen in order to steal her back, but I'd make sure that didn't happen.

Will Imogen agree, though?

I thought back to the way she'd frozen up when I'd tried to hand her the phone and the fear in her face…

Yeah, her agreement might be a problem.

Perhaps it was time I asked her what the deal with her father was. Directly.

I finished up the last of my meetings then headed back to the King mansion in Vaucluse, darkness beginning to fall.

A kick of excitement hit me as the car approached the gates, which was strange since I'd never particularly enjoyed coming home before. I'd had the place renovated to the highest standards, but it was little more than a hotel room. Too many shit memories basically.

But not tonight. Tonight there was someone waiting for me.

Except when I got inside I couldn't find her.

She wasn't in the kitchen I almost never used, with all its stainless steel and white tiles. Or in the cavernous lounge with the windows that faced the ocean and the black leather sectional sofas. She wasn't in any of the bedrooms on the first floor, or in the gardens outside. Or by the pool on the terrace that looked out over the sea. Or in the massive bathroom with the bath big enough to be a hot tub all on its own.

Mrs Jacobs had gone home so I snapped questions at my security staff, but they swore she hadn't left the building.

Which meant only one thing.

She was upstairs. Where I'd told her she wasn't allowed to go.

Bad little one. That was where my bedroom and office were, my private space.

I stormed up the stairs, taking them two at a time but soundlessly. Because if she was up there after I'd explicitly told her not to, then she was up there for a reason. And if that reason was something I didn't want her to fucking do, then I wanted to catch her in the act.

My office was empty, same with the other couple of rooms, which left only my bedroom.

Silently I stepped inside.

One wall was glass, as was most of the side of the house that faced the ocean, and the light shining through it showed me nothing but an empty room, except for my bed that faced the huge windows.

I waited, barely breathing, allowing myself to become aware of the space around me, the breath of air on my skin, any change in temperature, the slightest of sounds. It was a trick I'd learned from Dad's old Head of Security and it had helped me on more than one occasion.

I moved through the room slowly, expanding my awareness outwards, listening.

Nothing.

I stopped by the big walk-in closet. The door was half open, exactly the way I'd left it this morning.

But there was the faintest of scents in the air.

Roses.

CHAPTER EIGHT

Imogen

I LEANED IN to the suit that hung from the rail in front of me and sniffed, the warm scent of sandalwood and cedar filling my senses.

It was such a delicious smell. I wanted to bury my nose in the lapels of Ajax's jacket and spend the rest of the evening breathing it in.

Okay, so it was a little weird, me being in his closet and sniffing his clothing, and I did feel bad about poking around in his private space.

It was only that after two days of being alone with nothing to do I was going stir-crazy.

After he'd left me that morning, I'd decided that the only way to figure out how to get him on board with the whole losing my virginity thing was to explore as much of his house as I could, see what I could discover about him. And then perhaps use it to my advantage.

Unfortunately, there wasn't much to discover. He had an industrial, minimalist aesthetic which seemed to involve no clutter anywhere and absolutely nothing personal, including no knick-knacks or family photographs.

So I'd asked what I could of his housekeeper, Mrs Jacobs, but she wouldn't give me any answers, getting annoyed when I attempted to press the issue.

So I'd tried to wait him out.

I swam in the pool. I walked around the gardens. I watched TV and a few movies. I peered through his library and the bookshelves full of books.

But I couldn't settle. Every passing hour was another hour of my freedom gone. Another hour closer to going back to my father and a life of no choices about anything.

It put me in a foul mood.

This wasn't just about sex and my stupid hymen. Or even revenge against my dad. This was about life. *My* life. And what was missing from it. Choice. That was what was missing.

And I wanted the very first choice that I made to be about Ajax. Learning more of his secrets. Discovering more of his touch, more of *him*. And the longer he stayed away, the hungrier for him I became.

That's why I was up here on the forbidden second level of his house. Because my curiosity had morphed into frustration and I hadn't been able to contain it. I couldn't stop obsessing about what was up there, thinking that if he'd told me to stay away, it must mean that there was something he didn't want me to see.

So on the third day I'd crept up the stairs.

The second level had been quiet, with the same kind of uncluttered, minimalist vibe that the downstairs had.

There was an office and a bedroom that both faced the ocean and made the most of the awesome view.

His office was a plain white room with a polished wooden floor and a huge slab of black wood that served as a desk, with a sleek silver computer on it. Book-shelves lined two walls, all stacked with business texts and filing boxes. But, unlike downstairs, there was a piece of art on the wall above his desk: a painting of a yacht on the ocean, sailing towards the horizon. The picture was simple and clean and beautifully done. I could almost smell the salt coming from it, feel the wind in my hair.

Why had he hung this picture here? What was it that he liked about it?

I was tempted to look at his books or have a nosey at his computer, but I did have a few scruples and decided not to in the end, moving into his bedroom instead.

That was a nice space, the only furniture a mas-sive bed that faced the wall of glass and a dresser. There were two photos on it, who I assumed were his brothers, Leon and Xander.

There wasn't much else in the bedroom but, since the door to the closet was open, I put my head in and had a quick look inside. That's when his scent hit me and that's when I stepped inside, moving to where one of his suits hung, wanting more of it and the warm feel-ing it gave me.

Yes, I was an idiot and sniffing his clothes was ri-diculous. But that scent reminded me of how he'd made me feel the night he'd kidnapped me. Safe. Peaceful. Yet excited too.

You should probably leave before he catches you here.

I straightened reluctantly. I really didn't want him to catch me on the second level, especially not in his closet with my nose in his suit.

Abruptly, fingers closed around my upper arm.

I froze, a burst of panic exploding through me.

The fingers tightened in an irresistible grip and I found myself being pulled gently but firmly out of the closet then pushed with the same irresistible gentleness against the closet door.

An expanse of white cotton was in front of me, a T-shirt pulled tight over a broad, muscled chest.

Oh, hell.

I went from panic to excitement in seconds as it slowly penetrated whose fingers were wrapped around my upper arm. And the scent that I'd been inhaling only moments before was now coming direct from the source.

'Little one,' Ajax rumbled. 'What the fuck are you doing in my closet?'

Embarrassment set fire to my cheeks and I wanted to sink straight through the floor.

Going through his things had turned out to be a really stupid idea.

'I'm sorry.' I stared at his chest because I couldn't bear to look up at him. 'I was just…uh…bored.'

'Bored,' he echoed. 'So bored that you had to come upstairs, where I explicitly told you *not* to go, and start looking around my fucking closet?'

He sounded pissed and he had every right to be. Being found intruding on his privacy didn't exactly reflect well on me.

'I… I'm sorry,' I repeated. 'I know I shouldn't have. But there wasn't anything else to do. I swam in the pool and watched all the movies. And I don't have a computer, and I—'

'Look at me when you're speaking to me.'

I didn't want to, but staring at his chest was stupid so I gritted my teeth and looked up.

His electric-blue gaze slammed into mine and all the air vanished from my lungs, sending my heartbeat tumbling over itself.

In the two days he'd been away, I'd told myself that surely I'd overstated his attractiveness; that he couldn't possibly have been as gorgeous and compelling as I'd made him in my head.

But I was wrong. If anything, I'd *understated* it.

He stood very close, looking down at me, and his fingers on my skin were warm, sensitising all the places that he wasn't touching.

Bloody man.

'That doesn't explain what you're doing up here.' He said each word very quietly, anger gleaming in his eyes. 'After I told you not to.'

My own anger rose, fuelled by my helpless response to him, not to mention a fair amount of embarrassment.

I should have locked it down, but I couldn't. I'd been trapped in his house for two days, with the timer on my brief window of freedom from Dad slowly ticking down, and I didn't have the emotional resources to get myself under control.

'I was curious,' I snapped, lifting my chin. 'And look, if you leave me alone for two days, you're going to have to give me something to do or else I'll find something on my own that you may not like.'

'What are you, a toddler?' His expression turned thunderous. 'This area is private and I told you it was out of bounds. What made you think you could just come up here and start looking around?'

Another wave of defensive anger went through me,

his tone reminding me of the way Dad would berate me for my behaviour, telling me I was an insult to my mother's memory.

It never failed to hurt me.

'You patronising asshole,' I said, stung. 'Don't call me that.'

'I'll call you anything I damn well please. Especially if you're poking about in places that don't concern you.'

'Yeah, I know,' I shot back. 'I said I was sorry. I was just curious about you, okay?'

He went quite still, like a big predator spotting prey, a kind of electricity gathering around him that made something inside me pulse with excitement despite my anger. 'Curious about me?'

My mouth had gone dry, my quicksilver emotions changing in response, the anger beginning to fade, excitement building. 'I wanted to find out more about you.'

'What more?'

'I don't know.' Another blush heated my cheeks. 'Anything really.'

He leaned down, his face inches from mine, his astonishing blue eyes filling my vision. And I could smell his scent again, warm and sexy and masculine. 'If you've gone through my stuff, there'll be hell to pay.' He moved his muscled body closer, his heat surrounding me. 'I'm sorry about the toddler thing, but understand me: I wouldn't allow my brothers up here, let alone the daughter of my enemy.'

My breath hitched.

He was so beautiful and I stared, my anger forgotten.

The sharp angle of his jaw was made even sharper

by the faint black line of his beard and his cheekbones were to die for. The blade of his nose was straight, though I could see a few faint scars bisecting one eyebrow, scar tissue pulling at the corner of one eye.

It was a fascinating face. One that contained secrets and mysteries.

His black lashes were thick, a perfect frame for those startling pale blue eyes and the anger glowing in the depths of them.

I didn't look away. I couldn't. 'I didn't go into your things, I promise.' God, I wanted to touch him again. To feel his hot skin and the prickle of his beard against my fingertips. 'I only looked and then I…had to go smell your clothes a little.'

He blinked. 'Smell my clothes?'

I wasn't embarrassed any more, not now he was right in front of me, overwhelming me with his physical nearness. A bomb could have gone off behind him and I wouldn't have noticed. 'What can I say? You smell nice.' Somehow, without my conscious control, my hand was lifting, my fingers brushing along his jaw, the delicious prickle of his whiskers against my fingertips. 'And…you feel nice too.'

Ajax became statue-still. You'd think I'd shot him rather than simply touched him.

I shouldn't be doing this. I should control myself better, especially when I'd already made him angry by intruding on his privacy.

But I couldn't make myself stop. My fingertips grazed the sharp plane of his jaw, the feel of his skin sending short, intense pulses of excitement through me. This was so new, so different. It was wondrous.

The anger in his eyes changed, becoming something

hotter. Brighter. 'What are you doing?' His voice was strange, deep and oddly husky.

'Touching you.' Helplessly, my gaze dropped to his fascinating mouth and I brushed the curve of his bottom lip. My God. It was so soft. Who knew there could be something soft about Ajax King? 'Is that okay?'

He was so still and he was staring at me so fixedly. Perhaps he didn't want this. Perhaps he didn't like it.

Control yourself, girl. You're an embarrassment.

Dad's voice echoed in my head like a warning and a part of me curled up in shame. Yet that wasn't enough for me to take my hand away.

He was fascinating, addictive. A temptation too great for me to resist and it had been so long since I'd touched another person, so long since I'd had any physical contact with anyone at all, and I ached. I'd been so isolated and I was so lonely.

This was my chance to take something for myself.

Every other woman got to choose their own partner so why couldn't I?

'Stop,' Ajax said in that strange voice.

Remember what happened the last time you made a choice.

Yes, I remembered. Cam.

The shame inside me grew larger. 'I'm sorry.' I snatched my hand away and looked at the floor. 'I didn't mean to touch you. I should have asked or something. I'm not very good at—'

'Look at me, Imogen.'

I took a breath and looked, the note of command in his voice irresistible.

The heat in his gaze nearly flattened me.

Desire burned in his eyes. He liked me touching him. I could tell.

My breath caught.

'It's not that I don't want you to touch me,' he said roughly. 'It's that you shouldn't. And you know why.'

Of course I did. The whole virginity thing.

'But…you can kiss me, right?' I stared up at him. 'Dad wouldn't know if you did.'

'No,' Ajax murmured. 'No, he wouldn't.' His attention drifted, falling to my mouth. 'But what I want doesn't matter.'

That puzzled me. Why would he think that what he wanted didn't matter? And what did he want anyway?

'Doesn't it?' I asked. 'Why not?'

Somehow he was closer than he had been a moment ago, though I hadn't seen him move. He still had his hand wrapped around my arm and I was so aware of it I was sure I could feel every line of his fingerprints on my skin.

He didn't answer, his gaze lifting to clash with mine again.

There was a pressure in the air around us, the relentless build of attraction getting stronger and stronger.

'Please,' I heard myself say. 'I've never been kissed before. Not properly. And I… I'd like my first proper kiss to be with someone I want.'

He stared at me another long, aching second.

Then he closed the gap between us and covered my mouth with his.

Shock held me motionless.

I'd thought he wouldn't do it, but he had, and now Ajax King was kissing me. Those beautiful lips I'd traced with my finger mere moments ago were now on mine and they felt…oh, God, *amazing*.

He must have been drinking coffee at some point, the taste dark and rich, combining with a heady flavour that was all Ajax. It was delicious. I couldn't get enough.

The kiss was hard and yet somehow soft at the same time, his tongue tracing the seam of my mouth, getting me to open for him. And I shuddered in helpless reaction, lightning striking all over my skin, sending goosebumps racing everywhere, leaving me helpless to do anything but give him what he wanted.

This was nothing like the brief brush of his lips in the car a few days earlier. This was as similar to that as a candle flame was to a forest fire.

His tongue pushed into my mouth, beginning to explore me slowly and deliberately, and with so much heat I began to shake.

I pressed my palms to his hard chest, gripping onto the warm cotton of his T-shirt, holding on tight. A deep moan of pleasure escaped me.

I didn't know what had made him change his mind, but I didn't want to question it. I just wanted more.

And he seemed to understand, moving so I was pinned between him and the closet door, deepening the kiss, controlling it with such effortless mastery I nearly swooned.

Correction, actual swooning was already happening, my knees weak, my hands clenching even tighter in the cotton of his shirt just to stay upright.

I couldn't control myself any more. It had become impossible. I'd been without physical closeness for so long, thinking about him constantly for two days straight, craving his touch so badly I couldn't stop.

I tipped my head back, opening my mouth to give him greater access, at the same time as I tried to kiss him in return, wanting more of his heat and intoxicating flavour. Wanting more of his touch and his scent and the feel of him against my skin.

But I had no idea how to get it.

I tried to pull him closer, tugging on his T-shirt, but he wouldn't move, making me groan in frustration.

But then he cupped my jaw in one of his big, warm hands and kissed me harder, deeper, nipping at my bottom lip, changing the angle, turning the kiss into something so unbearably erotic I wondered if it was possible to come from kissing alone.

It wasn't enough, though. I arched my back against the closet door, trying to press myself into his hard body.

He ignored me, lifting his mouth from mine and, when I tried to follow, his fingers on my jaw tightened, holding me in place.

I was panting and I didn't care. 'Don't stop.' My mouth felt deliciously swollen and a little bruised from that kiss. 'Please.'

The electricity in his gaze crackled over my skin, the heat burning in the depths of all that winter blue undeniable. There was a flush to his high cheekbones, a slash of red that told its own story, and I could hear his ragged breathing.

He wanted me. It was obvious.

'No,' he said.

CHAPTER NINE

Ajax

IMOGEN WAS LOOKING up at me, her eyes wide and dark, her delectable mouth all red from my kiss. Her hands were gripping the front of my T-shirt so tightly it was like she was afraid to let me go, her chest rising and falling fast and hard. The scent of roses and the faint musk of feminine arousal were winding tight around me, making my breath catch.

I shouldn't have kissed her. Why the fuck had I?

All I'd meant to do was ask her why the hell she was in my room after I'd explicitly told her she wasn't allowed up here.

But then she'd touched me. Despite my very real anger, she'd simply put up her small hand and those delicate fingers had run along my jaw, lightly, gently. And she'd looked at me as if she'd never seen anything like me before in all her life. As if I was fascinating to her.

People were afraid of me. They were never fascinated by me.

For some women my reputation was a turn-on and I was a trophy. Bedding the most dangerous man in Sydney had a certain status factor.

Yet there was no fear in Imogen, either of me or my anger, and it got me hard. The way she'd begged me to kiss her, because her first kiss should be with someone she wanted…

Hell, how could I deny her?

You wanted to kiss her. Two days and she still affects you as badly as she did the night you kidnapped her.

She did. That was a fact. And fuck, I *did* want to kiss her. So why shouldn't I?

It was only a kiss…

Except now I was hard as a rock and the scent of her was driving me crazy. And there was a part of me that had forgotten about the goddamn big picture. That wanted nothing more than to lift her against the closet door and fuck us both into the middle of next week.

Except her virginity was the leverage I needed against her father and if I took it, that leverage would be gone.

There are other methods you can use to get rid of him.

Sure there were. But those were Dad's methods and I didn't use them. I was better than that.

So what? You can fake a doctor's certificate if need be.

Yeah, but I'd given my word as a King that I wouldn't touch her and that still meant something.

You know White doesn't give a shit about your word.

He might not, but I did. The King name was mud in this town and my brothers and I wanted that to change. And that meant standing by our promises, keeping to the agreements we'd made.

And going back on my word would make me no better than Dad.

'No? Okay then.' The disappointment in her voice caught at me. 'I'm sorry. I shouldn't have asked for a kiss. I just…'

The skin of her jaw beneath my fingertips was very warm and her hair brushing the back of my hand where I held her was very soft. It felt silky, and I caught a faint suggestion of what it would feel like spread over my chest.

I couldn't lie, couldn't tell myself I didn't want her. But those big picture goals were more important than what I wanted for myself and always would be.

I couldn't sacrifice them for a couple of hours in bed with a woman, no matter how lovely she was.

'You just what?' I prompted, trying not to let myself become mesmerised by her pink mouth and the little mole just above it. She'd tasted sweet when I'd kissed her, and yet tart at the same time, the flavour lingering on my tongue. What would the rest of her taste like?

There was a worried look in her eyes, as if she couldn't decide on what to say. Then her mouth firmed. 'Okay, the truth is that I was hoping for some revenge on Dad. You know what he's been using me for, a trophy for his friends to build alliances. And he doesn't care how I feel about it. And I'm pissed off, Ajax. When I lose my virginity, I want it to be with someone who's my choice, not his. Someone I'm attracted to.' She kept her gaze on mine as she turned her cheek into my palm, nuzzling into it like a little cat. 'Someone like you.'

There was determination in those green eyes of hers. A hint of the strength that I'd seen when I'd first come up behind her in the bathroom at the ball. This woman wasn't only wide-eyed questions and restless energy.

She was more complex than that, which was both fascinating and intensely sexy at the same time.

'I'm your father's enemy, though,' I murmured. 'He's not going to like it.'

'I know. That's kind of the whole point. That's what makes it perfect.'

Revenge. Hell, that was a concept I could relate to.

I kept my hand where it was, against her cheek. 'But your virginity is vital to my plan working, remember?'

Disappointment flashed across her expressive face. 'In that case, you'd better let me go.'

I didn't want to. She could have her revenge, couldn't she? And maybe I could get a little something for myself too. Such as her, all silky and strokeable beneath me.

It's a slippery slope. You know this.

Fuck, I did know. It was the tiny slips that led to greater ones. Small actions that didn't seem like massive deals, that eventually brought you down. That's how I'd finally managed to bring my father down, after all.

And if I took Imogen, if I got rid of the only thing I could use against White, what would I have left?

The only other language he understood was violence and I could *not* go down that road again.

The disappointment in Imogen's eyes was loud and clear. But there was also something else under that, something that hooked into my chest and twisted hard.

'What?' I asked roughly, my hand still against her cheek, even though I knew better than to keep it there. 'Don't look at me like that.'

'You're the only one.' Her voice was hoarse. 'You're the only one who's ever made me feel like this.'

Ah, Christ. What was she doing saying shit like that to me? 'I'm not special, Imogen. How many men have you even met?'

'Enough.' She lifted her hand and put it over mine, holding my palm to her warm skin. 'Enough to know it's you, Ajax. It's all you.'

The sensation in my chest twisted even tighter. 'I can't.'

'Then let me go.' Her hand dropped away.

Yes, I should let her go. I *should*.

And yet there was a part of me that refused. A part that was sick of having to sacrifice everything I wanted all the damn time. After everything I'd done so far for my brothers and my city, wasn't I fucking owed something for myself?

You can't have it and you know that.

'I'm not any girl's first time.' My voice had roughened further, turning dark and gritty, and I didn't even know why I was saying it when I wasn't going to be doing anything with her. 'Not if you're after sweet and nice.'

'Who said I wanted sweet and nice?' Her gaze searched mine. 'What if I wanted…rough? And kind of dirty?'

As if she even knew what that meant. Christ, why was I standing here? Why was I *still* touching her?

'Do you?' I asked, as if I was going to go through with it, throwing away the only leverage I had.

'I've watched a few videos.' She nuzzled against my palm again and this time the edge of her teeth grazed the base of my thumb. Then she bit me gently, watching my reaction with undisguised interest.

I felt that small nip like she had her teeth against

the head of my dick, short, sharp and electric. 'A few videos don't mean shit, little virgin,' I growled, angry at myself that I couldn't seem to do what I should and let her go. 'If you haven't done it, you don't know what it means.'

Her cheeks flushed, but determination glowed in her bright eyes. 'Why don't you show me then?'

Step away from her.

'Imogen…'

'Is that a yes?'

The smell of roses was laced through with the scent of her arousal, the heat of her body so close, bleeding into mine. I'd got my housekeeper to get her some clothes the night I'd kidnapped her and clearly she'd helped herself to them, wearing a green T-shirt and grey yoga pants. When she sucked in a breath the fabric stretched tight across her perfect little tits, her nipples pressing hard against the cotton.

You're going to do this, aren't you?

I'd had to put aside all the things I'd truly wanted. A home. A woman I loved and who loved me. A family that wasn't rotten to the core.

I'd accepted that those things weren't for men like me. Not when association with me would turn them into targets for my enemies. I couldn't allow anyone to take that risk, nor could I allow myself any vulnerabilities.

I couldn't allow myself to slip down the slope that would lead me back to my father and all I'd done in his name.

But…this girl wanted me. I was *her* choice. And the way she looked at me, like I was a dream come true…

You'll put everything at risk just to fuck her?

I could make it work. Doctors' certificates could be faked. And if I could bring down Augustus King, then surely one afternoon with a beautiful woman wouldn't put anything at risk.

Somehow my thumb was brushing lightly over her cushiony lower lip, then easing into her mouth. The heat of her lips closing around my skin made my breath catch.

Green fire glittered in her eyes. She bit me again.

Electricity arced directly to my aching cock and it was all I could do not to slam her against the door, rip those goddamn yoga pants off her and sink straight into her hot little pussy.

'A couple of hours,' I growled, making a decision that I knew I'd regret but making it anyway. 'That's all I can give you.'

She nodded frantically, her breathing turning ragged.

'Good. Now listen, this is important.' I leaned down a fraction more, looking deep into her eyes, watching the flames in them leap higher. 'You need to tell me if anything doesn't feel good or if you don't like it. And especially if something is—'

Imogen bit me harder, cutting off everything I'd been going to say.

Fuck it.

I pulled my thumb from her mouth and covered it with mine, taking what I wanted for once in my fucking life.

Something for me.

And the moment my lips touched hers, she opened for me, hot and sweet, her tongue touching mine at first hesitantly and then with more demand. Then her hands opened on my chest and slid up, winding her arms around my neck, her small curvy body arching into me. A soft moan escaped her and I found myself putting one palm onto the closet door beside her head while I cupped her jaw with the other, leaning in as she tried to pull me closer.

She was raw demand and passionate heat, holding nothing back. And she tasted so fucking sweet. So fucking hot.

Beneath those wide eyes and painful honesty, she was primal.

Just like me.

Any resistance I had left burned to ashes right where I stood.

I let go of her jaw and slid my hand into her pale silky hair, curling my fingers through it and gripping on tight, pulling her head back so I could kiss her deeper.

She didn't protest, moaning as I nipped her lower lip, licking into her mouth and taking possession once again. Jesus, she was delicious.

Her arms around my neck tightened, pulling me even closer, and then she began to climb me like a goddamn tree, winding her legs around my waist, arching her spine, pressing her tits against my chest and tilting her hips so my dick was rubbing up against her clit through her clothes.

She stole my breath.

I pulled her hands from around my neck, pinning them back against the closet door above her head. Then I lifted my mouth from hers. 'If you don't want this to be over right here, right now, you need to slow down.'

She was panting, her chest heaving, her luscious

mouth pink and swollen from my kisses. 'But I don't want to go slow.' Her hips rolled against mine, her heat soaking through the yoga pants she wore and through the denim of my jeans. 'Oh… Ajax…' Her voice was husky and breathless. 'I need you…please.'

It wouldn't have taken much to rip all that material out of my way and get inside her. But I wasn't an animal. I'd take my own sweet time and give us both as much pleasure as I could.

So I settled my hips between her thighs and rocked against her, watching as her face became even more flushed, her eyes luminous. She moaned as I made sure the ridge of my hard-on hit her clit, grinding on it, making her shudder and tremble and pull against the hold I had on her wrists.

'Oh, God. That feels amazing.' She writhed slowly, moving her hips in response. 'But aren't you…? I m-mean, don't you…? Oh…'

'Stop talking and let me concentrate.' I changed my angle, rubbing my aching dick against her.

She tipped her head back, her eyes half closing in pleasure. 'But I think…' Her chest heaved. 'Oh… I might…c-come. And I don't want to, not yet.'

I leaned down and pressed my mouth to her throat, licking the salt from her skin, feeling her shudder in response. 'There's no limit to the number of orgasms you can have, sweetheart. So feel free.'

'But…don't… Oh, Ajax… *Ajax…*'

The sound of desperation in her voice was unbelievably fucking hot. So was the way she writhed and panted, arching her back, wanting more.

So I gave it to her.

Keeping one hand wrapped around her wrists above

her head, I pulled her T-shirt up with the other, exposing a delicate white lace bra. It was pretty, especially the way her pink nipples showed through the fabric. I took a second to admire it, then dragged one of the cups to the side, baring her. Then I bent to her hard nipple and licked it.

She jerked in my arms, gasping.

I licked her again, the salty-sweet taste of her skin as delicious as her kiss. Jesus, this woman. I could eat her up.

Hell, I would. Right now.

I drew her nipple into my mouth and sucked, feeling her body stiffen and hearing her breath catch. Then I nipped her at the same time as I began to grind against her once again, trying to go slow, to tease her, to draw out the pleasure as long as I could.

But she wouldn't let me.

Her legs tightened around my waist as she lifted her hips against mine and arched her spine again, encouraging me to suck on her harder, deeper.

'Yes,' she gasped thickly. 'Oh, Ajax, yes...'

She was so fucking sexy. That taste of her was in my mouth, her wet little pussy soaking my goddamn jeans.

Jesus, she was going to make me come like a bloody teenage boy.

I teased her nipple with my teeth until the words she was muttering became incoherent cries. Until she went suddenly stiff in my arms, calling my name as she came.

CHAPTER TEN

Imogen

I SHUDDERED IN Ajax's arms, mind-blowing pleasure ripping through me, making me feel like I was glowing, lit up from the inside by the sheer ecstasy of his touch.

Hell, if I'd known sex would be like this, I'd have tried a lot harder to escape Dad.

It's not just the sex. It's Ajax.

I had my head tipped back against the closet door and my eyes were closed, but now I opened them a crack, half afraid to look at him, yet at the same time half desperate too.

His eyes were cobalt with desire, his expression feral with possessive hunger.

My soul shivered in instinctive response.

I'd told him just before that it was him, that he was different, and that had been instinct. But now I knew for certain. This feeling inside me, this pleasure. It was all because of him.

For a second I tried imagining doing this with anyone else and I…couldn't. I'd wanted him from the moment I'd first seen him, on a visceral level, but he also made me feel safe and protected.

Yet he wasn't a safe man. He was dangerous. And that excited me for reasons I didn't understand. There was a physical energy that drew me to him, yet it was about more than that.

I affected him. I'd seen him trying to resist me and being unable to. I liked that. I liked that a *lot*. It made me feel powerful and strong, and it had been too long since I'd felt either of those things.

'Still with me?' His voice was rough black velvet brushing over my skin, dark and sensual with a husky edge.

And this time my body shivered along with my soul.

I still had my legs wrapped around his lean waist, the ridge of his cock nudging my throbbing clit. The pressure of his fingers around my wrists was getting me off too, as if part of me enjoyed being held helpless like this.

I should have been embarrassed by the way I'd clawed at him and climbed him, losing control of myself in a way my father would have despised. But the way Ajax was looking at me made all my embarrassment fade away.

'Um…yes.' God, I sounded croaky. 'Unless those videos were wrong, we haven't finished, though, right?' I couldn't quite hide my uncertainty, a part of me worried that this was all he was going to give me. That he might change his mind and leave me here, sated yet still starving.

He shifted, the hard ridge between my thighs brushing against my sensitive sex, sending a shockwave of pleasure through me, his free hand cupping my bare breast.

His palm was hot, searing against my skin, and

when he brushed his thumb over my nipple, still slick from his mouth, I groaned.

'No, we're not finished.' He watched me, gauging my reactions. 'After all, you're still a virgin.'

'Well, right?' A weird reaction was starting to set in, a burst of intense emotion sweeping over me, making me feel like crying.

Okay, now *this* was embarrassing.

I never cried. Not ever. Not even the day Dad had informed me that I'd killed my mother by being born and he'd never forgive me for it. And that if I ever wanted even a crumb of attention from him, I'd have to work for it.

Not that I'd ever think about that day again.

'I mean, this hymen isn't going to break itself,' I babbled, trying to talk away the vulnerability that was getting wider and larger inside me. 'And it's not going to be much of a revenge if—'

Ajax lifted his hand from my breast and laid his thumb against my mouth, stopping the flow of words. His gaze narrowed, focusing intensely on me. 'Little one, are you okay?'

To my horror, I felt my lower lip wobble.

This wasn't how it went in the videos. The women all moaned and gasped like they were enjoying themselves, but no one cried afterwards. No one talked about feelings.

I knew that wasn't the point—porn didn't have feelings attached—but my reaction still caught me by surprise.

Why was this happening? A combination of his physical closeness and the unstoppable pleasure he'd given me? The realisation that this was all centred around him somehow? Or was it something else?

Whatever it was, I didn't like it. I didn't want it.

'What's wrong?' Ajax took his thumb from my mouth. 'And give me the truth this time.'

I swallowed, trying to get rid of the lump in my throat.

Dad would be appalled.

He would. He hated my tears. He thought I didn't deserve to cry.

'Nothing.' Desperately, I tried to salvage the situation. 'I'm fine.'

But of course Ajax knew I was lying.

'You're not fine,' he said flatly. 'You were honest with me before, Imogen. Why are you lying now?'

Shit. I was such a failure. This was why I'd wanted to get away from Dad in the first place, because I could never be what he wanted me to be. I could never earn a place in his heart. And my inability to do any of that only got people hurt in the process.

'Okay, so you're right. I'm not fine,' I croaked pathetically, not even trying to hide it because what was the point? 'I feel…weird. Like I want to cry. But it's not you. It's nothing you've done. It's just…'

He didn't say anything, simply stared at me.

'Don't think that this means I don't want you to keep going,' I added, angry with myself for ruining the moment. 'I still need you to take my virginity, okay? I want my damn revenge.'

He remained silent.

Great, so I'd screwed up. I'd been too full-on. Too honest. Too emotional. Too…everything.

I should have remembered that there were always

consequences when I didn't keep myself under control. Consequences such as what had happened to Cameron, the poor guy beaten within an inch of his life.

My fault. I'd never even thought that asking him out would be a problem, I'd simply gone ahead and asked him, too caught up in my attraction to him. And he'd got hurt because of me.

Failing. I was always failing.

Ajax lowered my arms from over my head, chafing my wrists gently. Then he eased me down his body until I was standing on the floor.

His gentleness made the emotions crashing around inside me somehow even worse. I felt like a hurt child in need of comfort.

How humiliating.

I tried to muster up some anger but, before I could get good and worked up, he picked me up in his arms and carried me over to the huge bed that faced the ocean, putting me down on the edge of the mattress before crouching in front of me.

'It's okay,' I muttered. 'You can leave now.'

'Leave?' He frowned. 'Why would I do that?'

'Uh, because I'm being pathetic and emotional?'

He shrugged one powerful shoulder as if that didn't matter at all to him. 'You're not being pathetic. Emotional yes, but what you're feeling is normal. Sometimes it happens when sex is particularly intense.'

Well, it *had* been intense, that was for sure.

I swallowed past the lump in my throat. 'Has it happened to you? Wanting to cry after sex, I mean?' The question sounded stupid as soon as it came out of my mouth. Ajax King wanting to cry after an orgasm?

The idea was as ludicrous as Dad suddenly becoming Prime Minister.

Ajax didn't laugh, thank God. 'No, but I know it happens to some people.'

'Well, I don't want it to happen to me.' And I didn't. Not crying was about the only thing I'd managed to succeed at, the only thing that Dad didn't criticise me for.

Crying now would be one failure too many.

I blinked hard and looked down at my hands. 'I don't blame you if you don't want to do this any more. I didn't mean to ruin the mood.'

Strong fingers caught my jaw, tipping my face up.

He'd risen to his feet and was bending over me, his intense blue gaze blazing into mine. 'You're not ruining anything. Cry if you want to. Scream if you want to. Emotion doesn't scare me, Imogen. I'm going to fuck you either way.'

The words shot down my spine like shocks. His expression was uncompromising and it came to me all of a sudden that of course my emotions didn't scare him. They didn't matter to him *at all*.

Because he didn't care.

Something tight in my chest, something I hadn't realised was there, suddenly eased. Like a heavy stone being lifted away.

I could cry. I could scream. I could ask too many questions. Be too restless. Talk too much. Do whatever I wanted.

I could be myself and it wouldn't matter.

Because Ajax didn't care and that meant I didn't need to either.

There is no way you can fail, not here, not with him.

A tear slid down my cheek without my conscious control. Then another and another and, for the first time in years, I didn't try to repress them or swallow them back, or talk to distract myself from the ache in my heart.

I let them fall.

There was no judgement in Ajax's face, that I'd seen so often in Dad's. None of the distaste or the active contempt. He simply…watched, expressionless, giving me some time and a quiet space to cry.

Then, after a while, his grip on my chin tightened and he bent down over me and kissed me.

I tasted the salt of my tears and that rich, dark flavour that was all him, and I was suddenly hungry. Hungrier than I'd ever been in my entire life.

Opening my mouth, I let him in, reaching out to pull him to me. But he was already pushing me back onto the bed and following me down onto it. His body was heavy, solid with muscle and so hot it felt like I was lying directly under a furnace.

He felt so good.

I arched up, pressing myself against him, spreading my thighs so he could lie between them and curling my arms around his neck. I kissed him harder, deeper; kissed him like there was no tomorrow and no yesterday, only now. Salt and Ajax in my mouth, the taste of him imprinting on me so I'd never get it out of my head and never want to.

He kissed me back, demanding, pushing his tongue deep into my mouth. Nipping my lower lip, sucking on it. Licking and taking, conquering. And I let myself be conquered.

Our kisses became more desperate, the sound of our breathing ragged.

Abruptly, he pushed himself off me, going up on his knees, straddling my hips, and he reached for the hem of his T-shirt, dragging it up and over his head. The movement was sexy and when his T-shirt came off I nearly gasped.

He was a work of art. Not only was every muscle from his pecs to his abs cut and sharply defined, they were highlighted by the most incredible tattoos I'd ever seen. Thick black abstract lines running all over his torso, trailing down over the broad plane of his chest and curling around his lean hips, outlining every dip and hollow, every flex and contraction.

I pushed myself up, my breath already short and getting shorter, reaching for him, my palms landing on his stomach. He was smooth and hot, the muscle beneath rock-hard. And I could feel the tightening of his abs beneath my fingertips, the merest hint of the power contained in his magnificent body.

Desperate to touch as much of him as I could, I ran my palms up from his stomach to his pecs, the prickle of hair an added excitement. God, he felt incredible. I leaned in, nuzzling against his abdomen, loving his heat and the woody, spicy scent of him. Then I licked him, tasting salt.

He shuddered, his reaction firing my desire even higher. I tried licking him again, but he caught me underneath my arms and pushed me back down onto the mattress. And then I couldn't do anything but lie there as he virtually ripped my clothes off.

In the hundreds of romance novels I'd read, I'd always thought that the ripping of the clothes was figurative. Apparently not with Ajax King.

He tore my T-shirt clean down the middle and got rid of the fabric, pulling apart my lacy white bra with the same ease. Then he jerked away my yoga pants and knickers along with them, so I lay naked in the middle of the bed.

He paused a moment, his gaze electric, scorching me every place it touched. And it touched *everywhere*.

If I'd thought about it I might have been embarrassed. No one had seen my naked body since I was a child. But it didn't even occur to me. All I wanted was him, naked as I was, his skin against mine.

'Ajax,' I said hoarsely. '*Please*.'

He said nothing, watching me with those intense, unfathomable eyes. Then his hands slowly moved to the buttons of his jeans.

Too slowly.

I sat up and reached for them myself, but he knocked my hands away.

'Lie down.' His voice was full of authority and darkness. 'Lie down and wait patiently, and you'll get what you want.'

A frustrated sound escaped me, but I did what I was told.

I didn't like to stay still for long and lying there, my breathing fast and hard, the need inside me like an animal tearing at me in its hunger, felt like the most difficult thing I'd ever done.

Slowly, achingly slowly, Ajax undid the buttons of his jeans and pulled down the zip, spreading the fabric. I could see the long, hard length that pressed against the material of his black boxers…

My pulse began to accelerate, my mouth was watering, my breath catching hard in my chest.

Holy crap. He was huge.

I began to push myself up again, wanting to touch him and unable to keep still for much longer, but he got off the bed suddenly, jerking down his jeans and getting rid of the rest of his clothes.

I blinked, staring at him, utterly mesmerised by the sheer masculine beauty of him. All that muscle and power. All that strength.

And his cock too, big and thick and hard, curving up towards his flat stomach. I wanted to touch it, wanted to see what it felt like and whether it would be as hard as it looked, or as smooth.

But I didn't get a chance to touch because he was back on the bed, sliding his arms beneath me and gathering me up before covering me with his body, pressing me back down onto the mattress.

The slide of his bare skin over mine made me shiver and the weight of him… I didn't feel crushed or suffocated. I felt anchored. Safe.

I put my arms around him, smoothing my palms over his broad back, feeling his muscles flex as I stroked down his spine, glorying in the feel of him. His hips were positioned between my thighs, his cock lying against my throbbing sex.

So. Good.

His mouth found mine and he was kissing me again, deeply, hungrily. I tried to kiss him back but he'd moved on, kissing a path along my jaw and down my throat, licking and nipping at me like I was his favourite ice-cream and he was making a meal out of me.

I panted as he found my breasts, teasing my nipples

with his tongue then sucking hard on each one, making me groan and arch up into him. His mouth was so hot and the graze of his teeth on my skin made me moan.

His big hands glided over my hips, scorching, then over my thighs and between them, pushing them apart with an irresistible strength that I found shockingly erotic. And then his breath moved over my stomach, his mouth brushing the sensitive skin of my inner thighs.

Oh, God. He could not be doing what I thought he was doing. Could he?

I pushed myself up on my elbows, looking down the length of my body. He was kneeling between my legs, the predatory hunger on his face making me lose my train of thought.

'What are you doing?' I gasped, shuddering as he slid his palms under my butt, lifting me.

He merely pinned me with his mesmerising stare, one corner of his mouth turning up in the wickedest, sexiest smile I'd ever seen. Then he buried his face between my legs and the entire world exploded into flame.

I cried out, sensation swamping me as his tongue pushed deep into my pussy, licking and exploring. I'd seen this in the videos but I'd honestly never thought the pleasure would be quite this intense. And then his hold on me shifted, his thumb finding my clit, an added pressure that made me arch back on the mattress in ecstasy.

Oh, God. Oh, God. Could something be *too* good? Because this was. I had no idea how I was going to survive it.

Gently, he separated the folds of my sex with his fingers so his tongue could explore me deeper, the hungry sounds of masculine pleasure filling the room, making me go hot all over.

I reached down blindly and tangled my fingers in his hair, needing something to hold onto as he pushed me higher and higher. Every lick was a brush of fire, the pressure of his tongue inside me and his thumb on my clit almost unbearable.

The orgasm hit without warning, pleasure detonating like a bomb, making me cry out as the raw ecstasy of it overwhelmed me.

Then I lay there trembling with the aftershocks, my mind completely blown, feeling him move on the bed. The sound of a drawer being opened came and then the crinkle of foil.

A condom. Which meant…

I felt the brush of his skin, hot and smooth, on mine and then his body coming back to cover me again. I forced my eyes open to find him staring down at me, his gaze an intense electric blue.

And he kept on staring at me as he positioned himself, the head of his cock nudging at the entrance of my sex. Sliding his hand under my thigh, he hooked my leg up and around his waist, opening me up for him. Then he slowly pushed into me and I felt myself stretch around his huge cock, the unfamiliar sensation making me gasp and clutch at his shoulders.

I was expecting pain, but there was none. Only a strange pinch that made me stiffen momentarily before the feeling vanished. And then there was nothing but him inside me, thick and hard, sliding deeper, filling me up so completely I could hardly breathe.

His head was bent, his mouth at my throat, his teeth

finding the sensitive place between my shoulder and neck and biting down. At the same time he sunk himself into me as far as he could go and I lay there panting and shaking at the intense pressure.

It was unbearable. It was amazing.

He bit me again, his hips pulling back, making me feel every inch as he slid his cock out, then he was pushing back in, a slow, relentless glide.

My eyes rolled back in my head, moans coming out of my throat without my conscious control.

He was everywhere. Inside me. Around me. The taste of him in my mouth, the scent of him in my nostrils, the feel of him in my sex. I was drowning in him and, quite honestly, I didn't want to be saved.

He ravaged my throat as he began to thrust, deep and hard, taking no account of my inexperience.

Apparently he hadn't been kidding when he'd said he didn't do sweet and nice.

But that was okay. Because I'd told him that maybe I wanted rough and dirty and if this was rough and dirty, I liked it.

No, I *loved* it.

All I was conscious of was the intense pressure and the slow lick of pleasure that began to build. I lifted my other leg and wrapped that around his waist too, instinctively trying to meet his thrusts, grinding to increase the friction.

He growled into my neck, answering my unspoken need by upping the pace.

I dug my nails into his back, gasping as the pleasure began to intensify, wrapping my legs tighter around him.

There was nothing in all the world but this feeling.

Nothing in the world but him and what he was giving me. It was heaven.

He got faster, driving himself deeper, and I clawed at his back, desperation pulling tighter.

'Ajax.' I twisted under him, blind to everything but the need inside me, the pleasure almost frightening in its intensity. 'Please… God…please…'

'Look at me,' he ordered, heated darkness edging his tone. 'Look at me, Imogen.'

My eyes flicked open and I felt the collision as his sky-blue gaze met mine, an impact that shook me right to my core.

He moved harder, ecstasy winding tight around my soul, making me feel helpless and treasured and powerful all at the same time.

Then he pushed his fingers between us, finding my aching clit and pinching gently.

The jolt of delicious pain was all the ignition I needed.

The pressure inside me released in an incandescent burst of pleasure that swamped me, drowned me.

And the blue of his eyes was the only thing that kept me from being swept away.

CHAPTER ELEVEN

Ajax

I WATCHED THE moment her climax hit, a brilliant flare of emerald in her eyes, and I bent my head, kissing her again, taking her desperate cry of release into my mouth.

Then I moved hard and deep, her slick little pussy clenching around my cock and blowing my goddamn mind. She was so soft and hot against me, all roses and musk and husky pleas.

I should have been careful with her, but the way she was clawing at me, her thighs clamped tight around my waist, made me think she could handle what I was giving her.

So I let go, driving her into the mattress as I chased the orgasm that was just out of reach. But my little ex-virgin wouldn't let me go without her. She moved restlessly, panting and writhing, letting me know in no uncertain terms that she was building up to yet another climax.

But I didn't know how long I could hold out.

My cock was aching, every slide into her wet heat

making me grit my teeth not to blow it right there and then.

I'd never had this problem before, could always put off my orgasm for as long as I wanted to, but not with this woman.

The way she gripped me, digging her nails into my back so hard they were going to leave marks. The way she moved under me, clearly hungry for more. The way she looked at me, her iris a thin emerald circle around her dilated pupils, staring at me as if I was the centre of her universe.

She wasn't afraid and she wasn't wary. There was no hesitation or doubt. She didn't care about my reputation or my past. She was with me, hiding nothing. Giving everything.

I had no idea why that was so fucking hot, but it was.

Perhaps it was her responsiveness, how she was so into it. Into my touch and all the new feelings she was experiencing. Because, of course, this was all new to her.

I didn't remember my first time, though I'd been young. I only remembered Julie, another stripper who worked at one of the lounges Dad went to. She'd liked me and I'd liked her and she took me to bed. Showed me what I liked and how to please a woman.

But none of it had felt new.

Not like it was new to Imogen.

And there was something about that, something that got to me even though I didn't want it to.

So I tried to hold back, because I wanted to make her come again, but the feel of her satiny skin and the way her pussy was clenching around my aching dick was too much.

The orgasm burned like wildfire up my spine, a conflagration of pleasure that made me roar against her throat and sink my teeth into her shoulder, shuddering as it blinded me.

I lost myself for a while, only coming back when I felt her hands on my skin, stroking over my shoulders as if she couldn't get enough of touching me.

What the hell had happened? I'd never had an orgasm that intense before, not with anyone.

Imogen made an impatient sound, her breath soft against my throat, so I shifted, pulling out of her and adjusting my weight so I wasn't lying fully on her. Then I looked down.

Her face was deeply flushed, her eyes grass green. A sheen of sweat was up near her hairline and gleaming in the hollow of her throat, her pale golden hair tangled and spread all over the black linen of the bed cover. Her lovely mouth was pouty and full from my kisses…

She looked thoroughly seduced and so beautiful my breath caught.

'You okay?' I asked, my voice gritty and rough.

'Omigod, *so* okay.' Her face was full of awe, no trace of those earlier tears now. 'That was just…wow. Is it always like that?'

'Sometimes.' I ignored the fact that it had never been like that, at least not for me. 'Not always.'

'Lucky for me I got the "sometimes" then.' Her hands moved from my back to my chest, stroking over my pecs and down further, tracing my abs, her touch delicate and light. 'That's probably all because of you. You're amazing, did you know that?'

Jesus, she'd better not put me on a fucking pedestal just because I'd let her cry then made her come a couple of times.

'It's just sex, little one. It's not like I cured cancer.'

I hadn't moderated my tone, but she didn't seem to care, her full mouth turning up into a smile. 'You don't know. Sex like that *could* cure cancer. You might have a magic dick and not even know.'

This woman…

She'd cried earlier, those tears telling a story that I knew I wasn't going to like, yet now she was lying here beneath me, looking sexy and sweet and flirting with me as if she'd done this a thousand times before.

As if she'd never been kept a prisoner by her father or screwed, and screwed hard, by the son of her father's enemy, with no care given for the fact that she was a virgin.

Yeah, she was trouble.

And if you're not careful you'll get in deep.

Ignoring that thought, I pushed back a couple of golden strands of hair that had stuck to her forehead. 'Did you ever think that maybe it's got nothing to do with my dick? It might be that you have a magic pussy.'

Her smile got wider and she spread her hands on my chest, pressing her palms against me, making it obvious she liked the feeling of my skin on hers. 'Hey, that's true. I might. Still, me and my magic pussy are going with my original "you're amazing".' Her fingers made another journey over my abs. 'Can we do it again, please?'

I was getting hard again, her hands on me so good. A couple of hours only I'd promised her and hell, maybe I could stretch it out longer. Especially since I was only just getting started.

The consequences of what I'd done and everything that came with them could wait.

'I don't know—are you up for it?' I stroked my hand down her body, lingering on the soft curve of her tits and the flare of her hips, down to the heat and wetness between her thighs. 'You might be sore.'

She shuddered, parting her thighs to give me access. 'No, I'm not sore. *Oh...*' Her breath caught as I found her clit, brushing lightly over it with the tip of my finger, teasing her. Her lashes swept down and she arched her back. 'Ajax...that feels so good...'

The way she said my name and the way she gave herself utterly to what I was doing to her was like a drug. I couldn't get enough.

'Wait there for me,' I muttered, moving off the bed and crossing over into the en suite bathroom to get rid of the condom.

A minute later I was back and she opened her arms to me like we'd been lovers for years and not a mere half an hour.

For some inexplicable reason, it made my chest get tight.

Refusing to examine the feeling, I ignored it, coming back down onto the bed beside her before getting her beneath me once again. Her hands settled on my shoulders and she began to stroke me as if she had every right to touch me however she liked.

Yeah, and that was hot too.

'What's going to happen about your plan?' she murmured. 'I mean, now that I've been de-virginised.'

'I'll deal with it,' I said shortly, not wanting to think about it right now.

There was a silence.

She began to trace the lines over my left pec. 'Your tattoos are incredible. What do they mean?'

I'd got them when I was much younger, the lines outlining my muscles, highlighting my strength. Dad had hated them and so I'd loved them, a secret declaration that I wasn't my father's puppet, the way he seemed to think I was.

But I wasn't going to explain that to her, so all I said was, 'Nothing in particular. A tattoo artist friend designed them for me.'

'I love them.' Her fingers moved down my left side, a look of fascination on her face. 'Did it hurt? Do you think I could get one done one day? Where's the least painful place to get one?'

'You ask a lot of questions. What's up with that?'

Her exploring fingers slowed, her lashes sweeping down and veiling her gaze. 'I'm…not very good at keeping quiet when I'm curious about something.'

I looked down at her lovely face. 'Why should you be quiet when you're interested in something?'

'It's not only that. I find it difficult to sit still and I often don't think before I speak. I'm trying not to be so impulsive all the time and I know I need to control myself better, but it's…hard.' She paused, her attention on the black lines of my ink under her fingers. 'Dad doesn't like it and I try not to do stuff he doesn't like.'

I watched her face, saw the expression on it close down, the lovely green of her eyes darken.

'Why not?' The protective instinct inside me growled deep and low and it echoed in my voice. 'I thought you said your father didn't hurt you.'

'He didn't. But there are always consequences for not doing what he wants.'

'What consequences?' It came out as a demand, but I didn't bother to soften it. William White may not have laid a finger on his daughter, but he'd clearly hurt her in other ways.

Imogen sighed. 'A couple of years ago I tried to have something of a normal life, or as much of one as you can with twenty-four-seven guards. I signed up for a course at uni, joined a few clubs to meet people, that kind of thing. Anyway, there was this guy in my history class and I liked him. I'd never been on a date before so I asked him if he'd come out for coffee with me. He said he would, except…he never turned up for it. The next day I read in the paper about a man who'd been beaten and left for dead in an alley near where we were supposed to be meeting.' She dropped her gaze, staring ferociously at her finger following the line of my tat to my hip. 'I knew it was Cam. Just like I knew it was Dad who'd hurt him. He'd always warned me that I needed to be careful who I associated with and who I spoke to, but… I don't know. I guess I never thought he'd actually do anything.' A flicker of pain crossed her expressive face. 'It was my fault Cam got hurt. I should have remembered Dad's warning. I should have thought more about the consequences of asking him out.' Her tracing finger came to a stop. 'But I was so thrilled to have a conversation with a cute guy and I…forgot.'

My protective instinct sank its claws deeper, responding to the note of pain in her voice. 'It wasn't your fault,' I growled. 'It was your father who beat him up, not you.'

'I know that. But Cameron didn't. It was my responsibility not to put him in harm's way, because I know what Dad's like.' She swallowed. 'And it's not like Dad hasn't told me for years that I need to learn how to control myself.'

I shouldn't have cared what her father had told her. She was my prisoner, nothing more.

Yet the pain that threaded through each word caught at something inside me like an anchor catching on a rock.

Did this have anything to do with the way she'd cried earlier? With how she'd tried to repress it, seemingly angry at herself for getting emotional?

I'd have bet the whole of King Enterprises that it did.

'You're going to have to explain to me why your father thinks you need to control yourself,' I ordered, not caring that my voice had got rough and uncivilised. 'And then you're going to have to explain why you believed him.'

Her mouth got a stubborn look to it. 'Why? I don't have to if I don't want to.'

I caught her chin with my finger, tipping her gaze back to mine. 'Because I'm curious, Imogen. And you know what it's like to be curious, right?'

She let out an annoyed breath, flickers of anger in her green eyes.

Good. Let her be angry. That was better than her being hurt.

'Okay, fine,' she said after a minute. 'My mother died when I was born and Dad never got over it. He told me that it was my fault she died and that I'll never be like her. Never measure up to her. I'm too emotional, too impulsive. I didn't…deserve her.'

Jesus.

'Of course you deserved her,' I said fiercely. 'Don't tell me you believed all that bullshit?'

The stubborn line of her mouth softened, became more vulnerable. 'I didn't want to. But he's my Dad. He's the only person I've got.' A shadow shifted in her green eyes. 'I don't have anyone else.'

Sound familiar?

Yeah, it did. But my isolation had been self-imposed, while hers had been forced on her, the bright, inquisitive spirit I'd seen behind those green eyes compelled to get what it needed from a man who didn't give a shit about crushing it.

Poor little one. No wonder she hadn't cared about being kidnapped. Her mother was dead and her father had denied her the connection she was hungry for. A connection she needed.

I stroked my thumb along her jaw. 'You have me. And I don't care if you're impulsive or emotional or curious or any of that other bullshit, understand? You can be yourself with me, Imogen.'

Emotions shifted and changed like quicksilver in her eyes. 'Because I don't matter to you, right?'

I didn't miss the half-desperate note in her voice. It sounded a hell of a lot like she didn't want to matter, which was pretty much the opposite of what I usually got from women.

'You don't want to matter to me?' I asked, curious. 'Why not?'

'I don't want to have to live up to anyone else's expectations. I don't want to worry about disappointing anyone.'

The way she'd disappointed her father, clearly.

'You won't disappoint me,' I said. 'Not in any way.'

Colour rose in her cheeks and her gaze flickered. 'You were disappointed that I wasn't afraid of you.'

'Apart from that.'

'And that I got into your stuff.'

'Yeah, apart from that as well.'

'And I ask a lot of annoying questions.'

'I can handle your questions.'

She let out a breath. 'Just don't care about me, Ajax. Caring makes people do things they shouldn't.'

Hell, I couldn't argue. I'd had front row seats to that particular shit show. There were a lot of things I'd done that I shouldn't have.

Such as leaving your brothers to get hurt?

Ah, fuck, I didn't need that thought in my head.

'Don't worry,' I said. 'Caring about you is the last thing I'm going to do.' I tightened my grip on her chin. 'Don't forget, little one, I'm a monster. And monsters don't care about anyone.'

CHAPTER TWELVE

Imogen

I STARED INTO Ajax's eyes and something gripped tight in my chest.

Did he really think he was a monster?

But the answer was there in his stunning blue gaze.

Denial shifted inside me. I knew monsters—at least I knew one, my father—and Ajax wasn't like him. Not in any way.

The night he'd kidnapped me, instinct had told me that Ajax King wasn't a man I should be afraid of, and so far he'd done nothing to disprove that.

And, anyway, I wouldn't have let him touch me if I'd been afraid. I wouldn't be sitting here, lying on his magnificent naked body and tracing his tattoos if he'd been the same kind of monster my father was.

He radiated protective energy; I could feel it in my bones. In my heart. He might be hard and pitiless, with a violent, fearsome reputation, but he wasn't a man who'd hurt vulnerable people.

I was the daughter of his father's enemy and, despite catching me poking around in his personal things, all he'd done was tell me off.

Hardly the actions of a monster.

You don't know him. He could be just a different type of monster.

He could be. But if he was a different type, then it was a type that I found completely fascinating and utterly compelling.

And what made him think he was a monster anyway? What was in his past that made him think he was so dangerous? There were rumours about him, about how ruthless he was as a businessman. Many had expected that, as heir to his father's throne, he'd go down along with Augustus, yet he hadn't. In fact, he'd been the one who'd taken Augustus down, seemingly escaping the charges that had caught his father.

Curiosity gripped me, winding tighter and tighter.

How had he escaped the law? When he'd supposedly been his father's true heir? Had he been granted immunity of some kind in return for betraying Augustus?

What kind of man are you touching right now?

I stared into his eyes, looking deep, and he didn't flinch away. Blue fire blazed there, burning hot and strong. A man of conviction, determination. A man of strength and power, who'd given me space to cry. Who'd told me I wasn't a disappointment.

He was no monster.

I lifted my hand and touched his cheek. 'What makes you think that? You haven't done anything particularly monstrous to me.'

'I kidnapped you. And I'm going to use you against your father to get what I want.' His mouth curved in a predatory smile that didn't reach his eyes. 'And I don't give a damn about your feelings on the subject.'

I let my fingers trail down to the sharp line of his

jaw and then lower, down the side of his strong neck. 'But I told you I didn't want you to give a damn.'

'There are worse things than not caring about people's feelings, little one. You must know that. Especially considering your own father.'

I brushed my fingers over his throat, moving down the hard expanse of his chest, crisp hair rough against my fingertips. 'Have you beaten up people and left them for dead?'

'Yes.'

It didn't surprise me. The son of Augustus King wasn't going to be as pure as the driven snow.

I didn't look away, kept my gaze on his. 'Innocent people?'

A muscle leapt in the side of his jaw. 'Yes.' A slight hesitation.

I focused on him, all my attention zeroing in on his winter-sky eyes. 'Why?'

He reached for my hand and pushed it down, curling my fingers around his hardening cock. 'My father needed to be taken down so I did what I had to do.' His voice was like iron and just as cold. 'Are we done?'

It was clear he didn't want to talk any more, but that only made me even more curious. He'd done what he had to do. What did that mean?

'No,' I said. 'I want to—'

'Because I'd prefer you to concentrate on something else.' His fingers tightened around mine, pressing my fingers against his hard flesh. 'Like my cock, for example.'

Dammit. I wanted to push, but having him in my hand, hot and smooth and firm, was distracting. Too distracting.

'Why can't we talk about you?' I looked down, at where my hand and his were wrapped around his hard-on. God, he felt good. 'I told you about me.'

'Because I said so.' His tone was flat, no room for argument. 'If you disagree, you know where the door is.'

Frustration needled at me, making me want to let him go and sweep grandly out. But I couldn't quite bring myself to do so. When would I get this opportunity again? To hold him like I was doing now, explore him the way he wanted me to? Maybe I wouldn't.

I glared at him. 'That's not fair.'

He looked back, his gaze uncompromising. 'That's it. Get angry with me. Show me what a pissed-off Imogen looks like.'

'A pissed-off Imogen might look like me leaving you alone with your hard-on.'

'Do it then.' Challenge burned in his eyes. 'If you think you can.'

And it hit me again in that moment—truly hit me— that I *could* get pissed off if I wanted to. I could get angry. I could get really, *really* angry. And there would be no consequences, because there was no one to get hurt and no one to disappoint.

There was only Ajax and he didn't care.

The weirdest rush of exhilaration swept through me. Was this what freedom felt like?

I met Ajax's stare, squeezing him at the same time as I brushed my thumb over the head of his dick, not knowing what I was doing and not giving one single damn. 'You really want to test me?'

'Fuck,' he hissed, his body tensing, every one of

those carved muscles contracting deliciously under his skin.

Oh, crap. Had I hurt him? 'Sorry,' I muttered. 'Was that too hard?'

'Hell, no.' The flame in his eyes burned even brighter. 'Do it again. And harder. And never fucking apologise to me again.'

The breath went out of me. Did I apologise too much?

Of course you do. But you don't need to worry about that with him. He can handle it. Because he doesn't care.

My hand tightened around him, my gaze riveted to his face, watching pleasure draw his features tight and set the blue of his eyes blazing even hotter.

And when I rubbed my thumb over the head of his cock again, I discovered his skin was slick and getting slicker. Interesting. I took my hand away and put my thumb in my mouth. He tasted of salt and something masculine and indefinable, delicious.

His gaze followed every movement I made, his lips drawing back in a snarl, and I felt it again, my power over him, at the same time as I could feel and see his strength.

Nothing could hurt this man, not even me.

I could do anything to him, tell him anything, and he would let it slide off him. He would remain un-touched.

The adrenaline rush was back and I was moving be-fore I could think better of it, straddling him, putting my hands on his shoulders and gripping him. Then I covered his mouth with mine, kissing him with all the passion I could feel expanding inside me.

'Yes,' he growled against my lips, his voice so rough I could barely understand him. 'Unleash yourself on me, woman. I dare you to.'

So I did.

I let the passion unfurl and along with it my power. And I touched him everywhere. Tasted him everywhere. I found out what he liked, which was pretty much everything, and what his boundaries were: he didn't have a single one.

His control seemed to be limitless, even though I tested the hell out of it. I made him growl and I made him curse. I made him shake and pant and grit his teeth, but he didn't restrain me and he didn't stop me from doing anything I wanted.

I felt free. Drunk on him and the feel of his body, the taste of his skin.

It was the most incredible experience I'd ever had in my life.

We were both shaking by the time I ripped the condom packet open and rolled it down on him, drawing more guttural curses from him.

But he didn't move as I straddled him, putting his hands on my hips only to steady me as I slowly eased myself down onto his hard cock.

Then I sat there, loving the stretch and burn of him inside me and the way his blue eyes stared into mine, his jaw clenched and his body beneath me as tight as a wound spring.

'Ride me, woman,' he growled, low and deep. 'Ride me like you mean it.'

Woman. Yes, that's what I was. I was a woman. Not a child.

His woman.

I tossed my head back and I rode him, and he showed me the way. And then he gave me my head and I galloped, riding wild and free, until our skins were slick with sweat and the rough sounds of earthy, masculine pleasure mingled with my own gasps of delight.

Until finally he gripped me hard between his hands, making me scream as he roared my name, our voices echoing off the walls of his bedroom.

Then when we were done he rolled over, tucking me close to his chest. 'Sleep,' he murmured roughly in my ear. 'You've earned it.'

He was warm and his big body wrapped around me made me feel safe. And, even though I didn't want to, I found myself falling into sleep all the same.

I slept like the bloody dead.

So deeply that when I finally opened my eyes again I wasn't sure where I was. At least not until I reached for the big masculine body that I somehow knew would be beside me, only to find it gone.

I cracked open an eye, wondering why I was so annoyed.

The other side of the bed was empty. And then I remembered.

Ajax.

Pleasure swept through me, a sweet, sensual ripple that reminded me of the night before and all the things we'd done. All the things *I'd* done. My body felt like it had been put through its paces, muscles aching in unusual places and most especially between my legs.

But it wasn't a bad hurt. In fact, I wouldn't have minded more because I was even hungrier for him now than I had been the night before.

Was it normal to want someone like that, even after a night of having sex with them? Or was that just him?

You already know the answer to that one.

I scowled at the thought, just as Ajax walked out of the en suite bathroom wearing nothing but a pair of low-slung jeans and carrying a black T-shirt in one hand.

'Good morning, little one,' he said in that deep, husky voice of his. 'Or is it not so good, judging by that scowl?'

I lay there for a moment, staring at him. He must have had a shower because I could see the moisture on his skin, a drop sliding down one pec and slowly over the cut lines of his abs.

My mouth watered. I wanted to lick that drop off his skin and then lick the rest of him as well.

'You weren't here,' I said. 'That's what I was scowling about.'

A flame glowed in his eyes as he took in my obvious appreciation. 'I had a shower. Some of us have things to do today.'

'I could have joined you.' Only just missing a pout, I sat up. 'You should have woken me up.'

'I didn't want to wake you.' He moved over to the side of the bed and reached out, gently pushing a strand of my hair behind my ear, making me shiver as his fingertips brushed my skin. 'Stay here and I'll bring you breakfast.'

Oh, yes. Breakfast. Suddenly I was starving.

'Breakfast in bed?' I asked hopefully.

'Of course.'

'With you?'

The flame in his eyes flickered, his hand dropping away. 'Not this morning.'

Disappointment gathered inside me. 'It would just be for half an hour. Not long. I could eat really fast—'

'Your father wants to see you, Imogen.'

The words cut across me like a whip.

Suddenly I wasn't hungry any more.

'Oh.' All the good feelings I had were slipping away, leaving me with nothing but a core of ice.

I didn't want to see Dad. He was going to be so angry and that anger wouldn't be directed at Ajax. It would be directed at me. For shirking my duty, for the debt I owed to my mother's memory.

Why do you care? What can he do to you anyway?

I couldn't help caring; that was the problem. Dad was one thing, but I cared about my mother too. She'd died to give birth to me and that was a sacrifice I could never repay. It hurt. Every day, it hurt.

'I'm sorry,' Ajax said, watching me. 'I should have told you last night, but we got…distracted. He wants to make sure that you're okay and that I haven't touched you.'

'Uh, well, you kind of have now.' Restlessness filled me, the need to move becoming almost overwhelming. I shifted, hauling the sheet around me, but Ajax was suddenly there in front of me, his hand reaching out, a finger beneath my chin, tipping my head back.

'What are you afraid of?' he asked. 'I won't let him take you.'

I swallowed, my throat gone tight. 'I'm not afraid.'

It was a lie and we both knew it.

'He can't touch you, Imogen. I'll make sure of it.

All you have to do is tell him you're okay, and we're out of there.'

But being taken by Dad wasn't what I was afraid of. It was that I'd let him make me feel like shit again, let him use me again, and all because I couldn't bear the weight of the debt I owed.

'What about a video of me or something?' At least in a video I wouldn't have to see that contempt in his eyes. 'Would that be enough?'

'Talking to you was a condition of him leaving the city and taking some of his friends with him.'

Oh. Damn.

'So, hypothetically, what would happen if I *don't* see him?' I tried to sound casual, to not make it into a big deal.

The look on Ajax's face hardened. 'He might make himself difficult. Which means I'll be forced to take more extreme measures.'

My heart caught. 'What "extreme measures"?'

His expression become even more wintry, his eyes pale as frost. 'That all depends on how difficult he turns out to be.'

Okay, perhaps I didn't want to know what his 'extreme measures' were, nor did I want to put him in the position of having to take them.

'You don't need to do that,' I said quietly.

But the ice in Ajax's gaze glittered. 'Your father is a liability, Imogen, make no mistake. He's a threat to this city. And the safety of this city and the people in it come before everything.'

Conviction vibrated in his voice and I found myself staring at him, unable to look away. 'What do you mean, the safety of this city?'

He lifted his head, somehow becoming taller, broader. Stronger. 'My father hurt a lot of people. He murdered them, stole from them. It took me years to bring that motherfucker down and I've spent the last five mopping up the rest of the mess he left.' Beneath the ice in his eyes, a ferocious belief burned. 'No one else is going to take his place. Believe me, I will *never* allow another Augustus King to rise.'

The words were more than a promise. They were a vow.

'Wow, you're kind of like Batman,' I said, not a little impressed. 'Why?'

His expression twisted and for a second I glimpsed a terrible rage burning deep inside him. 'Why? Why do you think? It was *my* father who nearly ruined it.'

'So? That doesn't mean you have to clean it up.'

His expression became shuttered. 'Someone has to.'

'But why you?' I wasn't arguing with him. I genuinely wanted to know.

'Because there is no one else.' Turning away, he pulled on his T-shirt, covering up all those beautiful muscles and ink. 'Stay in bed,' he ordered as he stalked towards the door. 'Breakfast will be here in ten.'

Then he was gone, leaving me alone.

CHAPTER THIRTEEN

Ajax

'AJAX?' LEON'S VOICE sounded sharp on the voicemail message. 'What the fuck is going on? There are rumours going around that you've done something with William White's daughter. If so, you owe me a goddamn explanation.' There was some muffled cursing in the background and I could hear Xander murmuring something. 'Yes, I know that,' Leon said curtly, obviously to Xander. 'Call me, you bastard,' he added to me, then cut the message abruptly.

I flung the phone down onto the coffee table in front of me, fighting irritation.

I'd let them know I was going to be out of commission for the next week and that I wasn't to be disturbed, and yet here they were, disturbing me.

Did they really think I was going to call them up and explain myself? I never had before and I wasn't going to start now, especially when I knew the pair of them would disagree with my methods.

What they didn't know wouldn't hurt them and the responsibility would remain with me, the way it always had.

Protecting them was what I did. After all, my brothers were the reason I'd taken my father down in the first place.

And they got hurt. You let them get hurt.

I'd had to. I hadn't been able to go to Leon's rescue when he'd been kidnapped and tortured, or tell Xander the financial games he was playing were real. I'd had to let all that shit happen, because I'd have blown my cover and taking Dad down had been more important and I'd known it would save more lives in the end.

Yeah, sure. Nothing to do with the fact that maybe you're a monster just like him and always have been.

Ice twisted in my veins but I ignored it.

What if I was like Dad? What did it matter? My city was safe and so were my brothers. That was worth any price, wasn't it?

My phone vibrated on the table where I'd flung it, announcing another voicemail from White about when to bring Imogen to see him. My silence on the subject was obviously annoying the shit out of him.

Good. He could stay annoyed a little longer. Considering Imogen's response to the thought of meeting him, I wasn't in any hurry to set it up quite yet.

At some point I would have to, though. I wanted him gone and with the least amount of fuss, which meant getting this proof of life nonsense out of the way.

I could have denied him his request to see Imogen, but then he'd make leaving Sydney a problem and I didn't have either the time or the patience for pissing around with problems. In the kind of mood I was in, I'd likely do something I'd regret later, which wasn't a good idea either.

Music drifted from outside, a driving, thumping beat.

Imogen must be in the pool again.

It had been a couple of days since I'd left her in my bed and since then I'd busied myself with monitoring the situation with her father and his various cronies, organising the fake doctor's certificates that would confirm her virginity, checking with my contacts about White's movements, and reviewing the security surrounding my brothers and their wives, not to mention keeping tabs on what was happening with King Enterprises.

I hadn't had time to see her, but I'd made an effort to ensure she had plenty to do, instructing my housekeeper to organise a laptop for her so she could use the Net since apparently a home cinema, a gym and a library weren't enough.

Though it seemed that what Imogen liked best to do was swim.

I turned automatically to the windows, the side of the pool visible from the lounge area where I stood.

She was standing on the diving board in a green bikini that she must have found in those clothes I'd got my housekeeper to leave for her.

Her pale skin gleamed like a pearl in the sunlight, her hair a gilded skein of silk down her back.

She was poised on the edge of the board like a dancer or a bird about to take flight, her small curvy body graceful and lithe.

I'd told myself that the few hours we'd had in bed was all we'd needed. She'd had her revenge on her father, losing her virginity to a man of her choice, while I'd got a little something for myself for once.

It hadn't ended up being a big drama, not now the

virginity issue was being handled by those fake certificates.

I didn't need to go back for more.

Yet that didn't stop my stupid cock from hardening at the mere thought of those few hours or at the idea of reliving them.

Repeatedly.

When she'd unleashed herself on me, her curiosity and passion had combined into a force that was as unstoppable as it was irresistible. It had blown my fucking mind.

I'd never thought that a virgin exploring a man's body for the first time could be so erotic.

She'd started hesitantly then had gained confidence, becoming utterly fearless. Watching her bloom had been the hottest thing I'd ever seen. And knowing that I was a part of that had only made it hotter.

I stared out the windows, my goddamn cock getting harder at the sight of her and the memories that kept unreeling in my head.

I should go to a bar. Find a woman. Fuck away the need.

But the idea left me cold.

I didn't want just any woman. I wanted her.

On the diving board Imogen leapt but, instead of a graceful dive, she drew her legs up under her and wrapped her arms around them, bombing into the pool like a teenager, water going everywhere.

Then she surfaced a moment later, grinning like she was having the time of her life.

I moved before I could think better of it, shoving the huge sliding glass door open so I could step outside, the sound of the music deafening.

She had her back to me, gripping the tiled edges of the pool then pulling herself out.

A wooden sun lounger sat nearby, the speaker and laptop she was using to stream the music sitting on it.

I bent and hit a button on the laptop, cutting off the sound.

Imogen, who was now standing on the side of the pool, water streaming down her lovely body, turned around. 'Hey, who did—' She broke off, blinking as she saw me.

Colour rushed into her face and a smile like the sun coming out turned up her mouth. Then just as quickly the smile vanished and she frowned. 'You've been avoiding me.'

That fleeting smile, bright and instinctive, hit me in a place I wasn't expecting, a place I hadn't realised was vulnerable.

Fuck.

I scowled. 'Why would I avoid you?'

She shrugged then raised her hands to her hair, squeezing the water from it. 'I don't know—you tell me.'

The movement lifted her breasts, the thin fabric of her bikini pulling tight, drawing attention to those sweet little nipples. They were hard, the wet material outlining them perfectly.

I'd tasted them, rolled them in my mouth, tugged on them with my teeth. She'd liked that. I could still hear her cries of delight in my ears…

Christ, I could not be thinking shit like that. There was no need for a repeat. I had other, more important things to do with my time.

'I've been busy,' I growled, irritated both with my stupid cock and the need I felt to explain myself to her.

'Too busy to even say hi?' Her arms dropped and she wandered over to where I stood, apparently not caring that her bikini was very small, very wet, and I was getting very hard. 'That's kind of a dick move, Ajax.' Mercifully she folded her arms. 'I mean, I'm not asking for flowers and chocolates and love songs. A "hi, how are you doing" would be fine.' Her brows drew down. 'Or is vanishing usual for guys after they've taken a girl's virginity?'

She called you, asshole.

Yeah, and I did not like it. Not one fucking bit.

'You're my prisoner,' I said flatly. 'Prisoners are lucky to get food and water, let alone computers, libraries, pools and loud music.'

'No need to be a bastard.'

'I'm your kidnapper. What the fuck do you expect?'

She stared at me, her green eyes sharp. 'I know why you're angry. You're annoyed because you wanted me to come and say hi to you, right?'

Caught off guard, I couldn't think of a single response.

'Because all you had to do was say,' Imogen charged on, not waiting for me to speak anyway. 'I was around. It's not like I'm going anywhere.'

Holy shit. The bloody woman thought I'd been hanging around waiting for *her* to approach *me*?

She's right though.

No. Why would I do that? If I wanted something and it didn't interfere with my plans I went the hell out and got it. I didn't wait.

But you wanted her and did nothing.

'Like I said, I've been busy.' I gave her a hard stare.

'And I still am so turn your fucking music down so I can concentrate.'

She searched my face, her expression turning into something like…understanding. 'It's okay, I get it,' she said, even though I had no idea what she was talking about. 'But you told me not to hold back and I didn't. So why are you doing the same thing now?'

'Holding back?' I shoved my hands into my pockets, the need to grab her needling at me like an itch I couldn't scratch. 'What the fuck are you talking about?'

She let out a sigh, like I was being particularly dense, then closed the distance between us, reaching out to brush her fingers over the fly of my jeans. 'You're hard, Ajax.'

I stilled, her touch electric, stealing my breath. It took every ounce of will I had not to take my hands out of my pockets and take her on the pool tiles.

You can't. You can never have what you want.

'I told you all I'd give you was a couple of hours,' I forced out between gritted teeth, ignoring the voice in my head. 'And I fucking meant it.'

'I know. But…you still want me.'

I couldn't deny it, not when the evidence was pressing hard against the front of my jeans. 'I told you that what I want doesn't matter.'

A crease appeared between her brows. 'And I told you that it does. Seriously, Ajax. How does us having sex interfere with the safety of this city? My virginity is gone and you're dealing with the medical proof. Dad's never going to know. So what's the problem?'

The problem was the catch, and there was always a catch. I'd learned that particular lesson in my time as my father's heir and learned it well.

I'd wanted to protect my brothers, but doing so would have exposed me and then Dad would have taken me down instead of vice versa. More people would have got hurt. And he would have ruled Sydney unchecked.

Sacrifices had to be made and I was the one who'd make them.

There was no room for selfishness in my plans.

It's great how noble you can make yourself sound.

My jaw tightened.

Imogen shrugged. 'Oh, well, your loss.' Reaching around behind herself, she tugged at the tie of her bikini top and I wasn't sure what she was doing until the whole thing loosened. 'But you know where I'll be if you change your mind.' Pulling the fabric free, she dropped the top on the ground, her perfect little tits bare. 'I'll be in the pool.' Pushing her bikini bottoms down, she stepped out of them then straightened, giving me a look from underneath her lashes. 'Naked.'

Then she strolled to the side of the pool and dived in.

Every muscle in my body tensed.

The gall of the woman. Stripping naked and swimming in my pool like she didn't give a fuck. Like I wasn't standing there aching to get my hands on her and hadn't been aching for the past two days straight.

Like I hadn't been using bullshit excuses to stay away from her, when all I really wanted was to take her to bed and keep her there for the next week straight.

You think a prick like you can ever have what he wants?

I shoved the thought from my head, stalking over to the pool, drawn relentlessly by the woman in it.

She was floating on her back with her arms out, her

hair moving like silky golden kelp around her head.
Her eyes were closed, her naked body the most beautiful thing I'd ever seen. Pale skin, golden hair, soft
pink nipples…

Shit, if there was a catch, I couldn't find it. And
since when had I ever made sex into such a big deal?

Her arms moved lazily in the water and she hummed
a song I didn't recognise, oblivious to me standing on
the side of the pool wrestling with my fucking con-
science.

It was just sex. No big deal. Her virginity was gone
and I was handling that. Taking her to bed wasn't the
start of that slippery slope, the one that led back to
the violence of the days I'd left behind. Anyway, she
wanted me and who was I to deny her what she wanted?
What we *both* wanted?

I couldn't. I wouldn't.

I took a moment to kick off my shoes, then I dived
in after her.

CHAPTER FOURTEEN

Imogen

I HEARD THE SPLASH, felt the spray over my face and the movement of the water as Ajax dived in. And my heartbeat accelerated, adrenaline coursing through me.

Yes. My gamble had paid off.

For the past couple of days I'd been hanging out by the pool, hoping he'd come. Hoping that seeing me in my bikini might make him do…something.

Because ever since he'd walked out the morning after we'd slept together, he'd been avoiding me. And I hadn't been able to get him out of my head.

I hadn't expected that. I'd thought that once I'd got my little piece of revenge, that would be it. I'd be satisfied. But apparently that's not how it worked with Ajax.

One night had done nothing to put out the fire of my curiosity.

He hadn't been around so I'd used the laptop he'd provided to distract me, but all I found myself doing was surfing the Net looking for anything I could find on him. There were old news stories about his father's arrest and how they'd eventually caught Augustus due to some dodgy financial business dealings. Ajax had been involved with the takedown and I obsessively read everything about it, watched all the interviews that featured him. There weren't many, but in each one his expression was hard, his eyes glittering. He looked dangerous and mean, and said virtually nothing.

I couldn't stop watching.

The media viewed him with suspicion and, to be fair, he hadn't done anything to change their viewpoint. But I wondered why not. Because the man the media had painted him as—the violent heir who'd somehow managed to avoid conviction—was *not* the man who'd cupped my face as I'd cried, who'd held me close while I'd slept. Who'd insisted that protecting his brothers and his city came before anything else, including himself.

I wanted to know that man quite desperately. It consumed me.

I'd had intense passions like this before—the tropical fish I'd been obsessed with once as a kid that I'd lost interest in a couple of weeks after Dad had bought me a tank. Or when I'd suddenly been desperate to learn calligraphy, fascinated by the black curves and elegant straight lines, getting lots of pens and different inks, practising for a day before putting everything aside and never picking up a pen again.

Ajax was the adult version of my interest in tropical fish. Or my calligraphy. He was the Mandarin I'd tried to teach myself once, the astronomy I'd been obsessed with for a whole month.

He was a puzzle that only got more complex and more interesting the closer I examined him, and I suspected that sex was merely scratching the surface of who he was.

Whatever, I knew myself. I knew that my obsession with him wasn't going to ease until I'd satisfied my curiosity and the only way I was going to do that was to figure out a way to get close to him.

And obviously the best way to get close to him was through more sex.

I hadn't been able to stop thinking about the hours I'd spent in his bed. About how free he'd made me feel and how accepting he'd been of me and my quirks. How he'd actively encouraged me to be curious about his body and how it had fit with mine.

No one had ever made me feel as if it was okay to be myself the way he had.

So, after the first day or so of obsessing, I'd decided that I had to do something about it. Such as convincing him to take me to bed again.

Unfortunately, for that to work, he had to be around and he wasn't. Which meant I had to try something different—getting him to come to me.

I'd been thrilled when my little ploy of hanging out by the pool in my green bikini and playing loud music had worked. But then he'd been a dick, giving me all sorts of crap about how busy he was, all the while staring at me like he wanted to eat me alive and pretending he wasn't as hard as a rock.

So, to give him some incentive, I'd taken my bikini off. And, judging by the way he'd launched himself into the water, that was all the push he'd needed, which thrilled me down to the bone.

Still, I wasn't sure why he'd been denying himself what we both wanted and I'd already decided I was going to find out.

I was going to find out everything.

But maybe *after* I let him catch me.

I turned over on my front, making an attempt to swim away, but his fingers closed around my ankle and he jerked me towards him. I took a breath as I went under, then his hands closed around my hips and I was out of the water again, being pulled against his hot, hard body and held there, face to face with him.

'Tease.' The hunger in his eyes blazed.

'You can talk.' I spread my palms out on his chest, loving the contrast of his heat with the cool press of the water on my skin. 'I've been in agony for two whole days.'

'Agony?' His hands slid over my butt as he fitted my hips against his, the denim of his wet jeans rough against my sensitive bare flesh. 'You should have come to me.'

'I would have. If you'd been around.'

'I'm around now.' He squeezed me, not gently.

I gasped, the slight bite of pain adding to the rub of his wet clothing on my tender skin, the friction maddeningly erotic.

The feral look on his face intensified, as if he liked the sound very much. 'What's wrong, little one?' His fingers shifted under me, finding the folds of my pussy and brushing over them. 'Am I too much for you?'

'N-no.' Excitement made me stutter as I shifted restlessly in his grip. 'I can handle you. But I'm not sure you can handle me.'

He gave a low growl and suddenly I was being kissed—and kissed hard.

I shuddered with pleasure, winding my arms around his neck, holding on tight as his tongue pushed into my mouth, the dark addictive taste of him flooding through me. His kiss was raw, with an edge of danger to it that I found absolutely intoxicating.

Yes, God, *this* was what I wanted. What I needed. Not movies or books or calligraphy or astronomy, or any of the thousand things I'd spent the last fifteen years of my life using to fill the void inside me. The void I hadn't even realised was there until Ajax had touched me. Let me cry. Let me explore. Made me aware of what I was missing.

Him. I'd been missing him.

I tried to kiss him back, but he was having none of it, wrenching his mouth from mine.

'Ajax, please.' Disappointment crowded in my throat. 'I want—'

'No.' His voice was so rough it was almost unrecognisable, his gaze incandescent with blue fire. 'We've done what you want. Now it's time to do what *I* want.'

A couple of days ago he'd taken my virginity, let me make a choice and take my revenge. That night had been all about me.

Now he wanted it to be about him.

I could not wait.

'Y-yes.' Excitement burned in my blood. 'Show me.'

He smiled, ferocious and predatory. Then, without a word, he turned and carried me to the edge of the pool and set me on the tiles. Gripping the edge, he pulled himself out in one fluid, immensely powerful movement.

My mouth dried, my heartbeat going into overdrive as I watched him.

He stood there for a second, dripping water, then he began to pull his wet clothes off, dropping them negligently on the ground. His body gleamed in the sunlight, slick with water, the ink of his amazing tattoos stark against his olive skin.

I'd never wanted to touch anything as badly as I wanted to touch him.

I got to my feet and stretched out my hands like he was a fire I wanted to warm myself against, but he took a long, loping step towards me, a wolf on the hunt.

Adrenaline rushed through my veins, my excitement electric.

Slowly, he began to stalk me and I let him, backing away in the direction he wanted me to go, towards the nearest sun lounger. Then, when the frame pressed against the back of my legs, he picked me up and sat down on it with me in his lap, both of us facing the pool, my spine against his broad chest, his hard cock pressing between my thighs.

I trembled at the feel of him, at all that heat and coiled power in the taut muscles beneath me.

His hands urged me to lie back against him, my head on his shoulder, and then he smoothed his palms down my arms to my hips. They rested there a moment before easing lower, to my knees, sliding inwards to grip my thighs and gently pull my legs apart, spreading them on either side of his. He bent his legs at the knee, widening them, so his knees were holding my thighs open.

The position was exposing, the slight stretch of the sensitive tissues of my sex so hot I could hardly breathe.

He stroked over my stomach, one hand grazing the sensitised flesh between my thighs, the other lazily toying with my nipple, pinching it lightly.

I groaned, arching into his hands, desperate for his touch. But it was too light. I wanted more, harder.

'Ajax.' His name was a prayer in my mouth. 'Ajax, *please.*'

But he ignored me, turning his mouth into my hair and nuzzling against my ear. The press of his knees was hard against my thighs as his fingers stroked un-hurriedly through my folds, getting me hot, getting me wet.

He pinched my nipple harder then found my clit with his other hand and pinched that too. 'You're mine, woman,' he said roughly in my ear. 'You want to play this game with me, then that makes you mine for the duration. And you do whatever I want, understand?'

Oh, yes, I understood. And I was totally on board.

'Okay,' I panted. 'I'm fine with that. Just…more, please.'

His fingers spread possessively over my pussy and he pinched my nipple yet again, making me groan. 'That's not up to you. Not now.' His teeth grazed my earlobe. 'I'm going to give you something and you're going to put it on me.'

I nodded quickly, the intense pressure between my thighs an ache I was desperate to relieve, his light touches only maddening me further.

He pressed something into my palm—a foil packet still wet from the pool. He must have got it out of his wallet before he'd stripped.

I sat up and with shaking hands ripped it open, tak-ing out the condom. Then I leaned forward to put it on him—or at least I tried. He made it difficult by toy-ing with my other breast and teasing my clit with his finger, making me pant and tremble with the brutal, wicked ecstasy of his touch.

Eventually I got the condom on and then he was taking over again, holding me open with one hand while he gripped himself with the other, fitting the head of his cock against my slick flesh.

He pushed inside me and I cried out at the stretch of him, the slow, aching slide of his flesh into mine. Then he gripped me, holding me still, his hips pushing upwards, forcing himself deeper, his knees pressing my thighs wider apart.

Pleasure cut like a knife and I arched again, writhing helplessly against him, my hips jerking against the relentless push of his.

But he held me there, not letting me move, making me feel every inch of his cock as he slid it out then back in, driving upwards in a hard, brutal motion that had me shuddering.

My hands tried to find something to hold onto, settling on his forearms, my nails digging into his skin as he thrust harder, deeper.

The angle meant I couldn't quite get the friction I wanted and I'm sure he knew that. And took complete advantage of it, every thrust driving me further and further towards madness.

I could feel the orgasm approaching, so close and yet just out of reach. Moans escaped me, desperate cries for him to relieve the growing pressure.

But he didn't. He made me wait. Pushing and pushing and pushing, until I clawed at him, twisting in his grip. Then his fingers at last found my clit and he stroked me in time with his thrusts, the pressure firm, his cock inside me achingly hard.

I exploded around him, stars shooting behind my closed eyelids, my cries echoing around the pool. It was only then that he withdrew from me and flipped me over so I was lying face down on the lounger. Then he came behind me, gripping my hips and pulling me up on my knees, sliding into me from behind.

I buried my burning face against the linen cover of the lounger and groaned, my pussy oversensitive and still pulsing with the aftershocks. But he didn't stop and I didn't want him to.

That first time, up in his bedroom, he'd been holding back and it was only now that I understood how much. Because he certainly wasn't holding back any more.

He drove into me hard and fast, low guttural sounds of pleasure coming from him as he thrust, and I gripped tight onto the cushions, more stars exploding behind my eyes, a second orgasm barrelling down on me.

I loved it. I loved how he simply took what he wanted from me without asking. It meant I couldn't fail or disappoint him, because I didn't have to try to be something I wasn't, or make up for something I didn't do.

It was enough to be myself.

And then his hand slid around my hip and down between my thighs, finding my clit and stroking relentlessly, and I stopped thinking.

The orgasm broke over me, making tears sting behind my lids and sobs choke in my throat with the intensity of the sensation.

'You're mine, woman,' Ajax growled from behind me, shoving me rhythmically into the cushions as he fucked me harder. 'Understand? Only mine.'

Then his big body slammed into mine one last time before stiffening, his roar buried against my skin as he bit my shoulder.

CHAPTER FIFTEEN

Ajax

IMOGEN RELAXED BENEATH ME, her luscious body hot and pliant. She'd turned her head on the lounger cushions, her cheek flushed, strands of hair stuck to it. Sunlight struck gold sparks from those strands and the thick, soft lashes that rested against her skin.

She was panting.

Her pussy was clenching tight around my cock and I could taste her from where I'd bitten her shoulder, her skin salty and sweet. I could see the mark my teeth had left there too, a small bruise already darkening her pretty skin.

A dark, possessive satisfaction spread out inside me.

I'd marked her. She was mine. I wasn't listening to that fucking voice in my head telling me that I didn't deserve her. That she was somehow the start of the slippery slope I was going to fall down.

It didn't matter. I'd have to let her go eventually but, until then, she was completely and utterly mine. And it felt good. It had been a long time since I'd had any-thing that was mine. If I ever really had.

I eased out of her then put a hand on the back of

her neck, pressing lightly. 'You okay?' I'd been rough and demanding and she was, after all, extremely in-experienced.

'Yes,' she said in a scratchy voice. 'In fact, I don't think I've ever been better.'

I smiled. My little one was as insatiable as I was.

'Good.' I pressed a little harder. 'Wait there.'

I got off the lounger and went into the house, getting rid of the condom in the downstairs bathroom. Then I went back outside.

Imogen was curled up on the lounger cushions and as I approached she turned her head, looking up at me from underneath her lashes. She smiled, green eyes dancing in the sunlight.

That thing that kept catching me in the chest caught me again. Harder.

She turned over, lying on her back, then she flung her arms up over her head and stretched, her back arch-ing, her toes pointed like a dancer.

So fucking sexy. I was hard again, instantly.

'Little one,' I murmured. 'Are you trying to kill me?'

She opened one eye, clearly pleased. 'Is it working?'

'Maybe.' I grinned. 'Are you up for more? Because I'm not finished.'

Her eyes glittered, the hunger in them in no way diminished by the two orgasms I'd already given her. 'Good. I was hoping you'd say that.' She rolled onto her side, facing me. 'Tell me what you want next.'

Perfect. She was absolutely goddamn perfect.

I put her onto her back next then came over her on my hands and knees, my head between her legs so I could eat her out. Then I had her suck me at the same time, telling her she couldn't come unless I did.

She managed the task pretty well considering I had my tongue in her pussy the whole time, proving that the woman could clearly concentrate extremely well when given the right incentive.

After we'd recovered, I gathered her up into my arms and took her inside to the en suite bathroom next to my bedroom. Pulling her into the shower, I washed her, running my hands all over her satiny skin before lifting her up and fucking her slowly against the tiled wall until she sobbed with pleasure.

By that stage the day was edging into late afternoon and she was starving, and so was I. So I took her down to the kitchen, where I made us both a BLT.

She insisted on watching me closely as I cooked the bacon, her bright eyes alight with interest. Then she demanded to have a turn pushing the bacon around in the pan so I handed the spatula to her and let her try.

'Please tell me you've at least cooked something,' I commented as she poked at the bacon.

'Nope,' she said, completely unashamed. 'Not a thing. Dad had a lady who came and cooked for us. I never even thought about doing it myself.' She gave the bacon another poke then looked at me, her pretty face beautifully flushed. 'Can I cook something to-night? Like…an egg or something? I've never even boiled one.'

I leaned against the kitchen counter. 'You didn't learn how to do it in school?'

'No. I didn't go to school. Or high school. Dad hired tutors for me.'

Of course she hadn't. She'd been kept isolated and deliberately so.

I studied her face as she gave the bacon the same

fierce attention she'd given to my dick not an hour earlier.

Poor little one. She'd been alone for a long time yet she hadn't let it crush her spirit entirely. She was still curious, still interested, still alive to the possibilities of the world.

Unlike you.

Yeah, I knew what the possibilities of the world were. Violence. Murder. Torture. Pain. Betrayal. At least that's what they'd been for me.

She should have better.

The thought was like a meteor streaking across the front of my mind, blazing, full of light. And I had no idea why.

It wasn't my job to make her life better. She was my prisoner and now maybe my toy, but nothing beyond that. I'd keep her in my bed for a few more days and then I'd let her go.

'What did you want to be when you grew up?' she asked me suddenly. 'Like, when you were a kid?'

It was such an out-of-the-blue question that I answered without thinking. 'A sailor,' I said, memories of watching those boats on the water coming back to me. 'I always wanted to sail over the edge of the horizon, see what was on the other side.'

She smiled. 'That sounds so cool. Did you ever get the chance?'

'No.' I managed to keep the word casual and not full of any dark undertones. 'What about you? What did you want to be when you grew up?'

Her expression shifted, rippling with something that I thought was curiosity, and I tensed, waiting for her to push.

But she didn't. Instead she looked back down to the pan. 'What didn't I want to be? A nurse. A fairy. A princess. A firefighter. An ambulance driver. A doctor. A painter. An astronomer. A historian.' Her mouth turned up. 'I was interested in everything, which basically meant that I could never decide.'

That seemed to fit her quicksilver mind.

'You never found the one thing you really wanted to do?' I asked.

'Part of the problem is that I want to try everything.' She gave a little sigh. 'But then, once I figure it out, I lose interest.'

She was bright and I suspected there was an intelligence to her that her curiosity only hinted at. What would she be like if she didn't lose interest? If she found that one thing and concentrated on it?

She would be...formidable.

Yes. She bloody well would be.

'Why do you lose interest?' I asked.

She lifted a shoulder. 'I don't know. I just get obsessed by something and then, once I've found out all there is to know about it, it's like I'm...not interested any more. Or something else catches my attention.' Her small white teeth sunk into her lip. 'It's frustrating, to be honest.'

'Maybe you simply haven't found the thing that'll hold your interest yet,' I said. 'You're still young. The world is a big place.'

'You say that like you're eighty years old.'

'I feel eighty years old.' I found myself staring into her eyes. 'Especially when I look at you.'

Her mouth, with its tiny, adorable birthmark, curved. 'I know I'm young, or at least younger. And

Dad is always accusing me of behaving like a child, but...' The smile faded, darkness flickering in her eyes. 'I'm not. I'm Dad's daughter. And no kid should ever have a childhood like mine.'

That strange tightness caught in my chest again, harder this time. All I could think about was how different we were—light years apart in life experience—and yet how similar we were too.

Our fathers, hers and mine, enemies. Our childhoods twisted by the same kind of monsters. She'd been sheltered from it more than I had, but she hadn't escaped. It had touched her too.

I wanted to ask her how she'd coped, but I suspected I already knew; that quicksilver mind of hers had protected her, always moving, always finding something new to concentrate on, distracting her from the truth of her existence.

I'd had the protectiveness that lived in me, that I cursed sometimes for the way it drove me, the way it denied me.

But in the end it had been the thing that had saved me too.

'No, they shouldn't.' I reached out to cup her cheek. 'And you shouldn't have either.'

'He hurt other people worse. He never touched me.'

'Hurt doesn't have to be physical—you know that, right?'

She looked away, her skin soft against my palm. 'He had his reasons.'

Something stilled inside me. 'What reasons were they?'

'I mean, he was right—I'm not that great at controlling myself even now. And besides, he said I owed it to her.' She let out a shaky breath, staring down unseeing at the pan. 'My mum.' Another pause and I waited, because I knew there was more.

Her gaze lifted, the green sharp as glass. 'I killed her, you know.'

It took effort to keep the shock from my face. 'You killed her? What do you mean?'

'I told you, remember? She died having me. And Dad...never forgave me for that. He told me that if I hadn't been born, Mum would still be here, and that I owed him for her loss. That I...owed her too.'

Jesus. Her dad had laid that on her? The bastard. The *fucking* bastard.

I stroked her cheek with my thumb, the tightness in my chest aching at the pain in her eyes. 'You don't owe him anything, Imogen, not a damn thing. And you didn't kill her either.'

Her mouth got that vulnerable look. 'Dad thinks I did. If I hadn't been born, she wouldn't have had that haemorrhage and she'd still be alive.'

'He's wrong. Grief makes people do odd things and blame others when they shouldn't.' I'd seen enough of that in my lifetime. 'I'm sorry your mother died, but...' I paused. 'I think she would have wanted you to be born.'

Imogen had gone very still. 'She wouldn't have wanted to die.'

I stroked her again, feeling the softness of her. 'No, but she would have been glad that you're alive. That you're here.'

'You don't know that.'

'I know what it's like to want to protect the people you love. To sacrifice things for them.' I didn't understand what was making me say this stuff to her, not when she wasn't supposed to matter to me, but I couldn't stop myself. 'Your mother loved you, Imogen. And she would have sacrificed everything for you to make sure you existed. Even her life.'

A tear ran down her cheek and then another. 'But... why?' She looked at me as if she genuinely didn't have any idea. 'She didn't even get a chance to know me.'

'Why? Because you're beautiful.' I wiped away the tear with my thumb. 'And you're very brave. You're strong. And you're fiercely intelligent. Why wouldn't she?'

'But I... I'm not any of those things.'

'Bullshit. You've done nothing but be resolutely unafraid of me since I kidnapped you. Hell, no one talks to me the way you do—no one would fucking dare. Then there's how you took everything I had to give you in bed, all the while screaming for more. And now... I want to see what that amazing mind of yours can accomplish when you find something you want to focus on.' I brushed away another tear. 'Because I have a feeling that when you do you're going to work miracles.'

Shock rippled over her face, along with something else I didn't recognise. She stared at me like she'd never seen me before in her entire life.

'How...?' Her voice was scratchy. 'How do you know all this stuff?'

'My mother died when I was young too, but I had brothers,' I said quietly. 'And I would have done anything for them.'

Behind her, the oil in the pan began to smoke.

'The bacon, little one,' I reminded her gently. 'It's burning.'

CHAPTER SIXTEEN

Imogen

I ROLLED OVER and blinked as the early-morning sunlight fell over my face.

Ajax wasn't in bed with me, but that seemed to be normal with him. He hadn't been there the past couple of days when I'd woken up either, though I hadn't woken this early before.

He must have been up even earlier.

I slipped out of bed, finding one of his T-shirts on the floor and pulling it on over my head. The cotton was cool against my bare skin and it smelled of the dark, delicious male scent that was all him.

It gave me a little shiver of pleasure.

I couldn't have put into words how happy the past couple of days with him had made me.

After that day in the kitchen, when he'd said those things to me about Mum and sacrifices, I'd felt lighter than I had in years. And in the days that followed I felt lighter still.

It wasn't as if we did anything major. Just…spent a lot of time in bed, talking. Or watching TV. Or swimming in the pool. One evening I'd curled up in his lap in the library, his hand stroking through my hair as we read books together. I hadn't wanted to move, not once.

Being with him eased something frenetic inside me. With him it quietened, as if his presence lulled it.

He still hadn't talked about himself in any meaningful way, though, apart from that one comment about his brothers. His past and his thinking processes were still as much of a closed book to me as ever.

Which naturally made me even hungrier to know about them.

I crept out of the bedroom and paused in the hallway outside, glancing through the open doorway into the office next to the bedroom.

Ajax sat at the computer, leaning back in his chair, his long legs outstretched. He wore nothing but a pair of running shorts, as if he'd just come back from a workout. His skin gleamed, those incredible tattoos outlining the muscles I'd explored with my hands and my tongue for hours the night before.

He was so delicious. My palms itched, wanting to touch him.

You're never going to stop wanting him.

I shook my head at the thought. Of course I would. I always lost interest after a while. Sex with him was new and fresh and so it was fascinating to me. Once I'd explored everything he had to offer I'd be ready to move on, the way I moved on with everything.

Trying not to make a sound, I crept into the room and sneaked up behind him, hoping to surprise him.

Leaning in, I whispered, 'Caught you,' in his ear.

He didn't move and he didn't look round. 'If you want to catch me, you'll have to use something to mask your scent. I could smell you the moment you stepped into the hallway.'

'You could smell me?' I wound my arms around his neck. 'Seriously?'

'I'm used to people creeping up on me, little one. I've developed a few instincts to stop them from surprising me.'

That made sense. I didn't imagine he'd had a peaceful life.

'But didn't your father have guards to protect you?' I nuzzled against his neck. 'Like, lots of security? Mine did. I can't go anywhere without my guards.'

He was sitting there, apparently relaxed. But I could feel the sudden tension in his body. 'My father thought I needed to protect myself.'

There was a note in his deep voice that I couldn't identify.

I shut my eyes, brushed my mouth across his powerful shoulder, wanting to ease that tension somehow. 'Why? Isn't that what guards are for?'

He didn't say anything and it felt like the tension in him was seeping into the silence of the room, pressing in around us.

This was a painful subject.

Abruptly I wanted to talk about something else, ask him questions, distract him. I didn't want to hurt him.

But, before I could open my mouth, he said, 'I had to learn what it meant to be Augustus's son early. I'd always suspected he was a monster, but I had it shoved in my face when I was thirteen.'

A chill crept down my spine.

'You don't have to say anything,' I murmured. 'Not if you don't—'

He put his hand over mine where they rested on his chest and the rest of what I'd been going to say vanished from my brain. It wasn't a move meant to hold me still. It was almost as if he wanted the touch of my skin against his as a comfort.

'Dad took me to an old warehouse one day after school,' Ajax said, the words toneless. 'There was nothing in it but a man tied to a chair. I had no idea what was going on or what the man was doing there, but as soon as Dad walked in the man went white.'

The chill down my spine solidified into ice.

I might have been sheltered, but I wasn't stupid. I knew where this was going.

'I asked Dad what was happening and he said that the man in the chair was an employee of his who'd disobeyed him and then tried to leave. I asked Dad what he meant by "leave", but Dad told me it would all become clear.' Ajax paused, his grip on my hand tightening. 'Then he made me watch while he beat the man half to death.'

The ice filtered into my bloodstream, chilling me despite the warmth of his hand over mine and the heat of his bare chest.

His father had made him watch... At thirteen.

I laid my cheek against his shoulder, fighting the sick feeling in my stomach. My father might have hurt and manipulated me emotionally, but he'd never shown me his violent side. At least not until he'd hurt Cam.

'Dad told me that I needed to see what happened to people who disobeyed him,' Ajax went on expressionlessly. 'And those who wanted out. Then he said that I was a King and I'd be one for life, and if I ever betrayed him or escaped, he'd kill me. And my brothers too.'

I had no idea what to say. Because what could I say? To something as horrific as that?

So I did the only thing I could. I tightened my arms around him and spread my palms out on his chest, pressing down. Then I turned my face into his strong neck, put my mouth to his skin.

He'd been just as much a prisoner of his father as I had of mine, hadn't he? Dad had used my mother's death against me, while Augustus had taken Ajax's inherent protectiveness and used that against him.

And of course it had worked, because if I'd learned anything about Ajax it was that protectiveness lay at the very heart of him.

It was why he'd kidnapped me. To keep his city safe.

And by threatening his brothers his father had ensured Ajax's loyalty.

It turned my stomach.

'I hate him,' I said fiercely against his neck. 'He's a bastard for using your brothers against you like that. Jail is too good for him. I would have beaten him up first.'

Strangely, the tension suddenly bled out of Ajax's shoulders and he shifted, swivelling the chair around and pulling me into his lap.

'You're fierce, woman.' His sky-blue eyes met mine, direct and uncompromising. 'I approve.'

I settled myself against his chest, in the crook of his arm, and looked up at him. 'Well, it's true. And I'm glad you took him down in the end.'

An expression that I thought was regret flickered over his face. 'It took me too long.'

'But you had to be careful, right? I mean, otherwise he would have hurt your brothers.'

'It still took longer than it should. And I had to stand by while…'

I put my hand on his bare chest, feeling the strong beat of his heart, knowing that whatever had made him stop, it was painful. 'You don't need to say it.'

He searched my face for a long time. 'I had to stand by while Leon was kidnapped and tortured. While Dad used Xander to steal people's money. I couldn't do a thing for them, not without betraying myself and all the plans I'd put in place. Taking down my father was more important and I sacrificed my brothers to do it.' He stared at me as if I had the answer to a question he'd been dying to know the answer to. 'What kind of man does that?'

Grief twisted in my heart, for him and the childhood he'd had. For how his father had used him.

Was this why he thought he was a monster?

I lifted my hands to his face, holding him gently. 'You wanted to save people,' I said fiercely. 'Not just your brothers, but all the people your father hurt. All the people your father could potentially hurt too if he wasn't stopped.'

A shadow moved over his face. 'I'm not looking for forgiveness, Imogen.'

I dropped my hands, unexpectedly stung. 'I wasn't giving it.'

'That's not why I told you.'

I pushed the prick of hurt away. This wasn't about me. It was about him. 'So why did you tell me then?'

'So you understand. The end justifies the means. Every time.'

I swallowed. 'Yes, I get it.'

The hard look in his eyes softened. He brushed my

cheek with one finger. 'I'm not saying this to hurt you and I'm sorry if I did. I just want to be straight with you. You can't get too comfortable with me. I'm a man with only one goal and I won't change it. Not for you. Not for anyone.'

Hearing it shouldn't have made the hurt go deeper. He was being honest and I appreciated it. Not that I was going to get too comfortable with him in any case.

'That's good.' I tried to make my voice light. 'Because you know I'm going to lose interest in you soon in any case. I always do.'

His eyes gleamed, though whether it was amusement or something else I wasn't quite sure. 'You want to see something?'

'What?' Automatically I looked down at his shorts.

This time there was no mistaking his amusement, his laugh deep and rough and sexy. 'No, it's not that, not today.'

My hurt began to ebb, pleased by how I'd made him laugh. I flicked him a glance from underneath my lashes. 'Is there anything else as interesting?'

'Look at my computer screen and then tell me.'

I sighed and turned to look at the screen.

I saw what looked to be a 3D rendering of a building. 'What's that?'

'A new apartment block my sister-in-law is designing.' He leaned forward, gripping the mouse and shifting it, his bare skin and heat teasing my hyper-alert senses.

The building tilted and turned in response, giving a three-hundred-and-sixty-degree viewpoint.

Of course. He was in the property development business, wasn't he?

I sat up, my curiosity starting to kick in. 'Is your company going to be building that?'

'Yes. Eventually. If we get the returns we want on the luxury apartment complex that's going up soon.'

I reached out towards the mouse. 'Can I have a look?'

He nodded and sat back, letting me take control.

I studied the building from different viewpoints, zooming in, pleased when the inside plans opened up and I could see all the apartments. Simple, elegant spaces, designed to take advantage of the light.

I knew nothing about buildings, still less about architecture, but this building looked like somewhere I'd want to live myself.

'It's amazing,' I said, staring fascinated at the screen. 'Who's it for?'

'Families who don't have homes.'

I turned sharply to look at him.

His gaze was as uncompromising as it had been when he'd talked about his brothers. 'There are a lot of homeless people out there, families with nowhere to go. I've been liaising with the state housing officials and we're working something out. This building is as eco-friendly as it's possible to get and cost efficient to build, and hopefully will serve as a prototype for more.'

Saving his city. That's what he'd said he was trying to do, and not only from people who might threaten it. He was trying to make it a better place for the people who lived in it too.

'Who's going to pay for it?' I asked, trying to cover the giant lump in my throat.

'I will. I have plenty of money.'

'You're not a monster,' I said bluntly. 'You're like…

Batman and Captain America and Thor all rolled up into one.'

He lifted a hand to my face, brushing my cheek. 'Look at the building again. I want to know if you think there's anything more I need to do to it, anything I could add.'

I shivered at his touch. 'But I don't know anything about buildings.'

'You have an amazing mind, though.' His mouth turned up. 'Time to put it to good use.'

CHAPTER SEVENTEEN

Ajax

As I'd hoped, Imogen became totally engrossed in the apartment building that Poppy, Xander's new wife, had designed for me.

So much so that she barely looked at me when I finally left the room to go and do a few other things.

I took her coffee and toast an hour later, and this time she didn't even turn, merely muttering thanks as she frowned at the article she was in the middle of reading.

I smiled and left her to it, having a shower then going downstairs, yet another message on my phone from her father burning a hole in the pocket of my jeans.

There were a lot of those, each message more and more pissed-off sounding, demanding I let him see his daughter.

You've been putting it off.

I pulled open the massive sliding window in the lounge that led to the pool and stepped outside, making sure it was shut behind me. Then I walked over to where the tiled pool area met the cliff that plunged down into the sea. A small stone parapet marked the edge of the cliff and I stood near it, staring out over the sea as I took the phone from my pocket.

Yes. For the last two days I *had* been putting this off.

Because something was holding me back from granting White's request. And I wasn't sure what it was.

It wasn't the danger factor, not when I'd make sure her security would be airtight. In fact, I couldn't put my finger on exactly what was bugging me about it.

Whatever the issue was, I had to ignore it and luckily the conversation we'd had just now, up in my office, had reminded me of where my priorities lay.

Another thing puzzled me. Why had I told her about Dad and the beating I'd witnessed? About how I'd had to stand by and watch my brothers get hurt? Her comments about her own guards and the artless questions about why I hadn't been given the same treatment had somehow got under my skin.

Or perhaps it had simply been the way she'd put her arms around me, her soft lips against my neck. How she'd nuzzled against me, her breath on my skin and her hands on my bare chest. Her warmth and familiar scent had eased a tension I hadn't known was there. A tension that had nothing to do with sex.

It made me fucking uncomfortable. Maybe that's why I'd told her what I had. To make her as uncomfortable as she made me. So she knew I wasn't a man she could throw her arms around whenever she pleased or treat like someone safe. Who wouldn't hurt her if she got between him and his goal.

Like you hurt your brothers?

The truth shifted inside me, digging in, sharp like a knife.

Yeah, I wasn't that man and she had to understand that.

Hitting the button that would call her father, I waited as it rang once and then White's furious voice was answering.

'King, you bastard! I've been trying to—'

'Next week,' I cut him off curtly. 'Wednesday night. I'll send through the details of where and when to meet.'

'But I—'

'There will be no negotiation. You wanted proof of life, you'll get it. That's all.'

I hit the disconnect button before he could argue further.

There. It was done.

Next week she'd meet her father and once he'd ascertained that I hadn't hurt her or touched her, he'd leave Sydney.

And take her with him.

That had always been the deal. I'd never intended to keep her. My threat to make her mine had extended to her virginity only to ensure White's obedience.

I'd let her go and her father would take her to Melbourne or wherever he intended to set himself up, continuing to use her as his tool to build his pathetic little empire.

You're really going to give her back to him? What will happen to her if he finds out you touched her?

I lifted my head, stared out at the sea, at the yachts in the harbour, sailing to places I could never go.

He wouldn't find out I'd touched her; I'd made sure

of that. But as to letting her go… What other choice did I have? If I kept her, White would make things difficult. My investigations had discovered that he'd built quite the web and I didn't have the time to take it apart. Not when I had a whole lot of other projects on my plate. Especially that social housing project. It had been on the backburner for a while and I wanted to get it front and centre. Protecting my city was one thing, but doing something good for it was quite another.

Apart from anything else, I'd spent years dismantling my father's empire and frightening off other challengers. I wanted to do something meaningful, that wasn't about banging heads together.

Putting more distance between him and you? Yeah. Sure.

I ignored the thought.

No, I couldn't keep Imogen. She had to go back to her father in the end.

I'd tell her about the meeting with her father tonight, and ease the sting by taking her somewhere private, where she could enjoy being out of the house for a change.

I watched one of the yachts tacking slowly against the wind and smiled.

I had the perfect place.

A couple of hours later it was all organised, then I busied myself with finally dealing with my brothers.

I sent them a couple of texts reminding them I was out of contact and busy. The situation with White's daughter was being dealt with and they weren't to concern themselves with it. On pain of me being severely pissed with them.

Of course, within moments of the messages being

sent, both Xander and Leon tried to call me. I ignored them. I didn't want to talk to them. Once Imogen and her father were gone, then I'd tell them, but not before.

It wasn't till the late afternoon that I realised I hadn't seen Imogen.

I went upstairs to check if she was still in my office and she was, sitting in the same position I'd left her in that morning, staring hard at the computer screen. Some official-looking document was open on it and she was frowning at it.

There was something different about her and it took me a moment to figure out what it was. She was sitting still. Her foot wasn't jiggling and she wasn't humming. She wasn't shifting around or doing any of the other things I'd watched her do over the past couple of days.

Her attention was focused so fiercely on the screen it was as if she was trying to see inside to the electronics themselves.

I leaned against the doorframe. 'Little one.'

She didn't even look at me.

'Little one.'

She twitched, but didn't look away from the screen.

'Imogen,' I finally said, amused.

She glanced at me, blinked, then grinned. 'Oh. Sorry. Did you want something?'

'You've been sitting there all day. Did you even have lunch?'

'No,' she said slowly. 'I don't think I did. But I had a good look at your building and a whole lot of social housing stuff, what's available in New South Wales and the rules and regulations—that kind of thing.' Her eyes were shining. 'It's quite complicated. Lots of things to figure out. I mean, I guess you've done all that?'

I couldn't help smiling. 'I've done some things. Haven't had a chance to investigate others.'

'Do you want me to tell you what I discovered?' She turned back to the computer, hit a button and the printer whirred into life. There was already quite a stack of paper beside it.

Clearly, she'd been busy.

'Yes,' I said. 'But you can tell me tonight over dinner.'

'Okay. Let me know if you want me to do anything, because I might just stay here and—'

'No,' I interrupted. 'I'm taking you out.'

'Out? As in out of the house out?'

'Yes, out of the house out.'

She smiled the most beautiful smile. 'Seriously?'

There was an unfamiliar warmth in my chest that hadn't been there before, somehow called into life by her smile.

It had been a long time since I'd done anything to make anyone happy. The big picture didn't include individuals.

Certainly not individuals like this one, who smiled at me as if I'd handed her the fucking moon on a plate.

'Where are we going?' she went on. 'To a restaurant? Like, Asian food? I love Japanese. Or Indian—I love Indian too. Thai is pretty cool. But I don't really mind. If we have steak, though, it must have fries with it, because you can't have steak without chips, right?'

Adorable. Delightful. Exuberant. Full of interest and questions and excitement. And, despite how she'd been trapped in the prison her father had created for her, there was an optimism to her that I didn't have and probably never would.

She was everything I wasn't. Everything that was missing from my life.

Everything you need.

The thought sat there for one long moment and, no matter how hard I tried to ignore it, the damn thing wouldn't go away.

And the warmth in my chest just sat there too, getting bigger and bigger the more she smiled at me.

It was so easy to make her happy.

That's what you want. You want to make her happy.

'Ajax?' She was giving me a slightly concerned look now. 'Everything okay?'

Christ, how long had I been standing there staring at her?

'Be ready in an hour,' I said, my voice sounding a lot rougher than I'd intended.

'Yay.' She frowned. 'But where are we going?'

'It's a surprise.'

'Omigod, I love surprises! Do I wear a dress? I mean, there is a dress in those clothes you got me, right? What about shoes? Heels or flats? Do I need a jacket?'

I couldn't stand it.

Pushing myself away from the doorframe, I strode into the room and over to the chair, bending to take her flushed face in my hands. Then I kissed her hard, stopping her stream of questions.

Instantly her mouth opened under mine, warm and generous, and hungry. If I wasn't careful I was going to have her right here in this chair and, since I had a few things to do before we went out, that probably wasn't the best idea.

Releasing her, I stepped back. 'Wear whatever you feel beautiful in. I'll take care of everything else.'

'Can I bring those printouts? I promise I won't talk at you too long.'

'Yes. Bring them all. And you can talk at me as long as you want.' I didn't think I could say no to her. Not now.

What I did need to do was get out of this room and figure out where the fuck I'd put my distance.

Because one thing was for sure; I was going to need it if I was ever going to give her back to her father.

CHAPTER EIGHTEEN

Imogen

I WAS RIDICULOUSLY EXCITED.

Ajax still hadn't told me where we were going but, sitting next to him in the plain black car as it slid easily through the Sydney streets, I knew that, wherever it was, it was going to be fantastic.

I was out of his house. Outside. And sure, it wasn't like I was completely alone and able to do what I wanted, but I didn't mind that. In fact, having him beside me, all tall, dark, muscular and hot, made it even better somehow.

Knowing he'd organised this for me made it better too.

I'd tried to make an effort with my clothes since he'd obviously made an effort to organise this and, even though I didn't know where we were going, I thought I'd wear something sexy that we'd both enjoy.

A pretty green silk shift dress with spaghetti straps that felt nice against my skin. The look he'd given me when I'd come out wearing it had thrilled me.

He liked it. A lot.

Well, the feeling was mutual.

He was in his usual jeans—he never seemed to wear the suits hanging up in his closet—along with a black T-shirt and battered black leather jacket. Casual clothing that fitted him like a second skin, highlighting his height and powerful muscularity, making him look deliciously dark and broody.

I could hardly drag my gaze away.

His mouth curved as he caught me staring. 'Feel free to stare at me, little one,' he murmured. 'I don't mind.'

I flushed. 'I was wondering why you never wear all those suits in your closet.'

'Because I don't like suits.'

'So why did you buy them?'

Dark humour glittered in his gaze. 'Leon thought they would make me more…accessible.'

I grinned. 'He's right. You were very accessible the night you kidnapped me and you were wearing a suit then.'

'I'm not sure kidnapping you was me being accessible.'

'Well, I didn't mind it.'

'I'm glad.' There was a blue flame burning in his eyes now. 'Because I'm pretty fucking happy I kidnapped you.'

My cheeks heated, something inside me glowing at how blatantly appreciative the look he gave me was. 'I hope I won't be too overdressed,' I said breathlessly. 'Or underdressed. Or whatever.'

'You're perfect.' His smile was hungry and a touch feral. 'Completely perfect.'

It made me shiver in the best way.

I hoped we'd be somewhere private, where we could

maybe indulge our mutual hunger, but then the car pulled up and Ajax looked out the window.

'We're here,' he said.

Here turned out to be a marina with a lot of expensive sleek boats moored on long jetties that stretched out across the dark water. The place was brightly lit and there were a number of people moving among the boats, either unmooring or tying them up.

I peered curiously out the window. 'What are we doing here?'

Ajax's smile turned enigmatic. 'You'll see.'

My surprise turned out to be one of those sleek yachts that sat low in the water. It had a covered deck and an interior like a five-star hotel. Low, soft couches, gleaming wooden floors and windows on all sides. A table was set up on the deck outside, complete with silverware, crystal glasses, candles and a spray of roses. A wine bottle stood waiting to be opened.

I stared around in wonder. 'It's a boat,' I said after Ajax returned from talking with the yacht's captain, coming around the table to pull out my chair. 'A bloody boat.' I sounded ridiculous but I couldn't help it. 'I've never been on a boat before. Is it yours? Where are we going? Are we really going to have dinner here?'

'Sit down and I'll tell you,' Ajax said, amused.

Obediently I did, biting down on my questions, looking around at the marina. There were yachts with graceful sails and huge super-yachts—basically a rich man's playground.

Ajax had said he'd wanted to sail away over the horizon as a kid, so this boat had to be his, right? And now he was inviting me out on it. So cool.

His gaze was full of warmth as he sat down opposite me and it made my heart beat faster.

'It's not my boat,' he said, reaching for the wine bottle and opening it, pouring white wine into both our glasses. 'But I'm considering buying it. This is a test drive.' His blue gaze caught mine. 'And, as to where we're going, we're going on a tour of the harbour while we have dinner.'

Oh, I was up for that. *So* up. I'd been to the harbour, of course, but never without guards. Never on my own with someone I liked for company.

And I *did* like Ajax. Sure, he was uncompromising, not to mention arrogant and bossy. But his heart was in the right place. And he made me feel good. And he was really interesting. I liked the way his mind worked. He saw the whole, while I tended to focus on the different parts.

Such as him, for example. I was seeing different parts of him, but I had the sense he was only showing me the parts that he wanted me to see.

Not the whole of him.

And I wanted to see that very much.

Maybe I would tonight.

Ten minutes later we were cruising over the water, the bright crescent of the harbour bridge and the neon of the city skyline in front of us.

I couldn't stop staring. The city was beautiful and the scent of salt, the openness of the water around us and the warmth of the night pressing in made me feel alive in a way I hadn't before. As if there were possibilities in the air. Possibilities I hadn't thought about before because they were things I couldn't have.

Correction, things I thought I didn't deserve, such

as a normal life. A job. A place that was mine. Friends. A man I loved.

The thought sent a hot pulse of emotion through me. A man I loved…

Such as the man sitting opposite?

The man who'd kidnapped me, saved me. Who'd not only shown me pleasure, but shown me that I was worthy of it. Who'd allowed me to be myself and liked me despite it.

Or maybe because of it.

The man who'd told me that my mother's sacrifice had been worth it if it had allowed me to exist.

You're in love with him. You have been since the moment you met him.

My eyes filled with the stupidest tears.

'You look sad.' His deep voice wound around me, encompassing me in its rough warmth. 'What's wrong? I thought you'd like the yacht.'

I blinked furiously. God, I did *not* want to cry. I didn't even know why I was crying.

Sure, you do.

Yes. I was in love with Ajax King and I couldn't have him. Because if he didn't release me back to Dad, then Dad would stay, continuing to threaten Ajax and his family. Continuing to threaten the city Ajax had sworn to protect.

And I couldn't ask him to keep me. I couldn't ask to be put before everyone he cared about. That would be selfish.

I forced myself to smile, my heart aching. 'Oh, I'm just…happy to be outside and here,' I lied. Then, because I couldn't help myself, I added, 'With you.'

Something in his gaze shifted, his smile fading. 'I have to tell you something, Imogen.'

I swallowed. I knew what he was going to say; don't ask me how, but I did. Maybe it was simply the timing of me discovering I was in love and realising I could never have it.

'You're going to tell me that you've spoken to Dad and that I have to meet him,' I said. 'And then you're going to give me back to him.'

He was silent, staring at me.

Of course he was going to give me back to Dad. And that shouldn't have disappointed me in the slightest. I'd told him I didn't want him to care about me, after all.

'No,' Ajax murmured slowly. 'I'm not going to give you back to him.'

The shock was a hard jolt, like I'd curled my fingers around a bare electrical wire. 'W-what?'

'I changed my mind.' The intensity in his eyes burned. 'I'm keeping you.'

I'm keeping you…

A hot ball of emotion pushed against my ribs, constricting my lungs, making breathing hard.

I had *not* been expecting this.

'You can't,' I forced out. 'You can't keep me. Dad will—'

'I'll deal with your father.' For a second the warmth in his eyes was replaced with something cold. 'But you're not going back to him, end of story.'

'B-but where will I go?' I stammered. 'What will I do? How can I—'

'Did you miss the part where I said I'm keeping you?'

'No,' I managed. 'I just…thought you might be joking.'

'I'm not. I'm deadly serious.'

The hot ball of emotion got bigger, wider. 'But why?'

'Because he's a prick and he hurt you. And I want to make sure he never hurts you again. Plus…' a familiar flame leapt in his gaze '…I haven't finished with you yet.'

'What will happen to me when you do?' My brain was already leaping to the next thing. Because of course he wouldn't want to keep me for ever. 'When you finish with me, I mean. Dad's not going to go away just like that.'

'Leave him to me.'

'But I thought you said nothing was going to get in the way of you protecting your city? Not even me.'

He pinned me with that relentlessly blue gaze. 'I've never been able to have what I want. At least, I never thought I'd be able to. You were the first thing I allowed myself. And I want more. I want both. To protect my city *and* have you, and fuck, I don't see why I can't.'

The emotion in my chest was crushing. Like hunger magnified a thousand times, multiplied by need, turning into something so intense I couldn't breathe.

I loved him. But to ask for it in return was too much to ask of a man like Ajax. He was too driven, too focused on his goals, and he'd told me himself how important they were to him. Far more important than I'd ever be.

Dad never loved you. Why would Ajax King?

He wouldn't. And that was the truth.

'Why?' I asked, unable to help myself. 'If it's just about the sex—'

'It's not just about the sex. I want to keep you because you wanted me. Because I haven't had a woman look at me the way you do for years, if ever. Because you're the first person I've met who wasn't instantly afraid of me. Because you're beautiful. Because I'm fascinated by the way your mind works.' The blue flame in his eyes leapt higher. 'Because you're challenging as hell and because your optimism is so fucking bright it's blinding.'

My throat closed up. He'd told me similar things that day in the kitchen, when I'd burned the bacon. But I hadn't taken them in, not until now. Not until I saw the truth burning in his gaze.

I tried to swallow. Failed.

'I couldn't have what I wanted,' he went on, 'because anything I claim will be a target. But I can protect you. I *will* protect you.' The look on his face was naked with need. 'I want you, Imogen. Do you want me?'

Emotion burned behind my ribs, a bonfire of it.

How long will he want you for? And what will you do when it's over?

But the future had never been something I wanted to think about and I wanted to think about it even less now.

Now was all that mattered.

Now was all I had.

'Yes.' I couldn't lie, not even to protect myself. 'I want you *so* much.'

His eyes were a deep, endless blue, like that horizon he'd told me he wanted to sail over to see what was on the other side.

I wanted to sail over it too. With him. Because,

whatever was on the other side, I knew it would be endlessly fascinating. Endlessly challenging. I would never lose interest. Never.

'Stay.' Ajax looked at me as if the rest of the world didn't exist. 'Stay with me, Imogen.'

How could I resist?

'Okay.' My voice cracked. 'I'll stay.'

A look of intense satisfaction crossed his face. 'I told your father he could see you next week. Instead, I'll take the opportunity to tell him you'll be remaining with me.'

I wanted to ask him how he'd keep Dad off my back and protect his city as well, but I didn't. That was another thing I didn't want to think about.

'Okay,' I repeated shakily.

'Be sure, little one.' He looked so fierce. 'I'm very similar to your father in a lot of ways.'

No, he wasn't. Sure, he was a man who'd been brought up with a monster. And in order to take down the monster he'd had to become one. And that had been a heavy price.

He'd isolated himself. Denied himself. But that hunger for someone had never gone away—I saw it in his eyes every time he touched me. And I recognised it because I felt it myself every day.

I couldn't tell him how I felt, not without making it ten thousand times harder, but I wanted to give him something back.

I wanted to give him everything he'd given me.

'You know why I want to stay?' I said huskily. 'Because you're protective. Because you'd do anything for the people you care about. Because you're unself-ish. Because you give me great orgasms and make me

feel treasured. Because you're honest and you challenge me in a way no one else does.' I stared into
his eyes, into the heart of him. 'And because I think
you're as lonely as I am. And that you need someone
as badly as I do.'

CHAPTER NINETEEN

Ajax

SHE SAW RIGHT through me. She saw *me*.

I didn't know how, but she did.

Her steady green gaze didn't flicker, seeing the truth that lay underneath my armour. The vulnerability I'd tried to protect and keep hidden.

Not all that noble hero stuff—that was bullshit and I knew it even if she didn't—but she was right about one thing.

I did need someone. I'd *always* needed someone.

But it hadn't been until the moment she'd boarded the boat and smiled at me like I was everything she'd ever dreamed of that I'd accepted that the someone I needed was her.

I'd been trying for distance, but distance with Imogen was impossible.

Giving her back to White was impossible.

Keeping her was not only possible, it was the only thing that made sense.

It would piss White off and no doubt he'd retaliate, but I couldn't let her go back. I couldn't let that bastard use her or hurt her the way he'd been doing, making her feel like shit, like she had some debt to repay.

My city was important to me and the safety of my brothers too, but somehow Imogen had become important as well.

Having her was addictive and it wasn't something I wanted to give up. Fundamentally, she understood that, deep down, we were the same. Both of us hungry for something we'd never been allowed to have. So why couldn't we have it now?

It was wrong to keep her, because she would find no freedom with me. Simply through being mine, she'd become a target and those guards of her father's she'd hated would soon be her King security detail.

She would only ever be alone with me or at my house.

It wasn't the life she should have, but there was no other choice. It was either that or give her back.

You could let her go.

Every part of me tightened in instinctive denial.

Let her go back to what? She'd always be at risk from her father and, anyway, she was mine. Keeping her would ensure she stayed mine.

Imogen's eyes glittered like emeralds, green fire in the depths, a flame I'd never seen go out, not once. Her face was pale in the night yet it glowed with the strength of her emotion.

For me.

I wanted to tell her all the different ways she was right, that I did need someone, but that would take too long. What I really needed was to show her.

So I shoved my chair back and got to my feet, stalking around the table to where she sat.

She watched me come and when I bent and swept her up in my arms she took my face between her small palms and kissed me like she was dying of thirst and I was a cold glass of water.

The dinner I'd organised was forgotten.

I carried her into the cabin and down into the main stateroom, where there was a bed, and then I stripped that pretty green dress off her and laid her down onto it. I took all her sweet demand and gave it back to her, my hands on her skin, my mouth on hers, making the connection we were both desperate for and couldn't get enough of.

It felt easier after that.

We couldn't be bothered getting dressed so I brought dinner into the stateroom and we ate sitting on the bed, her printouts scattered on the sheets, Imogen talking nineteen to the dozen about everything she'd discovered on social housing.

I could have listened to her talk all night. Her mind was a beautiful thing, jumping from topic to topic, looking at every angle and analysing each one in greater depth than I ever had. I kept her on track, helping her gather all the various parts of her subject into a whole so she could see the big picture, while she gave me insight into smaller aspects I hadn't seen or had dismissed as being unworkable.

'You should manage the housing project,' I said, the idea gripping me and refusing to let go. 'You'd be good at it.'

Her eyes opened wide. 'Me? But I don't know what I'm talking about.'

She was sitting cross-legged on the bed, the sheet wound carelessly around her waist, her bare skin glowing from the lights coming through the portholes. Her cheeks were flushed with excitement, her eyes like jewels.

Beautiful girl.

Yours. All yours.

A satisfaction I hadn't felt for years stretched out inside me.

'But it wouldn't take you long to get up to speed. I think it would be perfect for you. Lots of different things to think about, lots of balls to keep in the air. And I'd be around to help and keep you focused.'

A crease appeared between her brows. 'Ajax, you can't put me in charge. I don't know the first thing about housing, or building, or project management. I have no experience of anything. I wouldn't even know where to start.'

'Like I said, I'd help.' I smiled at her. 'Little one, that brain of yours is a gift. It needs to be put to good use and I think you'd be perfect for this. The way you see things, all the details, plus those outside the square ideas. Shit, your energy alone is what this project has always needed, because I sure as hell don't have it. I had the idea, now I just need someone with vision to carry it out.' I brushed my fingers over her soft cheek. 'You have the vision. You have the energy. You have the interest. All you need is the confidence.'

'You really think so?'

'I wouldn't have said it if I didn't. Besides, choosing the right person for a job is part of what I do and I'm very good at it.' I let my hand trail down to her chin. 'I haven't been wrong about a person yet.'

'You might be wrong about me.'

'No.' I slid my fingers along her jaw and into her

hair, curling around the back of her neck, drawing her towards me. 'I don't think I am.'

She didn't argue with me, not after that.

Later, we came back out and watched the lights of Sydney drift by from the deck.

She nestled into me as we stood at the rail and I held her, her curvy body fitting perfectly against me.

And for the first time in my life I let myself think about a future that had all the things I wanted in it. A family with children, a wife.

The things my brothers had, that I'd never thought would be mine.

Do you really think that, after everything you've done, you deserve it?

An intense possessiveness gripped me tight, anger gathering along with it. No, I didn't deserve it and I sure as hell knew that. But I didn't care. I'd worked hard to ensure Sydney stayed clear of bastards like my father, to give my brothers a future after all they'd been through, and now it was my turn.

Next you'll start believing you're the hero she thinks you are.

So? Would that be such a bad thing?

A memory came back to me, of being in that warehouse with Dad, standing beside the broken and bleeding man in the chair, his hand resting on the guy's shoulder. Dad had smiled as he'd told me what was expected of me, how he couldn't allow disloyalty, most especially not from his own sons.

His gaze hadn't flickered as he'd held Xander and Leon's lives over my head, using them to keep me in line. And I'd let him.

You're no hero. Heroes don't let those they love get hurt.

I'd been thirteen years old. What the fuck else was I supposed to do? Becoming Dad's puppet was the only way I could save them.

Imogen was standing in front of me and now she leaned back, resting her head on my chest, her blonde hair bright against the black cotton of my T-shirt.

She didn't smell of roses any more. She smelled of my soap, plus something indefinable and sweetly feminine. Like she'd taken my scent and made it her own.

I leaned down and nuzzled against her hair, folding myself more protectively around her, trying to ignore the thoughts in my head.

I needed to get her home and safe, but there was plenty of time for that. Once I'd let her father know she'd be staying with me I'd have to review my security and deal with the threat he presented, but until then I could take this moment the way she did. I could live in the here and now, and not think about what was going to happen in the future.

Let her enjoy this taste of freedom while she could because, once her father knew she was staying with me, that freedom would end.

She deserves that freedom. She deserves better than you.

I shoved the thought away hard, slipping my arms around her waist and pulling her in tight to me.

She'd chosen me and I was keeping her.

'Being with me isn't going to be easy,' I murmured into the night. 'You understand that, don't you?'

'Yes.' Her voice was quiet. 'I'll be a target, won't I?'

'You will.' I didn't want to sugar-coat it so I didn't. 'And I have many enemies.'

'I can handle it.'

'It'll mean security. More guards.'

'I get that. I don't care as long as I'm with you.'

She will care. Eventually.

I gritted my teeth. 'I'll try and allow you as much freedom as I can. And maybe after I've dealt with your father—'

She turned in my arms, her head tipping back to look up at me. 'Don't hurt him, Ajax.'

The vehemence in her tone caught me off guard, as did the way she'd apparently read my mind.

That slippery slope? You're heading down it already.

'I'm not going to hurt him.' It sounded hollow to my own ears. Mainly because hurting him for what he'd done to her was exactly what I wanted to do.

Imogen just looked at me. 'Please promise me you won't put yourself at risk. He's not worth it.'

'If it keeps you safe, anything's worth it.'

'No,' she said quietly. 'It's not. Sometimes the end does not justify the means, especially if that end involves you being dead or in prison.'

She was wrong. The end was the most important part.

I stared down into her eyes. 'But what if it means your freedom?'

Her gaze didn't even flicker. 'I'm not worth that kind of sacrifice, Ajax, and I don't want to be. You've already had to give up too much. I don't want you giving up anything more.'

'Your mother thought you were worth that sacrifice.'

Her eyes darkened. 'My mother didn't have a choice.'

'Imogen,' I began.

But she reached up and laid her finger across my mouth, silencing me. 'No. This is one thing I'm not arguing with you about.'

So I didn't argue.

I bit the tip of her finger gently instead and then we found something else to distract ourselves with.

But I couldn't get rid of the feeling that somehow I'd just made a mistake.

For both of us.

CHAPTER TWENTY

Imogen

THE NEXT FEW days with Ajax were the happiest I'd ever had.

I spent a lot of time researching his social housing project and discussing how we'd approach it.

I still thought he was mad to put me in charge, but I couldn't resist how confident he was that I could do it. It made me want to show him that he was right to be confident, that I could.

With his help I put together a plan and it was exciting to see it take shape. There were so many details to get right. It suited the way my mind worked, especially when I thought of how to apply what I'd learned to other projects.

I really loved knowing that we were helping people too.

It made me feel like I was doing something valuable rather than mastering a lot of skills that ended up being useless.

But work wasn't all we did.

We talked, about everything from our favourite

pizza toppings to the price of property and whether the kids of today would ever be able to afford a house.

Once I asked him what he did in his spare time and he told me he never had any spare time. I told him that was bullshit, he must have some hobbies, and eventually he took me down to the beach below his house and the tiny boathouse at the foot of the cliff where he kept a small yacht.

He'd got it when he was young and had taught himself to sail, though he hadn't been able to take it out much since his father had kept him so busy.

I asked him to take me out in it so he did, and I sat in the prow, watching him work the sails and do things with the ropes, his strong hands sure on the rudder as we tacked across the blue water.

The sun turned his hair glossy black, his eyes the colour of the sky above us as he watched the sails fill.

His expression was concentrated but the lines of tension around his eyes and mouth, lines I'd never fully noticed before, had gone. And I realised that this, out here on the water with the sea and the wind and the sails, was freedom for him.

He had no one to worry about. No one to protect. All he had to do was keep an eye on the weather and concentrate on the boat.

Yet now he has another person to protect. You.

I didn't like what he'd told me that night on the harbour, how he'd do whatever it took to keep me safe. And I had an idea what that meant to Ajax, and it made me afraid for him. Afraid of what he'd sacrifice to protect me.

I didn't want him to have to sacrifice *anything*.

He'd already risked his soul to take his father down,

putting aside his own hopes and dreams along the way, ignoring the cost to himself.

It wasn't fair. He looked out for everyone else yet no one looked out for him. Sure, he had Xander and Leon, but they had their own lives. Did they know how much Ajax had done for them? Did they even realise what he was *still* doing for them?

The thought made me ache and the closer we came to the day where he'd tell my father I was his, the deeper the ache became.

Dad would never let me go and if I stayed with Ajax he'd make Ajax's life even more difficult than it already was. He'd probably force Ajax's hand, encouraging him to do something that would end up…

Well, I didn't like to think where that might end up because, wherever it was, it wouldn't be good for Ajax.

And, no matter what Ajax told me about me being worth the sacrifice, there was still a part of me buried deep that knew I wasn't. He was more important than my freedom and always would be.

Over the next couple of days, I made it my mission to figure out how he was planning on dealing with Dad, but he always changed the subject, or distracted me. Or simply told me not to worry about it.

He seemed to think that it was my safety that I cared about.

He was wrong. It was his.

The day before the planned meeting with Dad was a beautiful day and I made Ajax take me out on his yacht again.

I hoped he might be more forthcoming about what he was planning if he was in his happy place. Except, as the sails caught the wind and the boat skipped over the waves, Ajax grinning at how fast we were moving, I couldn't bring myself to broach the topic.

Then he pointed at something in the water. 'Look, Imogen.'

Distracted, I looked and saw a sleek grey shape cutting through the waves, keeping pace with the boat.

A surge of wonder went through me. 'Is it a dolphin?'

'I think so.' His voice was full of the same wonder, making me stare, because I'd never heard him sound that way before.

The expression on his face was the most purely happy I'd ever seen him. Then the dolphin leapt and he laughed, the sound full of delight. A boy's laugh. And in that second that's what I saw—a boy, caught up in the excitement and wonder of the moment.

My heart twisted like a wet towel being wrung out.

Out on the waves he was free and I could see that freedom written all over his face. In his smile and in his laugh. In the relaxed way he sat in the boat, the tension in his shoulders gone.

This was what he should be. This was how he should live.

This was what he should have—the freedom to be who he was, and that wasn't the dangerous man with the violent reputation that everyone was afraid of.

It was a boy who loved the wind in his hair and the sun on his face and the sight of a dolphin leaping in the waves.

I couldn't let him sacrifice that freedom for me.

'Did you see it?' Ajax grinned. 'Did you see him leap?'

My eyes prickled with tears. 'No, I missed it.' I

turned to focus on the shape of the dolphin in the water, blinking the moisture away.

If he wouldn't save himself then I would do it for him.

Because there was no one else who could.

He didn't seem to notice my overly emotional moment and when we got back to the house I made some excuses about having to work on my project plan and disappeared upstairs into his office.

But I didn't look at the project plan.

I emailed my father instead and told him I was coming home.

It was surprisingly easy to set up.

I'd tell Ajax I needed a car to go into the city for some spurious shopping trip and then Dad would meet me.

The thought of going back to Dad's prison made me feel cold and sick, but the thought of Ajax losing everything purely to protect me was even worse.

I could bear being Dad's trophy a few more years. It wouldn't be for ever. Eventually I'd find a way to get free. Tonight, though, I'd have to keep my plan secret because obviously if Ajax found out he'd try to stop me.

Arranging for a car wasn't a drama; in fact I was almost annoyed by how easy it was to convince Ajax that I needed a shopping trip. And then, when the car arrived, he barely looked up from his laptop as I came to say goodbye.

This would be the last time I'd ever see him and it hurt that he only gave me a quick glance as I bent to kiss him.

But that was good. If he'd seen the tears in my eyes

he'd have asked what was wrong and I didn't think I had the strength not to tell him.

So I only brushed my lips against his cheek, inhaling the scent of him one last time, imprinting him in my head for ever.

'See you soon,' he said, his gaze on his screen.

I didn't trust myself to speak, turning and walking through the door, letting the tears fall only once I'd got into the car.

I didn't want to leave him, but there was no other option.

I loved him and if there was one thing Ajax King had taught me it was that, unlike my father, who'd used my love to get me to do what he wanted, Ajax's love wasn't selfish. He loved his brothers and his city and he put them first. Before everything.

I couldn't do any less.

As the car pulled away I didn't look back, gritting my teeth and wiping away the tears.

We pulled up outside one of the department stores and I searched the footpath surreptitiously, looking for Dad's guards. He'd told me that they'd be waiting for me.

A man signalled from the crowd and fear caught me by the throat.

Ignoring it, I pushed open the door. 'I'll be five minutes,' I told my driver.

Hopefully he wouldn't come after me.

The streets were full of people and I had to bite down on the urge to scream for help as Dad's guard caught my elbow, beginning to usher me to another car, long and black and drawn up down the street a little way.

But I put my shoulders back as the guard pulled open the door for me and I lifted my chin, steeled my spine.

Then I got in and sat down, turning to look at my father.

Except the man sitting beside me wasn't my father.

'Hello, Imogen,' Ajax said.

CHAPTER TWENTY-ONE

Ajax

THERE WAS SHOCK in her wide green eyes, which I'd expected. They were also red from crying, which I hadn't.

My little one had been crying for me.

Pain sat between my ribs, like someone had sunk a knife into me, and I wanted to pull her into my arms and wrap her up tight, hold her and never let her go.

But that wasn't why I was here.

I was here to set her free.

'Ajax?' She sounded bewildered. 'What are you doing here?'

I glanced in the rear-view mirror and caught the driver's eye. Then I gave him a nod and the car pulled back into the traffic.

'I know what you were trying to do, Imogen,' I said quietly. 'I know you were coming to meet your father.'

She blinked and her mouth opened. Then she shut it again as if she couldn't trust herself to speak.

So I went on, 'I saw your email this afternoon.'

'No,' she said faintly. 'I deleted—'

'It wasn't deleted. One of the emails failed to send and it was sitting in my outbox.'

She'd gone very pale. 'I wasn't going to hurt you. That's not why I was going back to him.'

'No, I realise that.' I knew why Imogen had decided to leave. Given the type of person she was, only one explanation made sense. 'You're trying to save me, aren't you?'

Her eyes filled with tears. 'You can't keep me, Ajax. Dad would force you into doing something terrible to protect me and I can't let that happen. It's better for me to go back to him. Then we'll both leave Sydney for good and you won't have to worry about me any more.'

I wanted to laugh—if only it were that simple.

Letting her go back to White and make her grand gesture for me would have been the easiest way out of the situation. Certainly it would have been better for me.

Except there was no way in hell I could do that.

The past few days with her had only cemented her worth to me, made me more aware of how vital she was. And not just to me, but to the people whose lives she would one day change. Because she would change lives. She'd changed mine.

The moment I'd seen her email to her father I'd known that I couldn't keep her any more than her father could.

What Imogen needed was freedom.

She needed the chance to stretch her wings, find out who she was on her own terms, figure out for herself what she was worth, without her father holding her mother's death over her head.

Without me stifling her.

Because that would happen if I kept her.

I'd accepted the truth as I'd read her email to White,

telling him she wanted to come home. That she'd agree to return only on the condition that he'd leave me alone.

I'd wanted to save her in that moment. And I knew that saving her didn't involve keeping her here with me. It was only condemning her to more fucking captivity.

She deserved better than that. She always had.

'You're not going back to your father, little one,' I said gently.

She blinked, her eyes glittering. 'Then where am I going?'

'I'm taking you to the airport.' I tried to keep my voice steady, but the rough edge crept in all the same. 'There's a King Enterprises jet ready to go, with all the documentation you need. I have a friend in New York who's going to make sure you're set up once you get there.'

She was silent. A streak of red tinged her cheekbones, the glitter in her eyes not fear or sadness like I thought, but anger. 'No,' she said flatly. 'I'm not going anywhere. I *need* to see Dad. I won't let him put you in a position where you have to do something you'll regret.'

My jaw tightened. She was right to call me on that. It was the slippery slope staring me in the face—the one that would make me no better than Dad.

You are *no better.*

'Give me some credit, for fuck's sake,' I growled, ignoring the thought. 'You think I'd really put everything on the line just to get him out of the way?'

'Wouldn't you?' Her chin lifted. 'What if he hurt me? What would you do then?'

I gritted my teeth. 'I would—'

'Hurt him back. And you wouldn't care what happened to you after that. All you care about is that the people you love are safe.'

She's wrong. All you care about is yourself.

Fucking lies. If that was all that mattered, I wouldn't be sitting here ready to put her on a plane to goddamn New York.

'I'm not accepting that any more,' Imogen went on, not letting me speak. 'You protect everyone all the time and yet who protects you?'

'I don't need protection.'

'Oh, don't give me that alpha male bullshit,' she said fiercely. 'Of course you need protection. And I'm going to protect you whether you like it or not.'

I felt the knife in my chest twist. She was so strong and I kept forgetting that. Far from the delicate little thing she seemed, she was electric. She felt things passionately and deeply, and she didn't give up.

But this was one fight she wasn't going to win, not if I had anything to do with it.

'No,' I said. 'It's not happening and that's final.'

Her green eyes burned. 'Look, it'll be okay. I'm not the same person I was when you kidnapped me from that ball. I won't let Dad hurt me the way he did before. I'll figure out how to get away from him eventually and—'

'No.' I kept my voice hard and cold. 'You're not going to give up your freedom for me.'

'You can't stop me.'

'I can. I will.'

Her pale throat moved as she swallowed. 'Don't… do this to me, Ajax. Don't let it mean nothing.'

'It won't mean nothing. Because you won't be doing it at all.'

Anger had flushed her cheeks, made her eyes glow.

Her hair was in a loose ponytail at the nape of her neck and little wisps of hair were curling around her forehead.

She was so beautiful. Giving her up was going to hurt like fuck.

But I'd made my decision.

'Ajax,' she said hoarsely, 'I care about you. That's what I told you on the boat. You're worth ten thousand of my father and I'm not going to sit around and watch you—'

'And you're worth ten thousand of me,' I interrupted. 'That's why you're going to get on my jet and leave the country.'

Her eyes were liquid in the light coming from the freeway, but there was fire in them. 'You're wrong. You're worth the sacrifice, Ajax King. Don't you know that?'

No. You're not.

And that was the truth that had always been there, sitting inside me. I wasn't worth it and I knew it.

'Go and have a fucking life,' I said, ignoring her. 'Go and have the life you should have had.'

She stared at me a second then looked away. 'And what about Dad? What are you going to do about him? Because if you end up in prison, Ajax King, so help me I'll come back and…and… I don't know. Murder you or something.'

Tenderness caught at me, unexpected and sweet. Bittersweet.

I reached out, touched her cheek, her skin so soft against my fingertips. 'You won't murder me.'

She shivered at the contact, turning back to me. 'Tell me you won't hurt my father. Promise me, Ajax.

Promise me you'll do nothing that will end up with you in prison.'

I trailed my fingertips along her jaw.

You can't make that promise.

And if I didn't? Shit, I'd be no better than Dad.

Why fight it? Maybe it's time you embraced it.

'Imogen…'

'I won't go without a fight. I'll come home on the next flight and you won't be able to stop me.' Determination glowed in her eyes. 'If you want me to have my freedom then you have to keep yours. I won't go if you don't make me this promise.'

'Stubborn little one.'

'You're better than that. Promise me. Your word as a King.'

What could I say? That I wasn't better? That deep down there was a part of me who was just like my dad? Just as violent, just as ruthless…

You should claim your legacy. Once she's gone, there'll be no one to stop you.

I could. Except there was one thing stopping me and she was looking at me right now, demanding a promise that would hold me back from that slippery slope into the past.

She thought I was better. That was the rope that kept me from falling and I couldn't refuse to hold onto it, not without hurting her. And I would never, ever hurt her.

'I promise,' I said, staring deep into her pretty eyes. 'My word as a King.'

I'd broken that word with her father, but I wouldn't with her. It was an oath, a vow.

She seemed to understand, giving me a slight nod.

Then she pulled away from my hand, putting distance between us, turning to look out the window. 'Good. You can take me to the airport now.'

Her withdrawal was like the sun clouding over, leaving me in shadow. I felt cold. I wanted to reach out again and draw her back, let her warmth and brightness cover me.

But if I did, if I touched her again, I'd never let her go. So I stayed where I was.

The rest of the drive was spent in silence and neither of us broke it. There was nothing to say.

The jet was waiting on the tarmac, Imogen waiting with it while I spoke with the captain and the customs official who was handling the departure.

Once that was done I went to take her hand, only to check myself at the last minute. No, I couldn't touch her. That would be a mistake I wouldn't come back from.

If she noticed my hesitation she didn't show it, following along behind me as I led her to the jet and showed her up the stairs and inside.

The stewardess was there, making the cabin ready.

'Can you give us a few minutes?' Imogen said unexpectedly.

The stewardess looked at me and I nodded, so she went out, leaving us alone in the cabin.

Imogen turned to face me, a familiar glow in her green eyes.

It made everything inside me tighten.

'No,' I said before she could speak. 'Not now. Not here.'

She ignored me, closing the distance she'd put between us in the car, her hand reaching out, her palm flattening against my chest.

It stole my breath, froze me in place.

'I want one more thing,' she said softly, looking up at me. 'One last time with you.'

'Imogen—'

'Just one more time. If you're going to make me leave, you have to give me something to take with me.' Her eyes were liquid. 'Please.'

'I touch you and I might never let you go,' I said roughly. 'That's not what I want.'

'I know.' She swallowed. 'But you will let me go. And this would be for both of us.'

I didn't know where she got her certainty from, because God knew I didn't have it. But I couldn't refuse her.

My goddamn cock wouldn't let me.

I let her take my face in her hands and bring my head down, let her mouth brush over mine.

She tasted of salt and sweetness, and I had her in my arms before I could stop myself, crushing that soft mouth beneath my own. Taking and taking. Gorging on her because this wasn't going to happen again. I would never kiss her again. Never hold her again.

This was all I'd ever have and it was going to have to last me and so I fucking took it.

Two steps took us to the closed door of the cockpit and I pinned her against it, my hands shaking as I slid them beneath her ass and lifted her. She wound her legs around my waist, raining kisses all over my face, hot and hungry and desperate just like me.

I was instantly hard and I ached, but there was also a knife in my chest and she was twisting it with every kiss. Every touch. But I didn't let her go. I shoved up her little dress and slid my hand between her legs, finding the slick heat of her pussy. She was wet for me, shuddering in my arms as I stroked her.

I wanted to go slowly, to make this last so we had something more than desperation to take with us, but there was no time. Her hands were at the fly of my jeans, pulling down my zip and sliding inside my boxers, cool fingers on my cock.

I turned my face into her neck, biting and licking her skin, her taste more delicious to me than anything I'd ever eaten, finding her clit and stroking at the same time.

She gave a sob. 'Ajax…'

The knife worked its way deeper, a dull agony seeping through me. But it wasn't enough to stop.

I found my wallet and managed to get it open without loosening my hold on her, dropping it on the ground as I took out the condom.

She tried to snatch the packet but I didn't let her, ripping it open with my teeth and then rolling the latex down.

My hands were fucking shaking like she was my first time.

She is your first time. Your first time with a woman you care about.

I hadn't thought that would make it different. But it did.

I continued to stare into her eyes as I drew my hips back then pushed in deep. Again. And again. Harder. Faster.

We didn't speak, our breathing loud in the quiet of the cabin, and the world shrank down, getting narrower and narrower as the pleasure curled around us and wrapped us up tight.

There was nothing but this. Nothing but us. Me inside her, her around me.

Except she was going to let go of me and I had to make her.

How are you going to live without her?

The thought was as clear as the deep green of her eyes, and as vivid. But pleasure was dragging at me, choking me, and I shoved the thought away.

I would live the way I'd always lived. Cold and hard and certain. Wanting nothing. Needing nothing. Living for the big picture.

Except it wasn't the big picture I saw as she sobbed in my arms, the orgasm flaring in her eyes. I only saw her. And when mine hit, a deep, annihilating pulse of pleasure, for a second there was no past and no future. Only a perfect, shining moment of us.

Her and me. Together.

It took a supreme act of will to let her go, but I did. I was proud of myself for that, if nothing else. I moved like a fucking robot, lowering her to the floor, dealing with the condom and my clothes. She'd already smoothed down her dress, but she let me lead her over to her seat and buckle her in. I didn't rush, taking my time, savouring every last second of touching her.

But then it was done and I couldn't put it off any longer.

I kissed her one last time then I turned to go, moving towards the door of the aircraft.

'Ajax,' she said softly.

I paused, everything in me wanting to turn around

and grab her, take her back to my house and keep her there for ever.

'I love you.'

The knife in my chest found my heart and slid straight into it.

I walked away from the jet a dead man.

CHAPTER TWENTY-TWO

Imogen

NEW YORK WAS FINE. I had an apartment and a great job, one I'd found for myself—basic data entry at an office. The apartment was one Ajax had organised for me, and perhaps I should have found my own, but apartments were expensive and the one he'd found was too nice to give up.

I made friends and I went out to clubs and bars. Central Park for picnics and the Met for a dose of culture. I went shopping and to the theatre, discovered I loved musicals and the cheesiness of Coney Island. I even liked riding on the subway.

I enjoyed my life.

But there was an ache inside me. A space that wasn't ever going to be filled. An Ajax-shaped space.

After I'd first arrived, I'd thrown myself into my new life because that was what he'd wanted for me and I hadn't felt I could throw that away on feeling sorry for myself.

Besides, he'd promised he wouldn't do anything that would involve him going to prison so I could hardly do anything less than honour my promise to him.

Every so often I'd run a quick search to check on him, not to make sure of the promise he'd made—I knew he wouldn't break it—but to see if he was okay. Sure enough, he was. There were a lot of news stories about the King brothers and the waves they were making with their new luxury property development in Sydney.

I couldn't look at pictures of him, though, so I didn't. I pretended that my heart was fine and didn't have an Ajax-shaped hole right through the middle of it.

Once, I even tried to date someone, but it was an abject failure. He was a nice enough guy but he wasn't Ajax and after ten minutes of awkward conversation I told him I was in love with someone else and I was sorry I'd wasted his time.

Then I went home and consoled myself with my newly purchased vibrator and memories of Ajax beside the pool. In the bedroom. In the shower... Everywhere but the plane before I'd left Sydney.

The look in Ajax's eyes as he'd held me. The way his hands had shaken. The agony on his face as he'd kissed me goodbye.

The way he'd paused when I'd told him I loved him.

The way he'd walked out without a backward glance.

It was all too painful to remember so I didn't.

Six months after I'd arrived in New York, I got a phone call from an Australian number.

It was late in the day and I was at home, settling in for a night of crappy TV, and my heart nearly stopped when I saw the numbers on the screen. And then it started beating again, hard and fast, making my hands shake.

Was it Ajax? Or was it someone else? My father? Who else knew I was here? Who else knew this number?

I hit the answer button and a man's deep voice said, 'Is this Imogen White?'

It wasn't Ajax.

The combination of relief and disappointment was so bitter it nearly choked me. 'Yes,' I said, forcing it away. 'Who's this?'

'This is Leon King. I want to know what the hell you've done to my brother.'

Shock coursed through me. 'What? What do you mean?'

'Ajax has been a fucking bastard to deal with for the past six months, which, to be fair, is nothing unusual. But now he's shut himself up in his house and won't see either Xander or me.' There was a pause. 'We're worried about him.'

I closed my eyes, longing pulling at me, making the hole in my heart hurt worse than anything I could imagine. 'What makes you think I can help him?'

'Well, he got like this pretty much as soon as you left so I'm assuming it's got something to do with you.'

'It might not.'

There was a silence.

'I tried asking him about you,' Leon said, 'but he refused to answer any questions and at the mention of your name... Well, let's just say he wasn't happy.'

My voice didn't work, but I tried to speak anyway. 'I promised him I'd stay here. That I wouldn't come back.'

'Why not?'

'Because he wanted me to be free.'

'Christ,' Leon muttered, sounding exasperated.

'Look, I don't know what you two are to each other, but can't you come back to Australia and be free with him?'

'I promised,' I repeated, clutching the phone. 'I told him I'd stay.'

Leon sighed. 'Do you want to stay?'

I thought of the life I'd made for myself here. The job and friends and apartment. It was a nice life. It was everything I'd dreamed about. And yet…

There was something missing. Him.

My throat felt thick. 'Not really.'

'Then come back.' Leon's voice was flat. 'Come back and help him.'

The ache in my chest got worse. 'Can't you do anything for him?'

'You don't think I've tried? He won't listen to me and he won't listen to Xander. Which leaves you.' For the first time I heard a note of actual worry in his tone. 'Someone needs to help him, Imogen, because, God knows, if there's one man who deserves a fucking break it's my brother.'

A shiver went through me. When I'd left Sydney, I hadn't fought to stay. I'd gone to New York with only the most cursory of arguments. I'd told myself that getting that promise out of him was a victory, that leaving was the best thing for both of us.

Besides, he'd wanted me to go and I hadn't wanted to make myself into even more of a problem for him than I was already.

Lies. You know why you didn't fight.

It was fear. Fear that he didn't feel for me what I felt for him. Fear that I didn't deserve him. Fear that because my mother had died for me I didn't deserve to be happy.

Then again, if I wasn't, wouldn't her sacrifice have been in vain?

Ajax had told me she would have been glad that I existed and I was pretty sure she wouldn't have wanted me to exist unhappily. That wouldn't have honoured her memory.

You know what will.

Yes. There was only one way to honour that memory, only one way to repay the debt I owed her. And that wasn't with yet another sacrifice.

It was with happiness. With love.

With showing a man who'd given up too much that he didn't have to give up anything more. That if I deserved happiness then he did too.

Tears filled my eyes.

'Well?' Leon demanded, after I hadn't spoken. 'Will you come back?'

I didn't hesitate this time.

'Yes,' I said fiercely. 'Yes, I'll come back.'

That night I booked a ticket home and the next day I handed in my resignation at my job. And I packed up my life in New York.

But before I left I made one last phone call.

The phone rang for a while before it picked up, but my father's voice hadn't changed, hard and cold and suspicious. 'Who is this?'

'Hi, Dad,' I said. 'It's Imogen.'

There was a shocked silence. 'Where are you? Where the *hell* are—'

'I haven't got time for explanations,' I interrupted

firmly. 'I wanted you to know that I'm coming home. And when I get back I will be marrying Ajax King.'

'You ungrateful little—'

'And if you so much as touch me or harm Ajax or his family and friends in any way—and I mean *any* way, Dad—I'll take what I know about you and your business to the media.' I paused, letting that sink in, then I added, 'And I'll make sure *everyone* knows just what kind of man you really are.'

There was another long, shocked silence.

'Imogen,' Dad said and there was a hoarse tone to it that I'd never heard before.

'You'll leave Sydney,' I went on, 'and you won't come back. And in return I'll stay quiet. But the moment you hurt anyone I care about, I'll tell the world. And you'll never work in Australia again.'

I could feel his anger radiating clear across the Pacific. But all he said was, 'Okay. You have a deal.'

A day later I flew back to Sydney to reclaim the life I'd always wanted.

And the man I loved.

CHAPTER TWENTY-THREE

Ajax

SOMEONE WAS KNOCKING on the front door.

I ignored it the way I'd been ignoring all visitors to my house for the past few months. Instead I shoved the empty takeout boxes that were sitting on the coffee table to one side, put my laptop down, poured myself another liberal amount of Scotch, then stared at the screen.

I'd been putting off my housing project for too long and I couldn't put it off any more. I had to do something, because at the moment it felt like I was in limbo.

All I'd done since Imogen had left was take the boat out every day, trying to get rid of the dead feeling inside me, trying to shock it back to life with the things that usually calmed me. The wind, the salt, the sun. Ropes under my hands and the crack of the sails above me.

But even being out on the ocean didn't get rid of it.

Everything was muted and flat, what little joy I'd taken from life utterly gone.

I accepted it. It was all part of the sacrifice. And

knowing she was in New York and having the time of her life made it better.

I got updates from my New York contact about how she was doing, but after a while I told him not to send me any more.

It was easier not to know.

I'd flung myself into work, chasing down the last of my father's loyal lieutenants, mopping up the rest of his mess. It was hard work and I took a certain relish in it. But I made good on my promise to Imogen and left her father alone.

He'd tried to exact his revenge on me for placing his daughter beyond his reach, but I avoided it. I didn't retaliate, didn't engage.

She held me back from the precipice and I couldn't let her down.

Eventually White lost interest.

With Imogen gone, what was the point? For either of us?

My brothers tried to talk to me, but I didn't want to talk to them. There was nothing they could say that would make any difference.

They had the women they loved and if I was grateful for nothing else, it was that.

I was never meant to have the things I wanted for myself anyway and I didn't know why I hadn't remembered that.

I stared at the document that had come up on the computer—Imogen's management plan. She'd put so much work into it and had been so excited about it...

Pain shifted in my chest, so intense I couldn't breathe. It would fade in a minute and then I'd go back to being deadened and numb but, for the moment it lasted, all I could see was her face, luminous with excitement, her green eyes glowing.

For a second I tried to pretend that I didn't know why it hurt so much, but it was too hard and so I gave up.

I knew why it hurt so much.

I was in love with her. I'd probably fallen in love with her the moment her gaze had met mine in the mirror of the bathroom the night I'd kidnapped her.

No wonder I felt like a dead man walking half the time; she'd taken my heart to New York with her.

Not that love would have made a difference anyway.

Love was just another sacrifice I'd had to make.

The hammering on the door didn't stop.

Fuck. I was going to have to either keep ignoring it or answer the bloody thing.

Ignoring it took work though and for once I was glad of the distraction. Otherwise I'd have to think about who could take Imogen's place on the housing project and thinking about that filled me with rage.

Cursing, I shoved myself to my feet, stalking out of the room and down the hallway to the front door.

Who the fuck was it? And how had they even got to the front door? They'd have had to get past the guards at the gate so it had to be someone I knew.

I could have checked via the front door camera, but I couldn't be fucked looking.

God help me, if it was Xander or Leon disturbing me again I'd have their fucking balls on a plate.

I jerked open the door and the heart I thought was dead shocked suddenly back into life.

It wasn't Xander or Leon.

It was Imogen.

She stood on my doorstep, her gilt hair loose and gleaming down her back, wearing a simple turquoise cotton dress that gave her green eyes a tinge of blue and her skin a creamy glow.

I hadn't seen her for a whole six months and I felt like a man who'd been in the desert for years surrounded by nothing but sand, suddenly seeing green grass for the first time.

Fresh. Beautiful. Evidence of life…

'Hi,' she said, her familiar voice with its husky edge sounding shaken.

I couldn't think of a bloody word to say.

'Uh, are you going to invite me in?' She gave me a small hopeful smile. 'Or do you want to have this conversation on the front doorstep?'

'What the fuck are you doing here?' I demanded, graceless and rough, like I hadn't spoken for days.

She swallowed. 'I came back. Obviously.'

'But… I freed you.' My heart was thundering in my head, beating so loudly I could hardly hear a fucking thing. 'You were supposed to have a life.'

'And I did,' she said. 'It sucked.'

I stared at her, not understanding. 'What do you mean, "it sucked"?'

Imogen took a step forward and put her palm in the centre of my chest. 'Seriously, I'm not having this conversation outside.'

Her touch was pure electricity, delivering another shock to my heart and, before I knew what I was doing, I'd backed away from the door so she could come in, closing it behind her.

She made as if to remove her hand but automatically

I put mine over hers, keeping it exactly where it was, desperate for her touch.

Her skin was warm and I could smell her. Ah, fuck…roses.

I ached.

'You idiot.' Her eyes glowed with a familiar determination. 'Did you seriously think you could send me away and that I'd stay? I told you I loved you before I left. That hasn't changed.'

My jaw was so tight I could barely speak. 'You were supposed to stay in New York. Get a job and friends and an apartment and—'

'Yeah, yeah.' She waved a hand as if that was nothing. 'I did all those things. But I didn't leave Sydney because I wanted to, Ajax. I left to make you happy.'

Again, I could not think of one fucking thing to say.

'But you're not happy,' she went on, gazing up at me. 'I can see that you're not. And you know something? I'm not happy either.' Her hand pressed a little harder on my chest. 'Mum gave her life for me and I've spent a long time thinking that I didn't deserve to have anything because of that. But… I was wrong. You taught me that. She wouldn't have wanted me to be unhappy. That would mean she died for nothing.' Imogen's thumb moved caressingly over my skin. 'Her death needs to mean something, Ajax. And the best way I can think of to honour it is with happiness. With love.'

The ache inside me intensified. It was plain she believed every word she said. I only wished I could believe it too.

'If anyone deserves to have that, it's you,' I said roughly. 'But you can't have it with me.'

She didn't look away. 'Why not?'

My breathing was ragged from the effort it took not to grab her and hold her. Keep her with me. Never let her go.

'Because you know what will happen when you're with me,' I said. 'There'll be guards and security and threats and—'

'No, that's not what will happen.' Her finger was on my mouth before I could move. 'What will happen with you is sex and sailing and swimming. And food and more sex. And then some interesting projects that I can really sink my teeth into, and more sex, and then a dolphin or two, and then—'

I shook her finger away before the touch would overcome my control. 'Imogen, you're not listening.'

She pulled her hands from me and took my face between them. 'I am. *You're* not listening to *me*.' Her eyes were very green. 'I love you and telling me you can't be with me because you want me to be free is a bullshit excuse. You're scared. I can see it.'

Of course she did. She'd always been able to see right through me.

I said nothing. There was no point in denying it.

She searched my face. 'What are you so afraid of?'

'That promise I made you—remember it?' I met her gaze head-on. 'That was the only thing that kept me from hurting your father. The only fucking thing that stopped me from being just like him. From being like my dad. And yes, that makes me afraid.'

'It wasn't the only thing,' she said as if she knew it for truth. 'You wouldn't have done it anyway.'

'I wanted to. I wanted to hurt him so fucking badly for what he did to you.'

'But you didn't. You're not that type of man, Ajax.'

'I could have become him,' I went on, laying out just what type of man I was for her. 'I still could. I can feel it inside me, his violence. Christ, so much. I *hurt* people, Imogen. Including my brothers. Fuck, I just stood back and watched them suffer. How can I be allowed to have you—have anything at all—after that?'

'That wasn't your fault.' Her tone was quiet and absolutely sure. 'Your father threatened them, you didn't. And you did what you could to protect them.'

'But what if I didn't?' I couldn't stop the words from coming out, the secret truth I'd been trying to hide. 'What if I didn't do *everything*? What if there's a part of me that enjoyed it? What if there's a part of me that's just like him? That *wants* to be like him?'

She shook her head. 'You're not him, Ajax King. Not in any way. You don't hurt people—you protect them. I was the daughter of your enemy. You could have used my life to get Dad to leave Sydney, but you didn't. And those houses you're building, they're to improve people's lives.' Her thumbs stroked my cheekbones so gently. 'Everything you do is about keeping people safe, the way you kept your brothers safe all those years ago.'

'They weren't safe,' I almost spat. 'You don't know what they went through.'

'I think they would have thought it was worth it to see Augustus in jail.' Her mouth curved in a smile of such tenderness it hurt to look at it. 'Do you know that Leon called me in New York? He told me that I'd better come home, because something was wrong with his brother. They want you to be happy, Ajax. Don't you think you should honour them by, you know, actually being happy?'

My brothers. They were the reason for everything. Because I was the oldest and I had to protect them. And I'd told myself that I'd had to stand aside and let them get hurt in order to ultimately protect them.

The end justified the means, always.

But…what if that was a lie? What if there had been something in me that had let it happen? The same thing that had been in my father, who caused people nothing but pain.

'They don't know,' I said raggedly. 'They don't know that Dad threatened them. They don't know that I couldn't lift a finger to save them.'

'So tell them. Talk to them.' Her fingers were cool on my skin. 'But you'll have to let me stay first, because I'm not leaving you.'

That steely determination was in her eyes, her will as strong as mine.

She'd got under my skin the second she'd appeared, with her wide-eyed innocence, incessant questions and electric presence, and I had a feeling she would never leave.

But it wasn't her I was fighting. It was myself.

'I'll never be an easy man to live with.' My voice was cracked and broken, all the fight running out of me. 'I can't change my past and I'm possessive as fuck. And you're wrong. I'm a man like my father was through and through.'

That blindingly tender smile was a weapon, cutting me to pieces. 'Don't use him as an excuse, love. Don't let fear win. He destroyed things. You build them.

That's what you do. That's what you *and* your brothers are doing.'

Fear. Was I really letting it stop me?

I looked into Imogen's eyes, saw her love for me staring back.

It didn't seem possible that a man like me, broken and dark, violent and possessive, could catch a beam of sunlight in his hand and hold it for ever. And, because it didn't seem possible, I'd locked myself down, denied myself. Told myself I couldn't have it.

But then she'd come along and broken me wide open with her honesty and her trust. With her love. A love that terrified me because I wanted it so much.

She was right; I *was* afraid. And if I gave into fear he would win.

I couldn't let that happen. Because I had one thing he didn't: love.

Love made me keep my promise to her. Love kept me from the brink.

Loving her had saved me and it was still saving me, even now.

Love was the key. It wasn't a word my father would have said to anyone. He wouldn't have even known what it meant.

But Imogen did. And she'd taught me.

Love was the difference between me and my father.

Imogen was watching me and maybe she'd read my mind because she asked very softly, 'Do you love me, Ajax?'

All my fight was gone. She'd kidnapped my heart and she wasn't giving it back. And I couldn't lie, not to myself and not to her.

Not any more.

'Yes.' It came out low and guttural. 'I'll love you till I die.'

The warmth in her expression killed me. 'Then have me.'

'I'll never be good enough for you. I'll never deserve you.'

'You don't need to. What you deserve is happiness.'

I couldn't hold back then, couldn't keep the hunger at bay.

She'd brought me back to life and there was no way I could have that life without her.

I caught her in my arms, pulling her close, fitting her against me, and the constant ache inside me began to ease, like a part of me that had been missing had come back.

'Little one,' I murmured, nuzzling my face in her hair. 'I can't let you go again.'

'Good.' She pressed harder against me. 'Because I wouldn't leave. I'd camp out on your doorstep and play loud music and sing and generally make a nuisance of myself, and then I'd—'

I didn't let her finish. I kissed her instead.

Because I suddenly saw it, my big picture.

My big picture was her.

EPILOGUE

Ajax

'YOU'RE A FUCKING IDIOT,' Leon muttered, adjusting the rose in my buttonhole, because there had to be roses the day I married Imogen.

'Seconded,' Xander said, frowning at me. 'I can't believe you haven't told us this bullshit before.'

It had taken me a while, but I'd finally told them everything about my time as Dad's second-in-command—about his threat to their lives and how I'd had to stand back and watch them get hurt in order to protect them.

The timing wasn't great—I was getting ready for my wedding after all—but they seemed to take it well.

'Of course he hasn't,' Leon said before I could get a word in. 'Big brother thinks he knows what's best for us, right?'

Xander snorted. 'How long have you been torturing yourself with this then?'

'For fucking ever.' Leon adjusted the damn rose again. 'Jesus, Ajax. You should have said something.'

'If I could get a fucking word in?' I jerked my lapel

away from Leon before he ruined the rose. 'It isn't that simple.'

'Sure it is,' Xander disagreed. 'You just open your mouth and words come out of it.'

Prick. I was about to tell him exactly how not simple it was when something caught my eye out the window. We were in my bedroom at home and I could see the pool area by the cliff, all decorated for the ceremony that would take place in an hour's time.

A woman was hurrying after something white that was being blown across the tiles, another two women chasing after her.

She wore a simple white silk gown, a crown of roses wound into her gilt hair, and she was laughing. One of the other women running after her had long auburn hair, while the other had a riot of black curls.

Imogen made a grab for the white thing—her veil— and caught it, Vita and Poppy, my sisters-in-law, cheering as she held it up triumphantly.

'It's bad luck to see the bride before the wedding,' Xander said from beside me.

'Surely not today,' Leon murmured from the other side.

There was silence as we watched the women we loved fix Imogen's veil, their faces alight with laughter.

'Be happy, Ajax,' Leon said at last. 'If anyone deserves it, it's you.'

Xander didn't say a word, merely put his hand on my shoulder.

Down by the pool, Imogen looked up and caught me watching. She smiled and I felt my heart catch fire.

Turned out that my brothers knew what they were talking about.

Happiness *was* something I could choose and they were showing me the way.

So I chose it.

It really was that simple after all.

* * * * *

GOOD GIRL

CHRISTY McKELLEN

MILLS & BOON

For Lycia, godmother extraordinaire.
Thank you for being there.

CHAPTER ONE

Juno

ALESSANDRO RICCI IS phenomenal in bed.

At least that's what I've heard other people say about him. Unfortunately, I wouldn't know, for two reasons: firstly, I'm a virgin, and secondly, he refused to sleep with me when I asked him to.

It wasn't my finest hour.

The first time we met was at my father's fiftieth birthday party. Even amongst the plethora of filthy rich, gregariously glamorous socialites that had been invited he stood out like the Sirius star system on a clear night.

I was making my way, head ducked, through the throng of partygoers to a quiet corner to hide out for a while, needing a break from the excruciating, polite conversation that my bully of a father demanded I make with his friends and associates, when my shoulder bumped against something solid and unyielding. Turning to flash whomever it was a look of apology, my gaze locked with a dazzling pair of eyes and my whole world came to a screeching halt, air whooshing from my lungs and a wave of heat rushing up my neck to flood my face.

You see Alessandro Ricci isn't just handsome—he's *beautiful*. Stop-you-in-your-tracks, steal-your-words beautiful. His features appear to be perfectly symmetrical, though I know that's not physiologically possible. No one's face is perfect. But he's as close to perfection as you can get. His bone structure looks as though it's been carved by a master sculptor; every feature of his face is exactly the right shape and size. As if someone's taken the best bits of all the most attractive men in the world and put them together to create him.

And his body. It was enthralling to behold. Broad shoulders tapering down to narrow hips and long, athletic legs. He was a good few inches taller than me, and I'm no shorty, so I guessed he was well over six foot. He was wearing an exquisitely tailored suit, which clung to his body like it loved him, and a crisp white shirt open at the collar to reveal a V of tanned olive skin and just the merest promise of dark, downy hair on his muscular chest.

If you asked me to produce an image of the picture-perfect male figure, he's exactly what I'd draw.

Caught in that moment, like a wraith between worlds, I found it intensely difficult to look at him—he was that dazzling—but at the same time I couldn't bring myself to look away.

He in turn looked back at me—or rather assessed me—as if he was stripping me naked with his eyes.

Those incredible eyes.

It makes my body rush with a prickly sort of heat just to think about them now. They were a bright, iridescent green that seemed to glow with a deep, secret knowledge. As though he knew exactly what to do to me to turn me into a gibbering wreck. Instinctively I knew they'd be things I'd never experienced before. Hot, dirty, sinful things.

My whole body throbbed with an unfamiliar sensation that made me clench my trembling hands into fists in an attempt to centre myself.

No one has ever made me feel like that before. Not even Adam.

I'm sure it's something Alessandro must do to all women, though. According to the people I've asked about him, he's reputedly a world-class seducer and an incorrigible playboy but, even so, when he smiled at me like that it made me feel somehow special and most unusually—attractive.

I've always been compared unfavourably to my beautiful older sisters—I know I appear washed out and pale in comparison to them, like a photo that's faded in the sun—and this knowledge has rather knocked my confidence when it comes to attracting men.

I do have one outstanding feature, though—my hair, which reaches all the way down to the middle of my back and is a warm chestnut colour. But, honestly, I've never really liked it. It makes me stand out too much. I like to be able to position myself quietly on the sidelines and watch what's going on around me rather than thrusting myself right into the middle of things like Maya and April do.

I know—logically, and away from Sandro's mesmerising charisma—that the whole encounter had been a purely physical reaction I'd had to his pheromones, rather than a cerebral connection. I'm usually attracted to someone for their intelligence and enterprise rather than something as superficial as their looks—but it hasn't stopped me from still wanting things from him.

Wanting him to do things *to* me.

What exactly those things are, I'm not entirely sure, but I'd bet my first-class degree he'd know exactly what to do to push my buttons. He certainly had that air about him, as if he'd been born with the ability to give women pleasure and was more than happy to utilise it.

The scientist in me makes me suspect he'd make a fascinating anthropological study subject.

Anyway, after I finally managed to pull myself away from his tractor-beam gaze, I hid away in the nearest bathroom and attempted to bring my racing heartbeat under control. Staring at my flushed face in the mirror, I thought about the way he'd looked at me with such intense interest that I'd felt the sensual effect of it all the way down deep inside me. It had made my blood thrum and my skin goose-bump and I'd had a sudden impulsive craving to master that skill myself. As I reflected on how powerful having this ability would make me feel, a germ of an idea began to form in my mind.

After recently living through the pain of being rejected by the man I've had a planet-sized crush on for the past year—a man who has one of the greatest minds of our time and with whom I'm lucky enough to work alongside in the cardiovascular research department at St George's University of London—I'd decided it was finally time to do something about my sexual immaturity. I had to stop letting life happen to me and actively do something about getting what I wanted. I needed to 'woman up', as my sister Maya would say, no

matter how terrifying the idea of that was. And
here, in Alessandro Ricci, I just might have found
the perfect person to help me.

So that, my patient friend, is how Sandro came
to take a starring role in the sorry tale of my mor-
tifyingly misjudged attempt to lose my virginity.

It happened at a private party in Chelsea.

It's not the sort of place you'll usually find me
on a Saturday night. Most weekends I'll either be
at home working on my PhD thesis, or hanging
out with a friend, eating fine food and having involved conversations about the state of the world.
So walking through a dark, sultry room writhing
with half-naked bodies all gyrating to a thumping
dance track was definitely not on my usual 'things
to do on a weekend' agenda.

Maya had given me the tip-off that Alessandro was going to be at the party that night after
I'd confided in her about my interest in him and
she'd suggested it might be a good place to catch
up with him. She'd warned me that it definitely
wouldn't be my usual scene, but I'd assured her
that it was probably the ideal setting for what I
had in mind. There would no doubt be a dark and
seductive atmosphere and I'd hoped it'd provide
an opportunity for me to get close to him with the
bare minimum of conversation required.

Don't get me wrong; I might sound flippant, but I was terrified about the whole idea. So terrified I'd already drunk three straight shots of vodka before I'd even arrived at the party and had stashed a hip flask in my handbag in case I needed a top-up later. I'm not usually a drinker, so my head was pretty fuzzy as I pushed my way through the throng of hot bodies, all now swaying in time to a pulsing ambient techno track, searching for any sign of Sandro.

I'd deliberately worn the same outfit I'd had on at my father's party, in the hope that Sandro would be more likely to remember me, but I was already too hot in it and totally overdressed compared to the rest of the guests. The crepe top stuck to my overheated, sweaty skin and the band of the black ankle-length skirt that had fit me fine only a week ago dug uncomfortably into my middle. I'd been stress-eating up till the day of the party and I cursed my weakness as I tugged the button at the back of the skirt open to give me a bit of relief, pulling my top down to cover the gape of the material at the back.

Unable to locate Sandro in the next room, which was similarly besieged with partying guests, I was making for the door, intent on escaping to the bathroom to regroup, when I saw a familiar striking figure stride past the doorway to the hall.

It was him.

Shouting unheard apologies into the throbbing air as I pushed past the other partygoers, I dashed after him, reaching the doorway just as he began to climb the sweeping staircase at the end of the hallway, his long legs making short work of the stairs. He moved with such enigmatic grace that I stood transfixed for a moment and watched him, until it occurred to me I was going to lose him if I didn't grab his attention.

I tried to call out his name, but my throat was parched and scratchy from the overwhelming heat of the party, so I pulled the hip flask out of my bag and took a quick swallow of the fiery alcohol in an attempt to soothe it as I darted up the stairs after him. The liquid burned my throat and I inhaled sharply, the acrid fumes of it flooding my wind-pipe, making me splutter and gasp for breath. Eyes stinging, I gripped the banister and attempted to get a hold of myself as the alcohol rushed through my blood, mixing with the adrenaline the chok-ing reflex had produced. I felt spaced out as my intoxicated blood pounded heavily through my veins and for one fleeting moment I considered turning around and running out of there, back to the safety of my quiet, comforting flat...

A warm hand gently pressed my shoulder, jerk-ing me out of my whirling thoughts, and I lifted my head, my cheeks already flaming with the heat of my embarrassment to be caught like this, only to meet the gaze of the last person I wanted to see me in this state.

'Are you all right?' Sandro asked in a deep, husky tone, only made more appealing by the warm timbre of his Italian accent.

All I could do was nod stupidly, my eyes brimming with tears and my throat still on fire from the alcohol. 'I'm fine,' I forced myself to croak when he gave me a concerned frown. 'Just swallowed the wrong way.' I waved a finger vaguely at my throat.

'Would a slap on the back help?' he asked, his dazzling eyes searching mine, one dark eyebrow quirked.

'No, that's okay.' I swallowed hard and gave a small cough to clear my airway. 'Technically, you only need to do that when someone's got a foreign object lodged in their windpipe, otherwise you're just assaulting them for no reason.'

An indignant expression flashed across his face, as if I'd just rudely shot down his perfectly reasonable offer of help and basically called him an idiot in the process. I shook my head, frustrated with myself for sounding so prim and schoolmarmish.

'I'm Juno. We met—well, not met, exactly— bumped into each other—at least I bumped into you—on Wednesday night,' I said quickly to cover my gaffe. 'I don't know if you remember?' I added rather inelegantly.

I wondered what had happened to me. I wasn't usually like this. The mixture of alcohol, nerves and Sandro's befuddling presence appeared to be messing with my neural pathways.

'I remember. At Maxim's party,' he said, seeming to forgive me as a slow, sexy smile broke across his handsome face.

My insides did an excited flip. 'Oh, good, I was afraid you wouldn't. I'm not usually that memorable,' I said stupidly. This really wasn't going as well as I'd hoped. My plan to appear mature and sexually alluring had already metaphorically face-planted at his feet.

'You had your hair down then, though,' he said, kindly ignoring my flustered unsophistication.

I raised my hand to touch the base of my neck where my hair was nestled in a tight bun. I usually wore it like that, or in a plait, to keep it tucked away. I wear my long fringe swept across my forehead, though, so I can hide behind it if I need to.

'Yes, it was. But it's too hot to have it down here tonight.' I flapped a hand across my face. 'It's positively steamy in here.'

He gave me a quizzical smile, then reached out his hand to push my fringe out of my eyes. It was such an intimate, proprietary move, I sucked in a breath of surprise.

There was a movement out of the corner of my eye and I glanced round to see a man walking quickly past us, looking down at the mobile phone in his hand. I had the strangest impression that he'd just taken a photo of us talking, but I quickly dismissed the idea. Why would he want a picture of me? The gossip magazines seem to have absolutely zero interest in featuring me on their pages any more, unlike my glamorous sisters. Thank goodness. I can't think of anything worse than being hounded by paparazzi and having my personal life constantly picked over by the general public.

'Why so jumpy, Juno?' Sandro murmured.

When I turned back to look at him, his bright gaze tangled with mine and my stomach did another somersault.

'I'm not jumpy,' I squeaked.

'Really? Because you seem a little edgy to me. Is something wrong? Has something happened here tonight?' He stood a little taller. 'Has your date abandoned you?' His mouth tensed as if the idea of that angered him.

'No, no, nothing like that.' I took a deep breath, keenly aware that this would be a great opportunity to ask for his help. My heart gave an extra-hard thump as nerves rattled through me.

'Actually, I…er…came here on my own hoping to bump into you.' It didn't come out sounding quite as seductive as I'd hoped—in fact I sounded more like a mouse with a sore throat—but at that moment I was just pleased I'd been able to get the words out.

'Me?' He looked surprised, though I was pretty sure it was a feigned reaction. I imagined women must turn up at parties all the time hoping to bump into him.

'Yes. I have a proposition for you.'

'A proposition?' His eyes flashed with a teasing sort of mirth, but I could tell I'd piqued his interest from the slight tilt of his head and the way he moved fractionally closer to me. This gave me the confidence to carry on.

'I was hoping we could talk somewhere privately,' I said as a group of people spilled out of the nearest doorway and rowdily made their way past where we stood in the middle of the staircase.

'Okay, I'll admit, I'm intrigued. Let's find a quiet room upstairs.' He gestured for me to climb the stairs in front of him. 'Ladies first.'

I climbed the stairs in front of him on shaky legs, intensely aware of his dominating presence at my back. I imagined I could feel the heat radiating from his powerful body, even though logically I knew that wasn't possible. Every nerve ending in my body was on high alert and it was clearly messing with my sensory perception.

Heart thumping hard in my chest, I walked into the nearest bedroom, relieved to find it empty of people. He followed me in, closing the door behind him.

There was a small lamp on by the side of an enormous bed, bathing it in a low, warm light. I swallowed hard, suddenly terrified. A dissenting voice in my head was telling me I was crazy to even think of doing this but I knew I had to be brave and take action if I was ever going to get past my hang-ups about sex and men.

I dropped my bag at my feet and turned to look at him.

He was standing proud and tall a few feet away from me with his hands casually by his sides, giving me a respectful amount of personal space. The man was clearly a gentleman, which heartened me. Everything I'd heard about him had pointed towards this, but it was comforting to have it confirmed. Especially as I was now alone in a closed room with him.

'So, what can I do for you, Juno?' he prompted when I failed to say anything. I'd been so busy psyching myself up I'd left an uncomfortably long pause hanging in the air.

Clearing my raw throat, I pushed back my shoulders in an attempt to project confidence.

But no words would come. I began to panic. How the heck were you supposed to seduce someone—someone you barely knew anything about? I had absolutely no experience in these matters.

In desperation I thought back to the sex scenes I'd seen on TV, where women who want to initiate sex simply strip off in front of the guy and he seems to know exactly what she wants without her having to say a word.

My blood was thumping so hard in my head by this point, I was afraid Sandro would be able to hear it in the quiet of the room. He was certainly looking at me as if he was concerned about something.

'Are you okay?' he asked, his brows knitted together.

'Mmm-hmm,' I murmured, sucking in a steadying breath then grasping the bottom of my crepe top in my shaking fingers. Knowing I had to act fast before I lost my nerve, I attempted to slip it over my head seductively. Unfortunately, I managed to get the neck caught round my hair bun and ended up struggling to get it past my chin. The zip at the top of my skirt, which was already loose, decided to choose this moment to undo fully and the whole thing slithered down my legs and pooled at my feet, leaving me flashing my underwear-clad body at him while my head was still trapped in my top.

Needless to say, it wasn't the elegant disrobing I'd been aiming for.

Finally, I managed to get myself untangled and dropped the offending article onto the floor, my face now flaming with embarrassment.

'What are you doing?' There was amusement in his voice, but I ignored it, desperate to get past this humiliating preamble and on to what I'd come here for.

Unfortunately, it seemed I was actually going to have to say the words.

I swallowed hard, my throat now as arid as my sex life. 'I want you to…to…have s-sex with me.'

He stared at me for a moment, then the corner of his mouth kicked up into a bemused smile.

'Just like that? No getting to know each other first?' He folded his arms. 'Why the rush?'

'Because I'm a virgin and I don't want to be any more,' I blurted, taking a shaky step closer to him and managing to kick my bag in the process. My small silver hip flask slipped out of it and slid onto the floor between us.

He looked down at it, then back up at me with one dark eyebrow raised.

'Are you drunk?' he murmured darkly.

'No,' I lied, kicking the hip flask back under my bag and taking a couple more sauntering steps towards him, hoping to distract his attention away from it.

'I've heard you're amazing in bed and I thought you'd be the perfect person to help me out. I want to learn from the best,' I said in as confident a tone as I could muster, desperately hoping that appealing to his vanity would yield results.

He leaned one shoulder against the wall, his arms still folded. The insouciant slouch he affected only made him look more intimidatingly sexy.

'So you've come here tonight because you want me to get rid of your virginity for you? Is that what you're saying?' he asked, his eyes assessing me so thoroughly now a delicious sort of shiver shimmied across my bare skin.

I screwed up all my courage and forced myself to meet his gaze. 'Yes, that's exactly what I'm saying.'

He let out a low, baffled breath. 'Why me? We don't even know each other.'

'Because when you looked at me at the party on Wednesday it seemed like you found me attractive. And I find you attractive, in a physical way, so I thought it might be mutually agreeable…'

There was an awkward pause before he spoke again. 'Agreeable?'

'Yes. Um, fun. And…er…sexy.' I could barely believe I'd just let those awful words out of my mouth. And I was supposed to be the genius of the family.

'Well, if you find me attractive in a *physical* way, how could I possibly refuse?' he asked, deadpan.

Once again I cursed my lack of confidence in these matters. Get me on my subject and I could talk with utter self-assurance for hours, but here I was just steadily digging myself into a deep, dark hole with no idea how to pull myself out.

I decided being honest was the only way forward from here.

'No. Look, sorry, this is coming out all wrong.' I pulled my arms around my body, intensely aware of how exposed I was. 'As I'm sure you're painfully aware, I'm really not experienced at negotiating this kind of thing.'

'You don't say.' The drawl of his words made his amusement very clear.

I tried to shake off my frustration. Getting het up was unhelpful. I needed to be cool, like my sister Maya would have been if she'd been in this situation. I attempted to channel her as I forced myself to stand a little taller and saunter up to him, looking him right in the eye.

'I feel like there's a connection between us. Chemistry,' I murmured, trying not to sway on the spot.

He frowned, looking confused, and opened his mouth as if he was going to refute what I'd just said but then closed it again. There was a tense pause while he stared hard at me, his dark brows drawn together tightly.

My blood was pumping so hard through my veins, I could hear the swoosh of it in my ears.

'Look, Juno, you seem like a lovely woman, and I take it as a huge compliment that I'm at the top of your list, but it's a no,' he said finally. 'I don't sleep with virgins. Especially not drunk virgins. I prefer to go to bed with women who know what they want and can handle having sex just for fun.'

Disappointment made my eyes sting with held-back tears. 'It could be fun with me,' I fired back, desperation straining my voice.

He just shot me a look that clearly said *desperation* was exactly what he was trying to avoid getting entangled in.

Frustration surged through me. I'd made a total fool of myself tonight and for what? A big, fat negative result.

'God! What is it with me and men? How am I supposed to get experience if no one will sleep with me?'

I took one last stumbling step towards him, pressing my hand against the wall next to him to steady myself. His wonderful, spicy scent flooded my senses, making my mouth water and my head swim.

'Please, I'll do whatever you say. Whatever you want. Just name it. Is there a favour I could do for you? Or would money help? Or—er—something else?' I asked hurriedly, agonisingly aware that offering him money was a stupid and offensive thing to do. 'L-l-like a promise to help you out when you next need it?' I rushed on, hoping he wouldn't take umbrage at my slip.

'You're offering me money?' His eyes were narrowed now in distaste.

'No, not money. Ignore that. I didn't mean it the way it came out—'

'You didn't mean it to sound like you were hoping to *pay* me to have sex with you?' His voice was filled with reproach.

Shame crawled up my spine. In that horrible moment I imagined I could actually sense his male pride putting up its fists.

'I'm sorry…'

He waved away my apology with a dismissive sweep of his hand before I was even able to finish it. 'Even if I do find you attractive, I wouldn't stoop to sleeping with someone who thinks so little of me,' he said, his voice dangerously low. 'I think you should go home before you say something stupid to someone else here. They might not be as forgiving of your crassness.'

Before I could utter another word, he'd marched out of the room, leaving the sound of his disgust ringing in my head.

I was so humiliated I wanted to cry. I couldn't believe I'd handled that so badly. Made such an utter mess of it. Because I had. A total mess. In fact, I don't think I could have done a worse job at persuading him to help me.

Which was why I was absolutely astounded when I picked up a voicemail message from him the next afternoon asking me out for a drink.

CHAPTER TWO

Sandro

IT HADN'T BEEN the best of weeks.

First I lost out on buying an old dilapidated building in Shoreditch, that my friend Jon and I had intended to turn into affordable studio space for artists, to a grubby property developer. Then the pretty redhead from Maxim's party treated me like some brainless piece of ass. That had been especially irritating, because when I'd first realised it was her at Harry's place in Chelsea I'd actually been pleased to see her. The evening had been a bust up till that point. I'd found myself surrounded by the same familiar faces and boring conversations, so the sight of her had lit something inside me.

I've always been a sucker for redheads and when I'd spotted her at Maxim's party—an event I'd been attending in my father's place while he

was away in Rome on important family business—
I'd been intrigued by her air of sweetness. I could
tell by the way she held herself that she wasn't confident and worldly like the majority of the women
there and it had made me want to take her away
somewhere safe to protect her. And perhaps do
other things too, if she'd been willing. She's an attractive woman, after all. I'd particularly enjoyed
the way her porcelain-pale cheeks had flamed with
colour when I'd smiled at her.

I love making women blush. It gives me a real
kick of pleasure. In fact, any instinctive physical reaction I can tease out of them gets me hot:
accelerated breathing, a damp sheen of sweat on
an upper lip, dilated pupils, a coquettish eyelash
flutter. I love it all. Because I love women.

All women.

They're such fascinating, exotic creatures.

And they usually love me right back.

So when she'd made it clear she thought I was
just some man whore, it had really pissed me off.
It had been obvious she wasn't interested in me
as a person when she'd asked me to take her virginity. I was just a throwaway cock she'd be using
to fix a problem and I hadn't been prepared to be
treated like that. Her disrespectful approach had
actually made me fucking furious, though I'd tried
not to show it. I never show my real feelings to a

woman, not any more—not when I know how it can strip you of your power and control—which is probably why, after I'd left her in that room, I'd gone downstairs, drunk half a bottle of whisky and ended up getting into a pointless fist fight with one of Harry's friends over some stupid fucking comment he'd made about a woman I'd been talking to. I can't even remember what it was now.

Normally I'd laugh off any kind of provocation, putting it down to jealousy or crossing someone's path at the wrong moment, but added to Juno's suggestion that I wasn't the brightest spark in the fire, it had blown something inside me and I'd lashed out.

The moment I woke up this morning with a thumping head and a horrible sense that I'd overstepped a mark, I regretted the whole thing.

I regretted it even more when my father summoned me to his Knightsbridge house later that day and showed me just how far the consequences of my actions had reached.

'This,' he said, gesturing angrily towards his open laptop, 'is unacceptable.'

The screen had a gossip article from one of the popular society pages on it. There was a picture of me with an ugly sneer on my face caught right after I'd punched Harry's friend in the face. It made the whole incident look much more brutal than it had actually been—I'd been too drunk to do more than glance my knuckles off his chin— but the look on the guy's face told another story. He looked afraid of me.

Shame sunk through my chest to nestle heavily in my gut. That wasn't me. I'm not a violent person— quite the opposite, in fact. I'm a lover, not a fighter. But this picture said differently.

'Well? What have you got to say for yourself? I thought you'd stopped fighting when you were a teenager,' my father barked. 'Your mother is dis- traught and the last thing she needs right now is more stress when she's so busy helping to orga- nise your brother's wedding. The press has been calling me for a comment about it. I told them in no uncertain terms that *that* wasn't going to happen.'

The good reputation of the family name is ev- erything to my father. He lives and breathes it. And he expects me and my brothers to do the same. My oldest brother took this so seriously he's now on the path to marrying into the highest echelons of Italian nobility—of which we are currently only lowly-ranking members—and my father is ada- mant that none of us does anything to jeopardise it. Our inclusion in his close family circle and all that comes with it depends on it.

'It wasn't as bad as it looks…' I began to argue,

but my father clearly wasn't in the mood to hear excuses.

'I want you to go back to Italy until this blows over. And I don't want to see anything about you in the papers there either. Unless it's a positive article. In fact—' He moved to his laptop and scrolled down the page until he came to another photo. This one also had me in it, but this time I was smiling and brushing hair out of the eyes of a pretty redhead who was gazing up at me as if totally entranced by the intimate moment we're sharing.

Juno.

My heart sank.

'This one's suggesting you're having a relationship with the youngest Darlington-Hume girl,' my father said, flashing me a questioning look.

My whole world started to tumble past my ears. She was one of Maxim's *daughters*. I hadn't realised. She'd looked so different from her sisters and she certainly hadn't acted like a Darlington-Hume—a family my father holds in very high regard indeed. In his estimation, they're the fucking *essence* of English high society.

And I'd basically told her to take a running jump when she'd asked me for help.

'I wouldn't call it a relationship,' I replied carefully. I wasn't entirely sure where he was going with this so I was treading carefully. I really didn't want to be banished to Italy for long. I have important plans here in England and I need to be around to put them in motion. Plus, this is where all my friends live now. Italy will be a social desert.

'You could do a lot worse than having a Darlington-Hume in your bed. The family has an excellent if mercenary reputation, but you can't get more inner-circle than Maxim.' He nodded, seeming to make up his mind about something, and my gut knotted as I predicted what he was about to demand of me.

'Take her to Florence. Stay in Maria's apartment. She's going to be in Sweden for the next few weeks, and she's worried it might be broken into again, so it would be good to have you there looking after the place. Let the press know you're there and make sure you're seen out and about in the right places. Get your reputation publicly back on even ground. Then you can come back.'

'I'm not sure she'll want to go to Florence with me.'

'I don't give a shit what she wants. Just make it happen. Prove to me, for once, that you're worthy of the Ricci family name, like your brothers.'

There was no point in arguing with him. I knew from experience that, when my father demands something, there's no way of getting out of it. He's hard-hearted enough to cut me out of the family if I don't play ball, and won't hesitate to stop me from seeing my nephews and my mother. That's the last thing I want. It would devastate her. I've disappointed her enough for a lifetime.

So a trip to Florence it was.

With Juno Darlington-Hume.

Assuming I could convince her I've changed my mind about helping her out after the contemptuous rejection I threw down at her feet the night before. I suspected it was going to take a monumental amount of charm and a shit-ton of good fucking grace to talk her round. Luckily, those are qualities I have in abundance.

So when I got home I swallowed my pride, sourced her number from a friend of a friend and called her, leaving a message on her voicemail, inviting her out for a drink.

'So in your message you said you had something you wanted to talk to me about,' Juno says warily, once we're seated in a booth in a chi-chi little cocktail bar in a backstreet of Soho that I'd chosen for its seclusion from the bustle of central London, and hopefully prying eyes. I don't want word going round about us until Juno's agreed to the proposal I'm about to lay out for her.

She's pointedly ordered a virgin cocktail and I've had to bite my lip so as not to make a joke about the car-crash conversation we had last night in case it upsets her.

This whole situation needs to be handled very carefully.

I give her my secret-weapon smile and lean forward, spreading my hands on the table and locking my gaze with hers. 'I want to apologise for the way I spoke to you last night. Your request took me by surprise and I didn't handle it well.'

She stares back at me as if I'm speaking a foreign language and I panic for a second that I've slipped into Italian.

Seeming to snap out of her trance, she shakes her head. 'You really don't need to apologise. I'm the one that should be apologising. I don't know what I was thinking, demanding…what I did…like that.' She looks down at the table as if she can't bear to maintain eye contact with me. 'You were right. I was drunk and totally out of line.'

Her shame-faced confession sends a wave of relief through me and I sit back against the red velvet banquette, feeling a little more in control of things now. I can't help but forgive her. It's pretty clear the Juno of last night wasn't the real her. It was just a glitch. A drunken mistake.

'How old are you, Juno?' I ask her gently, hoping to draw her out of her shell and gain her trust. Her shoulders are rigid and her chin dipped as if she's pulled herself inward for protection. It makes me want to smooth my fingers down her spine to help her relax. She doesn't seem to be able to look at me. Instead she's playing with the cocktail menu, lining it up with the edge of the table.

'Twenty-two.'

'Why are you so eager to lose your virginity? Twenty-two isn't old to still be a virgin.'

She takes a stuttering breath and finally looks up at me. 'Because it seems to me that in order to be sexy you need to have had sex. At least, all the women I know that attract men's attention are the ones that are really comfortable in their own skin. They ooze sex appeal. And none of them are virgins.'

'How can you be sure?' I ask, picking up the whisky sour I've ordered and taking a sip.

'I've asked them.'

The drink gets caught in the back of my throat, making me cough.

'Wow. So, what, you've just gone up to them and asked the question?'

'Yes. For research purposes.' She shrugs. 'I like to investigate my subject thoroughly. It's important to have all the information to be able to make an informed hypothesis.'

I frown, then flip it into a reassuring smile. 'I

don't think you have to have had sex to be sexy. At least, not in my experience.'

'Yes, well, unfortunately not everyone shares your viewpoint.' She looks down at the table again.

'Ah. So there's another guy involved in this?' I hazard a guess.

She visibly bristles. 'Actually, I don't think that's any of your business.' Her cheeks are bright pink and the expression in her eyes is defensive.

I hold up my hand. 'Wait—you want me to take your virginity but you won't tell me why?'

Her throat moves as she swallows. 'That's correct.'

I shake my head and frown, concerned about what I might be stepping into the middle of here.

'I'm really not comfortable with saying yes to this unless I know why you want it. We need to be able to be open and honest with each other. It's important we trust each other if we're going to get that close and intimate,' I say slowly, trying to sound as if I'm looking out for both our interests here.

She stares at me for a moment, then nods, and I can tell from the pained expression on her face that she's been struggling with what she's about to tell me. My gut clenches and I stretch back in the seat to ease it. It's a troubling feeling and not something I've experienced much. I usually only get it when I come across a woman I really like but can't have. Or one that I'm not supposed to have, at least.

'Okay, fine. I suppose it is better if you know the whole story.' She takes a shaky breath and splays her hands on the table, staring down at her fingers as she begins to talk. 'There's this man—Adam Cormack—he's a lecturer at St George's University where I'm doing my PhD.' I see her swallow and a small pinch appears between her brows. 'And I...er... I like him...a lot.'

'But he's not into you?'

She shuffles a little in her seat. 'Well, he *likes* me, I think. We've been on a few dates, but I think he's concerned about how...er...inexperienced I am. He's a bit older than me and I think he's looking for someone more like him. Well, not a *man* like him, but someone with the same sort of life experience as him.'

I smile. 'You mean he doesn't want to fuck you because you're a virgin?'

The frankness of my words seems to shock her and her face flames, bright splashes of red highlighting her pale cheeks.

'Yes,' she mutters. 'But in a much more gentlemanly way than you make it sound.' She's having trouble meeting my eye again and picks up her cocktail, taking a big gulp, then pushes her shoulders back in an obvious attempt to appear more confident, but it just looks stiff and awkward. My heart goes out to her. Her shyness is actually a real turn-on, if I'm honest.

'He's the only man I've ever felt this strongly about,' she murmurs. 'And I've decided it's time to stop hiding under a rock, get out there and go for what I really want. And if that means showing him I'm worldly and mature enough to handle a relationship with him, then that's what I'm going to do.'

I have a moment of unease where I worry that I'm about to take advantage of her heartache, but I push it firmly away. She came to me first, after all.

Clearly she's sensed my concern, though, because she says, 'Look, do you think you can help me or not? Because if you're not interested I'm going to go and find someone who is.' As if to prove her point, she stands up and reaches for her bag.

Panic ripples through me. I can't let her walk away. I need this to work out.

'Perhaps I could help,' I say quickly, holding up a hand to halt her. 'If we can agree on a couple of conditions.'

Her eyes widen with hope and she sits back down in her seat. 'I'm listening.'

'Okay.' I nod. 'I want you to come to Florence

with me for a week, go out on some dates with me there, so we can get to know each other first. I don't know what you've heard about me but it's not my style to just jump into bed with a woman without getting to know her a little first. And honestly…' I lean forward, giving her a friendly smile '…I think you'll be more comfortable with the whole situation if we handle it that way. With a little class.'

'Classy sounds good.'

'You know, that way you could put some photos of the two of us looking happy together on social media. You never know, Adam might see them, assume you're dating me and realise what a fool he's been passing you up. Believe me, there's nothing like jealousy to motivate a guy to action,' I add as a further incentive.

She shakes her head, wrinkling her nose in disdain. 'I despise the whole social media circus and avoid it as much as possible. I loathe the idea of everyone knowing exactly where I am and what I'm doing all the time. And I really hate having my photo taken. I had a horrible experience with the press in my teens.' She shudders. 'Death by public scrutiny.'

'Right,' I say, feeling my heart sink. 'Okay, then, no photos.' At least, none she'll be aware of. I'll have to make sure that the photographers

I call will be discreet. I try not to feel bad about not telling her we're basically going to be courting the Italian press while we're there. It sounds as if it'll be better if she assumes they're following us off their own bat. It'll be less complicated that way. And it'll seem more natural if she looks genuinely surprised to be photographed with me. Anyway, they'll be positive pictures. They'll make her look good. I'll make sure the photographers agree to that when I call to tip them off about where we'll be.

'Why do we need to go all the way to Florence?' she asks, apparently confused by that particular detail, which I guess is understandable.

I play it cool and give a nonchalant shrug. 'I've promised to house-sit an apartment there for a couple of weeks and after that I'll be too busy to help you.'

'So if I go out with you on a few dates first, you'll help me out with my...*issue*?'

'I'll teach you anything you want to know about how to please a guy in bed. When I'm done, believe me, this guy Adam won't be able to resist you.'

I see her throat work as she swallows hard and a spike of disquiet pierces my chest.

'My only caveat is no full sex,' I add, to try and exonerate my guilt. 'I'll let him have that honour.

You'll be grateful to me later when you realise what a big emotional deal it is to lose your virginity to someone you care about.'

She frowns, thinks about it, then asks, 'Did you lose yours to someone you cared about?'

'No,' I grunt, unwilling to go any further with that line of conversation. 'So I know what I'm talking about. There's plenty of other stuff we can do, though,' I murmur, giving her a teasing smile and moving my leg gently to press against hers. I'm rewarded with another full-face blush and, predictably, my cock springs to attention.

'Why are you doing this for me?' she asks, her voice sounding a little husky now. 'Especially after the horrendous way I acted last night.'

'Charity begins at home, right?' I take another sip of my whisky then smile at her over the rim of the glass, feeling guilt gnaw at my insides. 'And because I can't resist a challenge like this, especially when it involves someone as pretty as you.' I lean forward in my chair, ignoring the uncomfortable tension building in my chest. 'It'll be my absolute pleasure to help you out, Juno.'

This, at least, is the God's honest truth. I pause and take another sip of my drink to give myself a moment to refocus my thoughts on the issue at hand and stop them from wandering towards all the physical delights I'm going to take great satisfaction in introducing her to.

'Just so we're clear, it'll just be for the time we're in Florence. After that we'll go our separate ways. You towards your lecturer guy and me back to the uncomplicated lifestyle I love.'

From the look on her face, I can tell she's seriously thinking it over.

'I have a lot of work to do for my PhD, though. I can't be away for too long,' she says slowly, almost to herself.

'Bring your laptop with you. You can work during the day and hang out with me in the evenings.'

'Would that work? I need quiet to be able to concentrate.'

'Sure. I can entertain myself when you're busy,' I say, trying not to think about how bored I'll be sloping around the city on my own. I guess I should consider it karmic payback for losing my cool and punching that guy in the face.

'My father's mistress's apartment, where we'll be staying, is right in the centre of Florence and it has a study where you can work in the daytime without being distracted,' I reassure her.

She blinks at me, her eyes wide with astonishment. 'You know about your father's mistress? And you're prepared to stay in her flat?'

I shrug. 'Of course. She's a lovely woman. I

get on really well with her. They've been together for years.'

She shakes her head, looking utterly scandalised now.

'Doesn't your mother mind?'

Again, I shrug. 'I don't think so. Their marriage was arranged for convenience so I don't think they've ever really loved each other. They're very fond of each other, though, and they work well together as a team, so I don't think they'll ever split up. Not when the family's reputation is at stake. Reputation is everything to my father.'

Her expression tells me she's still completely baffled by the idea of that but I guess you have to live it to understand it.

'So are you up for it, Juno?' I press, wanting it absolutely confirmed.

She nods, confidently this time. 'Yes. I accept your conditions.' She leaves a small pause before adding, 'I've not had a holiday in ages because I've been so focussed on my work—which isn't particularly healthy, I know—so I suppose it'll be good for me to take a break away from London.'

'Great. Then we'll fly out tomorrow.'

'Okay. Tomorrow.'

I raise my glass, and when she does too I clink mine against it. *'A nuove esperienze.'*

'To new experiences,' she repeats.

'You speak Italian?' I ask, impressed.

'Yes, some. Enough to avoid any embarrassing misunderstandings, I hope,' she replies, grinning shyly for the first time since she arrived. She has a killer smile and the sight of it warms my chest.

I don't quite know how it's happened, but I seem to have landed on my feet here. I now get to spend the next week in bed with this enigmatic woman and all in the name of doing the right thing.

Yeah. This could actually turn out to be a lot of fun.

CHAPTER THREE

Juno

WE FLY OUT to Florence in Sandro's family's private plane the following afternoon, though we only just make our scheduled take-off slot, because he was half an hour late picking me up from my flat in his low-slung Italian sports car and has to put his foot down to get us to the airport.

He seems totally unconcerned about his tardiness, though, and throws me the merest of apologies when I raise my eyebrows and pointedly look at my watch.

He's such a cool customer. I wish I could be so nonchalant.

Upon boarding the plane we're shown to our seats—two large, cream leather armchairs positioned next to each other in a cabin that only holds six more. It's a small plane but beautifully upholstered with silk wall linings and soft wool carpets.

We take off only minutes later and I settle in for the two-hour journey sitting next to Sandro, my pulse on a high tickover as I breathe in his delicious scent and think about how much closer I'm going to have to get to him over the next week—though not, it seems, as close as I'd initially hoped.

At first I'd been a bit miffed that he was still refusing to take my virginity but, the more I thought about it, the more I'd come round to his point of view. He was probably right. It was a hell of a thing to ask of him and I'll most likely be glad to have more of an emotional connection with the person I finally lose it to. Someone I'll be in love with, perhaps.

In the meantime, I hope just by hanging out with him some of his charisma will rub off on me. And, if not, I have a week to study the way he acts and interacts with people, which I can then apply to my dealings with Adam when I get back. Perhaps he will hear about my 'relationship' with Sandro, realise I'm not the ingénue he thought I was and regret calling a halt to our burgeoning relationship after only a couple of dates.

I can only hope.

Once the plane is on a steady course we're served drinks by one of the elegantly dressed cabin crew. I watch Sandro out of the corner of my eye while I pretend to read the guidebook to Florence that I'd picked up the day before in the bookshop round the corner from my flat in Notting Hill. He rolls his cut-glass tumbler round and round in his hands. He has a restless sort of energy about him, as if he finds it hard to sit still and is always on the verge of getting up to do something else. He was the same in the bar where we had the drink and I agreed to this proposal. He flipped the drinks menu round and round in his fingers as we talked, as if he needed something to do with them. It made me wonder whether he'd been a smoker and now needed something in his hands with which to distract himself. As he twists the glass I marvel at the perfection of his long fingers with their square, blunt nails and wonder how he'll touch me with them, how it'll feel to have his hands on my body. *All over* my body. I squirm in my seat as a wave of heat rushes through me, pooling at the juncture of my thighs.

Right at this moment I can totally sympathise with his need to move about.

Just sitting still next to him in our plush leather seats, I can feel the attraction pulling taut between us. At least from my side. He's brought out a plethora of physical reactions in me. My heartbeat is accelerated, my skin hypersensitive and rushing with sensation and there's an insistent throb between my thighs that's steadily building the longer

I sit here—as if my body craves something with which I'm not providing it.

It's a hot, heavy *want*.

'You know, I've never understood why people rave so much about sex. Practically speaking, it seems like it'd be a messy and uncomfortable thing to do,' I mutter out loud to try and distract myself from these alien feelings.

He turns to look at me with a quizzical expression in those piercing eyes of his.

'And how can people let it wreck their lives?' I add nervously, realising I now have his full attention. 'It's just a physical act, right? Perfectly natural, and obviously imperative for continuing the human race, but surely it's not something to destroy a marriage over? What drives people to do that—to cheat on their partners? Just for the thrill of sex with someone else? I don't understand how it can be so overwhelming an urge that people are willing to do pretty much anything to get it.'

He shrugs. 'Passion is an irrational thing.'

'Passion? But that suggests emotions, feelings.'

'Not necessarily. It can be a basic human urge. That's a totally different thing.'

'So you think it's possible to have sex with someone without having feelings for them?'

He sits round in his chair, his knee brushing mine and sending an electric thrill of sensation through my whole body. 'I think it's perfectly possible. Otherwise I wouldn't have agreed to my part of the bargain. What I think you're talking about is something different. More than just the physical need for sex. When people cheat there are always other feelings at play. Insecurity about what they have or low self-worth. Or perhaps a fear they're missing out on something they'll regret not experiencing in years to come. I think, for others, the rush of sex with someone new after years of fucking their partner the same, predictable way can be like taking an addictive drug. That's just pure laziness, of course. There's no reason for sex to get boring. You have to work hard at being creative.'

'Are you creative?' I ask, though I think I already know the answer to that.

'You bet your sweet ass I am,' he confirms with an underwear-melting smile.

'I knew you'd say that,' I mumble, my throat tight with nerves.

'Are you suggesting I'm predictable?' he teases.

I can't help but grin, which breaks the tension.

He grins back and for a moment I'm lost in the dizzying intimacy of the moment.

I clear my throat. 'Have you ever felt that sort of passion for someone?'

For a second he glances away, up towards the ceiling. 'No.' Sitting back in his chair, he moves his leg away from mine and fixes me with a serious expression.

'You know, now might be a good time to talk about your expectations for the next week. I want to make sure we're both on the same page.'

Instinctively I tense at the sudden change in conversational direction.

'Okay.' I swallow hard. 'Well, I want you to do everything to me. Show me everything,' I say with feigned confidence. I don't want him thinking for a second that I can't handle this. I need to get it done so I can move on with my life and stop living under the shadow of my naivety.

'Everything?' He raises both eyebrows.

'Yes, I want to know all there is to know. Get it all ticked off.'

'Do you have a list you'd like to work from?' The smile he flashes me is teasing.

I roll my eyes at him. 'Very funny.'

'But, seriously, any hard limits I should know about?' he asks, his expression turning serious again.

I think about it for a moment. 'I don't want you to strangle or suffocate me, and I don't like the idea of being spanked.'

'Shame.' His grin lights up his eyes. 'Pain can actually be very pleasurable. It can give you really intense orgasms when you do it right.'

'Okay, well, I'll have to reserve judgement on that. But definitely no whipping.'

'Okay, fine. No whipping.'

I can tell from the look on his face that he's finding my sexual naivety amusing and it's irritating me.

'It's all right for you to sit there smirking, but I have no idea about these things,' I mutter. 'I'm learning from scratch so you're going to have to give me a break.' I'm shaking with both adrenaline and frustration. It's really unlike me to stand up for myself like this, but I know I need to do it if I'm going to maintain any vestige of control over this situation.

He puts up a hand in apology. 'I'm sorry. You're right. I'm being an asshole. I promise not to tease you any more. Not about your lack of experience anyway.' His eyes glitter with mischief. 'There are plenty of other ways to tease you that I think you're going to like a lot.'

I squirm in my seat as more heat surges between my legs and my knickers grow damp. At this rate I'm going to slide right off this chair in a pool of lust. And he's not even touched me yet.

We make it to the apartment in the early evening, doing the journey from Peretola airport to the centre of Florence in another powerful open-top sports car, whose roaring engine makes it impossible to conduct any conversation.

Our home for the next week is on the top floor of a grand apartment block right next to the Ponte Vecchio. Our windows look out over the quirky bridge with its jumble of jewellery shops clinging like limpets to each side with the help of precarious-looking wooden struts, and on across the wide Arno river to the deep russet-red-roofed buildings beyond. It's a magnificent city and I stand for a moment, drinking in the sheer unique elegance of the place.

'Let me show you your room,' Sandro says, beckoning me to follow him with one crooked finger.

I'm relieved to find he doesn't expect us to share and give a delighted smile as I look around the beautiful airy room with its Art Deco furniture and enormous, cushion-strewn bed.

'It's wonderful,' I say breathily. This room also has a view of the river and I push the wooden shutters open as far as they'll go to drink it in some more.

Turning back, I see he's moved to stand right next to the large bed and is watching me with an intensely thoughtful expression on his face. My pulse immediately picks up and my breath catches in my throat.

Is he going to start my first lesson right now?

The idea both thrills and terrifies me.

I move closer to him on shaky legs, telling my-self not to be nervous, that he'll take good care of me like he promised. Based on all my dealings with him so far, it's obvious he's absolutely the gentleman I'd hoped he'd be.

Even so, my heart is racing and my palms are sweaty.

He continues to look at me as I get closer, his fingers beating a silent rhythm against his thighs.

'S-so, do you want to get started right away?' I ask, nerves making my voice tremble.

A frown crosses his brow, then vanishes behind a smile. 'So eager.'

'Well, I've not come all the way to Italy just to sightsee,' I joke, but it comes out sounding a bit defensive.

He shakes his head and walks over to meet me in the middle of the room. Reaching out his hand, he pushes my fringe out of my eyes and I just stand there blinking stupidly at him.

The air crackles between us, as if the tension is charging it with electricity.

'You know, anticipation is a powerful aphrodi-siac,' he murmurs, sweeping his thumb over my cheek so softly I wonder whether he's actually touched me or if the mere promise of it has set all my nerve endings on fire. My whole body is one big throb of need and I stare up into his beautiful eyes, losing myself in the perfection of them.

His gaze drops to my mouth and my lips tingle as I wonder what it would feel like to have his mouth on mine. His wide, firm mouth.

I swallow hard, my throat a desert.

'Get changed. We're going out,' he murmurs, his gaze flicking up to meet mine again.

I stare at him for a moment, trying to process what he's just said through my haze of lust.

Then it finally sinks in. He's not interested in taking things any further right now. He wants to get out of here.

A strange mixture of relief and disappointment threads through me, quickly followed by panic as I wonder what the hell I'm supposed to change into.

I had no idea what sort of clothes I should pack for such a strange trip so I bundled one of everything I owned into my case, telling myself I could always go shopping if I needed anything else. But thinking over my sad collection of lingerie and demure clothes brings home to me just how much I've neglected that side of my life. I've never really thought about owning underwear and outfits that a man might find attractive; my top priority has always been comfort. And it's going to show.

Still, it's not as if I have to impress Sandro to entice him into bed—that side's already covered under our agreement—a thought that kept me tossing and turning in bed all night.

But I want to fulfil my part of our bargain and, in order to show I'm taking our dates seriously, I'm going to have to make an effort.

'Where are we going?' I ask, hoping for some sort of clue about to how to pitch the outfit.

'Out for dinner, and then who knows?' he says with a twinkle in his eye.

Okay, that's really not very helpful. I'll just have to wing it.

I nod and smile anyway, not wanting to appear difficult and needy. 'Give me twenty minutes.'

He flashes me one more of his heart-stopping smiles then exits the room, leaving me wondering how I'm going to pull 'Italian chic' out of the bag.

Mercifully, it seems I don't need to worry on that score. When I appear in front of him twenty minutes later in the only smart black dress I own— which is about as far from fashionable as you can get, with its high neck and mid-calf-length skirt— and with my hair in a neat, high bun, he gives me an approving look.

'You hungry?' he asks.

I nod, realising I'm actually ravenous.

'Good. Then let's eat.'

* * *

The restaurant he's chosen is in the Piazza Santa Croce, right next to the basilica, which regally presides over the wide paved square and turns out to be only a short walk from where we're staying.

As we stroll up to the buttery yellow frontage of the eatery, with its canopy shielding the patrons from the low, setting evening sun, I realise it has a long line of people waiting outside. I'm about to suggest we try somewhere else nearby when Sandro takes my hand and breezes past everyone, striding straight up to the *maître d'* at the door and introducing himself in Italian. As they talk, I notice a movement in my peripheral vision and glance round to see a man standing a few feet away, holding up a camera with a huge zoom lens that he's pointing right at us. Instinctively, I shudder and squeeze Sandro's hand. He looks round, spotting the guy, and immediately draws me closer to him, sliding his free arm around my shoulders and pulling me against his hard, muscular body as if to protect me. He leans in to nuzzle my ear. 'Just ignore him.'

Lust overrides my discomfort at being photographed as I breathe in his alluring scent and feel his warm breath glide along my neck.

Drawing back to look me in the eye, he shoots me a reassuring smile and I grin right back, feeling safe enveloped in his arms. A flash goes off and when I turn to look the guy is already scurrying away towards a motorbike parked nearby.

'Damn it,' Sandro mutters. 'Don't worry, he's probably just taking photos of everyone he sees here in case they turn out to be newsworthy.' He gives me a small squeeze, which only presses me closer to him, and my heart thumps with pleasure. 'Let's go inside—they have a table for us,' he says, releasing me from his protective embrace and gesturing towards the *maître d'* who's patiently waiting to get our attention.

'But what about those people waiting in the queue? Aren't we pushing in ahead of them?' I ask, nodding towards them.

'It's okay, the owner is a friend of my father's. He always has a table for a Ricci.'

'Oh. I see. Okay,' I say, smiling apologetically at the people still waiting as we stride into the restaurant in front of them, feeling a sting of shame. Using my name to get a jump on others really isn't my style.

'This is the hottest place to eat at the moment,' Sandro says as we're led to a table positioned next to one of the windows that looks out onto the grand square. 'That's why there was paparazzi outside. They often hang around there in case anyone of note turns up.'

I guess with Sandro being part of the Italian aristocracy, albeit a younger son and therefore an untitled member, he's probably a person of real interest here in Italy. Plus, he's such a good-looking man, women will no doubt buy a magazine with him in it just to be able to gaze at his handsome face. I'm actually feeling pretty lucky right now to have the real thing sitting right there in front of me. He's wearing an open-collared black shirt tonight, which works beautifully with his tanned skin and dark hair. He looks so delicious I could eat him up.

The succulent-looking wild boar fettuccini we ordered has just arrived when we're approached by a short, stocky man who is clearly 'somebody', judging by the way he swaggers over to us.

'Giorgio,' Sandro says when he sees him, standing up to give the man a hug and clap on the back.

'Alessandro—good to see you,' the man says in Italian, returning Sandro's effusive physical greeting.

It's unusual to see men embrace like this in England so I'm always a little taken aback by how physical they are with each other in other parts of Europe.

'This is Juno,' Sandro says in English, sweeping his hand towards me.

'Juno, wonderful to meet you,' Giorgio says, taking my hand and kissing the back of it.

I can't help but grin at the pomposity of the gesture.

Sandro and Giorgio exchange pleasantries about their families for a minute or so before Giorgio says, 'You've heard about my new club opening up in the city tonight, right?' He looks between us expectantly.

'We hadn't,' Sandro says.

'You must come! It will be full of beautiful people like yourselves. Come. I'll put your names on the guest list.'

Sandro glances over at me. 'What do you think, Juno—you want to go?'

I'm so caught up in the moment I just nod, even though I'm not sure I'm really up for going out clubbing tonight, especially not dressed as I am. 'Sure. That sounds fun,' I say, not wanting to sound like a killjoy.

'Great! Here's the address,' Giorgio says, handing Sandro a flyer. 'See you there later.' He gives me a slow wink, then slaps Sandro on the shoulder before striding away, back to a large party at a table on the other side of the room.

A murmur of conversation flows around the restaurant after he's left and I could swear everyone's talking about us.

'You okay?' Sandro asks after we've taken a few mouthfuls of food.

'I feel like everyone's staring at us,' I mutter under my breath, picking up my water glass and taking a sip.

He leans forward and smiles. 'That's because you're so hot.'

I snort with mirth and the liquid I've just drunk comes out of my nose.

'I didn't mean you had to cool yourself off by spraying water everywhere,' Sandro teases.

I groan and put my head in my hands, peeking out at him from between my fingers. 'Oh, God, I'm no good at this.'

'At what?'

'Being sophisticated.'

He waves a hand. 'You're doing just fine.'

'It's just not very *me*.'

'Why do you say that?'

I let out a low sigh. 'I'm not like my sisters. They've always been great at projecting a confident public image. They can play the part. Not me.' I shake my head sorrowfully.

'They're like fire and ice, though,' I continue nervously when he doesn't say anything, just looks at me with that piercing gaze of his. 'They *really* don't get on. I'm not entirely sure why. No one ever tells me anything of any consequence. They treat me like the baby of the family, even though I'm only two years younger than Maya. To be honest, where my family's concerned, I think I'd rather not know what's going on in their heads. I don't really feel like I fit with the rest of them. When she was alive, my mum always said none of them could figure out where I came from.'

He reaches over and gives my hand a squeeze. 'I was sorry to hear she passed away.'

'Yeah, thanks,' I say, allowing the grief I still feel to this day to sink through my body. I let it sit there in my heart for a moment, acknowledging it but not letting it overwhelm me, before tucking it away again.

'I was only thirteen when she died and my father just sort of checked out—not that he's ever paid much attention to me—so April stepped into her role, though she's not exactly the mothering type. She's very brittle, and can be quite cold sometimes—something I think that benefits her in the male-dominated business world she works in—but it makes me suspect she's quite lonely in her love life. In fact, I don't think she even really has one. I know she goes out on dates with men, and I'm sure she sleeps with some of them, but they never last. It's like she's built an emotional wall around herself, perhaps because she feels like she needs to be responsible for Maya and I, though she really doesn't. Maya can definitely take care of herself and she really doesn't need to worry about me. I'm fine.'

It must have sounded insincere because once again he reaches over and puts his hand on my arm. 'Are you sure about that?'

I sigh, feeling the weight of my anxiety about how difficult I've found it letting people into my heart, then shrug that off too. I mustn't dominate the conversation with my personal angst; it's not fair on Sandro.

'Yes. At least, I will be once you've taught me how to be a master seductress,' I joke, picking up my fork again and finishing off my meal.

I feel him watching me as I eat but I don't look at him again until I've put my fork down and wiped my mouth on my napkin.

'You want to get out of here?' he asks, nodding at my empty plate.

'Yes,' I say, liking the idea of having a break from the intensity of sitting opposite him. 'Good idea. I could do with some fresh air.'

So after Sandro's settled the bill, which he insists on paying, we take a walk across the square and look around the basilica, enjoying a few minutes of cool relief from the balmy evening air. I'm acutely aware of his presence, even when he's on the other side of the building, and I find myself drawn back towards him after only a few minutes on my own gazing at the beautiful Renaissance art. He's a work of art all on his own.

'So, do you still want to check out that club?' Sandro asks as we exit the church into the now dark night-time air. I nod, recognising that I really should be making more of an effort to be the sort of party girl he's used to being with.

'Sure, it sounds like fun.'

'I promise you, it will be. Giorgio's clubs are something else,' he says with a loaded grin and I worry for a moment about what we're about to walk into.

When we get to the club—which turns out to be in the middle of a row of bars and restaurants round the corner from our apartment—the bouncer on the door looks me up and down as if he's assessing whether I'm cool enough to be let in. My face flushes hot with embarrassment, as I suspect he's about to decide that I'm not, when Sandro steps forward and gruffly tells him our names, protectively sliding his arm round my waist and pulling me close.

After that we're waved straight through.

The magic of *who you know.*

Inside there's a chrome and black lacquer bar in the middle of the room with a large crowd of people standing around it and a small dance floor off to one side which is heaving with dancers. On the other side of the room are high tables and stools, which are currently all occupied. It's a popular place all right.

'Let's get a drink,' Sandro suggests, already heading to the bar. For some reason all the other patrons turn to stare at us as we approach and there's something strange about the way the men are looking at me, almost as though they're sizing me up. Do I really stand out so much in my demure cocktail dress? Surely I'm not making that much of a fashion faux pas?

Once we have our drinks, we stand by the bar and I watch the crowd of people around me. They're all so confident and full of life, laughing and flirting with each other. I have a pang of longing to be one of them. To be part of a scene that I feel welcome and comfortable in. It must be lovely, being so assured of yourself and your place in society. I turn to look at Sandro, who's staring over at the other side of the room where there's a long, green velvet curtain pulled across what appears to be a doorway. A tall, burly bouncer is guarding it and, as I watch, he gives a nod to a man and woman who approach but stops a small group of men from entering.

I wonder what can be going on behind that curtain. Is there a smoky room full of card sharps back there, perhaps? Or a cool nineteen-twenties-style speakeasy, or a jazz cabaret? My heart leaps with excitement. I'd love to walk through that curtain and into the middle of one of those things.

'Is there a poker game going on back there?' I wonder aloud to Sandro.

He gives me an indulgent sort of smile. 'Not exactly.'

'So what *is* it?' I ask, irritated that he apparently knows and is enjoying the fact that I don't.

'It's a playroom.'

'A what?' I have a vision of a room full of adults all playing with train sets and building blocks. It's a weird idea, but then people can have strange fetishes—or so I've heard.

'There are beds in there where people are having sex.'

'In—in front of each other?' I choke out.

There's that indulgent smile again. 'Yeah. Some people get off on that.'

Suddenly I can barely breathe. This is the sort of thing that only happens in stories, though, right? Surely people don't actually have sex in public in real life?

From the look in Sandro's eyes I'm guessing I have an awful lot to learn about 'real life'.

'Want to go in and check it out?' he murmurs.

My first instinct is to say *hell, no* and get

straight back to the safety of our apartment, but something in his face stops me. He wants me to see it. To experience everything there is to know about sex. Just as I told him I'd wanted to on the plane.

So I swallow down my fear and give him a shaky but affirmative nod.

He nods back. 'Okay, then.'

Taking my hand, he leads me towards the doorway. I think for a second we're going to be denied entry, as the bouncer looks us up and down, but then he holds back the curtain for us to slip through. I feel a rush of fear about what we're about to see, but I keep walking, allowing Sandro to lead me inside.

And straight into an orgy.

I stand there, frozen in shock, my heart pounding in my chest as though it's trying to break out and escape as I stare at a huge circular bed in the middle of the room upon which a big group of people is doing all manner of unnerving, intimate-looking things to each other.

I jump as Sandro slides his arm around my waist.

'Quite a sight, huh?' he murmurs into my ear.

I nod stupidly, but no words will leave my mouth. My body seems to be petrified. Despite my determination to throw off my prudishness while I'm here in Italy, I know for a fact right now that I'm not going to be able to handle being here. I really don't want to stay. I really, *really* don't.

Panic wells in my gut as I watch the surreal scene of entwined limbs and heaving bodies playing out before me. What if Sandro expects me to join in with this? I won't be able to. There's no way. An unnerving tremble that began in my hands seems to be spreading through my whole body now. I can't move. I'm too terrified even to take a step. I have a sudden mad vision of one of the people on the bed reaching out and dragging me into the mêlée, where I'll be suffocated under a pile of naked bodies.

I'm uncomfortably aware that Sandro is looking at me and I turn to meet his gaze, seeing a slight frown on his face.

'Are you okay?' he asks.

I can't even shake my head because my neck is too tense.

My expression must have alerted him to my discomfort because gently he draws me back behind the curtain with him, the security of his embrace helping to unfreeze my limbs. Cupping my face, he looks into my eyes, then frowns and sighs.

'I shouldn't have taken you in there.'

Now I'm behind the curtain with the sex show safely hidden on the other side, I'm finally able to speak. 'It kind of blew my mind,' I mutter.

He rubs his hand over his eyes, then shoots me a look of concern. 'I wasn't expecting you to join in with it, you know. I just thought you might find it interesting after the conversation we had on the plane about not needing to be in love to have sex. You said you wanted to understand and experience everything, so I thought it'd be a good opportunity to see other people being totally uninhibited in the pursuit of pleasure. I thought you'd be able to handle it, but clearly I read the situation wrong.'

'That's the understatement of the year,' I mutter, my humiliation turning to frustration with myself.

He lets out a low, exasperated sigh. 'Yeah, okay. We should go home.'

'Home?' I panic for a second that he means he's going to dump me back in London and my time with him will be over before it's even begun. That I've blown it by pretending I'm okay with our deal, only to prove tonight that I'm really not.

Am I a lost cause?

I want to cry.

'Back to the apartment,' he says gruffly.

I relax a little, but only a little. I can't look at him now, though. I'm so dispirited.

'Yes. Okay. Let's go back,' I mutter, pretty sure this signals the end of our deal. How can he possibly hope to help me when I freak out so badly at the sight of other people having sex?

I'm so convinced I've ruined everything, I fully expect him to ask me to pack my things and leave as soon as we get back to the apartment.

Shame and disappointment take turns to sink through me.

So much for my sexual liberation.

CHAPTER FOUR

Sandro

SHE DOESN'T SAY a word on the short walk home.

I feel like such an asshole, I can't even bring myself to make any throwaway conversation.

How could I have thought it would be a good idea to take her into that playroom? I guess I assumed it'd be okay because she's been acting pretty offhand about what we've come here to do. In the bedroom earlier I sensed she was keen to get on with it, but I held back because I wanted to take things slowly, to have some build-up—to show her I wasn't the easy lay she thought I was. I imagined going to that club might create some anticipation. That she'd get all hot and bothered at the things she'd see there. In my mind, it had been just an extension of foreplay.

It's crystal fucking clear now, though, that all that confidence she's been projecting about having sex has been a front and I've been too distracted by my determination to control the situation to notice.

She's so subdued as I let us into the apartment that I'm afraid she's beating herself up now for not being more gutsy.

My chest aches at the anxiety I've caused her.

I need to make it up to her, *pronto*.

'Let me run you a bath,' I suggest as we kick off our shoes in the hallway.

'A bath?'

From the look on her face, you'd think I just suggested she go skinny dipping in the Arno.

'*Sì*. To help you relax after your shock.' I throw her a teasing smile, hoping a bit of humour might lighten the mood.

She blinks at me, then nods. It's a jerky movement and I'm suddenly terrified she's about to cry.

'I'll fix you a glass of wine to drink while it's running,' I say, turning away quickly and heading for the kitchen.

There is a low pull of shame in my belly as I yank open the fridge door. I can't stand to see a woman cry, especially if it's of my making. That's one of the reasons I don't do long-term relationships. No emotional fall-out to deal with.

I find an ice-cold bottle of champagne and pour a generous measure into a flute. Pausing for a moment, I take a breath and give myself a good talking-to before heading back to deliver the drink to her. I find her in the living room, perched on the edge of the sofa as if she's expecting me to throw her out any second and is primed to leave.

'Here you go,' I say, holding the glass out to her.

She takes it with a small, grateful smile and I nod, relieved she's not burst into tears in my absence.

'I'll go and run that bath,' I tell her, heading straight out of the room before she can reply.

I fill the enormous tub almost to the brim and add lots of lavender-scented bubble bath for good measure. Then I light all the candles that are positioned in colourful little semi-melted mounds around the edge and turn off the main light, casting the room into a soft, comforting glow.

If that doesn't help her relax, I don't know what will.

Except for an orgasm, of course. But that's the next step in my plan to win back her good favour.

She looks at me with wary eyes when I come out to tell her the bath is ready, murmuring her thanks before slipping off, her shoulders hunched and her chin dipped.

While she's in there, I pace the room, agitation making me antsy. I know I've got a lot of making up to do to restore her faith in me. The last thing I want is for her to decide to go home tomorrow, convinced I don't have her best interests at heart. My father would not be pleased to hear I'd pissed off the youngest daughter of Maxim Darlington-Hume in twenty-four hours flat.

And, to be honest, I'd be gutted not to get the opportunity to get to know Juno better. I've really started to like her. She's such a smart, fascinating woman who clearly has her own issues with family, which has made me feel closer to her. It seems we're more in sync than I'd initially thought.

Twenty minutes later she emerges from the bathroom wrapped in an oversized towelling robe with her long hair freshly washed, dried and hanging in a smooth sheet down her back. I have a strong urge to wrap it around my hands and pull her close, to drag that robe from her curvaceous body and do all manner of pleasurable things to her. But I know I need to tread carefully here. I don't want to spook her again. This requires some careful handling.

'I thought you might have gone to bed,' she says in a quiet voice, tapping the brush she's carrying gently against her thigh.

I move towards her, holding up my hands in a peace offering. 'I wanted to make sure you're okay.' Taking the brush from her, I gesture towards the nearest sofa. 'Sit down. Let me brush your hair.'

'Seriously?' she says, her nose wrinkled in surprise.

'*Sì*. I want to feel it in my hands.'

'Uh, okay.' She sits on the seat nearest to her, turning her back to me, and I sit down behind her and take the long swathe of her hair in my hand. It's beautifully lustrous and feels soft and smooth against my skin. I forcibly have to stop myself from letting out a groan of pleasure as the strands slip through my fingers.

I begin to smooth the brush down her hair, from her scalp to the very ends, and I smile when I hear her let out a small sigh of pleasure.

'You like having your hair brushed?'

'I love it. Though you're the first person, other than my hairdresser, that's ever done it for me.'

'It's such a beautiful colour. Like autumn bonfires.'

She lets out an *mmm-hmm* sort of noise, but doesn't say anything else.

'Why do you keep it tamed all the time?'

She leaves a small pause hanging in the air before answering, as if she's deciding whether or not to tell me the truth. 'Honestly, it draws too much attention to me when it's down, and I find that hard to handle.'

I shake my head. 'Well, I think that's a travesty.'

Her breathing quickens as I continue to stroke

the brush through her hair and after a few moments I see her visibly begin to relax, her shoulders dropping and her back arching as if it's giving her real pleasure now.

'I'm sorry about tonight,' I mumble quietly into her ear.

She tenses a little and I move the brush back up to her scalp and run it from the crown of her head to the base of her neck until she relaxes again.

'You know, I think I freaked out so badly because I was afraid you might expect me to do sexual things with you in front of all those people,' she says in a small voice.

I stop what I'm doing and get up from the sofa, moving to sit in front of her instead so I can look into her eyes.

'That's not why I took you in there, I swear. I genuinely thought you might find it "fun and… er…sexy".' I flash her a humbled smile, hoping she'll realise I'm referencing the first awkward conversation we'd ever had about sex. That I'm suggesting we're both as bad as each other.

I'm relieved to see her smile back, even if it is a little restrained.

I rub my hand over my face, wishing I could take tonight back and start again. So much for my reputation as a world-class seducer of women.

'It's not that I didn't find it sexy, exactly,' she

murmurs. 'I was just surprised by how full-on it was.'

I nod. 'I guess I'm a bit desensitised to how extreme that place would seem to the uninitiated. But we don't have to go anywhere like that again,' I promise her. 'And from now on I want you to tell me immediately if something makes you feel uncomfortable. Communication is really important. I want you to feel safe and in control, okay?'

'You still want to help me?' she asks, sounding surprised.

I stare at her, dumbfounded. 'Of course I do. Why wouldn't I?'

Her shrug is awkward. 'I don't know. I guess I thought you'd be disappointed with me for being such a wimp and not want me here any more if I'm not going to be any fun.'

'I don't think you're a wimp, Juno.' I lift my hand to her face and smooth my thumb over the soft skin of her cheek. 'I just think we need to take some time to get to know each other. To figure each other out. What I really need is for you to be open and truthful with me when we're in bed.'

'I'll try, but I don't think I'm going to be good at sexy talk.' She glances down and frowns at her hands which are so tightly linked in her lap the tendons are standing out.

'It doesn't have to be sexy. It has to be honest.

If you don't want to do something, or don't like something, you have to say so. Don't do it just to try and make me happy or to spare my feelings.'

I feel her begin to tremble under my touch and I can see from the fast tick of the vein in her throat that she's nervous.

'We'll only go as far as you're comfortable with. And we'll take it slow.'

'In the interest of being honest, I have to tell you... I'm nervous about how inexperienced and... *ordinary*...you're going to find me,' she blurts, colour rising to her cheeks. 'I know the kind of women you usually date and I'm pretty sure I'm not going to compare favourably to them.'

I shake my head, mystified that she'd be concerned about that. 'Juno, you're a very attractive woman with an incredible body.'

She won't look at me now though and just shakes her head.

'What happened to you to make you doubt how fucking *sexy* you are?' I ask roughly.

'I'm sure you don't have any experience of being made a fool of, but it strips you of your confidence,' she says quietly.

'Who made a fool of you?'

There's a small pause before she answers. 'My first boyfriend, when I was sixteen.'

She lets out a long-suffering sigh.

'I'd had men trying to get close to me before I met him—because of my family name and the attention it brings—but I genuinely thought Malcolm liked me for *me*. He was twenty-three and seemed so mature and cultured. He was also really possessive and attentive, telling me all the time how beautiful he thought I was. And even though I know I'm no real beauty I lapped it up. I really needed to believe it at that point in my life.

'Truthfully, I'd taken my mother's death really hard and he seemed so understanding about how hollow and lost I felt. Like he understood me and had my back. That he cared. He seemed so sincere. And I…believed at that point I was in love with him. I planned on losing my virginity to him. I thought what we had was real, you see, and I wanted to trust him with it, to prove to him how much I cared about him too. But then I found out from a friend that he was only dating me because I'm a Darlington-Hume.'

She pulls a disgusted face. 'She overheard him talking about the sacrifice he was making being with the runt of the litter instead of someone "more in his league", like one of my sisters. He told his friends he was "taking one for the team" by pretending to be in love with me so he could reap all the privileges that come with my family name—to benefit both himself and them, if they were nice to him. It was all a power trip. He thought being with me would open all sorts of doors for him. Once I started asking around about him, it turned out that pretty much everyone knew he was like this, except for gullible old me.' She shakes her head. 'I was utterly heartbroken and it put me off dating for a long time.'

'What a prick!' I say roughly, furious on her behalf. I know exactly the type of guy she's describing—someone who's happy to wreck a woman's self-esteem just to get ahead.

I try not to think about the fact I'm also using her for her name right now. It's not as if we're in a relationship and I'm pretending to be something I'm not—or to care about her more than I do. This is an entirely different scenario. No one's going to get hurt here.

I watch her playing with the cord of the dressing gown as she continues to speak. 'I've never had a lot of confidence in my looks. Somehow I ended up with the trifecta of bad luck in that department in my teens. After my mother died I started comfort eating and put on a lot of weight. Then my face broke out in acne. Basically, I was an overweight, spotty redhead and I got bullied a lot at school by some of the other girls. And then, later, by the press. Journalists seemed to love drawing unfavourable comparisons between my sisters and I. You've met them, right? They're beautiful—knockout beautiful—and so confident with it. I'm just not like that, no matter how hard I try to be.'

'Well, as I said, I think you're a very attractive woman and I'd very much like to get to know your incredible body better,' I murmur, pushing her fringe out of her eyes and cupping her face, forcing her to look into my eyes so she can see how serious I am. That it's not just a line I'm reeling out. Because it's really not. I genuinely find her extremely fucking tempting. She's not like the women I usually date, sure, but I like that she's different.

She's trembling hard now, but I can tell from her expression that it's with anticipation rather than nerves. But, still, I want to be sure.

'Is that okay with you, Juno?' I murmur, my heart racing as I wait for her answer.

I want to touch her so badly now I feel knots of tension building in my muscles. I want to put my mouth on her soft, warm skin and prove to her just how amazing her body is.

'Yes,' she says softly. 'That's okay.'

Juno

He's going to kiss me.

I can feel his intent as he strokes his thumb

gently over my cheek, sending ripples of pure plea-sure across my skin.

My lips tingle with expectation as I stare down at his mouth, wondering how it will feel against mine. His lips look firm, but so soft. I imagine he kisses well. Really well.

I'm nervous about him seeing me naked, but I know I have to get over it if I'm ever going to move past this sexual glitch I'm stuck on, so I push the worry to the back of my mind. He'll take good care of me. I know he will. I trust him. The whole reason I wanted to come to Sandro, apart from the physical attraction I feel for him, is because I know I don't have to worry about him only doing this to try and get something from me. He doesn't need the benefit of my family name—he already has enough power and money through his own family connections.

But he doesn't kiss me. Instead he gently parts the dressing gown I'm wearing, exposing my breasts to his gaze. His appreciation is clear in his eyes, which gives me the confidence to stop myself from covering right back up again and to let him do what he wants to me.

I watch him as he drops his head to kiss the swell of one of my breasts, running his tongue in soft sweeps just above my nipple, then tracing a gentle circle around the aureole. My breasts feel heavy and engorged and I drag in a sharp breath as he sucks down hard on my nipple, drawing it deep into his mouth, sending a wave of pure, electric sensation straight between my legs as if the two areas are connected.

'Oh…whoa…that feels so good,' I gasp.

He pauses for a moment and raises his dark head. 'Yeah? You like that?'

'Yes. Don't stop!' I plead.

He moves to the other breast, giving it the same treatment, making my head spin and my whole body flood with dopamine. The heavy, insistent throb in my core intensifies.

'Do you feel it in your pussy?' he mumbles against my skin.

I suck in a shocked breath at the intimacy of the question, then force myself to answer. 'Yes.'

He nods and I feel him smile against my breast. 'Good.' The sensation of his exhalation buzzes my skin and I can't help but smile as well.

'Your body has more erogenous zones than you think,' he whispers, sliding his hands down over my hips and round to my buttocks. Grasping me firmly, he lifts me up and drags me further down the sofa, so I'm now lying prone beneath him. I feel the heat of his hands through the material of my robe as he moves them lower to find the hem. His fingertips skim over the sensitised skin behind my knees—a place I never thought in a million years would be so sensitive to touch—and I let out a gasp as flames of desire flicker up my thighs to join with the heat already pounding through my pelvis.

One by one, he walks the fingers of one hand up the inside of my leg, his mouth still hovering over my breast with erotic intent, and I begin to drag in short, sharp pants as I feel him getting closer to the place I ache to be touched. He's casting some sort of spell over me. In my haze of lust I think I'd probably do anything right now to get what I want. What I *need*.

'You know, the whole of your pussy is one big erogenous zone.' He goes on to prove this as his fingers finally reach their destination and he walks them over my mound, pressing firmly on each side and opening me up to his exploration. Each small pressure sets off little bombs of erotic sensation through me, as if all the nerves in my body have accumulated in my vagina and are having a war with each other. But he doesn't touch my clit, which throbs with longing to join in.

I almost sob with frustration as he walks his fingertips further up my torso and away from where I desperately need them to stay.

Moving up the sofa so we're now face to face, he looks into my eyes and I realise he's checking if I'm still okay with all this.

'Please…yes…' is all I can say. I know I want something more, but I'm not sure how to ask for it. I need him to tell me.

'Have you ever found your G-spot?' he asks, his gaze searching mine.

'What's a G-spot?' I pant.

His smile is wicked. 'So much good stuff to learn,' he murmurs as his fingers glide lower again.

This time he parts me fully and I gasp as he gently penetrates me with one long finger. I'm so turned on it slips easily inside me, bringing with it another riot of sensations. He slides it deeper, watching for my reaction the whole time, and I have to close my eyes because it's too intense, too intense…

And then he hits a spot that makes me see stars and I jerk beneath him, trying to get him to touch it again.

'There?' he murmurs.

I nod and he finds it again, pressing hard in short pulses.

'Oh, oh, oh!' is all I can say.

And then his thumb glides over my clitoris and I think I'm going to die with pleasure. But it's not enough. Not quite. I need something…something more…

As if he senses my inner battle, he whispers, 'Tell me what you need, Juno. Say it, whatever it is. Say the words. You have to tell me what you want or you're not going to get it.'

A fierce blush burns my cheeks, but I'm determined to ignore it. I'm not going to let it stop me from getting what I want. I don't want this to end. I have to have more.

'Faster,' I force out. 'I need it faster. And harder.'

'Good girl,' he says with a smile in his voice and does as I ask, increasing both pressure and tempo until I think I'm going to go crazy with the joy of it. I'm so close to the brink, after a whole day of my body being primed for his touch, that I know it's not going to take much more to break me apart.

I begin to match his movements, unable to stay still, pushing myself harder against the pressure of his fingers. A low, guttural noise is building in the back of my throat, but I'm too far gone to care.

And then, as if I'm hitting a high I've been unable to reach before, the intensity of the sensation shatters and wave after wave of pure pleasure washes over and through me, making my limbs jerk involuntarily and my breath stutter in my throat. I'm unable to focus on anything but the sensation of the orgasm as it rushes through me over and over again. I let out a loud groan of relief as it finally begins to subside and turns into a gentle buzz of satisfaction.

My world comes back to rights and I open my eyes to find Sandro staring down at me, his expression one of awe, as if he's never seen anything more absorbing in his life.

And suddenly I'm shy again and intensely aware of how vulnerable I just allowed myself to be. I squeeze my eyes shut, hiding in the darkness I find there, taking a moment to centre myself. When I open them again, he's smiling at me.

'Fuck. That was so beautiful to watch,' he mutters roughly, drawing his hand away from between my legs and gently pulling my robe closed to protect my modesty.

My body gives a throb of regret at the loss of his touch.

'And that concludes your lessons for today: how to ask for what you want,' he murmurs.

'Really? You want to stop now?' I ask. I was expecting him to ask for his own orgasm in return, so I'm surprised to find he doesn't seem to want that. At least not tonight, I guess.

'More tomorrow. I promise. Time to sleep now.' He rolls away from me, and off the sofa to standing, then holds out a hand and helps me up too.

My legs feel like jelly and I have to hold on to him for a second to steady myself.

'You've not got your sex legs yet,' he jokes.

I can't help but giggle, it's so absurd.

'Thank you,' I whisper, glancing up at him with a smile and giving his arm a squeeze.

'It was my pleasure. I think you're going to make a very satisfying student.' He pushes a rogue strand of hair away from my face and grins at me. 'Now go to bed. You must be exhausted.'

'I am,' I say, yawning to prove the point.

'Then I'll see you in the morning. *Buonanotte*.'

'You're not going to bed too?' I ask.

'Not yet. I'm going to sit up a while,' he says.

I nod sleepily, grateful he doesn't expect me to stay up too. My whole body is achy and heavy-limbed from such an intense experience and I desperately need to sleep now.

He's wrecked me.

I can only imagine what a mess I'm going to be at the end of my week here with him.

CHAPTER FIVE

Sandro

I DON'T SLEEP well alone in my bed.

The memory of Juno losing herself plays over and over in my mind and, no matter how many times I jerk off, it's not enough. I can't sate this insistent urge for something more.

Her mixture of sweetness and smarts seems to have me by the balls. Not to mention that gorgeous, curvy body of hers.

Despite my firmness about not wanting to take her virginity, I have to admit, there's something really fucking appealing about the idea of taking her on a sexual journey. She's so pure and uncorrupted, it's driving me crazy knowing there'll be no climax to this scenario. At least, not for me.

I roll out of bed the next morning feeling agitated and full of a nervous energy I have trouble keeping under wraps some days. It's always been like that for me, as if my body produces too much adrenaline sometimes. It used to get me into trouble a lot when I was younger because it makes it impossible for me to sit still and concentrate. My teachers at school hated me for it. Now, though, when I feel like that, I relieve it by working on my latest sculpture till my whole body aches and I'm too tired to keep my eyes open. But I can't do that while Juno's here.

I'm going to have to think of a good alternative.

It looks as though she'll be getting more than her fair share of attention from me today. Not that I'm complaining, and I suspect she won't be either, judging by the way she responded to me last night.

The memory of it gives me another raging boner and I decide it's time I went to find her.

The door to her bedroom is closed so I tap lightly on it, wondering whether she's still asleep. It's only seven a.m. so there's a good chance she is. I've always been an early riser, even after a late night out partying.

'Juno? Are you awake?'

'Yes,' she calls back in a throaty morning voice, 'but I'm not dressed. I've just got out of the shower, so I'm only wearing a towel.'

My mind jumps immediately to those incredible breasts of hers. I imagine them glistening with water and how I'd like to lick every drop from her skin… 'Great, let me see,' I say, trying to keep my tone playful and light when all I want to do is barge in there, rip that towel from her body and do filthy things to her.

There's a short pause, and I worry for a moment that she's gone right back to being shy with me again and is going to refuse me entry.

'Okay, you can come in.'

Relief ripples through me and in that moment before I turn the handle I have a vision of her lying naked on the bed with her legs spread for me and a suggestive smile on that wonderfully expressive face of hers. But, as I push open the door, I know in my heart that that's unlikely to be the case. She's going to need a lot more encouragement to let go of her insecurity and start having more confidence in how fucking sexy she is.

As I suspected, she's actually standing in the middle of the room, looking a little awkward, with her towel wrapped tightly around her and her arms folded across her chest.

'Buongiorno, cara,' I say, keeping my eyes firmly on hers so she doesn't think I'm ogling her in her undressed state.

Sunlight is streaming in through the partly open shutters, bathing the room in a soft, golden glow. I glance at the rumpled bed, imagining her in it, tossing and turning—just as I did last night, unable to sleep—touching herself to try and relieve the same ache with which I'd had to contend.

'Morning,' she replies. Her cheeks are pink but the expression in her eyes is bright and friendly. 'Did you sleep well?'

'Terribly,' I admit, strolling over to where she's standing and leaning down to kiss her on both cheeks, taking the opportunity to breathe in her fresh, clean scent.

'Sorry to hear that. I slept like the dead,' she says, her voice coming out a little breathy.

My cock gives a throb of interest, but I ignore the urge to pull her towards me and kiss her hard. I don't want to spook her. I need to take this slow.

'I like you all wet,' I murmur with a grin.

Her eyes widen and her cheeks deepen in colour as her gaze flickers away for a second before returning to mine. She lets her arms drop down to her sides as if forcing herself to relax.

I smile, loving the warring reactions I'm drawing from her.

'I just need to dry off, then I'll be right with you,' she says.

'Let me help you with that,' I suggest, reaching out to loosen the towel from where it's wrapped across the top of her breasts, grasping both ends when it comes apart and holding it up so it's still covering her body. I'm fully expecting her to stop me, so I'm delighted when she doesn't. Instead she looks at me with a wide, trusting gaze, her eyelids only flickering closed for a second as she stands there meekly, waiting for me to do what I will with her.

Blood pounds through my veins as the powerful sense of absolute control rushes through me.

Droplets of water have pooled in the dip of her collarbone and they sparkle in the dappled sunlight as I lower my mouth to kiss her there, sweeping the dampness from her skin with my tongue.

She drags in a sharp breath and I feel the pulse in her neck begin to race as I trace my tongue along it and up to the small hollow behind her ear.

Her hair is damp and cool against my cheek as I gently bite her earlobe.

A low, gratified moan rumbles in her throat and my cock hardens fully in response.

Gathering the towel in my hands, I begin to rub it gently over the top of her back then lower to the swell of her buttocks. I kiss under the line of her jaw, then down the long column of her throat, feeling her swallow against my lips as I gently press them against it.

Letting go of one side of the towel, I bring it round to the front of her body and dab it over her shoulders and the tops of her arms, then move down to the water-speckled skin of her chest and the top of her breasts.

She's letting out little pants now, as if she's enjoying this, but just to make sure I ask, 'How does that feel?'

'Amazing,' she whispers. 'Like the whole of my skin is super-sensitised.'

'Good,' I whisper back, smiling to myself. If she's turned on just from being touched like this, what I'm about to do to her is going to blow her mind.

She inhales sharply as I get to my knees and begin to sweep the towel lower, over the tops of her breasts, then her nipples, which are standing erect and are rosy-pink after the heat of her shower. I have the strongest urge to draw one into my mouth and feel her squirm with pleasure, but I restrain myself, ordering myself not to get distracted.

As I move lower, swiping at the smooth skin of her stomach and gently dabbing into the hollow of her belly button, her fingers curl into fists at her sides.

I guess she's beginning to suspect where this is going.

Avoiding the place I'm most interested in for the moment, I get down on my haunches and move the towel in soft, smooth strokes from the tops of her thighs right down to her ankles, then back up again, pushing her thighs gently apart as I go so she has to spread her feet a little more widely apart, exposing more of her beautiful pussy to my hungry gaze. I let my breath fan over her as I work, seeing her skin turn pink under my attention and feel the muscles in her legs vibrating as I work the towel over them again.

'Relax. I'll be gentle with you, I swear,' I murmur.

She lets out a rough groan of frustration. 'I know I've still got a lot to learn about all this.'

'There's really not that much to learn. Once you've figured out what you do and don't like, it's pretty straightforward from there.'

'Really? Because it seems like a minefield to me. People make such a big deal about it.'

'Only people who are too afraid to ask for what they really want.'

'What do you want?' she asks with hesitation in her voice, as if she's worried it's too personal a question.

I smile, pleased she's asked me.

'I want to go down on you. I want to put my mouth on your hot, sweet pussy and make you moan with pleasure. I want to feel you come on my tongue.'

I hear her breath hitch in her throat and when I look up she's gazing down at me with wide, startled eyes.

'Relax, *tesoro*,' I urge her again. 'Trust me. Be proud of your amazing body. Let go.'

'But I don't know how.' Her voice jangles with nerves.

'Stop thinking and let yourself *feel*. Nothing else matters right now, just this. Just my mouth on your pussy, my breath on your skin.'

With that assurance, I finally bend forward and run my tongue down the seam of her pussy lips and over the swell of her clitoris.

She drags in a loud, stuttering breath and I sense her hands ball into even tighter fists by my head.

Dropping the towel now, I use my fingers to open her up to my gaze, locating the tiny bud of nerves that's about to give her so much pleasure. It's already swollen with anticipation and my mouth fills with saliva. I tongue her there, pressing down gently at first, then sweeping around its circumference, finally moving on to lazily flick the tip of my tongue from the base to the top, feeling her shiver with delight.

'Oh, oh, oh!' she breathes. 'That feels amazing.'

'And it's only going to get better,' I promise her, bending forward to do it again, this time with a little more pressure, flattening my tongue to make my sweeps wider and longer at first, then bringing them back into tight little circles.

Her legs begin to shake and I put my hands on

her thighs and guide her backward until she's right in front of the bed.

'Lie down,' I tell her, giving her a gentle push of encouragement. I'm enjoying this so much I'm reluctant to take my mouth off her for long. I want so much to see her come, it's making me tremble.

As soon as she's comfortably lying back on the bed, I push her thighs open wider and lower my mouth to her pussy again, using the fingers of both hands to hold her open and fully expose her clit, before restarting the sweeps of my tongue against it, beginning slowly and steadily getting faster. After a few moments I feel her begin to move with me and I smile as I realise she's finally allowing herself to relax into the sensations and enjoy what I'm doing to her.

Her hands grip the duvet on either side of her legs as I bring her closer and closer to the release she's clearly desperate for now.

'Oh, my God… Oh, my God…' She pants as her back arches off the bed and she pushes herself against my mouth. I suck down, then lave my tongue over and over her, feeling her shaking, twisting and throbbing beneath me as she comes hard, a low, guttural moan piercing the quiet of the bedroom.

And I'm in heaven. There's nothing I love more than making a woman come apart, but for some reason it's even more satisfying with Juno. Perhaps because I was worried it'd be hard to get her to trust me and relax. But that wasn't the case here.

She certainly seems very fucking relaxed right now.

I look up to see her gazing back at me with a look of absolute wonder on her face.

'Oh, my goodness, what did you do to me? I thought I was going to implode with the intensity of it.'

I grin, delighted she's so appreciative of my skills.

'I dreamt about doing that to you all night.'

'Really?'

'*Sì*. And it was even more enjoyable than I imagined.' I get up off my knees and crawl over her, flopping down next to her on the bed and turning to look into her deep-blue eyes.

'I love the way you respond to me when you let go. It's so natural. So visceral. A real fucking turn-on.'

'Do you…want me to…do something for you?'

With difficulty, I shake my head. 'No. This is about you. What you want.'

'What if I want to give you pleasure?'

I wave the suggestion away, my head telling me it's the right thing to do but my body groaning in protest. 'You already have.'

She starts to protest but I cut her off. If I don't get out of here right now, I'm afraid I'll give in and take her up on her offer. But I really can't right now. We need to take this slowly, eke out the pleasure and anticipation of it.

Pleasure delayer, that's me.

'Get dressed. We're going out for breakfast,' I mutter roughly, turning away before she can see the war raging behind my eyes.

Juno

My body is still humming as we stroll slowly through the bright morning sunshine to a pavement café in the Piazza della Repubblica, where we can watch the bustle of the farmers' market going on around us. The place is alive with colours, smells and lively chatter and I sink gratefully into my chair and order a double espresso and a rich, buttery pastry for my breakfast, very much enjoying the feeling of being a part of this wonderful scene.

I'm absolutely famished and when the food arrives I can't get it into my mouth fast enough.

It's strange, but after my experiences with Sandro last night and this morning I feel as though something's changing inside me. It's as though I've woken up from a deep sleep to find everything feels about a hundred times more intense and, somehow, *real*. Life's brighter, sharper, louder and has more depth. Perhaps it's just the dopamine rushing through my veins, but something instinctively tells me that it's not just that. It's something else that I can't quite put my finger on.

Every time I glance over at him my whole body heats with the memory of what he did to it and I have to squeeze my thighs together to try and dull the greedy ache for more. I can't stop thinking about the way his dark head looked, moving between my legs earlier. My body gives another throb of longing and I shuffle impatiently in my chair.

What the hell is happening to me? I've never felt wired like this before—as if every nerve in my body is humming with electricity.

'So, what do you do with your time when you're not house-sitting for your father's mistress or teaching naive young women how to have a good time in bed?' I ask in an attempt to put the thought of sex out of my mind for at least a few minutes. I suspect it's going to become increasingly difficult to do that when I'm around him. He's sex personified.

'At the moment I'm trying to set up an affordable artists' co-operative in London with a friend of mine, but we're constantly being outbid by the big property development companies for the sort of premises we need. Ideally we want to find a big, airy building with large windows to let in lots of light, but of course those types of properties are also ideal for loft-style apartments.'

I frown in sympathy. 'Sorry to hear that. It must be frustrating to keep being outbid.'

'Yeah.' His expression darkens as he appears to reflect on exactly how frustrating he finds it. 'I have the money—my favourite great-aunt left a decent chunk to me—but I don't have much experience in buying property and there's no way I'm asking my father or brothers for help. They'd laugh me out of the room if I told them what I was doing. None of them think I've got the skills to pull something like that off.'

'Well, for what it's worth, I think you absolutely do have the skills. You're obviously dedicated to the idea and it sounds like you're trying your hardest to make it work against fierce competition. You probably just need a bit more time for the right place to come along, and a bit of luck so you can get in there first.'

He lets out a grunt that could either be a gruff acknowledgement or a dismissal of my optimism.

'So why an artists' co-operative?' I ask, in an attempt to flip the mood back to a less stressful subject.

He pauses for a moment before answering, his gaze on the empty espresso cup he's rolling between his hands. 'Because artists get a raw deal and I wanted to help others get a foot in the door. It'll provide a support network as well as a space to create.'

'Do you make art yourself?' I ask, still not able to make the connection with him and artists in my head.

'Yeah. I sculpt.' The expression in his eyes is wary, as if I might not find this a fitting activity for a man like him.

'Really?' I'm surprised by this admission. It really wasn't what I was expecting him to say. Not that I know exactly what I *was* expecting. I guess I thought he just drifted around, partying and giving women pleasure, and perhaps that he believed being philanthropic towards a bunch of cool artists would make him look good. How very shallow of me.

'Yeah. It's something I've loved to do since I was a kid, but my father discouraged it as a career. He doesn't think it's a masculine enough pursuit for a Ricci.' He shakes his head as if this has been a bone of contention for years. 'He wanted me to go into the family business like my older brothers but I couldn't do it. I couldn't sit at a desk all day in a stuffy office. It drove me crazy. I need to have space and be able to move about and breathe.'

'So you're actually an artist?'

He lets out a disparaging snort. 'Nah. I've never sold a piece and that's what counts, right? There's a lot of competition out there and I'm not great at the whole marketing side of things. It takes smarts I don't have. That's why I'm so keen to make this co-operative successful, so I can work with other people that can help me with that side of things, and I can concentrate on the stuff I'm actually good at.'

I frown at that. 'You know, you come across as a pretty smart guy to me.'

He gives another snort. 'Well, I can read and write, but I struggle with staying focussed on stuff that doesn't interest me. I'd never be able to run my own business like my brothers are going to. Not that I'd want that.' I can tell how much this affects his pride by the way his hands grip the coffee cup.

As if sensing my thoughts, he puts the cup down and sits back, waving a hand to show me he doesn't really care. 'I wasn't exactly a model student at school. I hated sitting still at a desk there, so my grades were awful. The only reason I passed the most basic of exams is because I was fucking my maths teacher at the time.'

He flashes me a wry grin but all I can do is stare back at him, shocked by this piece of information.

'How old were you?'

'Sixteen.'

'And how old was she?'

'In her mid-twenties.'

'And she asked you to have sex with her in exchange for giving you a good grade? That's such an abuse of power!'

He shrugs, as if it's of no consequence. 'I was getting really close to being kicked out, which would *not* have pleased my father. It would have reflected badly on the whole family. Though it wasn't exactly a chore—she was a beautiful woman… I liked her a lot.' He picks up the coffee cup again and examines it as if it's the most fascinating thing in the world. 'At the time, anyway. Not so much after I found out I wasn't the only one she was fucking.'

More horror slides through me. 'She was sleeping with other pupils too?'

Again he shrugs, his focus still on the cup. 'Yeah. One of the other guys that got into trouble a lot walked in on us kissing one day. He caught up with me later and told me she was a whore and that she'd been sleeping with him too. At first I thought he was just jealous and I got angry and lashed out. It turned into a pretty serious fight—

I broke his nose—which got me hauled into the headmaster's office. I refused to talk about what the fight was about, as did the guy whose nose I'd broken, even though I was threatened with expulsion. After my father had been summoned and convinced the headmaster keep me there—I suspect with the promise of a large cash donation—I confronted her about it. She acted as if she thought I'd known that's what she did and it wasn't a big deal. But I hadn't known. I thought I was special.'

He shakes his head and finally looks up at me, his eyes hooded. 'She was the woman I lost my virginity to. I'd thought that was special too, but it turned out I was just one in a long line of guys she'd "made into a man".'

My whole body feels hot with anger at the way this despicable woman treated him. 'Sandro, that's awful!'

He puts down the cup and waves a dismissive hand, but I'm sure I see a flicker of something dark in his eyes. 'It wasn't so bad. It taught me that I loved sex and that I was good at it. Seducing and pleasing women gave me a focus for all my pent-up energy.' His smile is full of humour now and I wonder if I've imagined the pain I'd seen. 'It turns out I'm very good with my hands.'

He winks at me and slides one hand across the

table to link his fingers with mine, but I can't bring myself to smile at his joke.

Because it's not funny.

In fact, none of what he's just told me is okay.

No wonder he hides behind this mask of non-committing playboy and doubts his intelligence.

'Hey, no need to look so serious,' he says, his smile dropping away. 'It was a long time ago.'

'Yes. But even so. It must have really knocked your sense of self-worth. And I'm guessing that's probably had repercussions ever since.'

He shrugs and looks away across the piazza, as though it's not a big deal.

'Sandro,' I say quietly, and wait for him to look at me again. 'What she did to you was awful. Wrong. Criminal, almost. You know that, right?'

He just raises an eyebrow at me. 'I guess it wasn't a great way to behave.'

'Have you talked to anyone else about it?'

He shakes his head. 'Only my father at the time, and he brushed it off like it meant nothing, so I've not told anyone else since. What's the point anyway? It was years ago.'

'So I'm the only other person that knows?'

I feel privileged that he's trusted me with something so personal, but also keenly aware I should try to help him recognise the effect it might have had on the choices he's made in his life ever since.

'Yeah, well, it's not something I'm particularly proud of so I don't go shouting about it to everyone I meet.'

'You have no need to feel guilty about it.' I stare into his eyes, trying to express how serious I am about that. 'You were young and she took advantage of you in the worst way possible. It wasn't your fault, or a case of you not being smart enough.'

He just gazes at me for a moment and I think I see something shift in his eyes. 'Well, thanks. I appreciate you saying that. But let's not talk about it any more. It's done with. I'm fine.'

I want to argue, but I can see from the closed expression on his face now that he really wants to change the subject.

So instead I reach across and gently stroke my thumb over his cheek to let him know I'm on his side.

Out of the corner of my eye I see a flash of light, as if the sun just caught on something reflective, and I turn to look towards where it came from. There's a group of people milling around a couple of stalls there, but I can't see what would have caught the light.

'You know, it's weird, but I keep feeling like we're being watched,' I say, shaking my head at how ludicrous that sounds.

'Really?' Sandro says, glancing over to where

I was just looking. 'Perhaps you've had too much coffee and sugar and it's making you twitchy.' He turns back to face me, his eyes gleaming with seductive mischief. 'Perhaps we should think of a way to burn off that energy. They have large bathroom stalls in this place, big enough for two.'

I can't shake the discomforting knowledge that he's using sex to distract me from something he doesn't want to face.

'Not right now,' I say, giving him an awkward smile.

'Okay, then, perhaps we should just go for a walk,' he suggests, looking a little miffed that I'm failing to respond to his flirting.

Tamping down on the feeling of unease that's swirling through my stomach, I give a nod of agreement. 'Sure, that sounds like a good idea.'

Sandro stands up and tosses some money onto the table for our breakfast. Is it my imagination or are his movements more jerky than usual?

We take a stroll down to the grand Piazza Duomo and once we're in front of the magnificent cathedral Sandro tells me from memory the fascinating history of the artwork as we walk around it. I soak it all in, aware that only a small part of everything he's telling me will stick in my brain.

His voice is so wonderfully animated and warm, I feel myself sinking into the pleasure of listening to him speaking. He has a seemingly encyclopaedic knowledge of the works of art and architecture of the buildings, and his interest in and respect for the artists is glaringly apparent. A warm glow of admiration builds in my stomach as he becomes more and more animated, his eyes shining with excitement. He's such an engaging person to listen to when he's on his subject.

And I thought it wasn't possible for him to be more attractive than he already was.

'How do you know all this?' I ask, gazing into his eyes, which are sparkling with exhilaration.

He shrugs. 'I guess I remember it because it interests me. Maria, my father's mistress, is an art historian and she talks to me a lot about it. We've toured the city a few times together when I've made trips here.'

Looking at the pleasure in his eyes, I have a sudden mad urge to reach up on my tiptoes and kiss him. And then, just as suddenly, it occurs to me that we haven't done that yet—kiss on the mouth, that is. He's had his mouth pretty much everywhere else on my body, just not my lips.

A slow roll of heat makes my skin tingle, and I feel myself flush, so I turn away and pretend to study the statue we're standing next to. 'And what about this one?' I ask.

He launches into its provenance but, despite

my interest in the history of it, I can't stop my mind from wandering back to the story he told me about his experience at school—how the teacher had used him and has probably made him feel as if the only worth he has is in taking women to bed. My heart squeezes in distress at the thought of this and I'm aware of a disconcerting swirl of shame growing in the pit of my stomach. Am I not reinforcing this belief for him by appearing only to be interested in him in a sexual way? The idea of that fills me with horror.

'You know, I really should get back soon. I have so much work to do,' I say determinedly, shooting him a look of regret. I don't want to cut our time short here, but the unease I'm feeling about our agreement is making me antsy. I need some time on my own to process how I'm feeling about it.

He frowns at me, clearly a little taken aback by my sudden withdrawal, then shrugs. 'Okay, if you want. That's cool.'

But I know it *isn't* cool. None of this is. And I need to figure out what to do about that.

CHAPTER SIX

Sandro

JUNO SHUTS HERSELF in the study as soon as we get back.

I'd hoped to be able to distract her and get her straight back to bed but it seems she's determined actually to do some work while she's here. Which leaves me with fuck all to do.

Just knowing she's in there and that I can't get near her is driving me crazy and I find myself pacing up and down the living area, not sure what to do with myself. I want to be with her again. I have an oddly intense craving to see that look in her eyes when she's listening to me talking again, as if she's absolutely fascinated by what I have to say. I love that I know more about the art here in Florence than she does. It gave me a real buzz to be able to impress someone as smart as her with my knowledge about it.

That doesn't happen a whole lot to me. Usually when I'm with a woman she's not interested in anything I have to say. It's my skill in bed she wants. It used to upset me when I was younger but now, in my mid-twenties, I've come to terms with the fact I'm never going to be the kind of guy from which people expect to hear anything of any note. It's always been like that and I thought it always would be. Until I met Juno.

She has a way of making me feel good about myself. I don't know how she does it exactly. It's as if she sees and responds to something in me that most people miss.

Her horrified reaction to my story about what had happened at my school shook me up, though. I'd never considered before that it had been anything other than a rejection from a woman that I'd thought, in my naivety, I'd been in love with.

My father hadn't made any kind of reference to it being an abuse of power so it had never occurred to me that it was. Her age and standing had been of no consequence to him, so it hadn't been to me either. In a way I think he'd actually been proud of me for apparently having seduced such an attractive woman and I'd taken that as a huge compliment. My father isn't an easy man to impress and I've not had many opportunities to do it in my life so it was important to me. I guess that's how I managed to talk myself into getting over it so quickly.

But Juno's reaction made me think about it in a whole different light.

I guess that's why I want to be with her right now. I want to talk to her some more about my life, to see whether there are other things on which she can give me her unique perspective. Even though I know she's only here to learn how to get her sex life on track I have this powerful urge to show her more of the real me. Which is unusual. Normally I'm totally focussed on disguising my soft under-belly for fear of being laughed at or rejected, but I don't believe she'd do that to me. She's too kind, too considerate—and such a genuine, determined sort of person—one who's prepared to put herself out there and be vulnerable, and to ask for help despite the risk of failure and humiliation. That kind of bravery is something I haven't come across very often. It's actually pretty fucking inspiring.

I pace a while longer, then have the bright idea of taking her a drink and suggesting she take a break. Surely it can't be good to work that intensely for that long?

Poking my head around the door to the study, I see she's sitting in front of her laptop with a pair of wire-framed glasses perched on her nose, staring intently at the screen.

'Juno?' I say when she doesn't seem to notice my presence.

She jumps a little in her seat then lets out a low laugh. 'Sorry, I didn't see you there.'

'Can I do something for you? Fetch you a drink, a snack? Bring you to screaming orgasm at your desk?'

She grins shyly and I'm delighted to see her cheeks flush.

'Just a cold drink for now, please,' she replies, to my disappointment. I'd really hoped she'd take me up on the orgasm. 'I need a while longer to finish this article I'm reading.'

I go to the kitchen and fix her an orange and soda, feeling disgruntled that I've not been able to tempt her to take a proper break. Maybe she needs a little more encouragement…

On the way back to the study I stop off in my bedroom and grab something I think she might actually feel forced to take a break for.

'What's your PhD on?' I ask her as I hold out the drink.

'Thanks,' she says, looking up from the screen to take it from me and swallow a few gulps of the cold fizzy liquid. Once she's done, she places it on the desk and leans back in her chair, stretching out her arms behind her and wincing a little as if her neck and shoulders are stiff. I try not to stare at the way her breasts press against the cotton of her T-shirt.

'I'm conducting research into sudden cardiovascular death in athletes and looking for a way to recognise early the signs of heart disease through the study of human genetics. If we have a better way to identify it, we've got more chance of catching it early and treating it.'

I sit down hard on the edge of the desk, a wave of awe rippling through me. 'Wow, that's really fucking cool.'

She smiles. 'It will be if I find a way to stop it happening.'

'Why did you choose that as a subject?'

A small frown pinches her brows. 'One of my friends in senior school was a brilliant athlete and one day, right out of the blue, she just fell down dead while playing hockey.' She swallows and I see the pain she clearly still feels about this flash across her face.

'It turned out she had an undiscovered heart defect. She was only fifteen and the sweetest, most caring person you'd ever meet. We'd been friends since infant school and she was my rock—the person I'd go to when I was struggling with who I was and how I felt about losing my mother. My whole world fell apart all over again when I lost her. So I decided to do something good and positive with my life to try and stop it from happening to other people.' She smiles, then turns back to the computer screen.

A throbbing sensation is growing in my throat, as if my heart has risen up from my chest to relocate itself there. This woman is truly amazing. She totally puts me to shame. What the hell have I done with my life up till now? Fucking nothing. I've been playing at being a grown-up. Even though I've been trying pretty hard recently with the artists' co-operative, I've still not managed to make it work. So at the age of twenty-five I've achieved nothing I'm truly proud of.

This has to change. It's time I grew a pair and made a monumental effort to make things work out. But in order to do that I have to start believing I'm smart enough. Clearly my attitude needs a serious adjustment.

But I guess, right now, I'm going to have to content myself with using the skills I've already honed to give her a reward for all the hard work she's been putting in.

My version of giving back to those in need.

And I want to see a smile back on that pretty face of hers.

'You should take a proper break for a while,' I suggest. 'It can't be healthy to sit at a laptop for so long.'

'I can't. I've got so much to do,' she mumbles.

'Perhaps you need a lesson in priorities.'

'Hmm?' is all she says to this, already engrossed again in what she's reading on the screen.

Okay. Time to get serious.

Getting up from the desk I move round to where she's sitting and pull the wheelie office chair backwards, away from the desk.

'Let me help you.'

She blinks at me in surprise, a cute little frown pulling at her brows. 'Help me? What do you mean?'

I don't answer. Instead I climb under the desk, then pull her chair towards me so she's back in her original position and I'm trapped under the desk. 'Spread your legs,' I instruct her.

'What are you going to do?' she asks with a nervous quaver in her voice.

'You'll see. Just do it.'

I think for a moment that she's going to refuse, but when she sees how serious I am she does as I ask, her legs quivering a little as she pushes them as far apart as the chair will allow.

'Now start reading what's on the screen aloud to me.'

'But it won't make much sense out of context...' she begins to argue.

I dismiss her argument by sliding my hands

between her thighs to find her underwear, which I tug to one side, exposing her beautiful pussy.

'What are you doing?' She gasps.

'Just read,' I demand, reaching in my pocket to find the vibrator I'd stashed there earlier. 'And don't stop, no matter what happens.'

She peers down into the gap between her body and the desk and sees what's in my hand. Her eyes go wide. 'What are you going to do with that?'

I smile and turn it on to vibrate. 'Something good,' I promise her. 'Now read.'

'Wait, Sandro, you really don't need to—'

'I want to do this, Juno,' I interrupt. 'It's going to give me just as much pleasure as you, believe me. Now do as I say.'

So she begins to read the technical-sounding article out loud, her voice shaking a little with anticipation. It shakes even more as I slip my hand back between her legs and gently strum the tip of the vibrator, first up one soft, creamy-skinned thigh, then the other. She lets out a breathy giggle of surprise, but to her credit she doesn't stop reading.

I'm rock-hard as I listen to the wobble in her soft, smoky voice and have to force myself to concentrate as I continue the buzz between her legs, this time moving the vibrator all the way up to stroke between her pussy lips.

She yelps in surprise and loses her thread for a

moment so I withdraw the vibrator until she starts reading again, then put it back in the same spot, smiling to myself when this time she doesn't stop, even though it's clear she's having trouble concentrating. Every time I glide it over her clitoris her voice jumps a little and I relish the way her words become more and more ragged and broken as she finds it increasingly difficult to keep reading out loud. My cock throbs against the confines of my trousers, but I doggedly continue with my task, determined to give her the reward I promised myself I would. Just seeing the way her body is twitching with the need to come is giving me tremendous pleasure.

And then her words start to slur and jumble together as if her brain is switching its focus fully to the sensations building between her legs and is no longer sending the right signals to her mouth.

'Oh, God, Sandro… Oh, oh, oh! I can't… I can't…' She squeaks as the sensation clearly reaches a peak and her body begins to shudder with her orgasm.

Her fingers gripping the arms of the chair are white as she rides the climax, and I push her back from the desk to see she has her eyes screwed shut and that her face is flushed with colour.

Very slowly, I remove my hand from between her legs and take a moment to enjoy her sexily dishevelled state. Her whole body is slack and floppy now in her chair.

My work here is done.

For now.

Finally, she peers down at me through half-closed lids, a small, slightly sheepish smile on her face.

'Whoa. That was intense,' she murmurs. But I can tell from the awe in her tone that she enjoyed it.

I smile at her and get up from my kneeling position. 'There's another lesson for you—how to stay focussed through distraction.'

'I'm not sure I did so well with that one,' she half-moans, half-laughs. 'But I have to admit,' she adds huskily, 'it's a great incentive to work hard while you're around if that's the kind of help I can expect to get.'

Juno

I wake up the next morning with a smile on my face.

After our lesson in 'maintaining focus under pressure' Sandro persuaded me to finish working for the day, which I have to admit didn't take much persuasion, what with my body and brain feeling like jelly, and we went out for food at a lovely family-run restaurant round the corner, away from the tourist trail.

Even though Sandro seemed happy with how sequestered it was from the bustle of the city, I'm pretty sure I spotted someone standing around on the pavement opposite holding up a camera in our direction when we were leaving. But I was probably just being paranoid again. How they'd known that the two of us would be there, I couldn't begin to imagine. I doubt very much a paparazzo would waste his time trailing around the city after us. We can't be of that much interest to the press here.

I push the worry about it out of my mind. It was probably just a tourist taking a picture of the quaint little backstreet and had nothing to do with us being there at all. Being around Sandro and his electrifying presence seems to be messing with my perception of reality.

Speaking of which, it really is time I figured out how to return some of the sexual pleasure he's been giving me. I'm intensely aware that I've barely even touched him. He must be beginning to get fed up with how unforthcoming I am in that department and I want him to feel as wanted as he's making me feel. Also, it's something I really need to get a handle on if I'm going to feel confident about making my own sexual advances in the future.

Frankly, I think I need to learn how to give a damn good blow job.

Picking up my phone, I put it on the private-browsing setting and go about searching the Internet for the best tips and hints on how to do this. Some time later I come up for air, my mind buzzing with information and my body with nerves.

Once again I feel the weight of my inexperience pressing down on me. How does one go about offering a man fellatio? Especially one who doesn't appear to be interested in getting an orgasm for himself. I want to do this for him, to show him I'm not a selfish lover, but also because I feel that he deserves it after all the work he's putting into giving me the confidence I need.

I don't want him to think it has to be all about me. I'm intensely aware that he's not really getting anything out of this. He's being so selfless. And that doesn't sit right with me.

I'd like to pay my way, as it were.

Walking into the kitchen, I find Sandro sitting at the breakfast bar dressed in a pair of navy chinos and a soft-looking grey T-shirt that stretches becomingly across his broad, muscular back. My heart rate immediately picks up at the sight. It's so unfair. The man could probably wear a bin bag and still look amazing. His hair is wet from the shower and shines a dark blue-black in the bright morning sunshine that's pouring into the room.

His hair is a thing of real beauty. It looks perfectly rumpled all the time, as if he's spent hours getting it that way, but I've not seen him touch it once. I think it just has the God-given ability to fall sexily into place without human intervention.

'Good morning, *bella*,' he rumbles in a just-rolled-out-of-bed voice and my body responds accordingly, sending a dart of pure need straight to my core.

'Morning,' I reply, annoyed that my own voice sounds so unattractively rough.

I flit around the kitchen, pouring myself coffee and buttering a piece of toast, before going over to join him.

He's been sitting there watching me the whole time, drumming his fingers lightly on the countertop. There's a restless sort of energy about him again this morning and, as I see him fiddle around with the teaspoon in front of him, winding it back and forth between his fingers, the action suddenly reminds me of a girl I was at school with who did the same thing with pencils. She also found it intensely difficult to sit still.

I smile at him as I sit on the stool on the other side of the counter. 'Can I ask you something personal?'

'Shoot.'

'Do you ever have trouble staying interested in tasks that take a long time to complete?' I have a suspicion I know what's going on with him now but I want to know more before I suggest it.

'I guess so. Sometimes. It depends what it is. If it's something I love—like my sculpting, or sex—I can focus on it for hours, or days, without needing to take a break.'

'But if it doesn't interest you?'

He stares down at the counter and shrugs. 'I can't make myself sit down and do it, no matter how much I tell myself I need to. I guess I'm just not as smart as you.'

He says this curtly and it's clear he's struggling with his pride, uncomfortable with admitting his perceived weakness to me.

'You know, it's not necessarily about being smart, it's more about being able to manage your concentration levels so you can stay focussed long enough on tasks in order to finish them.' I take a breath. 'Have you ever been tested for ADHD?'

'What the hell is ADHD?' He scowls at me as if I've just suggested he might have a horrible disease.

'Attention Deficit Hyperactivity Disorder. It would explain why you find it so hard to focus on certain tasks, like involved paperwork, or anything that doesn't really interest you. There are ways to manage it if it's affecting your life.'

I think I can actually feel him retreating into himself.

'I've never been tested for anything,' he says roughly. 'My teachers said I was just lazy and not cut out for learning.' He lets out a snort. 'And there's no way my father would publicly admit to one of his sons having any kind of learning disability.'

'That's a shame. It could have made a real difference to your time at school.'

He shrugs. 'Maybe. Maybe not. I don't think there's anything wrong with me, though, I just never enjoyed learning at school.'

I give him an acquiescing smile. 'I'm sorry. I didn't mean to suggest there was anything wrong with you.' My face is hot with dismay at having offended him. 'Anyway, you've clearly found a great outlet for all that energy you have.'

This seems to break the tension and he raises his eyebrows and gives me a provocative smile. 'Yes, fucking is a great way to expend some energy.'

'I was actually talking about your sculpting,' I correct him with a self-conscious grin. 'You know, I'd love to see some of it sometime.'

He assesses me for a moment, as if trying to

decide something. Such as whether I'm serious, or just saying that to be nice.

'Really. I'd genuinely like to see it,' I say.

After another moment's hesitation, where I'm sure he's going to refuse, he finally gives me a nod.

'Okay. I have some of them here.' He still looks a bit unsure, though.

'They're here? In the apartment?'

'*Sì*. I keep some of my work here. Maria lets me use one of her spare rooms as a studio.'

'Okay, great,' I say, jumping off my stool. 'Then let me see it.'

Sandro

My hands shake a little as I unlock the door to the room at the back of the apartment that I use as a temporary studio when I need to get the hell out of London and find some peace.

I usher her inside. I've not shown my sculptures to anyone but Maria and I'm nervous about how Juno's going to react. I have a nagging desire for her to like them. To think I have talent. It matters to me that she does. Especially after the conversation we just had about my struggles with learning. Her implication that it could be down to more than a lack of smarts needles at my mind. But I can't think about that right now. I'll give it some brain space later, when I'm alone. As much as I'd like it to be true, I'm afraid that it'll turn out not to be the case and I'll end up looking like an idiot for even suggesting it to anyone else.

The room my studio's in is small compared to the rest of the apartment but there's enough space for a work bench, which is pushed up against the wall, and for five of my sculptures, which sit on the floor so you can walk around them.

Three are of abstract shapes that change as you move round them, as if they flow into themselves like waves. One starts out as a bunch of different-sized curvy fronds at the head of the sculpture, like reeds in a pond, and becomes the body of a woman lying on her back as you move round to view the side of it. Another is a collection of arms reaching towards the sky as if waving at the sun, which then becomes a gnarly-looking oak tree as you walk around it. The majority of the things I make are made from interesting bits of wood I've found on beaches or in forests and then whittled or carved to make the shapes I need. Others are built from bits of scrap material and wire.

'You have to walk around them,' I say, bending down to turn on the floor lamps so she can see how the light transforms them.

She nods and begins to circle them, peering intently at each one as she does so. I can't read the expression on her face and the nerves jumping in my stomach make me queasy.

After she's studied every single one, she finally looks at me. To my relief she gives me a huge smile, her face lighting up with pleasure. 'Oh, Sandro, these are beautiful. You have to get them shown in a gallery. People will go wild for them.' Tears glint in her eyes and she blinks them back, seemingly embarrassed by her visceral reaction.

I love it, though, more than I can express. It's exactly the type of response I'd hoped for and it means a hell of a lot to me, coming from her.

Truth be told, I'm terrified to show them to anyone in the art trade for fear of being laughed out of the building for how amateurish they are. 'It's not easy. As I said before, there's a lot of competition, and you need good business skills as well as artistic talent to sell your work.'

'You know, I could help you with that,' she says, her expression deadly serious. 'If you'd like me to?' She peers at me from behind her fringe. 'Perhaps it can be my way of paying you back for helping me out.'

I try to ignore the sting of shame that reminds me she's already helping me out, only without her knowledge, and bend down to turn the lamps off again to give me a reason to break eye contact with her. 'You don't need to pay me back,' I mutter, glad she can't see my face now.

I hear her clear her throat, and when I turn round to look at her again she's moved closer to me, so close I catch the sweet, musky scent of her. 'Okay, well, maybe I could do…something else for you, then,' she says in a teasing sort of voice that I've not heard before. There's desire in her eyes, and determination, and my cock springs fully to attention in anticipation of what it might mean.

'Oh, yeah? What's that?' I murmur, unable to tear my gaze away from the expression in her midnight-blue eyes. It's mesmerising. I've never seen her like this before and it's doing all kinds of strange things to me.

Without saying a word, she undoes the button on my trousers, then tugs down the zip. 'Can I touch you?'

I give a jerky nod.

Her eyes don't leave mine as she slides her hand into the waistband of my boxers and takes a firm hold of my cock. I'm already hard, but as her cool fingers wrap around me another hard pulse of blood joins what's already relocated there.

She looks up at me with startled eyes. 'I have no means of comparison, other than pictures I've seen, but am I right in thinking your penis is very large?'

My smile is wide and wicked. 'Yes. I have a big cock.'

But to her credit she doesn't wimp out. Instead she drops to her knees in front of me, slides down my trousers and boxers and then boldly wraps her hand back around my shaft.

I suck in a breath, aware that I don't want her to think she needs to do this for me. I've deliberately not pushed for my own pleasure up till now to take the pressure off the situation, to allow her time to become comfortable with the idea of touching me, but to be honest it's been really fucking hard. As has my cock whenever we've been together.

'Juno, you don't have to…'

She looks up at me imploringly. 'I want to. I've never done this before and I want to experience it. Can I? Please?'

As if I could say no to this woman when she's on her knees.

'Yes.'

She explores me tentatively at first, as if she's fascinated by the weight of my dick and the way it feels in her hand. Then she wraps her fingers firmly around my shaft and starts to pump her fist firmly up and down, catching the sensitive end each time with the pad of her thumb, and any thoughts of ending this fly right out of my head.

'Fuck. That feels so good,' I groan as my sex-starved body jumps in delight. Then without warning she moves closer, unwraps her fingers and takes my cock deep into the heat of her mouth.

And that puts an end to any more thoughts of arguing for her to go slow. There's no way I'm going to be able to stop this now. It feels way too fucking good.

She's a little hesitant at first with her movements, but every time I give a groan of pleasure it seems to spur her on and her movements become more confident. She begins to explore and play with my cock, swirling her tongue around the head, then gently poking the end of it into my slit. Then back to sucking. She's using her tongue to lap me as she reaches the tip and the added pressure there is making me wild.

Fuck. This is not going to last long if she keeps doing that.

I try to think about something else…my sculptures that still need work, the gallery opening in the city I want to go to in a few days…but nothing seems to be working.

I decide the only option is to give in and let it happen.

'Wrap your hand around the base and squeeze a little,' I command, deciding I might as well make a lesson out of this too.

She does what I've asked and pleasure shoots

through my balls as she continues to work her mouth over me, taking me deep, then sweeping her tongue hard over the head of my cock. I sense my orgasm growing and grip the edge of the table to steady myself.

'A little faster,' I say, groaning with satisfaction as she does it. The mind-melting pressure continues to build, until the only thing I can think about is her hot mouth around my cock and the hard flicks of her tongue against it. And then I'm coming, spurting into the cavern of her mouth, my whole body on fire with relief, but she doesn't stop or draw away from me until I stop twitching.

When I finally get myself together and look down at her, she's grinning up at me like the cat that got the cream.

'You've really never done that before?' I mutter, my voice guttural and low.

'Never. But the Internet is a wealth of information.' She seems delighted that she's been able to make me lose my mind like that.

'You're a quick study.'

She shrugs, then smiles. 'I pride myself on doing my research properly.'

'Still, there's always room for improvement,' I cajole her, giving her a wink to let her know I'm teasing. 'And practice makes perfect, right?'

CHAPTER SEVEN

Juno

SO PRACTISE WE DO.

Over the next few days Sandro introduces me to all sorts of new physical delights.

I quickly come to enjoy sensory deprivation in the form of a blindfold and headphones playing loud music, especially when it goes hand in hand with the lavish use of Sandro's tongue, mouth and hands on my body. I also find, to my surprise— once I pluck up the courage to allow it—that spanking can actually be rather pleasurable. It's something to do with the release of endorphins into the bloodstream, he tells me afterwards, which heightened my orgasm and left me in a panting, shuddering mess of exquisite sensation.

The days fly by like that, with me working on my laptop during the day, him disappearing into his studio to work on his sculptures, then the two of us taking increasingly longer lazy lunch breaks in a nearby café before returning to the apartment to continue to feast on each other's bodies.

I'm bolder now with my advances and requests for what I want and Sandro seems pretty pleased with my progress. But he still won't take my virginity, much to my frustration.

Even though I'm very much enjoying our time in bed, I feel as though I'm missing something important. A closeness, perhaps. I think it's something to do with the fact we haven't actually kissed on the lips. I can understand why he might want to keep himself cut off from the emotional side of sex—we're going our separate ways soon, after all—but it leaves me longing for something more. Something I can't quite put my finger on.

I'm taking a break for a little while, after a particularly intensive hour of working, and to distract my whirring brain decide to go and see what Sandro is working on.

When I gently push open the door to his studio I see that he's in there working on a new piece, which seems to involve an awful lot of bright copper wire that he's meticulously twisting into amazing shapes to form what looks like the cascading branches of a weeping willow tree. He's so involved in what he's doing he doesn't notice me standing there, and I don't want to break his concentration, so I content myself with watching him work for a while.

It occurs to me, as I stare at the careful, sure movements of his fingers, that for once he seems completely calm. His usual restless energy is noticeably absent and instead he appears to be completely serene and deeply focussed on the task at hand. It's as if he's channelling the whole of himself into his art.

Something about that makes my heart lurch in my chest.

It's a truly awe-inspiring thing to behold and I experience a wave of pure admiration for him. I have a mad urge to do something—*anything*—to make him see just how unique and incredible his creative talent is. That he shouldn't listen to his father and let him influence his feelings about his sculpting.

I want him to be able to see himself in the way that I see him. To *know* how good he is. To accept that there's so much more to him than just being good in bed. That there are different types of intelligence.

I watch him for another moment or two before leaving him to it, determination to help him recognise his talent for what it is surging through my veins.

I'm not sure how I'm going to do it yet, but I know I'll find a way.

* * *

On Friday night I'm fully expecting Sandro to want to go to the hottest new restaurant, bar or club, so I'm surprised when he suggests we call for takeaway pizza from the local pizzeria and eat it at home.

While we're waiting for the food to be delivered, he drags me into the bedroom and introduces me to the delights of nipple clamps.

The painful pleasure from the clips mixes with the delicious sweep of his muscular tongue over my clitoris, which does something magical to my body, as if the two areas are connected and feeding off each other's stimulation. Whenever he increases pressure in one area, I feel it in the other one too, until I'm gasping and moaning uncontrollably, unable to concentrate on anything other than the intense sensations he's creating in me.

Afterwards, I lie panting for breath after an orgasm that seemed to go on for ever, and when I look up at him Sandro is watching me with a perplexed expression on his face.

'What's wrong?' I ask, wondering if I've committed some sort of post-orgasm *faux pas*.

'I was just wondering why you came to me for help—other than hearing about my amazing reputation in bed, that is. I can't believe you don't have men asking you out all the time.'

I let out a snort of surprise, which I quickly cover with a small cough. 'That's kind of you, but I don't really. Not any more. I try to keep well out of the limelight now, after what happened with Malcolm, and I'm extremely wary about the men that approach me.' I swallow. 'Actually, the reason I came to you was because I knew there wouldn't be any danger of anything like that happening with you. And because I like and trust you.'

He's looking down at the bedspread now with a frown and for a second I wonder whether I've spooked him with that final comment. Was it verging on too emotional?

'And hopefully you find me just about tolerable too?' I joke, hearing the nervous quaver in my voice.

'More than tolerable,' he says, looking up now and giving me one of his heart-stopping grins. 'And I feel privileged to be the person you trust enough to help you get past your hang-ups.'

I smile back, though a strange, heavy weight seems to have lodged somewhere in my chest.

I push it away.

'Well, I really couldn't see any of the men I know agreeing to such a preposterous-sounding request. I probably would have given them heart attacks if I'd suggested it. Not that there are many to choose from. The two men I've dated since Malcolm were both really gentle and unassuming. Beta, I suppose you'd call them. Unthreatening. Thinking about it now, I suppose I was attracted to them for that very reason. They made me feel safe, which was important to me after what happened. Neither of them were exactly proactive when it came to initiating sex.'

'Lazy bastards,' Sandro hisses with a disgusted wave of his hand.

I smile and shrug. 'Maybe. My last boyfriend, Hugh, was the sort of person that would stay put until someone moved him and I was too insecure about sex to make anything happen myself.'

'It sounds like you need to adjust the preferences on your dating profile.'

'I don't have a dating profile. I only ever meet men through work.'

'Like this guy you're so keen to impress—*Adam*, is it?' He says the name as if he's offended by it.

'Yes,' I reply, a little bemused by that. He's not even met him so his insinuation that he's not worthy of my attention is a little misplaced.

'What is it about him that gets you so hot?' he asks. There's an aggressive undertone to his voice now, as if he feels a need to compete. He's such an alpha male.

'He's one of the brightest minds in our area of research. I've had some really enlightening conversations with him about my PhD topic. He really knows his subject. And he's clearly going places. I wouldn't be at all surprised if he ends up with a Nobel prize.'

'A Nobel prize, huh?' Sandro raises a derisive eyebrow as if he doubts this very much.

'Probably,' I say, bristling a little on Adam's behalf.

'He sounds to me like the kind of guy that thinks way too much of himself. Especially if he's happy to pass up the opportunity to be with a smart, attractive woman like you.'

'He really doesn't,' I argue, although thinking now about the dates we'd gone on, he'd mostly talked about himself and asked very little about me. 'He's a busy, in-demand guy who everyone holds in high esteem and wants a piece of. Especially women. He has every right to be a bit full of himself. He's worked hard to be top of his game, so he's entitled to be picky about who he chooses to spend his time with. And how,' I bluster, though I'm less sure of myself now.

'And this is the guy you're so desperate to get into bed?' Sandro mutters with such distain I feel a shiver of indignation run the length of my spine. 'He sounds like a total narcissist.'

I feel myself getting hot with irritation. 'Actually, he's exactly the kind of man I want to spend the rest of my life with—someone who'll be able to look back on his time and know he's made a difference to the world. Someone who'll stimulate me intellectually.'

The door buzzer goes and he rolls off the bed to go and collect the pizza. 'Well, before you propose marriage to him, can I recommend you check he can stimulate you in bed as well? I think you're gonna find that's just as important,' he says as he exits the room.

'That's the plan,' I call after him, with a confidence I'm not feeling any more. It's funny, but it occurs to me now that ever since I've been here in Italy with Sandro I've not given Adam a second thought. Until just now when he mentioned him.

I guess that's the power of Sandro's charisma coming to the fore.

Meeting him has really opened up my eyes to how sexual impulses can befuddle your brain and cause you to act in all sorts of uncharacteristic ways.

Hormones have a lot to answer for.

But I have to keep my head on straight. We're only going to be together for another couple of days. The trouble is, after talking to Sandro about him, I'm beginning to wonder whether Adam really is the sort of man I should be chasing. Whether he'll give me the kind of love and affection I'll need from a long-term partner. Whether he'll make me feel alive, like Sandro does when I'm with him.

I push this rogue thought from my mind. I'd be crazy to start imagining there could be anything more between Sandro and I. He's made it clear he loves his free, non-committed lifestyle and I need someone steady in my life, not someone who's going to forget I exist the moment I walk out of the door.

Sandro

For the first time in my life I'm wishing that time would slow down instead of speed up. To my surprise I'm really enjoying having Juno here with me in Florence. Things come to life when she's around and she has a way of brightening up the room whenever she's in it, as if she emits some kind of positive force. It seems to be infecting me too because I find myself smiling all the time. And the sex is incredible. I've never been with anyone so openly and honestly responsive. There's no pretence with her. No acting cool. No game-playing. She finds such joy in learning new things. It's inspiring and refreshing.

And I don't want it to end.

I'm also having a hell of a job maintaining my

determination that she should lose her virginity to someone else. I've come close to giving in a couple of times, when she's had her hand wrapped around my cock and all I can think about is how amazing it'd feel to thrust it inside her hot, tight pussy. But I don't want the responsibility of being her first. No matter what she thinks, there would always be an emotional attachment between us because of it, and I don't want that.

It could make things way too fucking complicated.

Speaking of complicated, my father calls me that night in a good mood to congratulate me on the successful job I'm doing of rehabilitating my image. Apparently there's been a lot of interest in his social realm about Juno and I, which surprises me, but then I suppose we'll be viewed as a pretty unlikely couple and people are always curious about that sort of thing.

I'm actually really regretting the phone calls I've been making to the paparazzi now, after getting to know Juno better. I'm hoping she won't see any of the pictures that my father tells me have come out in the Italian press. Luckily she seems completely uninterested in reading gossip pieces or looking at social media so she should miss them.

But I'm worried about any possible backlash

when she gets home. I'll feel like shit if the press starts to hound her there. So we'll need to be more low key from here on in. No more tip-offs to the paparazzi. The only trouble with that is there's a new gallery opening in the city tomorrow night, which I'd really like to attend, and they have a famous, well-respected Italian artist exhibiting so the place will be crawling with press.

But there's no way I'm going to sneak out and leave Juno at home. I don't want to lie to her about where I'll be. I've already done enough skirting around the truth as it is.

I'm walking towards the kitchen to fetch myself a stiff drink when I hear the sound of Juno's voice coming from her bedroom. She's left the door slightly ajar and through the small gap I can see her sitting up against the headboard, talking to someone on her mobile.

I know I shouldn't eavesdrop, and begin to walk away, but the sound of my name stops me in my tracks.

'...having a really amazing time. He's not at all what I expected.'

There's a small pause and I take a couple of quiet steps back to her door and peer through the crack again to see a frown cross her face.

'Maya, don't say things like that! You clearly

don't know a thing about him if that's all you've got to contribute.'

There's another pause, where she taps her fingers restlessly against the bedspread while she listens to her sister's response.

'Actually, he's an incredibly astute, sensitive and generous person. And oh my God, Maya, is the guy talented!'

Another pause and a frown.

'As a sculptor!' She shakes her head at what she clearly feels is her sister's crass misunderstanding.

'He's shown me some of his work and it's knockout. I mean, the man is incredibly talented. He should be exhibiting it. I know people would fall over themselves to buy his pieces.'

A warm feeling is rising through me, beginning deep in my belly and rushing up through my chest. Her praise is like a drug, rushing through my veins, making me high on happiness.

I listen in for another minute, unable to tear myself away now, but when the talk appears to turn to a discussion about their father I slowly back away and go to fix myself that drink.

Though strangely, when I get to the kitchen, I realise I don't need it any more.

Saturday night rolls around and I leave it to the last minute to tell Juno about the gallery opening.

'You don't have to come,' I say, trying to make it sound as if I don't care either way.

'No, no, I'd love to go with you,' she says, her eyes shining. 'Hey, you should take some videos of your sculptures so you can show them to people there. There might be some useful contacts you can tap up. My father always says he makes his most important deals outside of the boardroom. It's probably the same for artists. You need to meet socially with the people who could support and promote you. Dazzle them with that Ricci charm.'

She gives me that heart-melting, warm smile of hers.

I try to smile back but my facial muscles seem to be frozen. The idea of failing in front of her makes me feel sick.

'No. I'm not ready to show them to anyone yet,' I say gruffly.

She looks a little shocked at the forcefulness of my tone.

'I'll do it soon. Just not tonight,' I add to save her feelings.

'Sure. Okay,' she says, giving me what feels like a pitying smile.

I bristle, but don't react, though I'm aware of a familiar shame sliding through me.

We get to the gallery an hour after it opens its doors. I've deliberately made us fashionably late in the hope we'll miss the photographers—not that I think Juno would recognise it as such. As she's come to discover, I'm a terrible timekeeper.

Juno smiles at me as we step inside, giving my hand a squeeze, and we make our way through the thick throng of people standing around chatting and clutching flutes of champagne.

I smile back at her, marvelling at how well she fits in with this crowd. She's wearing a simple but elegant forest-green slip dress, which she bought on one of our excursions a couple of days ago, and she's pulled her hair into a loose knot on the top of her head with her fringe clipped up away from her eyes for once.

She's not hiding here tonight and is actually making eye contact with the other guests. I know how hard she finds it to socialise with people she doesn't know, so this behaviour both surprises and gratifies me. She's doing it for me. I know she is.

We tour the gallery, looking at the art and making small talk with one or two of the other people there who are doing the same thing.

'There's the gallery owner,' Juno whispers into my ear a few minutes later, nodding first at the information programme she picked up at the door, then towards a lean, balding man who is holding court in one corner of the room.

I feel a tightening sensation in my chest.

'Yeah, I see him,' I mutter, but don't make a move that way, and I can't look at her in case I see disappointment in her eyes. I really can't handle that right now. But this isn't the right time to try and push for an exhibition of my work. I need more time to prepare.

'I'm going to find the ladies' bathroom. Back in a mo,' she says, handing me her glass to hold and striding stiffly away.

I watch her go, frustration swirling in my gut, then turn to scope out the room to distract myself from the gnawing feeling of guilt that joins it, smiling at the women who turn to look at me.

For the first time in my life, their interest leaves me cold.

Juno

I walk up to the gallery owner with my heart in my throat. I so desperately want this to go well, but I'm afraid of making a mess of it and consequently making Sandro angry. But I have to do it. It would be an absolute travesty for his talent to go to waste. For him to let his father's prejudice get in the way of what could be a really successful future as a professional sculptor. He just needs a break—for someone to give him an opportunity to prove himself—and, after that, I know he'll fly.

'Excuse me,' I say to the guy, who is surrounded by a throng of arty types, all crowded round listening to him talk.

He turns to look at me and my stomach gives a horrible swoop of nerves. If this doesn't work, Sandro's going to be furious with me. But it will work, I tell myself. It has to.

'It's a beautiful gallery you have here,' I say with a smile. 'Juno Darlington-Hume,' I add when he gives me a perplexed look. 'I'm here with Sandro Ricci. I'm his manager.'

He nods, clearly recognising the name. 'Have you seen Sandro's sculptures?' I ask, bringing my phone out of my pocket and opening the video app where I've stored some short videos that I took of the sculptures when Sandro was taking a shower.

'I didn't know he sculpts,' the owner says, bending to take a look at my screen.

'He's really good,' I say, 'And he's looking for somewhere to exhibit them.'

The guy nods and takes my phone from me, peering down at the video of my favourite sculpture, then clicking through to look at more of them.

I hold my breath as I wait for his reaction, crossing my fingers and praying for good news.

'These are very interesting. I'd like to see them. Give me a ring next week and we'll set up a meeting,' he says, handing me a business card.

My hand shakes as I take the card. 'Thank you. We'll do that.'

I walk back to where Sandro is standing, my legs wobbly with relief. He watches me approach with a dark expression on his face.

My throat tightens with tension. I'm worried he'll be offended that I took such liberties with his work and I give a small cough before speaking. 'I showed him your sculptures, pretending that I was your manager. He wants to see them.' I hold up the card I've been given. 'He said to call him next week to make an appointment.'

My heart hammers in my chest as I wait for his response. He's frowning at me as if he can't believe I'd had the nerve to do that.

'You showed them to him without my permission?' The fury in his voice makes me quake.

I give a tense shrug and tilt my head to one side, feeling tears of disappointment pool in my eyes. 'I was just trying to help. Please don't be angry with me. They're so beautiful, Sandro. They deserve to be seen.'

He stares at me for a moment longer, then lets out a rough groan deep in his throat. 'You make it really fucking hard for me to be angry with you when you look at me like that.'

'So you'll call him?' I ask in a shaky voice.

'I told you—I'm not ready to show them yet,' he

says tersely, taking the card from my outstretched hand and crumpling it into a ball before pocketing it.

I open my mouth to protest, but then close it again. He has to want to do this himself. As frustrated as this makes me feel, I know it'll probably be counterproductive to push him any harder on it. The will to make it work has to come from him.

'Let's get out of here,' Sandro mutters. 'We can't stay now.'

I allow him to lead me out, feeling tension in the bunched muscles of his arm that he's slung around me, which he drops as soon as we're out of sight of the gallery. We walk back to the apartment in uneasy silence, my blood pulsing hard through my body. Perhaps I shouldn't have interfered. But I had to. It was a great opportunity and I would have regretted not trying to help him later. I know I would.

He lets us in through the door and shucks off his jacket, still not saying a word to me.

'Okay, maybe I shouldn't have done that without asking you.' I can hear the anxiety and a hint of resentment in my voice as I shut the door behind us. 'But you're so talented, Sandro, and sometimes we all need a bit of a push from the outside.'

He stares back at me, his dark brows drawn into a frown. Angry tension buzzes between us.

I want to cry.

'Please don't be angry,' I whisper, barely able to get the words past my painfully constricted throat. 'There's so much more depth to you than you believe. Your father and that awful teacher did you such a disservice, letting you think you're not good enough. That you're not smart and sensitive and talented. Because you are. You are!'

I can see a muscle working in his jaw and watch as he swallows, his Adam's apple bobbing in his throat. I want to lean forward and kiss him there, nuzzle his soft warm skin, make everything okay between us again. But I don't. Instead I wait, my heart fluttering like a caged bird.

Then without a word he reaches out and pulls me firmly against him, lifting his hand to cup my face. His dazzling eyes stare intently into mine, flashing with frustration, hurt then finally acceptance, and my stomach does a slow somersault.

I sense that we're tipping over some sort of edge. Something's changing between us. There's a fizzing sensation in the pit of my stomach and my heartbeat thumps hard in my throat as the tension builds.

And then, suddenly, he brings his mouth crashing down onto mine and kisses me hard, his lips firm and assured. I shudder with pleasure as I feel the hot slide of his tongue penetrate my mouth.

It's the most wonderfully intimate sensation in the world, and the most terrifying. I sense myself falling down some sort of rabbit hole from which I'm pretty sure I won't be able to climb back out. All I can think about are his lips owning mine, his tongue searching out the most intimate spaces within me. He moves against me and I lose my balance and take a stumbling step backward, feeling my back hit the wall behind me. He pins me there, his hard body pressed firmly against mine, his arousal digging into my stomach sending great waves of need between my thighs, but there's also something else. Some strange buzzing sensation against my leg.

What the hell is that?

Finally we break apart, gasping for breath, our bodies pressed wantonly together.

'Is that you vibrating or me?' Sandro asks in a voice heavy with lust.

And I realise that it's my phone in my bag that's been caught between our legs.

'I think it's me,' I say, automatically reaching for my phone in my flustered daze to check the screen, grateful for a moment to recover from the intensity of our kiss. A kiss that meant a lot more than it should have done.

'Oh!' I say, looking down at my screen, confused by what I'm seeing.

'Who was it?' Sandro asks in a concerned voice, glancing down at the screen too.

The name *Adam Cormack* is written there.

'Why's he calling me on a Saturday night?' I ask dumbly into the silence.

Sandro pushes himself away from me and folds his arms in front of him. 'It's probably a booty call,' he jokes, though his voice has a sharp edge to it.

'What's a booty call?' I ask.

'It means he wants you to go over to his place for a fuck,' he says roughly, not looking at me now. His body language is stiff, as if he's retreating from me—from the situation—as though he's worried he's interrupting a private moment between Adam and me. Which is ridiculous. It's him and I who were interrupted.

'Well, he needs to do much more than just call me to get me to do that,' I say lightly, feeling uncomfortable.

'Yeah, you make him work for it,' Sandro says. But there's something very wrong with the way he's acting now—as if none of this is of any consequence to him. It's all just part of another lesson he's giving me.

I try not to care, but my heart weighs heavily in my chest and my body yearns to be pressed up against the strength of his again.

'I guess there's still a lot for you to teach me,' I

say, pressing my hand against his chest, trying to rescue the previous mood. His heart beats a steady rhythm against my palm. 'Let's go to bed,' I suggest, going for a teasing tone in my voice.

But, instead of smiling, Sandro lets out a grunt of disgust.

'That's all I am to you, isn't it?' His eyes are full of an indignation that shocks me. 'Just a real-life blow-up doll to practise on and manipulate.'

'What? No! Of course you're not. That's not what I mean to imply.'

He steps away from me and strides towards his bedroom, the muscles across his shoulders pulled tight with tension.

I catch up with him as he steps into the room and I lay my hand gently on his back, horrified to feel him flinch under my touch. 'Sandro. Please don't be angry with me.' Hot tears begin to gather in my eyes again. But I don't want to cry in front of him. I don't want him to think I'm that emotionally weak.

He turns back to stare at me for a beat, a muscle ticking in his jaw, then a look of shame flickers across his face.

'*Shit*. I don't know what made me say that. I'm just feeling messed up tonight.' He wraps his arms around me in a tight hug and carries me to the bed, laying me down and joining me there. Rolling onto his back, he reaches for me and deftly lifts my body on top of his so we're lying chest to chest. 'But you know how to shut me up, right?' he murmurs darkly, skating his hands down to my hips and pulling up my dress, then urging me to shuffle up his body. As I do this, his fingers find the sides of the lacy knickers I bought at the same time as the dress and he tugs them down my legs.

'Sit on my face,' he demands.

I hesitate for a moment, wondering whether I should do it or insist we talk about what just happened first. But he doesn't seem to want to talk, and I don't know what I'd say to make this situation better anyway.

'Do it, Juno. I want you to smother me with your pussy,' he urges. 'Teach me it's not okay to speak to you like that.'

Again, I hesitate. It's not my style to be forceful in bed, but I know that's something I need to work on, and I want to give him what he's asking for.

So I shuffle further up the bed on my knees until I'm positioned right above his mouth and dip down to press myself against him. I feel his groan of satisfaction vibrate between my legs and deep into my core, then the powerful thrust of his tongue inside me. I cry out from the pleasure of it. It's such a lewd, intense feeling, and I find to my surprise that I love the idea of being in control of this, knowing he's captured beneath me, a prisoner to my whim and my body. The feeling of power is heady and I begin to move with the rhythmic thrust of his tongue.

Sweat pools between my shoulder blades and runs down my spine as his fingers grip my hips and we move together, faster and faster, me using him purely for my own pleasure. Teaching him that I'm on top now. I'm the one in control. That he has to give me what I want.

And oh, God, I think I'm losing my mind. I want this to go on and on and on. But I also want more. I need more. His tongue alone isn't enough. There's still an aching void inside me that needs to be filled, to be satisfied. To connect with him.

My trance breaks as I suddenly become aware that his grip on my hips has become harder and more urgent, and I realise to my horror that he's having trouble breathing.

I jump off him, distraught that I've let myself get so carried away. That I'd not noticed I was hurting him.

'Sandro, I'm so sorry. Are you okay?' I cup his face and stare into his eyes. 'I'm so, so sorry!' I can hear the panic in my voice. I can't believe I let that happen. That I wasn't thinking about him at all. Only about myself and my pleasure. And my power over him.

But, instead of looking relieved or angry, he flips me over so I'm now on my back and kneels over me, shaking his head and kissing my cheeks, my forehead, my mouth, to calm me.

'Never apologise!' he growls against my skin. 'Never apologise to me.'

He pulls my dress roughly over my head and lands hard kisses over my breasts and stomach, moving ever downward till he's back between my legs. He puts a hand under each of my buttocks and lifts me up while bringing his mouth down between my legs again.

'I worship this pussy. I fucking worship it.' He hisses against my mound, my clitoris, my vagina. His tongue laves me again, pushing open my folds and expertly finding the spots that give me the most intense pleasure. I buck up towards the touch of his tongue, wanting it harder, deeper.

Sensing my need, he pushes a finger inside me. But it's still not enough. I ache for more. I need more.

'Please, Sandro. I want to feel your cock inside me. Please! I need it. Please!' I beg him through heavy sobs of breath. I'm aware of the desperation in my voice, and it seems he is too, because he stills his motion and raises his head to meet my gaze.

We stare at each other for long moments loaded with unsaid questions and answers.

'Are you sure?' he whispers, his eyes intense with a plea for me to be totally honest with him.

'Yes. I'm sure. I want it. Please, Sandro. I need you to help me. Please just help me out with this.'

This seems to be enough to convince him because he gives a sharp nod, then leans away to open a drawer at the side of the bed and take out a little foil packet.

I watch with wide eyes as he quickly gets undressed then rolls on the condom and moves back to kneel between my thighs, our faces now level and his bright eyes gazing into mine.

'Ready?' he whispers, his voice a sweet caress all of its own.

'Yes. Ready,' I say, drawing in a steadying breath.

I feel him line up our bodies, then there's a pressure between my legs which is strange, wonderful and frightening all at once. Then without another word he slowly pushes inside me, bringing with him a sharp pain that makes me wince and ball my fists.

'Are you okay?' he murmurs, holding still and stroking his thumb over my cheek in a soothing motion until I feel the pain begin to subside.

'Yes. I'm great.' I smile up at him, my head hazy with all the new sensations I'm feeling. And there are many.

He gently draws back out, then pushes into me

again with slow, careful strokes, watching my face the whole time, checking my reaction. Checking I'm okay.

And I am okay. More than okay. I'm in heaven. Now the pain has receded, having him inside me feels like magic. It's the most wonderfully connected state I've ever been in. It's intense, but the sensation both excites and arouses me. Makes me yearn for even more. And then, when he moves his hand to where our bodies connect and presses down firmly on my clitoris, I can't help but let out a low keening sound of pleasure.

He continues slowly to move inside me until I'm able to match his rhythm, my breath leaving my body in small gasps as he pushes me closer to the edge of the orgasm that's beginning to grow deep inside me.

Our bodies slide together, moving in perfect sync, and as the pleasure grows, beating a steady, inimitable rhythm inside me, I begin to lose all sense of my surroundings. It just becomes him and me, suspended together in our state of bliss.

And then it breaks over me, my release rushing through my head and flashing in my eyes. For those few seconds, I think I stop breathing.

As the feeling begins to subside I slowly become aware of him again, the hard press of his body against me and the softness of his skin as it slides against mine. I love it. I absolutely love it. And I love the sounds he makes as he continues to thrust inside me, caught up in his own world of pleasure.

A few strokes later he lets out a low guttural growl and shouts, 'Fuck, Juno! Fuck!' His whole body shudders above me as he climaxes and he pushes himself as deep inside me as he can, holding us there locked together, as close as we can get to each other.

After a while he carefully slides out of me. 'Are you okay?' he asks, pushing an escaped tendril of hair out of my eyes.

Words seem to have completely deserted me so I just nod and smile.

'Let me run you a bath,' he murmurs, rolling away from me and getting up out of bed.

I lie there, listening to the water running, feeling spaced out and unreal.

'It's ready for you,' Sandro says, coming back into the room a couple of minutes later.

'Thanks,' I reply, getting out of bed and wincing a little as I realise I'm a little bruised.

As I pass him in the doorway to the bathroom, I lean up to give him a gentle kiss on the lips, pressing my body close to his. 'Thank you,' I whisper.

He smiles, but there's something in his eyes that sends a small jolt of unease through me.

'It was my pleasure, *bella*,' he murmurs, then turns away before I can question him about it.

I wash quickly, then spend a couple of minutes luxuriating in the warmth of the water, letting it soothe my aching body.

Well, that's it, I think to myself. I'm no longer a virgin. I don't know quite how to feel about it. In some ways I still feel exactly the same, but in others, ways I can't quite describe, I feel as if I've just taken a big jump forward in my life.

Coming out of the bathroom, I see Sandro has changed the sheets and is lying naked in the middle of the bed, his hair wet from the shower he must have taken.

He grins at me. 'I thought you might like a come-down cuddle,' he says in that beautiful husky voice of his.

There's no way I can refuse that, of course, so I get onto the bed and snuggle up close to him, breathing in the fresh, citrusy scent of his shower gel, amazed to feel my stomach fizzing with lust again.

But it seems he's keen we don't do anything else tonight and pulls me towards him so my back rests along his front, spooning me tightly against him. I'm aware of the soft exhalation of his breath on my neck, and the heat of his body pressed securely against me, and in my blissed-out state I sense myself beginning to drift off to sleep almost immediately.

I wake some time later and find to my surprise and delight that he's still in bed with his arm tightly wrapped around me. It's the first time he's ever slept with me and the discovery that he didn't get up and leave the moment I fell asleep makes my chest feel as if it's turning inside out.

And for the first time since we got here I'm scared—not about being here in bed with him, but about the fact I'm not going to be here with him for much longer.

CHAPTER EIGHT

Sandro

I KNEW THAT taking her virginity had been a mistake the moment it was over.

Not that it wasn't the best, most exhilarating mistake I've ever made.

After holding myself back for so long it had been a blessed relief finally to be inside her. But that, of course, now came with its own problems— namely the emotional connection I've been trying to avoid since we got here, not to mention the guilt of having given in to my needs when I'd instructed myself to let her keep her virginity for someone she was in love with.

But after seeing her reaction to Adam's call, and then hearing her tell me she thought I was smart, sensitive and talented, something snapped inside me. Something primal took me over and I pushed aside all my perfectly logical arguments. In that moment I decided he didn't deserve the honour of being her first if he hadn't recognised what an amazing woman she is.

I wanted it to be a great experience for her, one she'll be able to hold on to for ever and remember with warmth and happiness. And I wanted to be the one to give that to her.

I'm certainly going to remember it, no matter what happens next, because it was truly amazing for me too.

This whole week with her has been amazing.

Spending time with Juno has helped me find a calmness I've never experienced before. I think it's because of the way she listens to me—like she really understands and is interested in what I'm saying—and she treats me with such respect and compassion.

I don't want her to leave. Not yet.

Now we've finally fucked, I feel it's my duty to introduce her to all the different positions available. I wouldn't be doing her any favours if she left thinking the missionary position is the be all and fucking end all.

'Hey,' I whisper as she begins to stir in bed next to me. I've been lying here with my mind racing for the past half hour, wondering how to handle things this morning, but as soon as she opens her eyes and looks at me I simply say, 'Stay here for another week with me.'

'What?' she asks blearily, blinking the sleep out of her eyes and struggling to sit up.

'I can't let you go back to London when you still have so much to learn,' I say, pushing her rumpled hair away from her face. 'A whole new world of sex has just opened up now you've handed in your v-card and I don't want you going off half-cocked thinking you know it all. I feel it's my duty to complete your education.'

I wait with bated breath as she stares at me for a few moments, as if she's having trouble understanding what I'm saying. 'You really want me to stay for another week?'

I shrug, trying to look as if it's not a big deal to me whether or not she does. 'Sure. That ought to be enough time to get you straight.' I raise a teasing eyebrow.

There's another heavy pause while she appears to think about it. 'Well, I guess I could keep working from Florence. It seems to have been okay doing that so far,' she says slowly, still sounding a little unsure. 'And it's done me the world of good being away from London for a while.'

'Great, that's settled, then,' I say, sliding my hand around her waist and pulling her warm, naked body against me, already rock-hard at the thought of all the new scenarios I'm going to introduce her to.

She giggles as I push my cock against her belly, signalling my intent.

'And then I really should get back. I've got so much going on back at home, so many responsibilities,' she murmurs without much conviction. I get the impression she's trying to sound offhand about staying on but that really she's just as taken with the idea of a whole week of fucking as I am.

'Then I guess we shouldn't waste any time,' I whisper against the crook of her neck as I begin to kiss my way down her body, my blood already rushing with the thrill of all the pleasure to come.

We spend the next few days happily twisting ourselves into ridiculous contortions, in between bouts of laughter and shouts of pleasure, as we find new ways to make each other lose our minds.

By the time the middle of the week comes around I think we've done the entire Kama Sutra and have made up a few of our own positions too.

I've never had so much fun with a woman and I wake up each morning feeling the dread of time slipping away from me.

I watch her with hooded eyes as she gets dressed on Friday morning, gracefully slipping on her underwear and brushing out her beautiful long hair.

It's less than two weeks since we first arrived here, but she seems like a totally different person now. She's lost the timidity I saw when we first met at that party in Chelsea. She's standing taller now, as if she's proud of her body and pleased with the pleasure it can give her—and other people, though I don't want to think too hard about that.

'Let's take a trip out to Montaione for lunch today,' I suggest, wanting to capture her interest before she sits down to do more work. I want to spend the whole day with her. It feels important that we do that, now we only have a couple of days left together. 'It's only thirty-five kilometres away and it has some amazing views of the Tuscan countryside.'

'I should really work…' she begins, predictably, but then to my surprise she checks herself. 'But I'm not going to today. I can catch up another day. Lunch sounds wonderful.'

I smile, deciding to make sure the experience is as memorable as possible.

The *taverna* I've chosen for lunch is perfect. It's up high in the hilly town and has sweeping views over the vineyards and olive groves from its terrace.

From the simple menu we select large bowls of fresh, green salad dotted with succulent chopped tomatoes and juicy slices of chicken breast and wash it down with ice-cold white wine produced in the region. A white canopy flaps in the gentle breeze above us as the sun beats down heavily on the terracotta tiles.

'Ah, this is heaven!' Juno exclaims after our empty plates have been taken away.

'Would you like anything else to eat?' I ask, nodding towards the dessert menu the waiter has left for us.

She pats her stomach. 'I couldn't eat another thing. In fact, I could probably do with walking my lunch off.' She gives me a mock-piteous look, which I can't help but smile at.

'Yes, poor you. Let's take a stroll through the trees to the south of here,' I suggest.

Once outside the town's border, we stroll along the quiet country lane and through a thick forest of trees until we come out into fields of long grass dotted with vibrant red poppies, their magnificent heads bobbing gently in the breeze.

I watch her stride through the field, her arms flung wide and her fingertips brushing the tops of the plants. She turns to look at me with an expression of such ecstasy, my whole body rushes with joy. She looks so perfect there in her white sundress, her normally pale skin now toasted a light honey from a week and a half in the Italian sunshine. Her hair gleams like burnished copper in the sunlight and I take a mental picture of the scene, wanting to remember it for ever.

A little farther along, there's a lone tree standing in the middle of the field, its branches casting a long shadow over the ground.

'Let's sit under that tree and take a break,' I suggest.

She nods, flapping a hand in front of her face. 'Good idea—a bit of shade would be most welcome right now.'

Once we're under the tree, she lies down on the cool earth with a satisfied sigh and I go to join her, immediately rolling on top of her and caging her with my body. I have an urgent need to be close to her, to soak in every molecule of her being.

'How do you feel about al fresco sex?' I murmur into her ear as I bend to kiss her throat, which gleams with perspiration.

'I feel good about it,' she murmurs back, her fingertips lightly brushing over my back, sending desire rushing up and down my spine. 'But won't someone see us?'

'Not with the grass so high,' I reassure her, sliding my hands down her body to find the hem of her dress and kissing her deeply, her mouth hot and wet under mine.

It only takes moments for me to shrug off my shorts and T-shirt, suit up and be inside her. I feel the fresh air on my back and breathe in the heady mixture of Juno's unique scent—sex and the organic smell of the earth around us—and in that moment I know there's nowhere else I'd rather be.

Afterwards, when we're both sated and damp with sweat, we slowly get dressed again, then stroll back through the poppies, enjoying the sensation of their caress on our bare legs. I really don't want to leave this place, but I know we have to. That this is going to end soon.

We're both quiet on the journey home, lost in our own worlds, sun-kissed and sexually satisfied.

I push away a niggle of despondency as we drive back into the bustle of the city, the magic of the afternoon already slipping away.

We've not talked much today, but it's been a comfortable quiet between us. A wordless under-standing of just *being*. It strikes me again how much calmer I feel when I'm around her, like the usual whirlpool of thoughts and overabundance of adrenaline lessens to a more manageable level.

But then that could be down to all the sex we've been having. That would take the liveliness out of anyone.

Juno excuses herself to take a shower as soon as we get back and I'm fixing myself a cold drink in the kitchen when my mobile begins to ring.

Tension lodges in my gut when I see it's my fa-

ther calling. What the hell does he want? I'm un-
reasonably annoyed with him for ruining my cosy,
secluded bliss with Juno today and I almost ignore
it. I stop myself at the last second from pressing
the 'reject call' button, though, because I know
from experience that my father doesn't like to be
ignored and won't put up with it for long. He'll
just call again in half an hour, then every half hour
after that till I pick up.

'*Pronto,*' I say after clicking the 'answer call'
button.

'Sandro. I want you to go to a charity ball at
the Hotel Magnifica Vista in Piazza della Signo-
ria tonight. Take Juno with you and make sure
the press get some good photos of the two of you
together,' my father says without ceremony. 'I've
had word from your brother's future parents-in-
law that they're pleased with your relationship with
her. It shows you to be a more responsible character than they'd had you down as. It's good for both
their and our public image if it looks as though the
family playboy is finally settling down.'

This would be fine if there was any chance of
that happening, but the sinking feeling in my gut
reminds me that Juno isn't and probably will never
be interested in settling down with a 'playboy'
like me. As she's pointed out a number of times,

she needs more intellectual stimulation than I can offer her.

Trying not to let my torment colour my voice, I say, 'We can't make it tonight. We have plans.' No way do I want to waste one of the last nights I have with her at some tedious charity ball.

'Then change them,' my father barks. 'I want you there.' My stomach sinks even lower. I know what the likely outcome will be when he gets like this; it's his way or the highway, which in real terms would mean excommunication from the rest of my family.

I try not to sigh with frustration, but the pause I leave clearly does the job anyway.

'I hope we're not going to fall out over this, Sandro,' my father says in a dangerously low voice.

'No. We're not,' I concede, running through the issues in my mind. First, I'll have to talk Juno into going—which could be pretty tricky, because it's just the sort of thing I can imagine she'll hate to go to—then I'll have to find some way to persuade her to have her photo taken, which she'll also hate and probably refuse to do.

Frustration and guilt swirl in my gut.

'Good,' my father says, clearly already sure of his victory. 'There's a tuxedo of mine in the closet of the spare room you can wear. Make sure you both look the part.' Then he hangs up without even saying goodbye.

Wearily I drop the phone down onto the counter, then jump when I see movement in my peripheral vision.

'Whoever that was, I get the impression they're not in your good books right now,' Juno says with a grin.

I try to smile back, but fail. I just can't summon the energy for it. I feel drained and edgy now.

'It was my father. He wants us to go to a charity gala to represent my family this evening.'

Instead of looking displeased, I'm surprised to see her smile again. 'We can do that.' Her brows pinch together as she studies my tense expression. 'Unless you really don't want to.'

I sigh and rub my hand over my face. 'He didn't exactly give me much choice.'

'Then we'll go,' she says, her eyes glowing with a compassion I've come to love.

'Are you sure? It'll be really fucking boring and stuffy.' I don't want to mention that we're expected to pose like stuffed mannequins for the camera at this point. I'll tackle that little glitch later.

'Sure I'm sure. I'd love to help you out.' She moves closer to me, bringing with her the scent of sunshine on her skin. 'After everything you've done for me, I think it's about time I paid you back.'

'Okay. If you really don't mind.' I lean down and kiss the top of her head, pushing away a surge of guilt about the things I've already taken from her that she doesn't even know about. 'Let's get changed and get it over with.'

Juno

'It's a black-tie do, so we'll have to get trussed up for it,' Sandro says as I turn away to go and get ready for this impromptu night out.

'Oh, God, I don't have any clothes for that sort of party,' I say, suddenly realising the folly of being so quick to agree to this. But I don't want to let Sandro down when he needs me. Not after everything he's done for me. And I want him to be happy. Very much so. So much so, I'd rather not think too hard about it.

He frowns, then waves his hand towards the bedroom we're not using. 'Borrow one of Maria's dresses.'

'Really? She won't mind?'

His expression is unconcerned. 'Not at all. My father bought them all for her anyway.'

'Okay, then.' I nod assertively, as if there's nothing at all weird about me wearing one of his father's mistress's dresses out on a date with him.

'Would you do something for me?' he asks as I go to turn away again.

'Of course.' As if I could deny him anything when he's looking at me like that.

'Wear your hair down tonight.'

I raise my hand to touch where I've caught it in a ponytail at the nape of my neck. 'Okay. If you like.'

'I do like,' he says, strolling over and reaching behind my head to pull the band out so my hair falls freely around my shoulders. Leaning forward, he nuzzles into my neck and I hear him take a deep breath through his nose.

'Are you sniffing me?' I tease.

A laugh rumbles out of him. 'Yes. I'm the big, bad wolf and I want to eat you all up.'

Heat builds inside me at his covetous tone, making my body ache for him, as it always does. How am I ever going to go back to my normal life without him being in it?

'Hey… We'll still be friends after this…won't we?' I whisper.

I feel him stiffen then draw away from me. There's something in his face that makes my stomach swoop, but not in a joyful way. He looks wary suddenly. Have I gone too far? Asked for too much? We've been living in a make-believe land for so many days, I'm not entirely sure what's right and wrong any more.

'Sure, we'll be friends after this,' he says. But there's something not quite right about the way he says it.

Before I can summon the courage to question him about it, he gives me a terse sort of smile that doesn't quite reach his eyes and backs away. 'I'll leave you to choose your dress,' he says. And then he's gone.

I tell myself I'm being overly sensitive. Why on earth would he suddenly be acting strangely about being friends after this? That would be ridiculous. Surely?

As I look through the rail of beautiful dresses with slightly shaky hands, I realise that Maria is a size smaller than me and that I'll only just be able to squeeze into a small selection of the dresses and won't be able to wear any underwear for fear of terrible visible panty line. I'll just have to go without.

I smile to myself, wondering what Sandro would say. Knowing him, he'd probably love the idea of it.

It's funny, but I would never even have considered doing something like that before I met him. His influence seems to have given me more confidence than I'd ever imagined possible.

Half an hour later I walk into the living room to find him waiting there for me, dressed in a beautifully cut tux and looking as stunning as ever. My breath catches in my throat and every nerve in my body gives a little wiggle of joy at the sight of him.

'*Jesus*, you're so fucking sexy,' he growls, his eyes roving over my body, taking in the sleeveless, floor-length, gold lamé evening gown that flows over the curves of my body and forms a fishtail skirt at the bottom, making me look like a mermaid fresh from the sea. The slit, which is cut to mid-thigh, opens to reveal a tantalising flash of leg as I walk towards him. I've left my hair down, as requested, and it hangs down my back in soft waves.

And I feel it—sexy—I really do. For the first time in my life. And I realise that it's not because I've had sex but because I've finally started to feel comfortable in my own skin. To like and appreciate my body for all the wonderful things it can do and the ways it can make me feel.

He strides towards me, his eyes intent on mine. 'Look what you've done to me.'

I gasp as he wraps his hand around my wrist and pulls me against him so I can feel the hardness I've magically conjured.

Desire twists through me, amplifying my nerve endings into tight strands of need.

I feel his heartbeat against my chest and breathe in the alluring fresh scent of him.

'We should go,' I say hurriedly, before I give in to my cravings and encourage him to strip off the dress I've only just managed to put on.

Sandro

I can't take my eyes off her. She's fucking *mesmerising.* There are plenty of beautiful women in the grand ballroom of the hotel, but I'm totally uninterested in checking anyone else out. They have absolutely no draw for me. It's Juno I want to look at, to be with, no one else. She's cast a spell over me with her kindness and compassion, her intelligence and drive. Her purity of heart.

I notice a bank of photographers on the other side of the room from where we're standing and slip my arm around Juno's waist, guiding her away from them. I don't want those vultures wrecking her mood. She seems so happy to be here. Every time I look at her she has a wide, brilliant smile on her face, which makes me smile in return. I wonder whether I've had anything to do with that. I hope so.

I suspect it's more about what she's discovered about herself recently, though—that's she as beautiful and sexy as I've been telling her she is. I think she's finally beginning to believe me.

A waiter glides by and I let go of her to reach for two glasses of wine, handing one of them to her.

'We should celebrate,' I murmur, staring into her deep-blue eyes and getting a little lost in the warmth I see there.

'What are we celebrating?' she murmurs back.

'You.'

'Me?' She looks confused.

'Yeah, you. For finally breaking out of your chrysalis and becoming a butterfly.' I cringe a little at how cutesy that sounds, but she doesn't seem to mind. In fact, I think she quite likes the idea of it.

'I couldn't have done it without you,' she says, sliding her hand up to cup my jaw and draw me towards her for a kiss. As soon as our lips meet I feel a rushing sensation all over my body. It's not just lust. It's something deeper than that. Something new and frightening.

'So now you can go back to your lecturer guy and seduce the Y-fronts off him,' I joke, trying to throw off the disconcerting way I'm feeling. But even as I say this I'm hoping she'll laugh at the idea of that. Tell me she's changed her mind about Adam—that she wants to stay with me, to continue whatever it is we've started here.

My stomach lurches when she just nods, smiles and says, 'I don't think he's the Y-fronts-wearing type. He strikes me as more of a boxer shorts kind of guy.' There's a faraway look in her eyes, as if she's picturing him right now, standing in front of her with a hard-on and a smile.

I feel sick.

I want to say something disparaging about him—point out that the guy doesn't deserve her if he hasn't taken the time to figure out what an amazing woman she is—but before I can formulate the words I feel a tap on my shoulder and turn to see an old school friend of mine grinning back at me.

'Francesco!' I say, giving him a jovial slap on the back. *'Come va?'*

'Bene,' he replies, returning my friendly greeting. 'Good to see you. I thought you were in London now?' He glances towards Juno and I turn to look at her too. She's gazing at him in fascination. Now, Francesco is a handsome guy, I'll admit that, but I don't think he warrants that much fucking adoration. The hairs on the back of my neck stand to attention as she flashes him a smile.

'Ciao, bella,' Francesco murmurs smoothly, stepping towards her and kissing her lightly on both cheeks. I can tell from his body language that he finds her attractive. Too fucking attractive for my liking. 'And who are you?'

'I'm Juno. I'm a friend of Sandro's.' She says this

so easily, I know in my heart that's exactly how she thinks of me. Just a friend—with benefits, sure, but still just friends.

'Hey, have you guys visited the Bargello while you've been here?' Francesco asks.

When we both shake our heads, he says, 'You must! I'm the curator there now and we've been doing wonderful things. You were always interested in art, weren't you, Sandro?' Before I get a chance to reply, he carries on speaking, looking directly at Juno, to my utter fucking annoyance. 'Come. I'll show you around *personally*. We have some amazing exhibits at the moment. You'll *love* them.'

'That would be wonderful, but I'm not going to be in Florence for much longer,' Juno says sadly.

'What? No, you must stay!' Francesco says, giving it the full works: big, sad eyes and a covetous hand on her shoulder. I recognise the move. It's one I've used myself to good effect.

'Maybe I'll make it back some day soon,' she says, clearly buying in to this crap.

I want to punch something. Probably him.

'I need another drink,' I mutter, and before either of them can say anything I stride away to the bar and order a double shot of whisky.

Turning back with the glass clutched in my

hand, I watch them from a distance, feeling my heart hammering in my chest.

What the fuck is happening to me?

Whatever it is, I don't like it.

Francesco moves his hand to brush an eyelash off Juno's cheek and shyly she smiles up at him.

Out of nowhere a veil of blinding rage descends over me. I bunch my hands into fists and drag in a ragged breath, feeling as if someone's just ripped my fucking guts out. I don't want anyone else touching her like that, seeing that hazy look in her eye, making her smile. I want it to be all for me, only me.

Not for Francesco—and definitely not for that fucking lecturer asshole back in England.

Unfortunately, she chooses that moment to look over towards where I'm standing and the smile fades from her face.

I see her excuse herself from Francesco and start to move through the crowd towards me.

Forcing a neutral expression onto my face is pretty fucking tough, but I think I manage it, because when she makes it over to me she gives me a tentative smile.

'Are you okay? It looked for a second like you were annoyed about something.'

'I'm fine,' I say, swatting away her concern

and staring over her shoulder at a small group of women by the bar.

She turns to follow my line of vision and I sense her tense as she spots what, or rather whom, I'm looking at.

'Do you know them?' she asks. Her voice sounds high-pitched and accusatory, as if she thinks I have a nerve to check out other women in the room. This riles me. She has no right to police what I do, not when she clearly thinks it's okay to make eyes at my friend in front of me.

I shrug. 'I've seen them around at parties. I may have slept with one or two of them.'

This is a lie, and I feel a sting of shame as I see her visibly tense at the insensitivity of my answer.

'It looks like you're not finding it hard to handle attention from men today either,' I add, feeling the need to defend myself. I wouldn't have been looking at those women if she hadn't been fawning over Francesco the wonder kid. Even as I think this, I know what a fucking tool I'm being. She's just testing her new-found abilities. Life has suddenly opened up to her and she's enjoying treading new ground. I get that.

But I also hate it.

I notice a photographer spot us from the other side of the room and start to head our way, his camera held up ready to take our photo. Panic shoots through me. I don't want to have to deal with that right now.

'Come with me,' I whisper into her ear, taking her by the elbow and quickly leading her out of the room. There's a sweeping staircase to our right that leads to more function rooms and the roof terrace. A good place to hide out for a while.

'Where are we going?' she pants as I urge her to climb the stairs in front of me. It reminds me suddenly of following her up the stairs at the party in Chelsea and I feel a pang of nostalgia for the life I had before we embarked on this crazy folly. But only for a second. What I have in front of me now is worth so much more. I'll never regret agreeing to help her. Never. Even if it does end up tearing my fucking heart out.

'I've never had sex on a roof,' I murmur as I come up alongside her on the landing. She looks at me with shock in her eyes.

'What? We can't have sex here.'

'Of course we can,' I say. 'We'll be discreet. No one will know.'

She pauses for a moment, as if needing to think about it, then nods, her mouth widening into a mischievous smile. 'Okay, then. I guess there's no harm in adding it to our catalogue of sexual experiences.'

Our. I like that word on her lips.

The door to the terrace is locked, but I pull out a credit card and jemmy it a bit until it unlatches.

Juno looks at me with awe. 'I had no idea I was sleeping with a master criminal.'

I give a nonchalant shrug. 'I spent a lot of time in my youth figuring out ways to escape from places.'

'Which places?'

'Locked detention-classrooms at the school I went to mostly.'

She shakes her head, her expression dismayed, but I'm too busy thinking about what we came up here to do to worry about her reaction.

It's a good-sized roof terrace with creeping plants clinging to an ornate, chest-height, wrought-iron railing that runs one length of the building. We both stand and stare at the cityscape in front of us for a moment, entranced by its higgledy-piggledy beauty.

'Wow,' Juno murmurs, walking to the railing, her hips swaying provocatively, her ass looking incredible in her tight shiny dress.

I stride over to stand behind her, pressing the front of my body to her back so she can feel exactly how much she's turning me on.

'Yes, wow,' I say, pushing her hair to one side and bending to kiss her elegant neck. I feel her shiver as I brush my lips over her skin. She smells amazing—clean and fresh, but with the spicy undertone of her own unique scent. My mouth waters as I move across to kiss her bare shoulder and slide my hands round to cup her breasts.

Pressing herself back against me, she leans into my body, using me for support. And it's another perfect moment. Her scent in my nostrils…her beautiful body under my hands.

I don't want it to end. But I know it's going to.

I'm suddenly overwhelmed with anger, bitterness and frustration.

Why wasn't I born with astounding intelligence instead of my useless fucking looks? Why can't *I* be the kind of man she wants to spend the rest of her life with?

There's only one reason she's with me right now and I guess I'll have to play that to my advantage.

I want to ruin other men for her. I want her never to have sex with anyone the way she has it with me. And I want her never to find anyone else to satisfy her the way I can.

I want her like I've never wanted anything or anyone before. Just as I'll never be the same again if I can't have her.

I ache for her, my body a throbbing mess of torment.

Skirting my hands away from her breasts and over her stomach, I bunch the skirt of the dress in my hands and lift it up till I can slide one hand between her legs. I drag in a guttural breath as I discover she's not wearing knickers, my cock jumping with excitement at the discovery.

'Not wearing any underwear out to a fancy party like this?' I mutter teasingly into her ear. 'Bad girl—wicked, filthy girl. I should punish you for that.'

She makes a sound, as if she agrees with me.

Gathering up her beautiful mane of hair in my left hand, I wrap it round and round my fist till I'm clutching it in a tight knot at the base of her skull. She's all mine to control now. With my right hand I slide my fingers between her pussy lips and find that magical bundle of nerves, running my fingertip gently over and round it.

I hear her gasp in pleasure as she jerks at the intimacy of my touch. 'Yes. Yes, just there, touch me there,' she urges.

She's already wet with excitement and I use the silky lubrication easily to glide two fingers into her pussy. Her body rocks against me, juddering with pleasure as I begin to finger-fuck her, sliding the pad of my thumb over her clit.

'An orgasm with a view,' I murmur and she lets out a throaty laugh, her body wiggling seductively against mine.

'I want you to fuck me,' she whispers, turning

her head to look me in the eyes. 'I want to feel your cock inside me.'

I've never been more willing to do something in my life.

I slide my hand away from her and release my grip on her hair, then quickly undo my tux trousers and pull out my cock, which I quickly cover with a condom that I stashed in my pocket earlier. Just in case.

'Spread your legs,' I instruct her roughly. As soon as she does this, I pull her hips back towards me and slide inside her, taking myself right to the hilt in one quick, smooth movement.

'Ooh!' she moans, but it's a happy sound. The sound of relief.

I begin to pound into her ruthlessly, possessing her entirely. I want her never to forget this. Never to forget me. To yearn for this time we've spent together for the rest of her life.

She's tight and hot around my cock, and is pushing her ass back against me now, taking my hard thrusts, her breath panting out of her throat in rough, vocal gusts.

'Sandro, I'm so close. Please, please…'

She wants my hands on her too. I know she does. She needs to come desperately, but can't quite get there. I'm totally in control of her pleasure and she's begging me for mercy…

And suddenly I'm coming—spurting hot and forcefully inside her. My head rushes with lights and colours and my whole body jerks with the ferocity of my orgasm. And I ride it, on and on, still thrusting inside her until the feeling finally begins to subside and my senses return.

Then the shame hits me.

I feel as though I've just regressed ten years.

Because for the first time in my life I've lost control of my own need. The one advantage I had, the thing I'm so good at, so proud of—the thing that drew her to me specifically in the first place— has just shattered into a million useless pieces.

'Oh!' she mutters. 'Did you come already?'

I hate the sound of confused disappointment in her voice. But I'm not about to let her see my distress.

Ignoring the insistent aftershocks of my orgasm, I spin her round and push her against the railings. Then I drop to my knees and lift her leg to hook it over my shoulder and suck down hard on her pussy, finding her clit with my tongue and lashing at it over and over again. She begins to jerk and twitch against me.

'It's too much, Sandro, too hard!'

Through the heat of my humiliation I force myself to be more gentle and take my time with her, slowing my movements until I feel her begin to move with me instead of against me.

Her hands grip my head, her fingers tugging at my hair, and I allow her to guide my movements, giving her the control for once, letting her win this.

A few more strokes of my tongue and she starts to come, making breathy, satisfied sounds in the back of her throat and gripping my hair tightly between her fingers until she's finally satisfied.

And I know in that moment that that's the end of it. The end of us. I've taught her everything she needs to know now. She's surpassed me. There's nothing more she can learn from me. So I've served my purpose. Now I have no unique selling point.

I don't want to look at her. My heart is thumping so hard I think it's going to break my ribs. I can't speak. I can barely breathe.

Adrenaline shoots through my bloodstream, making me antsy, and all I can think about is getting out of here. Getting away from the curious look on her face and the gnawing sadness in my gut.

'Are you okay?'

The confusion in her voice only adds to my sick feeling of guilt. Whatever I say right now, it won't be enough to stop this falling to pieces right in front of me.

I'm itching to get out of here now. So instead of answering her I take the coward's way out.

'Let's go back to the apartment. I think we've had about as much fun as we're going to have here,' I say.

CHAPTER NINE

Juno

I FEEL DREADFUL. My head's a cloudy mess and my body is tense with mortification.

I'd not meant to sound so critical when, for the first time ever, Sandro had come before I'd had a chance to. But I'd been so close to orgasm, with him hitting the perfect spot inside me, it was extremely frustrating when he suddenly stopped.

Not that he hadn't made it up to me.

But now there's a strange, fractious sort of atmosphere between us. It hums in the air like a dangerous swarm of insects just waiting to strike. My heart races as we make the short drive home, with Sandro sitting tight-lipped beside me, his powerful body rigid and his concentration fully focussed on the road ahead of us.

Perhaps he's deliberately withdrawing from me now our time together is nearly up.

My heart contracts painfully at the thought of leaving Florence. Of leaving him.

How can I even think about going back to my steady, closeted life in London when I know there's so much more for me out here? With him. Not that *that* had ever been on the cards. He's been pretty clear all the way through that he's not interested in having anything serious with me. And why would he choose me anyway? I'm nothing like the women he's dated in the past. I don't have the pizzazz or street smarts he seems to go for.

I wonder whether he's beginning to worry that I've become too emotionally attached to him and that's why he's going cold on me—to make it easier on us both when I leave. It wouldn't surprise me. He's incredibly intuitive like that.

In fact, now that I've finally grown up, I realise he's actually the kind of man I'd like to spend the rest of my life with. Someone who excites and inspires me, brings me out of my shell, encourages me to explore new facets of myself without judgement. There's so much more depth to his character than I'd given him credit for when we first met. I'm actually ashamed of myself now for judging him on such superficial terms. Clearly there's a lot going on with him that he's not been able to express because of the strictures of his family's expectations of him.

'Sandro?' I ask tentatively. 'Is everything okay?' I've already asked him this once but he ignored the question.

This time he gives me a nod, but it's terse, and so unlike the warm responses I'm used to getting from him.

Tears burn at the back of my eyes, but I'm determined not to let them fall. I don't want him to think I'm trying to emotionally blackmail him. That wouldn't be fair at all. Not after what he's done for me—without ever asking for anything in return.

I suppose I should start to get used to the idea of letting our time together go. But it's such a horrible thought I immediately push it away.

Not yet.

Luckily, there's a free parking space right outside our building and Sandro pulls into it and we both get out of the car.

I'm still so deep in thought I don't realise what the bright flash of light that nearly blinds me is for a second.

'Fuck off!' Sandro shouts at the photographer who's just run up to stick a camera right in our faces, pushing me behind him to try and shield me from the lens. 'Leave us alone, you piece of shit!'

The guy just leers at him with a contemptuous expression. 'You've changed your tune. Last week you were begging me to take photos of the two of you. What's this meant to be—some kind of stunt to eke out your popularity in the gossip columns?'

'I said fuck off!' Sandro says again, this time stepping menacingly towards the guy.

The photographer takes a step back, dropping his camera to his side, as if he's afraid Sandro's about to snatch it. 'You fucking celebrity social-ites make me sick.' And he spits on the ground at our feet before stalking away.

I stand rooted to the spot, paralysed with confu-sion. All through that shocking incident I was mostly upset by the blatant disregard for our privacy—it brought back all those old feelings of humiliation from my teens—but now the guy has gone his words begin to penetrate my brain and a heavy feeling of dread sinks through me.

'Sandro?' I say shakily. 'What did he mean by that?' My heart's thumping a heavy, painful beat against my ribs.

'Nothing. Don't worry about it,' he says gruffly. But I'm not going to let him fob me off. I reach up and put my hand on his jaw, turning his face to-wards me so he has to meet my gaze.

'What aren't you telling me? Why did he accuse you of asking him to take photos of us?'

There's a guilty look in his eyes now and cold panic spikes my chest.

'*Did* you call him?' I demand, with a sudden rush of fearful anger.

'Yes,' he replies hotly, turning away from me so I can no longer see his eyes.

I stare at his rigid back as he strides towards the door to our building.

'What? But…but you told me I was being paranoid about photographers following us round the city. You've actually been setting it up to happen?' I shout after him.

'Let's talk inside,' he says, glancing around as if he's worried there'll be more press hiding in the shadows, taking down our every word.

He heads up the stairs before me, not slowing his pace so I can keep up with him as he usually does. I'm out of breath by the time I reach our apartment and my blood rushes thickly through my veins as I try to prepare myself for what I'm about to hear. I'm already vibrating with tension, knowing it's not going to be good. Why would he do something like this to me? I just can't reconcile it with the Sandro I know. It has to be a mistake.

He's already inside as I walk through the door on shaky legs.

'Why?' Anger permeates my voice, along with panic. 'Why would you do something like that when you know how much I hate being photographed by the press?' I ask him.

He doesn't answer, just kicks off his shoes and shrugs off the tux jacket, then starts to walk towards the living area.

'I need a drink,' he mutters, his back to me.

'Sandro? Talk to me!' I demand, running to catch up with him and putting my hand on his arm to try and stop him.

'Because my father told me to!' he shouts back.

I physically recoil, horror sinking through me. 'Why would he do that? I don't understand.'

'Because I needed to give the press some good pictures of us together in order to navigate a *situation* I created,' he says, roughly shoving his hands through his hair.

'What situation?'

He sighs and rubs at his forehead. 'A photo of me appeared in the society press the day after the party in Chelsea and my father wasn't happy about it.'

'Why wasn't he happy? What's the photo of?'

'I got in a fight at the party after you'd left. A guy there insulted a woman I was talking to so I hit him.' He holds up both hands. 'But I swear to you, it's not like me to lose it like that, which is why I didn't mention it. I didn't want you to think I was a violent person and walk away from our deal. I was just in a bad mood that night and I overreacted.'

'Was the bad mood because of me? Because of what I…implied?' The idea that I'd set this awful chain in motion horrifies me.

'No, of course not,' he says, batting away my words. 'I was drunk and the guy was out of line. But my father wasn't pleased about it getting into the press and wanted me to make amends. Which is why I needed you to act the part of adoring "good girl" girlfriend to help me convince him I was serious about restoring the family's reputation.'

'Why didn't you just ask me to go along with it?' I ask, not quite able to believe I'm hearing this.

'Because I thought you'd refuse after what you said about your experience with the press. I thought you wouldn't agree to come to Florence with me, and I needed it to look real. I was afraid it wouldn't look right if we were both pretending.'

'Oh, I don't know, I can be a good little actress when I need to be. I've done it all my life. Pretending I'm okay when I'm not,' I spit angrily.

'Well, I didn't want to ask you to do that.'

'No, because you're too bloody proud to ask for help, aren't you?' I jab my finger at him. 'So you lied to me instead.'

'I never meant to lie,' he shouts back. 'And I didn't think you'd ever find out about it.'

'So you've just been pretending to find me attractive all this time? Playing dumb to gain my sympathy, when actually you're a smart, conniving con artist. You're the one who's been manipulating *me*.'

'Playing *dumb*? I fucking knew it. That's all you care about, isn't it? How many degrees and awards someone has.' The look in his eyes is so full of fury, I take a step backwards and wrap my arms around my body.

Shame slides sickeningly down to my gut as I remember how I misjudged that side of things before I met him.

'How much of what you told me about yourself was made up?' I counter in defence.

'None of it. It's all true, every word,' he bites back.

'How do you expect me to believe that now though, Sandro? How can I believe anything you say to me?'

All those memories of us together, where he'd shown me affection and been so kind, take a dark turn in my mind. Were all of them fake? They hadn't felt it at the time, but maybe I'd been kidding myself, wanting them to be real. Wanting him genuinely to like me as I am.

Had I gone and fallen all over again for the same trick that Malcolm had played on me?

Panic and pain well inside me, making my head throb. I really want to cry, but I'm not going to give him the satisfaction of an emotional response.

'You were so offended when I accidentally mentioned money to you, when we first talked,' I blurt, using my anger to hold myself together. 'But you were more than happy to whore yourself out for a few photographs in a newspaper. For publicity.'

I can see a muscle working in his jaw. 'Yes, but only to restore my reputation and my family's good name.'

'Oh, well, that's all right, then, as long as your reputation's safe!' My voice is heavy with sarcasm.

Another horrible thought strikes me. 'You only asked to me to stay on longer because you knew there'd be more photo opportunities, didn't you?'

He shakes his head. 'No. I wanted you to stay because I liked having you around. I didn't call the press at all this last week.'

'I don't believe you.'

'Well, it's true. You have to trust me.'

'Well, I don't. I don't trust anything you say now I know how you used me.'

He takes an angry step forward and points at my chest. 'Well, you used me too. I was just a warm body to fuck to you, wasn't I? Just practice for the real thing. For someone with more intelligence. You weren't here for me as a person. You were here for what you could get from me.'

'I didn't mean to make you feel like that,' I argue, but the heat of my shame rushes to my face and shows me up for the selfish bitch I really am. Of course that's exactly what I did at first. I treated him like a sex object, not someone with feelings and his own insecurities. I naively thought he couldn't have any because of his beauty and popularity.

'Well, anyway, it's over now. You don't need me any more. You can go back to that lecturer and blow his mind with your expertise in bed.'

His eyes are totally devoid of emotion now, which sends a shiver of fear down my spine. Was this really the way things were going to end between us, after everything we've shared? Could he really turn his back on me and walk away so easily? Anger and frustration flood through me.

'How can you treat me like this after everything we've shared? Everything I trusted you with? All those humiliating stories…' I whisper, my voice a rough croak. 'I can't believe you think it's okay to have used me like that. And after what that teacher did to you, the way she made you feel about yourself, how she abused your trust and smashed your pride to pieces… I thought you'd never do that to someone else. And I gave you my virginity because I genuinely thought you cared about me.'

This seems to get through to him because I see his shoulders tense and a glimpse of something like shame on his face. 'You *asked* me to take your virginity, remember? You *begged* me.'

'Yes, when I thought it actually meant something to you. Because it meant something to me. *You* meant something to me.'

'But I don't any more?' I can't read his expression now. He's withdrawn too far into himself.

I swallow painfully, my throat tight with sadness. 'You're not the man I thought you were.'

'Juno...'

I stiffen as he moves towards me, his arms raised as if he wants to pull me into a hug against his body. But I can't let him. I can't give in to my physical response to him. That's what got me here in the first place. It was a mistake then and it would be a mistake now.

'Don't touch me,' I snap. 'Don't even come near me.'

He drops his arms and folds them across his chest instead, staring down at the floor between us.

'Look, I know you've never wanted a real relationship with me. I'm not stupid. You told me that from the off.' I take a deep, shuddering breath. 'So I guess this is the perfect time to end this charade.'

'So you can go back to Adam?' He sounds disgusted, as if I'm making a huge mistake by ignoring his disdain for the guy, but I don't care about his opinion any more. Why should I? He didn't care about my feelings when he was calling the press.

'Probably,' I say in frustration. 'Maybe I will give him another chance. At least he was man enough to be honest with me.'

I see him jerk back, as if I've physically wounded him.

'Fine. You do what you want. I'm going out.'

He strides past me to the front door and roughly shoves his feet back into his shoes.

'Where are you going?' I ask, panic chasing through my body. I suddenly don't want him to leave in anger like this. I want to find some way to work it out. But I'm afraid, deep down, that there's nothing either of us can say right now to make this horrible situation better.

It's pretty damn clear that it's over between us.

'It's none of your business,' he replies, confirming my fear. And then he's gone, slamming the door behind him and leaving the apartment ringing with the shocking sound of his departure from my life.

On unsteady legs I walk back into the living room, slump down onto the nearest sofa and curl myself into a ball. My heart is racing and a heavy blanket of dread presses down over my entire body.

All the confidence that's slowly been building in me over the last two weeks has drained away because I know now that what we had wasn't special at all. That I wasn't special. He was just stringing me along till he got what he wanted.

And I lost my virginity to him, even after all his warnings not to—to save it for someone I cared about, and for someone who cared about me. But I begged him to do it anyway, like the guileless sap that I am. I chose not to listen, blinded by my infatuation with him, thinking, like a total idiot, that he felt the same.

Even now I can't quite believe it has all been a lie. It seemed so real. Felt so real. But it can't have been, not if he's been lying to me all this time.

He played me, like the expert player he is.

What was I thinking? I've been so naive, assuming I could shield my heart from him whilst blithely giving him everything else I had.

My heart thumps heavily in my chest as I realise I've gone and done the most stupid thing in the world.

I've fallen in love with him.

CHAPTER TEN

Juno

HE DOESN'T COME back that night, or the next morning.

At nine a.m. I drag myself out of bed and pad into the kitchen, hoping I'm wrong and that he's snuck in quietly, while I've been dozing for a few restless minutes, and gone to sleep in his own bed.

But when I tentatively push open his bedroom door his bed is conspicuously empty.

My heart plummets with sadness.

I don't even want to think about where he went last night. Images of that sex club we visited on our first night here flash through my head and I try to push them away. He wouldn't do that to me, would he—go straight out and find someone new? Or is he, at this very moment, curled up in some other woman's bed, his powerful body pressed up against her, or inside her…?

I shake my head fiercely, trying to dislodge the

horrible image I've conjured. I burn with jealousy. But it's tinged with anger. The thing is, I have absolutely no idea what he's capable of, because the Sandro I thought I knew doesn't actually exist.

After the torment of being rejected by every single man I've ever had a connection with—even my bloody father—I thought I'd finally found someone who genuinely liked me for *me*. Not because of my family name, but for *me*.

But I was wrong.

So I guess it's time to go home and try to pick up the pieces of my life. At least I have my work to plough my energy into, though I suspect I'm going to have trouble concentrating on it when it feels as if my chest's been split in two.

I give him one more hour, tidying the apartment and stripping my bed, even though I know the cleaner will come in soon to do it. But I need something to do, to take my mind off the waiting and the horrible, sinking feeling of dread in my stomach.

When the alarm on my phone goes off, signalling that the hour's up, I pack my case, leaving out anything I've bought while I've been here. I don't want any reminders of my time here once I've gone. It will hurt too much to look at them. To feel that connection to Sandro that I know now I never really had.

The taxi I've called is waiting outside for me when I walk out of the apartment block for the last time and I shield my aching eyes from the sun as I make my way towards the car in a sort of dream-like trance, allowing the driver to take my bags and put them in the boot for me. I'm functioning completely on autopilot now to get me through this.

The trip to the airport takes longer than I remember it being on the way here. But then everything seems to move at a much faster pace when Sandro's around.

An insistent bubble of grief rises to the surface as I think about him, but I push it firmly back down again. I'm not going to fall apart until I'm safely back in my apartment where I can wallow for a while before putting myself back together, piece by piece. I have a terrible feeling it's going to take a very long time to do that, though—if I ever manage it.

How am I meant to forget him, and what we shared? It doesn't even seem possible right now. I suspect he'll always have a piece of my heart for ever.

Finally, we reach the airport, but it seems the gods really aren't smiling on me at all at the moment because there's a baggage handlers' strike and all flights back to London have been cancelled. I'm too drained to try and organise another means of transport home right now, though, so I book into the airport hotel and get straight into bed there, pulling the covers up to my chin and staring at programme after programme on the television, barely taking any of it in, but desperately trying to stop myself from thinking about him.

I must have fallen into a deep sleep at some point in the early hours of the morning because I wake with a start to find the sun has risen on a new day.

The reason I woke so suddenly, it turns out, is because my phone is ringing. I reach over to pluck it from the nightstand to see who's calling me.

Half of me aches for it to be Sandro, calling to apologise and tell me he loves me and can't live without me. That he doesn't want me to leave. Telling me to come home. But the new, more worldly half of me knows that that's not likely to happen.

That side is right, of course. Even so, cold disappointment slides through me when I see it's not Sandro who's calling me, it's my sister April.

I almost don't pick up, not sure I can keep it together enough not to alert her to my destroyed state of mind. I'm scared that if she asks me how I am I'm not going to be able to lie and I'll start to cry, and I'm pretty damn sure that once I start I'm not going to be able to stop.

But I'm not a little girl any more who doesn't

face things that frighten her. So I press the button to accept the call and my world crashes in a little further when my sister tells me that our father's been in a bad car accident and might not live out the day.

Sandro

I stagger back into the apartment around mid-morning, the day after our fight, feeling like shit.

I spent the whole night walking around the city, too ashamed of myself to come back and face her, finally only giving in to the drag of sleep at dawn and taking a nap on a bench in the Parco delle Cascine.

I know I have no right to expect to find Juno still here waiting for me to get back, but still as I go from room to room... I hope.

My gut twists painfully as I open her wardrobe to find that it's empty, apart from the couple of things she bought while she was here. Her case has gone, as has her washbag from the bathroom.

She's left me.

I slump against the wall next to the sink and slide down to the floor, putting my head in my hands, feeling totally wrecked. A hollow shell of myself.

How could I have let this happen?

I am such a *fucking idiot*.

A *shallow* fucking idiot.

I was so proud of myself when she told me that out of all the men she'd researched I'd come out at the top of her list. My sexual reputation had been everything to me at that point. In my mind it made up for my lack of academic prowess, business acumen or any kind of serious drive or ambition, but I know now that it doesn't. Not for Juno. She needs more than that. She deserves more.

My insides clench with disgust at myself.

I've allowed myself to be my father's puppet all my life, but I'm fed up with putting on a show for people now—just being a pretty face, an arm for women to hang off. I don't want to be that person any more. I want to be someone who's respected for more than their family name and looks, even if it means going out on my own. But I don't want to make a success of my art just for me; I want to do it for her too. I want to feel worthy of being with someone as smart and accomplished as Juno.

I want her to be proud of me.

So I'm going to change. For her. I'm going to do all the things I've been too scared to do for fear of failing, and even if I do fail, over and over again, at least I'll be moving forward.

And maybe she'll recognise that as a strength

and a good reason to give me a chance at being a proper partner to her.

Jesus, I hope so. Because I don't know how I'm going to live without her.

Finally, I allow myself to put a name to the way I feel about her.

It's love.

I love her.

I've known it for a while, of course, I just haven't wanted to admit it to myself.

But I have now. And I know what I need to do to let her know it too: I have to swallow my pride and allow myself to be vulnerable. Just like she did.

It takes me a few days to put everything into motion and then there's nothing left but to go back to London, find her and ask her to forgive me. To beg her for another chance, even though I probably don't deserve one after the shitty way I behaved.

Once back on English soil, I call the friend of a friend who originally gave me Juno's number, but he doesn't have her address. It seems the rest of the people I know from London's social scene don't know her well enough to have it either, because she rarely makes an appearance at the events and parties they go to.

But now I've made up my mind to do this I know I have to see her right away.

I rack my brain, trying to remember the name of the university where she works, pacing the floor until I manage to break through the fog in my head and access a memory. I remember now that it was named after one of the saints—fitting, really.

I use the Internet browser on my phone to look through the possibilities and when 'St George' comes up my brain sparks. That's it. St George's University. In a department that has something to do with heart attacks in young athletes. Another search finally leads me to the department I need and its address in London.

With adrenaline rushing through my veins I leave my apartment and run outside to hail a cab.

Juno

After a horrendous day of worry about my father's condition, where I'd paced around Peretola airport waiting to get on a flight back home, I finally hear from Maya that he's out of surgery, out of danger and already demanding to be discharged from hospital.

It seems even life-threatening injuries can't keep my autocratic father down for long.

Joking aside, though, I'm hugely relieved to hear he's all right and as soon as I get the good news I finally allow myself to cry out all the tension I've been carrying around with me like a ten-ton weight.

It takes me another few hours to secure a seat on a plane back to London then two hours in the air and two more till I'm finally back at my apartment in Notting Hill, where I crawl straight into bed. The next day is spent visiting my father in hospital and supporting my sisters, so by Thursday I'm totally shattered when I finally drag myself in to work.

I probably should have called in sick, but I can't stand the thought of being alone in my flat with just my heartache to keep me company. So I brave the tube, and the curious questions from my colleagues about where I'd been on holiday, and smile politely as they tell me how well I look. Even Adam makes a point of stopping by my desk to check in with me.

I listened to the message he'd left for me that fateful night a few days ago and decided answering it could wait till I got back. Needless to say, it hadn't been a booty call.

From the way he looked at me just now, however, I'm beginning to wonder whether the next one will be.

I won't be taking that call, though. Not a chance. From our short conversation earlier it became patently clear to me that there was nothing there for me any more. No attraction whatsoever. *Nada.*

I'm just making myself an extra-strong cup of coffee in the break room when I hear the sound of loud male voices in the corridor outside. I almost drop my mug when I realise I'm listening to the beautiful, haunting sound of an Italian male's voice. But it can't be Sandro's, can it? Why would he be here, right now?

'Yes, I'm he,' I hear another voice reply and I make an involuntary squeaking noise when I place Adam's voice as the other male. So an Italian man is asking for Adam. This doesn't bode well.

Putting the mug down, I rush out into the corridor, my heart racing, to see the extraordinary sight of Sandro, looking as dauntingly handsome as ever, staring down at my rather cowed-looking colleague.

'She's an amazing woman and you're a fucking idiot for turning her down,' Sandro is saying in a loud, commanding voice. 'I can vouch for that personally. I just wanted you to know that.'

'Erm…okay,' Adam says, holding up his hands and backing away, clearly perplexed and perhaps a little bit scared by what he's found himself entangled in here.

'And the reason I know that,' Sandro continues, his amazing eyes flashing with a passion that makes me catch my breath, 'is because I made the same stupid mistake as you did. And if she doesn't forgive me I'm going to regret it for the rest of my fucking life.'

'Sandro!' I call out loudly, aware of some of my other colleagues sticking their heads out of their offices to see what the drama is all about.

He turns to look at me and the moment our eyes meet I know it's all going to be okay. That he's suffering the same way I am and that he wants what we had back. He wants me back.

Not that I'm going to let him just waltz in and sweep me off my feet without making him work for it first.

I watch with my heart in my mouth as he slowly walks over to me. My body reacts in its usual wanton way whenever he's near me and I flush with heat and longing for him.

Stepping back into the break room, I beckon for him to follow me.

'Why are you here?' I ask as soon as I've shut the door on the curious faces of my colleagues.

'Because I love you,' he says without preamble, moving closer to me, the delicious scent of him that I've missed *so much* winding through my senses. 'And I wanted to *tell* you that I love you and that I'm a fucking selfish idiot. I know that now, but I'm going to change. For you, Juno—and for me, but mostly for you. And I'm begging you to forgive me. I want you back. With me. Where you belong.'

My whole body is shaking with relief and happiness now. 'You love me?' I say, wanting to hear him say it again.

'Yes. I love you.'

I nod and fold my arms, not sure I'm going to be able to maintain my cool, but determined at least to try for a few more minutes. To torture him for just a little bit longer, as his absence from my life has been torturing me for the past few days.

'Just tell me one thing. Was it an act at first? Were you pretending for those first few days to have fun with me?'

'No, Juno, of course not,' he says fiercely, lifting his hand as if wanting to touch me, then dropping it again, clearly feeling it's not the right time when I tense a little.

'Surely you know that, deep down?' he pleads, his eyes dark with apprehension. 'I loved having you with me from the beginning. That's why I wanted you to stay on another week. I couldn't stand the thought of you leaving.'

'But you were just following your father's orders when you initially agreed to our deal?'

He shakes his head. 'When I started to get to know you I genuinely wanted to help you, Juno, I swear. It wasn't just about appeasing my father.'

'I wish you hadn't lied to me, Sandro.'

He nods. 'Me too. I'm so sorry. I hate myself for it. Please believe me. I wanted to tell you, but I thought you might leave if you knew what I'd done, and I really didn't want you to go. And I couldn't stand the idea of you hating me. I already thought I wasn't good enough for you and admitting to what I'd done would have proved it. I stopped calling the photographers as soon as I knew they'd taken a few pictures of us at the beginning of the first week, hoping that would be enough. But it seems people are more fascinated by us than I imagined possible.'

I can't stop the corner of my mouth from quirking at that. 'I guess we are an unusual match.'

He frowns. 'Not that unusual. We're extremely compatible in all the ways that matter.' He gives me a slow, seductive smile now and I feel the heat of my longing for him intensify.

'I imagine people looking in will be wondering why someone as intelligent as you would go for a no-talent playboy like me,' he adds, looking away from me now, down at his hands.

His insecurity tugs at my heart. 'You have a huge amount of talent—you just haven't had a chance to show it off yet. As I've said from the beginning, you have to get your sculptures in front of people, then you'll see I'm right.'

'Actually, I have a confession to make about that,' he says, looking back into my eyes.

'Another one?' The tremor in my voice must have given away my concern because he shakes his head and smiles.

'A good one, I promise. After you left, I called the guy from the art gallery and showed him my sculptures. He's agreed to exhibit them for me next month.'

I can't help myself. I fling my arms around him, grateful for the excuse finally to hold him close. 'That's wonderful!'

'I never would have done it if it wasn't for you,' he murmurs into my hair, wrapping his arms around me and pulling me close. Leaning back to look me in the eyes again, he reaches up and pushes my fringe out of my face, sweeping his thumb across my cheek in the tender way I've come to love. 'I wanted to prove to you that there's more to me than I've let you believe.'

'I always knew there was more to you than you wanted me to see,' I say with a smile.

'Yeah.' He nods. 'I think you saw through me right from the start, my clever girl. You saw the real me. The side of me I've hidden from other people for years because I was ashamed of myself for not being smarter or more successful.'

'You have no reason to be ashamed.'

'I know that now.' He smiles and strokes my face again. 'In fact, I've made an appointment to speak to a professional about getting tested for ADHD and to figure out some methods I can use to help me when I'm struggling to concentrate.'

I blink at him in surprise. 'That's great.'

'It's a start.'

Staring up into his amazing eyes, I know I can't hold myself back any longer. It's time to tell him how I feel. 'You know I'll always be there for you, don't you?' I murmur. 'Because I love you too.'

He lets out a low moan of relief, dropping his forehead to mine. 'Thank God!' He lifts his head again, then presses his mouth to mine, sliding his tongue into my mouth in such a possessive way I shiver with delight.

When we finally come up for air a few minutes later, he says, 'And you know I'll be there for you too, right? *Always*. That's how it's going to work from now on.'

'So, no mistresses and no affairs,' I say forcefully. 'I can't stand the thought of sharing you with someone else.'

He looks taken aback. 'I wouldn't do that. I wouldn't need to. I don't want anyone but you, my smart, beautiful, kind girl. You're everything I want. I love you. That's the difference. Only you.

And I'm going to devote my entire life to making you happy.'

'I already am happy.'

He solemnly shakes his head. 'I can't believe I tried to dazzle you with sex to distract you from my shortcomings. That was never going to work. You always saw straight through me.'

'Oh, I don't know,' I say, grinning mischievously. 'I seem to remember being pretty dazzled—in fact, so dazzled I might need a reminder about exactly how to do it.' I give him a mock frown. 'It's been a few days and I'm beginning to forget some of the lessons you taught me.'

He grins back, then reaches down and turns the lock on the door. Then he lifts me up, walking us over to the three-seater sofa on the other side of the room.

'Coming right up,' he says, and kisses me hard.

* * * * *

COMING SOON!

We really hope you enjoyed reading this book. If you're looking for more romance, be sure to head to the shops when new books are available on

Thursday 2nd May

To see which titles are coming soon, please visit

millsandboon.co.uk/nextmonth

MILLS & BOON